the
heights

LOUISE CANDLISH

the *heights*

ATRIA PAPERBACK

New York   London   Toronto   Sydney   New Delhi

SIMON &
SCHUSTER
CANADA

Simon & Schuster Canada
A Division of Simon & Schuster, Inc.
166 King Street East, Suite 300
Toronto, Ontario M5A 1J3

Originally published in Great Britain in 2021 by Simon & Schuster UK Ltd.

This Simon & Schuster Canada edition March 2022

SIMON & SCHUSTER CANADA and colophon are trademarks of Simon & Schuster, Inc.

For information about special discounts for bulk purchases, please contact Simon & Schuster Special Sales at 1-800-268-3216 or CustomerService@simonandschuster.ca.

Interior design by Erika R. Genova

Manufactured in the United States of America

1   3   5   7   9   10   8   6   4   2

Library and Archives Canada Cataloguing in Publication
Title: The heights / Louise Candlish.
Names: Candlish, Louise, author.
Description: Simon & Schuster Canada edition.
Identifiers: Canadiana (print) 20210215747 | Canadiana (ebook) 20210215755 | ISBN 9781982177560 (softcover) | ISBN 9781982177591 (ebook)
Classification: LCC PR6103.A53 H45 2022 | DDC 823/.92—dc23

ISBN 978-1-9821-7756-0
ISBN 978-1-9821-7759-1 (ebook)

This book is for all the friends I didn't see during its writing,
including Mats 'n' Jo

part one

Killing Time

Opening lines are hard to write, says Felix Penney, and he of all people should know. The author of three writing manuals and nine crime novels, he is one of the most high-profile creative writing tutors in the UK, with a prestigious class at King's College London.

"How will you start your feature?" he asks me, deftly preempting my questions for him.

"With the setting," I reply, playing along.

"Nice choice," he says. "A good, safe entry point for any narrative."

And so, with Mr. Penney's blessing, picture if you will a small library on the outskirts of a midsize Berkshire town. It's a standard underfunded community space with scuffed furniture and a pair of antiquated radiators leaking just enough heat to stop the cold from creeping to the bone. Dust motes hover in the thin winter sunlight.

I'm here to sit in on a session run by Penney that is fast

gaining a reputation beyond these book-lined walls and, as his students arrive, I count myself extremely fortunate to have so little in common with them. For this is a course designed to explore the impact crime has had on their lives. Violent crime, for the most part.

"Take ownership of everything you've been through," Penney urges his class. "Dig as deep as you dare. You'll be amazed by the power you have to unearth the missing pieces of your story."

"I still don't know how to begin!" complains one woman, something of a slow starter given that this is the third time the group has met.

"No one ever knows," Penney sympathizes and he inspires her by reading aloud the first chapter of another student's work, one who is progressing rather better.

As he reads (the opening line is a doozy, just you wait), I find my gaze resting on the author. Sharp-boned and fair-skinned, she's not as beautiful as she once was—by my reckoning, she's closer to fifty than forty these days—but she has a quality to her that's impossible to tear your eyes from. A charisma, a pathos.

I recognize the face, of course. And, to an extent, I already know the story.

At least, I think I do.

Michaela Ross, *Sunday Times* magazine,
December 2021

SAINT OR SINNER

by Ellen Saint

one

KIERAN WATTS HAS BEEN dead for over two years when I see him standing on the roof of a building in Shad Thames.

It is October 2019, a Monday that should be unremarkable.

For those who don't know the area, Shad Thames is a historic parcel of riverside London just southeast of Tower Bridge. Think step-back-in-time wharves with winches and walkways and cobbled alleys running red with the blood of bygone crimes (okay, that's in poor taste. I apologize).

For those who don't know the *man*, Kieran Watts is the monster who destroyed my life. Whose actions will torment my soul until my dying day, and perhaps even beyond—I wouldn't put it past him. He is the reason I am writing this, the reason I am here. As I once said to my daughter, Freya, not missing the look of revulsion on her face: *I will never forgive him.*

I mean it. *Never.*

So, I'm in Shad Thames for work. It's been raining overnight and the riverside palette is all soot and stone, rust veining the dark-painted ironwork. My new client is called Selena. She's in her early thirties, white British mixed with something chic and southern European. She works in finance, which explains her acquisition of a fifth-floor flat in Jacob's Wharf, one of the east-facing warehouse conversions overlooking St Saviour's Dock. Though beautiful, the apartments have inconveniently small windows, calling for lighting expertise beyond what your average sparky will dispense, and I've been brought in by the architect commissioned by Selena to do her refurb. This first meeting is for me to get a sense of her lifestyle and personal aesthetic. Naturally, she wants it both ways—the candlelit romanticism of smugglers conspiring in shadowy corners *and* the radiant, flattering light beloved of the millennial narcissist (her words, not mine).

But you don't need to hear about that. Rest assured I'll light her beautifully. What's important here is what happens *after* the consultation.

We are sitting at her breakfast bar by the window, with cups of espresso and shortbread cookies she claims to have baked in the microwave, when she says, "You wouldn't need your trickery up there, would you?" And she gestures to the building directly opposite.

It's a slender modern structure slotted between two warehouses, its top protruding like an elongated head on broad shoulders. Each floor has a large lozenge-shaped window overlooking the water, with a second full-height one to the right running up the building in a reflective stripe. Though all its units must get their share of natural light, the top flat has what looks like an atrium or skylight behind a roof terrace that spans the full width of the building.

"There must be a great view of Tower Bridge from that terrace." I bite into a cookie and sugar grains melt on my tongue. "It's an unusual building, isn't it?"

"Went up in the early nineties, apparently," Selena says. "I don't know how they got permission to build so high."

"Oh, it was the Wild West back then. Some of us remember it firsthand." I raise my eyebrows at her and she does the same back. I smile.

Seek out people who improve your mood, Ellen, a counselor once advised, but it was too soon then. I understand better now.

"It's the tallest building in Shad Thames, I think," she says. "And *he's* the king of the castle, look."

Craning to glimpse the man who has come out onto the terrace and stands at the clear glass balustrade, I find that my first thought, as it always is when I witness someone poised inches from a sheer drop like that, is, *He's going to throw himself off.* He's going to lean forward, look down, and hear the call of the void, exactly as I would. Then he'll jump.

I say as much to Selena and she exclaims in horror. "But why would he want to jump?"

"Not him, *me*. If I were standing where he is. Don't worry, it's nothing to do with feeling suicidal. It's a condition. They call it high place phenomenon."

"What, it's like vertigo?"

"That's more a sensation of spinning—like in the movie. This is a kind of irrational impulse. But not everyone has it." I gesture to our man on the roof terrace, as still and poised as an elite diver about to go for gold. "*He* obviously doesn't."

"Well, it wouldn't be the best place to live if he did," Selena says, with a smirk, as he turns and walks the length of his terrace to its river-facing corner.

That's when it happens. The impossible. The grotesque. There's a self-consciousness to the way this man lifts his chin, an exaggerated bounce to his step, that I recognize. That makes me put my hand to my mouth to muffle a gasp, my heart punching a savage rhythm in my chest.

It's him.

The desire to flee collides with a compulsion to keep my eyes fixed on him, to learn all that I can in the time available. Absorb the clues. The distance between us is too great for me to be able to make out his features, though I can see his hair has been bleached, and he's a good twenty pounds lighter than I remember from when I last saw him, almost two and a half years ago.

No, it can't be him. If there's any link at all, this must be a relative of his. He said he had no family back then, but that doesn't mean none existed. This could be a cousin or a half sibling, someone he never even met.

He stretches his arms to the sides and raises them above his head, bringing his palms together in some sort of meditative pose. He was never so composed in the past—even in court, he fidgeted constantly. I feel bile slide through my throat and up into my mouth.

"You okay?" Selena asks, a stitch of concern between her brows. "Is it the vertigo thing? Let me close the window . . ."

I swallow, drop my hand from my face. "No, no, I'm fine. Do you . . . do you know that guy?"

"Not to speak to. I've seen him, though, in that café on Mill Street. He always buys the biggest bucket of coffee. Wait, maybe we did speak once, I don't remember. Why?"

"He reminds me of someone." It's a struggle to control my facial muscles and I feel myself grimace. "Someone I didn't think was . . . in London."

Selena moves to the window for a better look, obscuring my own view. "He looks pretty young, doesn't he? Must be a banker. No, something in tech — a banker wouldn't still be at home at ten in the morning. Or maybe he's a rich overseas student, there are so many of them around here. Russians, mainly."

I silently burn for her to get out of the way, but by the time she does, he's disappeared. "Where did he go?" I ask, foolishly.

"Back inside. Don't worry, he didn't jump. If he *did*, would he land in the water? These walkways are pretty narrow."

As she leans steeply out of the window to remind herself of the dimensions of her own building's waterfront, I suppress a shudder and get to my feet.

"Time for me to get going."

She walks me out and I step into the lift gratefully, like someone being airlifted from a war zone. Only now, alone in that mirrored box, do I allow myself to receive at full voltage my anguish at the memory of a boy called Kieran Watts and the power he had over my son, Lucas. The sheer predictability of Lucas's response to his God-given cool.

Of course, by this stage in the game — middle age — we know cool is just another way of saying restless, reckless.

Careless.

The lift gives a queasy little lurch before coming to a stop. The doors part and I step out. The lobby looks the same as it did when I arrived, but the floor feels like sand moving beneath my feet and I press a hand to the exposed brick wall to steady myself.

It can't be Kieran Watts, I tell myself. *And if anyone can be sure of that it is me.*

Because I'm the one who killed him.

two

THAT GOT YOUR ATTENTION.

Well, hopefully. Otherwise I might as well give up this writing lark right now and sign up for some other form of therapy. Get my catharsis by an easier method, because this one is hard, really hard. Already I feel as if I'm using bodily fluids for ink—the blood of my son, the tears of my daughter. My own bottomless tap of adrenaline.

So I'm the first to admit that what was set in motion after that visit to Jacob's Wharf was basically one disastrous mistake after another. I can hardly deny it, can I? But at least hear the story from the horse's mouth. Appreciate the context.

Let me take you back to when I first met this man, in September 2012. He was a child then, or a man-child, as they are at sixteen, and he'd joined Lucas's school for sixth form, a "cared for" pupil who by law rose to the top of the admissions list. And quite rightly, too—don't get me wrong, with any other disadvantaged youngster I'd have been as compassionate as you'd expect of a parent at Foxwell

Academy, Beckenham. The catchment was a classic suburban bubble of wholesome parenting, all scratch cooking and helping with the homework; soft clean sheets and fluffed pillows. We wished everyone's kids could have the same advantages, we honestly did—just so long as it wasn't at the expense of *ours*.

"Does he live in a children's home?" I asked Lucas, when his head of year emailed us with the news that our son had been assigned as a buddy to this vulnerable new classmate. I wasn't aware of such a residence in our area, but I knew from a feature I'd read in the *Guardian* that they were often friendly, cozy places, nothing like the bleak institutions of public imagination.

"No, he's got a foster mum," Lucas said. "A woman called . . . I don't know, something funny. Over in South Norwood."

"Quite a way to come for school."

"He gets the tram. And he's going to learn to drive as soon as he's seventeen. His foster mum's paying, so yeah."

So yeah. Lucas always used to finish a sentence that way. Even now, I feel a twist in my gut when I hear someone with the same verbal tic.

He didn't know the details of the new boy's birth parents, but I soon heard on the grapevine that the mother had had learning difficulties and drug issues and hadn't been allowed to keep him. His grandmother had taken him for a few years, but, following her death from cancer, he'd been in a series of foster placements. He'd scored unexpectedly well in his GCSEs and his current placement had been extended so he could take A-levels. Lucas, at this time an academic star with a reputation for being a team player, was a natural choice of buddy for a youngster whom I pictured as diffident, if not damaged.

"I hope you're being kind," I said. "He's had a tough start, poor kid."

"Suppose."

"Does he seem sad?"

"Sad? Kieran? No, he's a real laugh."

Lucas was a typical sixteen-year-old kid, not exactly renowned for his empathy—or maybe it was just that his generation took everything in its stride. Identity politics were taking off then and, amid a dizzying array of new ways to be defined, not living in a traditional nuclear family was so old-school as to be scarcely worth a mention.

Lucas's own family arrangement certainly raised no eyebrows. He lived with me, his stepfather, Justin, and half sister, Freya, in a lovely old Edwardian villa a mere fifteen-minute walk from his father's flat on a 1980s housing estate. He shuttled between us—we always use that word, don't we? *Shuttled*—or, in reality, strolled, while smoking the roll-ups he hoped we didn't know about.

Before I go on, I ought to describe Lucas's appearance, because most people have only ever seen the photo the papers used, the one of him on the beach in Greece. Damp hair, bare shoulders, a huge grin splitting his tanned face. Breathtakingly alive. During that first term of sixth form, he was only three or four years off the age his father had been when I met him and the resemblance was striking. Lucas had the same ink-black eyes and silky dark hair swept from his face like a spaniel, while his heart-shaped face came from my side of the family. He looked young for his age, I'd say. (Later, when the actor Timothée Chalamet came on the scene, Freya said he would play Lucas in the movie of his life, but I don't suppose we'll ever see that. Not unless someone buys the screen rights to *this*.)

As for Kieran, I heard him before I saw him. Letting myself into the house one evening after work, a few weeks into the new term, I caught the sound of a great rattle of laughter coming from the den, a rich baritone I couldn't place. I poked my head around the door and, finding Lucas with his friend Tom, game consoles on laps, asked if they wanted a snack. Only then did I notice a third boy, sitting on the floor on the far side of the sofa.

"Hi, I don't think we've met before. I'm Lucas's mum, Ellen."

"Hey." He offered me neither his name nor any eye contact.

Lucas took pity on me. "This is Kieran, Mum."

"Oh, so *you're* Kieran? I've heard a lot about you."

The new boy laughed, mockingly, though it was not clear if he was mocking me or Lucas or simply the notion of anyone choosing to talk about him at all.

Smiling, I stepped further into the room to see him. I admit I was surprised by his appearance. Right from the start there'd been a daredevil theme to the anecdotes about him—he'd scaled the high gates that stopped pupils from leaving the premises at lunch time; he'd skidded down the center of the tram when rainwater got in and received a round of applause from the other passengers—and I'd imagined some tall, golden-haired athlete, as heroes often are at that age. Kieran Watts was nothing like that. Short and fleshy, with deep red hair that he had a habit of tugging at and skin bumpy with acne, he was, at first glance, many people's idea of *un*heroic.

The boys were playing *Grand Theft Auto* V or whatever the big violent game was that year, and seemed to be waiting out an internet interruption, so I lingered to chat. "You're new to Foxwell, aren't you, Kieran? Settling in okay?"

"It's all right," he said, as if dismissing an idiotic question.

"The teachers there are so great, aren't they?"

Kieran sent a glance Lucas's way and mouthed what I was fairly sure was "What the fuck?"

"I'm not sure he's that bothered about the teachers," Tom explained (I liked Tom).

"Well, he should be," I said, cheerfully. "Where did you do your GCSEs, Kieran?"

Again, Lucas spoke for him. "Not round here. His old school was in Croydon. Horville Senior, wasn't it?"

"Whoreville, with a 'w,' " Kieran drawled and the other two snickered.

"Wait, the connection's back," Tom said, brandishing his controller.

"Fucking *yes*!" Kieran yelled, with sudden energy. "Let's go!"

I withdrew. It was clear from this interaction that the boy lacked any interest in making a good first impression, but I doubted this was anything to do with his being in foster care. Plenty of kids were self-conscious at this age and hid behind swearing and juvenile banter. Even so, I didn't like the idea of Freya overhearing quips like that "whoreville" one.

Half an hour later, Tom came to say goodbye and Lucas called to me from the hallway. "Going out!"

"Where to?" I asked, hurrying from the kitchen, and he shot me a look of adolescent terror: *Don't show me up in front of my friends.*

"Mate of Kieran's."

"Where does he live?" I asked.

"K?" Lucas prompted.

"What? West Croydon way," Kieran said.

"That's miles away! What about dinner, Lucas?"

"I'll be *out*, Mum!"

As the door closed in my face, I could only stand there gaping, a mother in a teenage movie stupefied by her own irrelevance. But not before catching a parting look from my son's new friend, a look that bristled with dislike and contempt. They call it a death glare, don't they?

Well, let me tell you it was so deadly, so chilling, I actually shivered inside my merino wool jumper.

three

BUT WHAT'S A LOOK, you might ask? This was Beckenham, not *Goodfellas*. Kieran was a disadvantaged child, I was a privileged adult: it was my moral duty to give him the benefit of the doubt.

I certainly wasn't going to say anything to Justin—not yet. Over the course of our twelve-year marriage, I'd developed a finely tuned instinct for when to involve him in my neurotic obsessions—as Vic called them when we were together—and when to nurse the matter privately.

I have a strong feeling that as you read on, you'll come to re-gard Justin with immense admiration, maybe even pity. You'll say he's one in a million and far too good for me. And I would agree with that. But he's not too good for our daughter and that's all that counts now.

When Justin and I met, queuing for the vending machine in the basement of South Beckenham Technical College, I was still with Vic, living in our little flat in Sydenham. I was taking an adult education class called Basic Electrical Understanding, an essential qualification for my future career in lighting, while Justin, who worked for a corporate education company, was making a supervisory visit to an engineering course running at the same time. I knew at once we were sympatico. Where Vic had grown irritable with me ("For God's sake, don't be so hysterical, Ellen" had become a common response by then), Justin was good-humored and rational. He was like a psychologist who could never be dismayed by odd behavior, only pleased to have the opportunity to decode it.

As the machine spat out cups of scalding dishwater and the strip lighting flickered at migraine-inducing speeds, we joked about having found ourselves in the least glamorous coffee spot of our lives. Then we competed to name the *most* glamorous.

"I just came back from Singapore and there was a rooftop café there that'd be pretty hard to beat," Justin said. His face had a kind of honesty to its construction, I thought, all straight lines and agreeable angles, and his gaze was steady.

"I'll take your word for it," I said. "I wouldn't be able to go to it—and if I did, the caffeine would bring on a heart attack." I told him of my condition, using the French term, *l'appel du vide*, which sounded more romantic, like the affliction of an artist or a poet.

"Is that why you have the platinum hair?" he asked. "A nod to Kim Novak?"

"Not at all." I ran my fingers through the short strands, slightly stiff from a fresh bleaching. "I just like this color. Anyway, it's the James Stewart character who has vertigo. Kim trots up tall towers without a care in the world."

"It's so long since I've seen that film," he admitted, something deepening in his smoke-gray eyes. The association was made there and then, I suppose, between glamour and frailty, and I know I benefited from that.

"What's *your* Hitchcock phobia?" I asked him, as we dangled our plastic cups by their rims to avoid burning our fingers.

"Well," he said, smiling. "I can't say I'd be overjoyed if a flock of crows came flying at me."

| | | | | |

So yeah, back to Kieran. Not long after that first meeting came the night of Freya's birthday dinner. It was a Saturday in October and she'd turned twelve the day before. I remember sourcing a vintage green-and-yellow toucan lamp for her gift. As far as I know, it's still on her desk now.

I popped my head round Lucas's door to remind him we were about to leave. As usual, I made no comment about the maddening disorder of his room or the miasma of a week's worth of unventilated odors. "Are you almost ready?"

"What for?"

"Freya's birthday meal."

"Oh." He looked puzzled. "I thought that was yesterday."

"That was her tea with her friends. Tonight, we're going to Ichi Ni for sushi."

"Oh," he said again. Sushi wasn't his favorite; on *his* birthday, we went for burgers. Part of the mythology of our blended family was that Freya had the more sophisticated tastes of the better-off child while Lucas carried the legacy of a humbler start in life. "I'm not actually free."

"Why not?"

"There's a party at Mac's place. I've said I'll go."

"Who's Mac?"

"Mate of Kieran's."

"At Foxwell?"

"No."

"Where's he from then?"

"You mean his school? What's the difference?"

Lucas could keep this sort of thing up for hours, which wasn't helpful right now. "Well, call him and say you can't go. This is your sister's birthday celebration. It's nonnegotiable."

Freya emerged from her room, changed and ready to go. "I don't mind," she said, anxious to avoid a row.

"What's the problem?" Justin asked, from the foot of the stairs.

"Lucas isn't coming," Freya called down. "He's going to a party."

Justin came up to join us. "Can't you go along after dinner?" he suggested.

Lucas groaned. "If we eat quickly, I suppose, yeah."

And so the nonnegotiable was renegotiated and we moved the reservation forward half an hour, arriving to a half-empty restaurant.

"Do we *have* to have a table in the window?" Lucas complained, choosing to sit facing me, with his back to the street, and then spending half his time swiveling to look out at it. Before he'd shoveled the last of his katsu curry into his mouth, a car pulled up outside and issued a series of long and short hoots.

"I think that's your distress signal," Justin said, amused, and I strained to see who was at the wheel. No one in Lucas's year could feasibly have passed their driving test yet, so it had to be an older friend or sibling. I had no trouble recognizing the boy who jumped out of the passenger seat, however. Spotting Lucas in the window, Kieran marched over and pulled a stupid face at him through the glass, in response to which Lucas tossed down his fork so violently it fell to the floor and, barely saying goodbye, made his getaway. I expected

Kieran to meet him at the door, but instead he stayed where he was and stared across Lucas's vacated seat straight at me, that clownish expression supplanted by an insolent victory smirk. This continued even as Lucas could be seen behind him, squeezing into the back seat of the car. Only at the sound of the car horn did Kieran finally join them, keeping his right hand behind his back as he turned, middle finger raised. Since Justin had his back to the window and Freya, shy of her older brother's friends, kept her eyes on her plate, I was the only one to see this gesture of contempt, which was no doubt just what Kieran intended.

"Who was that you were glaring at?" Justin asked me.

"No one," I said, smiling for Freya's benefit.

"It was Kieran," she told her father. "Lucas's friend."

"I hope so, otherwise we've just witnessed a kidnapping," he said and the two of them laughed.

"Anyway, I wasn't glaring," I said, my cheeks scorched like sunburn. *He* was glaring. "I'm just disappointed Lucas had to leave halfway."

"You wouldn't like it if he wasn't invited to anything," Justin pointed out, correctly.

"Yes, Mum, you'd *hate* that," Freya weighed in. They were a team, those two. It had always been the case that when we broke into pairs I'd naturally be with Lucas and Justin with Freya. Now that Lucas couldn't get out of the door fast enough, did that mean I was on my own? Had we entered an era of two against one?

"Shall we have pudding here or go to the gelato place?" I said, and their matching eyes met at the obvious change of subject.

"Gelato, please," Freya said.

| | | | | | |

That night, in the shower, I pondered whether to air my grievances to Justin. Only as I did up my pajama top and wandered into the bedroom did I make my decision.

"Did you *really* not see the way that Kieran character looked at me?" I said.

Justin, already in bed, didn't look up from his thriller. Its title was *Die Trying*. "No, I had my back to him."

"Well, it was really threatening. I didn't want to say in front of Frey, but he gave me the finger as well."

"What?" He glanced up, brow lifting. "Are you serious?"

"Yes." I got into bed, kicked out the duvet, and stretched my toes. "And he waited till the exact moment neither of you could see. Only me."

Justin looked doubtful. "But why would he do that?"

"I have no idea. Motiveless malignancy? I've certainly done nothing to offend him."

"Maybe you misunderstood," Justin suggested. (I swear that will be on my gravestone: *Here Lies Ellen Saint. Maybe She Misunderstood*.) "Or could it have been directed at his crew in the car?"

"His crew?" I chuckled. "No, I don't think so. Anyway, he's obviously a bit of a . . ." I cast about for a kind alternative to the ones that sprang to mind—*lout, brute, troublemaker*—". . . free spirit, and I'm not sure that's what Lucas needs this term, is it? You heard what the Head of Lower Sixth said at the induction meeting, A-levels are a leap, and the boys can't wing it anymore."

I admit I was ambitious for Lucas. He was naturally bright—his teachers' reports backed me up—and the sort of classic all-rounder the top universities loved. "I know Kieran's supposed to be some sort of computer whiz, but I don't get the impression his priority is the academic side of things." It was safer to reference schoolwork over any social concerns. I didn't want to be caught in the act of casual snobbery, even with my own husband.

Justin closed his book. "Is Lucas in classes with him?"

"Only for geography. Not maths or biology, though."

"I guess he has to decide for himself who he wants to hang out with." In the lamplight, Justin's gaze was ambiguous: was he sympathizing with me or warning me off? I couldn't tell. "Make his own mistakes," he added.

"So you *do* think Kieran's a mistake?"

"I know hardly anything about him. But if he is, then Lucas needs to be the one to come to that conclusion, not us."

"That doesn't mean we can't try to steer him away if it looks like he's falling in with a bad crowd."

Justin smiled. "What, there's a whole crowd of Kierans, is there?"

"I'm not sure, but he certainly seems to know a lot of kids from other schools." Rougher schools, full of boys like this Mac (why hadn't I demanded an address for him?). I thought of the crush of kids in the car; there couldn't possibly have been enough seat belts to go around. "It's a different group," I added.

"The Motiveless Malignants? Let's try not to get too *Daily Mail* about this, eh?"

He fell asleep easily, as the even-tempered do, while I stayed awake right until I heard footsteps stumbling up the path and a key turn in the door.

Lucas, home safe.

four

Leaving Jacob's Wharf, I have my hand on the door, ready to pull it open, when it's suddenly shoved towards me and I hear myself cry out.

"Excuse me." The incoming figure, a well-heeled older woman carrying a canvas Tate Modern tote straining with groceries, holds the door with a show of keeping her distance.

"Sorry," I say. "You gave me a fright."

She does not reply. Some people are instinctively repelled by skittishness, I've found.

Outside, I take a moment to compose myself. I can't spend the foreseeable future cringing. Before I make any decisions, I need proper confirmation that the man I saw is him, that I'm not losing my mind.

I cut through Butler's Wharf and cross the footbridge over St Saviour's Dock, the river a churning gray expanse to my left. From the bridge, less is visible of the building opposite Selena's than I'd hoped, the angle allowing a frustratingly partial view of that rooftop perch. I follow the passageways to Mill Street, where the entrance to the building is easily identified. The Heights, it's called. The name is carved on a stone panel, letters in lowercase, with an elongated riser on the "h." There appears to be only one flat per floor and, in a grandiose touch, each has its own brass plate and button, the kind you might find on an old Venetian apartment building. The name for the top flat, number 10, is S. Harding and my breath catches in my throat when I see that. Harding is my maiden name. A coincidence or some sort of sick tribute? Some sort of *joke*.

To the right of the building, there's a narrow lane leading underground, presumably where parking and other services are situated, and to the left, there's a gated passageway connected to a fire door. Though none of it looks particularly high-tech, all zones are accessible only by keycode.

I have a sudden idea. First, I check I'm not wearing anything Kieran might recognize from years ago—my charcoal-gray mac was bought in this year's sales, the furry bucket hat a recent birthday present from Freya—and then I keep my head down and press the buzzer for Flat 10.

Nothing. Beneath my feet, the paving stones gleam in the thin light, rivulets of rainwater trickling between them. I press a second time. Again, nothing. Why doesn't he answer? No longer than ten minutes has passed since I saw him, so where could he have gone? A horrifying thought strikes: if I saw him, doesn't it follow that he might have seen me? Come to hunt *me* down.

Holding my nerve, I try the other buzzers until someone answers and invites me to leave my package inside. The door releases and my boots clatter onto marble. To my immediate right is a slate-topped console table with a few Amazon boxes already stacked, ahead there's a lift, and to the left are two doors, one signed to the stairs and the other marked "No Entry." I keep my head down. Though the building predates the mania for police-standard surveillance and is too small for a concierge, it's not impossible there's a maintenance worker somewhere on the premises or a service monitoring video footage remotely.

At the sound of the lift groaning into motion, I slip through the door to the stairs and peer through the glass panel as the lift opens and a young woman emerges. Then, before I can change my mind, I climb the stairs. It's an enclosed staircase, with one small round window per floor looking onto the featureless brickwork of the neighboring building, so nothing to trigger my fear. But at the tenth floor, when I push through a fire door onto the landing, there *is* a problem: directly ahead is a narrow full-height window overlooking the water. Clear floor-to-ceiling glass this high can bring on panic, my brain mistaking it for an unprotected drop. I need to avoid looking at it and focus on the apartment door instead, on the chrome "10" set plum in the middle.

Only now, knuckles just inches from knocking, do I ask myself what it is I intend to happen here. Do I expect to be asked in? To *talk*? The thought of being close to him—the thought of his being *alive*—causes a crawling sensation on my scalp and I let my fist drop. For a full minute, I do nothing but wait and listen. Then I take a step closer and actually put my ear to the door.

That's when I catch it: the sound of breathing. Soft, rhythmic, human. Spooked, I skitter off to the left and, before I can orientate, I'm right up against that strip of glass, palms flat, ten stories above the dock. As the water ripples below, there's the illusion that it's the building that's moving and I hear myself moan in terror. Then the glass seems to dissolve and I'm stepping into the void, I'm speeding headlong, Selena's question spinning in my head: *Would you land on the walkway or in the water?*

Knees soft, I stagger backwards, my hands clawing the walls as if searching for something to grip on this pitching ship, past the flat door and back to the stairwell. Whatever nerve brought me up here has vanished and I stumble back down the stairs, exiting the building without looking back. I tear down Mill Street towards Tooley Street, then straight on and across Tower Bridge Road. Seeing a coffee shop in a side alley, I duck in, order an Earl Grey to go. *Breathe.*

Only as I wait do I make the connection. It's the same café where I killed time the morning Justin took Lucas and Freya to the top of the newly opened Shard, before the four of us went for lunch. Seventy-two floors and as high as it got—still gets—in London. I remember my irrational gratitude when the group reappeared, how I hugged both my children tightly, and I feel the imprint of my son again now, the narrow bones of his torso, the jut of his chin against the top of my head.

Collecting my tea from the server, I find I'm crying, something I haven't done in public in a long time.

By the time I enter the soaring space of London Bridge Station, I've calmed enough to find my phone and leave a voice mail for the first person—the only person—who needs to know what just happened.

"Call me as soon as you get this. I mean it, Vic, it's urgent!"

five

I SHOULD EXPLAIN THAT although Vic has often been misreported as my ex-husband, we were never married. We were twenty-three when we had Lucas and under no pressure to formalize our new family—in any case, we were never going to withstand the earthquake of a baby, with or without smoked salmon canapés and a band cranking out soft rock covers.

But we stayed close after we split. In fact, our relationship improved, the parenting discussions that had begun to be a source of dispute between us now serving to unite us. Vic followed Justin and me to Beckenham and we co-parented in a style that would now be labeled "conscious" or "authentic" but that we considered basic common sense. The best for Lucas.

And all of a sudden "the best for Lucas" concerned Kieran.

"What do you think of Lucas's new bestie?" I asked, when we met for a quick drink near the station. He's an attractive guy, Vic, one of those wiry, magnetic types. Whatever cool is, he has it. Mind you, as I said, by this point Lucas had grown to look like him, to match him in height, which I suppose must have created a kind of nepotistic beauty bias.

Vic's job as a manager for a leasing company required a certain level of presentable attire, but out of work he wore the battered jeans and vintage band T-shirt of a student and on this occasion, if I remember, it was The Doors. I noted, but did not comment on, the progress of the hipster beard he was growing; it undoubtedly meant he'd secured another meeting with an investor to pitch his craft beer idea.

"I assume you mean Kieran?" He grimaced over the top of his pint. "What do *you* think?"

"I think he's a complete waster," I said.

"Right. Nice of the school to consult us before they saddled our son with some problem kid."

"If it was only at school, it wouldn't be so bad, but it's out of school, as well. They're inseparable."

"We need to keep an eye on it, definitely," Vic said. "He's bad news."

"I'm so glad someone agrees with me," I told him, and I felt the particular shame of an unattractive prejudice reinforced. "I've found him very rude, but Justin thinks I'm imagining it. There's the whole foster placement thing and I think he finds my attitude a bit un-PC."

"He might feel a bit less PC himself if Freya was the one following him around like the Pied Piper," Vic said.

"Oh, without a doubt." Though this was fondly said—we both knew that Justin adored Lucas as much as we did—it felt disloyal to be talking like this.

Which is a joke when you think of the secrets Vic and I would keep from Justin later.

| | | | | | |

Frighteningly quickly, it began to feel as if Lucas was hardly ever at home, even on school nights, and when he was, he and Kieran were joined at the hip. There was still the odd gaming session in the den, but where Tom or other kids would leave for homework or family meal times, Kieran would always suggest going on to some party or hangout. Though there were no more overtly hostile gestures towards me (or not that I saw), I grew to loathe the distinctive spring in his stride — as if he hadn't quite learned to put his heels to the ground — as he led my son down our hallway and out of the door, off to wilder neighborhoods.

The Find a Phone app didn't exist then, or if it did, I hadn't yet heard of it (for Freya, later, yes, we tracked, but I think that's understandable). Instead, we relied on texts from Lucas to say he was safe. Good old-fashioned trust. Vic was very good about picking him up from parties and Lucas seemed to prefer that option, maybe because Vic's company car, a black Mondeo, could be passed off as a taxi, whereas I looked too much like a neurotic mum in my high-end silver Jeep with the "Child on Board" sticker I'd never got around to removing.

Occasionally an old red Corsa would pull up in the middle of the night to deliver Lucas home and this, I learned, was the car of Kieran's foster mum, Prisca.

May I take this opportunity to say I liked Prisca, still do, in spite of all that's happened between us, the impossibility of true accord. I met her that first term of sixth form at parents' evening, when we were both in the queue for the geography teacher. She was in her early fifties, about five five, dressed in a shapeless hooded jacket and knockoff Uggs. Compared to the typical Foxwell mum, who was ambitious and managerial in her parenting, she had the approachable, good-natured air of a grandparent.

"You're Prisca," I said, as the boys peeled away from us, and she agreed that she was and that I'd got the pronunciation right—*Priss*-ka. "I'm Ellen."

She seemed unsure what our connection was.

"Your Kieran is chums with my boy, Lucas."

Accustomed to a culture of flattering others' kids at every turn— "He's a *charming* boy," "She could be a model," "He's so clever he'll walk into Oxford" (you get the picture)—it felt strange when Prisca failed to compliment Lucas even in the smallest way. Then again, I wasn't about to lavish praise on Kieran either. "They were buddied up to help Kieran settle in," I reminded her.

"Oh, yes, that's right. Foxwell's very good like that," she said. "Kieran's old school was a bit more sink or swim."

"Is that why he transferred?"

"All sorts of reasons." Though she had an open, even guileless manner, she was adroit at closing down my lines of inquiry.

"Do you have other kids besides Kieran?"

"Not at the moment. Mind you, it's a full house with a teenager and their friends, isn't it?"

"Yes," I said, though I was finding the opposite now Lucas was out so much. I proposed we exchange numbers, which she agreed to with the air of someone who knew how to pick her battles. And, as the queue for the teacher moved and Prisca summoned Kieran for his turn, I couldn't help feeling that she regarded me as a battle not worth picking.

| | | | | | |

In late November, Lucas turned seventeen. "How about hosting a soirée for your birthday?" I suggested, and he laughed at the word. I'd found that such *High Society*–speak was more acceptable to him than my trying to be down with the kids. ("Anyone who still says 'down with the kids' is not," Vic said.) "We'll take Freya to Grandma and Grandpa's, so you can have the place to yourself for the night."

"Maybe," Lucas said.

Maybe, yes. The offer of an empty house was never going to be passed up. Beyond stringing lights in the kitchen and conservatory in the hopes of demarcating the party zone, I kept my interference to a minimum. A casual reminder to him not to advertise the event on social media. Of course, I knew better than to issue any more specific sanctions regarding the guest list, since they'd only be disregarded. It went without saying that Kieran would be there.

There being no known temperance movement in their sixth form, Lucas's guests would need booze and Justin and I favored the approach of supplying it directly rather than leaving them to ship in their own 40 percent proof vodka.

No drugs and no smoking, we said, but we weren't idiots. We were under no illusion that those little canisters of NO_2 wouldn't find their way in too.

"You're not worried your house'll get trashed?" my friend Sheridan asked me. She was the mother of Jade, a girl Lucas liked who was, in my view, a natural match for him: attractive, charming, academic. They hadn't overlapped in year eleven, but now had two subjects together. "Or the bedrooms used," she added.

"Out of sight, out of mind," I said, more with a sense of hope than any real insouciance. "Vic, Lucas's dad, will be on call in case of emergencies."

Her face brightened. "Oh, yes, we know Vic."

Which meant Jade must now be hanging out at Vic's flat too. I could only dream that she'd displaced Kieran.

"My sister-in-law just set up a hidden camera at my niece's sixteenth," she said.

"A camera?"

"Yeah, you know you can do it on an iPhone now? There's this motion detector app thing you can use."

"That sounds a bit creepy," I said. There were no locks on the doors in our house, even the bedrooms. Would a row of closed doors deter the rampaging hormones of teens? It was doubtful.

Sheridan pulled a face. "I have no problem with creepy. You wait, Ellen, you'll find out."

"What do you mean?" I said, surprised.

"Er, your other child? The one with two X chromosomes?"

"Oh, yes. Sorry, I'm a bit preoccupied with Lucas." And as we laughed, I thought of all the mothers out there worrying themselves silly. It was a full-time job in itself and it didn't seem to matter if the children were technically adults. They were always our cubs, always in need of our protection.

| | | | | | |

Having said that, I remember that night away as one of the last of the carefree times. We drove down to the Kent coast to meet my parents in St Margaret's, the tip of England closest to France, and Freya, Justin, and my mother walked up to the South Fireland Lighthouse while I stayed in a café in the bay with my father. He was in a wheelchair following hip replacement surgery.

Though the sight of that cliff-edge path unsettled me, I loved my home coastline and its colors—grass-green, ocean-blue, chalk-white—have always been my favorites. Over the years, I painted the Tanglewood Road house in endless variations of them; there isn't an interior design scheme in all the world to match it.

The walkers returned, cheeks touched with high color and hair blown into madcap shapes around their heads. "It was quite gusty up there," Justin reported. "For a minute there I thought we were going to be knocked off our feet!"

"I don't want to hear," I said, smiling.

"When did my mum know she had a fear of heights?" I heard Freya asking her grandma as they queued at the counter.

That was how I characterized my disorder to the kids: a fear of falling, not the urge to jump.

"It was when she was about five or six," Mum told her. "We were walking on a different stretch of the cliff path and she held my hand so tightly I had bruises the next day."

"I like being high up," Freya said. "When I grow up, I want to live in a tall block of flats. Kieran wants to as well."

"Who's Kieran?" Mum asked, setting their drinks on the table. We accommodated the new seats in a tight huddle.

"A new friend of Lucas's." I sent her a look. "He was recently in trouble for climbing onto the roof of the school."

"He says when he leaves home, he's going to live in a penthouse in Central London," Freya said.

"He'll need to improve his grades if that's going to happen." I hoped I didn't sound too scornful.

"Is Lucas still thinking about Oxbridge?" my father asked.

"I hope so. If he does all the extra reading he's supposed to. Not tonight, though, obviously."

The conversation moved on to Freya's school grades and then to the cream tea we planned to eat when we got home. There were scones and clotted cream, and a neighbor of my parents had just dropped round a jar of homemade rhubarb jam.

Rhubarb jam, so English! The whole thing strikes me now as the very picture of security and support and love. Smug, you might say, but I really don't think so. I was too much of a catastrophist to ever be smug.

| | | | | | |

In spite of a reassuring text from Vic, when we pulled up at the house on Sunday evening I still half expected to see jagged gaps in the front door where the original stained glass had been. But it was intact. Inside was also impressively untouched. Friends who'd stayed over had helped clear up in the morning, Lucas explained, Jade's name buried casually in the list.

Meanwhile, no parents had left voice mails about stomach pumps at A&E, no neighbors queued at the door to complain of a pounding sound system or scratched cars.

"Did you have fun?" I asked Lucas.

"Yeah, it was good."

"How many people?"

"Thirty, maybe."

"Double that," Justin said. "Did anyone vomit?"

Amid theatrical *urghs* from Freya, Lucas just grinned.

I took our bags up to the bedroom, immediately noticing the spicy cedarwood scent of my perfume, a bottle of which stood on the chest of drawers under the window, its lid off. The window had been cracked open and I caught the faint smell of weed on the curtains as I went to close it.

Remembering Sheridan's warning, I searched for more clues of occupancy. I wasn't proud of myself for running my fingers over the not-quite-smoothed-out duvet and examining the short red hairs I found there. I didn't need a hidden camera to tell me who had been in here. I stripped the bedclothes in a matter of seconds, but I knew I couldn't strip my mind of the image of Kieran Watts rolling about on our bed with a girl or perhaps even alone. Lighting up, spraying toiletries, prowling the room.

No care for the space he inhabited, the people he used.

Killing Time (cont)

What do we know of Ellen Saint? What do we remember of her brief prominence in the British media?

She is a tigress of a mother, that comes first. That was what fueled Lock Up Longer, the campaign for stiffer prison sentences that she launched in 2015 in partnership with a national tabloid. Less well known are her business credentials as a lighting consultant, her once-thriving roster of affluent clients. (It's too easy to talk of her story as one of light and dark and it is to her credit that she resists the temptation in her own account.)

She grew up in the North Downs, near the famous white cliffs of Dover, a problematic base for someone with a phobia of heights. Hers is a form known as "high place phenomenon," characterized by a sudden compulsion to jump that may seem at odds with the sufferer's normally conservative relationship with risk. Asked about it in a newspaper interview, she said, "I have intrusive thoughts about high places, yes, but I've never acted on them." She added, "Actions are what count. People should not be judged for their thoughts. Heaven knows, if we were, I for one would be serving back-to-back life sentences at Holloway."

Something else we know about Ellen Saint: she's held on to her sense of humor.

Sunday Times magazine,
December 2021

six

I'D LIKE TO EMPHASIZE that it was very rare for me to feel animosity like this—make that unprecedented. I could probably count on the fingers of one hand the people in my adult life that I've truly disliked.

And for my nemesis to be a seventeen-year-old boy! I should have known better. I should have *done* better. But whether or not self-improvement on my part would have altered the outcome, I really don't know.

As for Lucas, if any doubt lingered in his mind that I would have preferred a version of his sixth-form life without Kieran Watts in it, then it evaporated after the ferry incident.

It was the spring term by then and the two of them were supposed to be on a geography field trip to the Wye Valley. At 7 p.m., I got a barely decipherable text from Lucas telling me they were back and he was at Kieran's and would eat there. I was in the bath an hour or so later when Justin took a call from the police explaining that the boys had been escorted from a cross-channel ferry arriving in Dover, having been caught smoking cannabis on one of the decks.

"A cross-channel ferry? They've been to *France?*" There was a split second of confusion—had the school changed the field trip destination?—followed by furious understanding. They'd phoned in sick and gone on this unauthorized jaunt instead.

"Thank God it was only dope, the police don't bother with that so much these days," Justin said. "They've been let off with a caution, but they're in no fit state to make their own way home. I thought maybe your mum could take them in while we talk to Prisca and decide how to mobilize?"

It was arranged that my mother would pick the boys up and keep them overnight, then Justin would drive down early to collect them. He knew I'd be too emotional to drive. Mum echoed this sentiment when I phoned to speak to Lucas.

"He's not making much sense, Ellen. Let him sleep it off and get to the bottom of it tomorrow."

I knew exactly what was at the bottom of it—or rather *who.* The whole caper smacked of the rule-breaking Kieran specialized in. It meant nothing to him to party on a school night, climb onto the roof of a public building, or, apparently, take a drug-fueled day trip when he should have been in class.

I hardly slept that night, already awake when Justin prepared to leave for his daybreak taxi service. Outside, the blackbirds and robins were in full voice, but all I could hear was the contemptuous jangle of Kieran's laughter seventy miles away, making it seem like Justin's rescue mission was just another overreaction on the part of other people's parents.

"I assume you'll drop Kieran home first?" I said, from bed.

"Actually, no. His situation is slightly more complicated," Justin said. "He drove them down in Prisca's car and so I'm picking her up and taking her to get her car from the port. Then she'll follow me to your parents' and collect Kieran."

I jerked upright. "He *drove* them down? You mean alone, just him and Lucas?"

"As I understand it, yes."

"Didn't Prisca notice the car was missing? Or the keys?"

"She was at work, apparently."

"He's still got his L plates, Justin! Learners aren't supposed to drive on the motorway unless they're with their instructor."

"I don't know which route they took," Justin said, infuriatingly matter-of-fact. "Maybe they stuck to B roads."

"Any route is illegal on their own!" I cried. If I was irate about the drugs and the truancy, I was terrified by this.

"Prisca says he's taking his test in a couple of weeks," Justin said. "Apparently he's a natural."

A natural delinquent. "Why didn't you tell me this last night?"

"Because you were upset enough as it was." Justin turned from me. "Look, I need to get going. I'll phone you when I get there."

I fought hard to conceal my internal commotion when Freya came down for breakfast. I hadn't forgotten that remark of Sheridan's, humorous though it had been: *Er, your other child?* Lucas was my priority, thanks to this parlous new influence, but the last thing I wanted was to neglect my daughter. I made her waffles and Nutella, a sure sign that I was burying bad news.

"When's Lucas coming back?" she asked.

"Later this morning."

"Is he in trouble?"

"A bit, but nothing for you to worry about."

"I'm sure he didn't mean anything, Mum."

Maybe that was the problem, I thought. Maybe it was better to mean something by your misdemeanors. I dropped a kiss on the top of my daughter's head and watched as she smoothed her hair flat, wiping off my touch.

| | | | | | |

The school phoned at nine thirty to question Lucas's absence. I'd forgotten to send an email before the 9 a.m. cutoff.

"I'm afraid yesterday's absence was unauthorized, as well," Tracey from the school office told me. "The message needs to come from the parent's email address, not the pupil's."

Then why didn't you investigate this yesterday? "I understand," I said. "He'll be back in after lunch. I'm sure he'll be able to explain himself."

"I'll book in ten minutes for him with his head of year, Mrs. Shipton, shall I? Three thirty, if you could tell him."

"Of course. Will that be with Kieran or on his own?"

"Kieran?"

"Yes, Kieran Watts?"

There was the sound of tapping on a keyboard. "You're right, Kieran *was* off yesterday, but fully authorized. He won't need to see Mrs. Shipton."

"I see."

As I waited for them to return, I texted Sheridan.

> Did you know anything about the kids bunking off to go to Calais yesterday?

> No, thought they were in the Wye Valley.
> Who?

Not Jade. Just Lucas and Kieran.

There was a longer pause before her next message:

Kieran. Say no more.

Lucas thinks the sun shines out of his arse.

Yep. Jade too.

I gathered from this that she shared my distaste. I suppose, by then, I was keeping a mental note of allies.

Justin and Lucas got home just after one. Despite having obviously showered—urged by my mother, no doubt—Lucas was wearing yesterday's clothes and looked grubby and gritty-eyed. Justin had to leave immediately for the office and so I confronted our young offender alone.

"It's okay to say no to Kieran, you know. Let him find someone else to be his partner in crime occasionally."

Lucas's face twisted in annoyance. "Why do you always want to blame him? Maybe it was *my* idea."

"Was it?" I demanded. "Was it your idea to steal Prisca's car and drive seventy miles to Dover, when neither of you have the correct license or insurance? Was it your idea to get on a ferry to France without saying a word about it to your parents or teachers? To send lying texts to cover up where you really were? Was it your idea to buy and use illegal substances?"

"It was just a bit of weed! You're making it out to be some big crime."

"You'll need to sound a lot sorrier than that when you explain yourself to Mrs. Shipton this afternoon," I snapped.

"What?" Lucas was outraged. "I'm not going into school."

"You damn well are. I've said you'll be in after lunch and you're booked in to see her at three thirty. On your own, as well. Your great mate Kieran got Prisca to phone him in sick. *His* slate is clean."

It was impossible to tell whether he already knew this or not. I suspected not. He assumed his footloose, spontaneous friend was making life up as he went along, not plotting to cover his tracks. As his eyes welled with childish tears, I softened my stance.

"Look, they know nothing about your alternative field trip or your brush with the police, so I suggest you keep it that way if you don't want to be suspended. Just say you were ill, but your parents forgot to send the email."

Great. Now I was urging him to lie. No one was coming out of this well.

"I've made you a sandwich. Eat that, then go and get your stuff, I'll drop you in the car."

Lucas threw me a furious look before stomping to the kitchen to eat. When I heard him on the phone—I guessed to Kieran—it was all I could do to stop myself from going in and dashing the phone from his hand.

After I'd run him to school, I rang Mum to thank her for her overnight services.

"There's something not right about that other boy," she said.

"What do you mean?"

"The way he looks at you, it's cold. Emotionless. I knew straight-away he must be the one you told us about."

I'd forgotten I'd complained to her about Kieran on the phone once or twice—I hoped Freya had not been within earshot.

"I think you're right to keep Lucas away from him," she added.

I sighed. "Apparently without much success."

"Can you speak to the school about separating them?"

"They're the ones who pushed them together in the first place. Anyway, it doesn't work at this age. Forbidden fruit and all that."

"What does Vic say?"

"I need to call him next," I said, slightly ashamed that I needed reminding.

In the event, Vic was fully supportive of my stance, including both the cover-up I'd briefed and the punishment I planned to dole out. "No nights out, no parties, no nothing, for a month. And I suggest we make it clear Kieran is no longer welcome in either of our homes."

"Fine by me," he agreed, with only the subtlest note of "Good luck with that" detectable.

Lucas, returning from school with a printout of the school's policy on reporting absences, listened in sullen silence as I outlined the new rules. His only response was a muttered "You're ridiculous" and I decided I could live with that.

As for Justin, once the inconvenience of the rescue mission had been forgotten, he was typically pacific about the whole thing.

"This is the kind of thing parents laugh about years later." He adopted an exaggerated elderly croak: " 'Remember the time young Lucas got the ferry to France and was caught smoking grass on the deck? Met off the boat by the police, he was!' We won't be able to remember Kieran's name then, you wait. 'Who was that kid we thought was such a terrible influence? Kevin, was it?' "

Perhaps if it had been Jade with whom Lucas had absconded, I might have been able to share in the smiles. She'd have been shamefaced, at least, and I'd have reasoned that a police caution nipped any wayward instincts in the bud just in time to knuckle down to the serious study required if they were both to go to good universities.

But Kieran, no. I couldn't get on board with Justin's comic projection.

Nor did I believe we'd ever forget his name.

And I was right about that.

seven

I'M ALREADY BACK IN Beckenham, halfway between train station and home, by the time Vic phones me back.

"I got your message," he says, and there is a familiar agony in the silence that follows as we hear the words that would for so many years have naturally come next. *Lucas all right?* or *Lucas on his way?* Or, in the age of Kieran, *I need to talk to you about Lucas.* Our son was always the reason for the call—the link that made us a chain.

Still is.

"What's up?" he says. "You sounded a bit upset."

"It's Kieran Watts. He's back." Only as I speak does it occur to me that I had a second option this morning when I left Vic that message: I could have kept this information to myself. Spared him the pain.

But it's more complicated than that, as he and I both know.

"I mean, he's *alive*," I add, lowering my voice as if at risk of being overheard. "I saw him, Vic. I saw him this morning."

There's silence on the line. All I can hear is the slap and scuff of my boots on the pavement.

"Well, it can't have been him, can it?" Vic says, finally, and where I had expected outrage, or at the very least bafflement, there is nothing but pity in his voice, pity at the distress my misapprehension has caused me. Not only that, but dragging and clinking sounds start up in the background, telling me he's working as he talks. Loading or unloading boxes of Common or Gordon beers for his next farmers' market or music event or sports meeting (the UK is your oyster when the product you're selling contains alcohol). I've already lost his full attention and it is crucial that I use a measured, sane tone if I'm not to squander what's left. "Obviously I can't explain it, but the fact is it happened. *I saw him.*"

Vic sighs. "Where?"

"On the roof terrace of a building in Shad Thames. It's called The Heights." I've already decided not to tell him that I tricked my way in and went up to Kieran's flat. It sounds much too incautious. Recalling my lack of strategy, my empty-minded vigilance as I stood outside his door, and the way I bolted like an animal, I shudder.

"Where were you?" Vic asks.

"In the building opposite, just across the water, about five floors down."

"Five floors? So not very close, then."

"Close enough to recognize someone you know well," I protest. "You know them by their mannerisms, their posture. Their gait."

"Their gait," he repeats and I know he's thinking, *That's a new one.* "Come on, Ellen," he says, gently. "It's not like we haven't been here before."

This is true. Several times, we've had discussions like this, each leaving us unnerved but ultimately accepting of the fact that it couldn't possibly have been Kieran. Just an episode as real-seeming and fraudulent as déjà vu.

He looked so exactly like him, I almost fainted, but when he stood up, he was way too tall . . .

I could have sworn it was him, but then I realized he was too young. He looked like they did when they were seventeen . . .

That terrible "they" had silenced us, laid to rest that last misjudgment, almost a year ago. "I actually think we're wired to see him," Justin told me on that occasion. "Especially you and Vic. It'll probably go on for the rest of your lives. It's the part of us that believes in miracles and magic. The soul, I suppose."

I found his theory very consoling.

As I turn into Tanglewood Road and its fiesta of autumnal foliage—oh, how I miss it!—Vic's kindly skepticism resumes in my ear: "Plus, well, Freya's just started at uni, hasn't she? So it's only natural . . ."

Natural that the emotions associated with Lucas's first term at university have bubbled to the surface, he means, bringing with them flashbacks and hallucinations. Ghosts.

"Things can seem the way we want them to," he adds and the abrupt crunching sound of his van doors shutting, followed by a call goodbye to a colleague, makes me lose my patience.

"Why would I *want* to see Kieran? Wouldn't I rather it was any one of the other seven billion people on the planet? More to the point, *how* have I seen him? Look, meet me after work and I'll take you there. You'll know it's true the moment you see him."

"I can't, Ellen." He sighs, mournful notes in his breath. He's sure I'm wrong but that doesn't mean he isn't aching too.

"Is India expecting you home?" I guess. There've been numerous partners in the near two decades since we broke up, but I can tell India is different. She has real sway, this one.

"No, but I'm heading up to Birmingham for a face-to-face with a new customer. I'm literally just loading up and about to hit the road."

"Okay, tomorrow then? In the morning?"

"I can't do tomorrow either. I'm staying the night and won't be back till lunchtime. Sorry, but it's a crazy time for me. Trade events and markets almost every weekend. With a new business, I just can't turn anything down. I'll call you when I'm back, yeah?"

"Fine," I say, over the sound of his van engine starting. "I'll get you proof."

"Proof?"

"Yes, a photo or something."

There is a sharp intake of breath, a warning coming. The engine is killed. "Ellen, promise me you won't go back and confront him. This younger generation can be very sensitive. You don't want this person reporting you for harassment."

"This person" who is not who I say he is, he means. But he has a point about avoiding confrontation. "Dangerously impulsive," that was what the judge called Kieran. Heedless of the welfare of others. It was hotheaded of me to approach his apartment without knowing if there was a single other soul in the building who might come to my aid if things turned violent. And that panic attack at the top window: what if I'd fainted and come round to find that monster bearing down on me?

"Promise me," Vic repeats and I hang up with a bitter laugh.

It's like he doesn't know me.

| | | | | | |

I don't tell Justin. I can't risk both of them doubting me. And while it feels impossible not to involve Vic, I can certainly protect Justin — for the time being. Of course, he notices I'm distracted within five minutes of arriving home from work. First, I don't know if I want a drink or not, then I'm not sure how hungry I am. Our home, my pride and joy for so long, restful and comforting, feels like a stage set, designed to deceive.

"You okay, El?"

"Fine."

He cracks open a can of Common or Gordon pale ale (we are subscribers to Vic's popular monthly plan) and pours me a glass of white, which I drink with obvious urgency. "You sure?"

"Yes." I try to hide my alarm that the man opposite me, my *husband*, looks less familiar than he did this morning. I size him up: square face, with the smooth Saint jawline; once nut-brown hair now liberally salt-and-peppered; gray eyes faded with fatigue. In spite of his efforts to keep himself in shape—running, cycling, the usual MAMIL stuff—he looks older than his forty-nine years (mind you, we all look older than we are in this story—you can take that as read).

No, it's not he who has changed since this morning, it's me. My senses have been hijacked.

We eat sausages and mash for dinner. Since our resident pescatarian left for uni, we've reintroduced meat. Justin tells me about his day: an e-learning presentation that told him nothing he didn't already know; a lunch he could have taken or left; something about apprenticeships that rescued his mood just in time for the commute home.

"How was your meeting?" he asks. "The one with the new client."

Justin is unflaggingly supportive of my business. I used to work for an events company, lighting jobs on a scale a hundred times bigger than anything I do now—sports events and conferences and weddings—but there came a time when I knew I could no longer manage. To master the epic, you have to be strong, complete, and I was broken.

My business is small, but steady. Modest commissions, bite-size achievements. The occasional location might trouble me, but the architects I work with know not to come to me with high-rise work, those off-plan developments where you have to go up in construction elevators to units with great windowless holes in the walls, open to the elements.

"Fine," I say.

"Where's she based?"

"Shad Thames. Right on the water, near Butler's Wharf."

"It's nice there. Pricey."

"Yes." Especially penthouse flats with outside space. I feel confusion rise and mingle with my frustration at Vic's denial. How the hell can a loser like Kieran afford an apartment like that? The rent must be thousands a month. Has he latched on to some unsuspecting woman? Does she know about his past? The googling I indulged in this afternoon yielded no mention of him since the press reports of his disappearance in July 2017. Nothing to his name at all. Which is exactly what I would have expected and what Vic assumes is the case.

Justin spears the sausage I've pushed to the edge of my plate in favor of more wine. "Did you see Frey's picture today?" he says.

"Huh?" We have a family WhatsApp group. You're probably familiar with the dynamic: Mum keeps it going, day after day, striving to stay relevant in her newly flown chick's life; child humors her with cute titbits; Dad throws in a line or two because he knows it's important to contribute. It's not like that for us. Instead, there's constant easy banter between father and daughter, with the odd interjection by me.

He passes me his phone to show me a picture of Freya's desk in her room at Warwick, where she's in her first term of a history degree. There are piles of books, a scattering of devices, her toucan lamp, rewired just before she left.

I feel a stab of love in the pit of me, followed by a strange hollowing. "I'm so glad it's going well for her," I say. "Nothing for us to worry about."

Watching my husband smile with an ease that's only recently returned, all I can think is that I neither want nor need this retrograde infusion of pain from Kieran Watts. It is like a drug administered against my will, alcohol force-fed in rehab by some perverse, sadistic doctor.

Well, I will not allow it. I will not allow him to tear us apart a second time.

eight

I WON'T TROUBLE YOU with every individual example of Kieran's toxic influence, the ones that sound negligible in isolation but cumulatively turned me gray. Suffice to say it was soon obvious that our response to the cross-channel jaunt had done nothing to curb the pair's taste for partying—and only made Lucas more secretive.

Once released from captivity, he simply took his antics off-site. On weekend nights, he'd stay over at a friend's house and return the next afternoon dead-eyed and smelly, dashing off an hour's schoolwork before abandoning study for gaming. Kieran no longer came to play in person, of course, but I'd hear his voice through the speakers, trading war stories with Lucas about blackouts, whiteouts, blowouts—I really don't know what they were called. "Wavey," that was a word Kieran used a lot. *I was so fucking wavey last night.* He spoke in a patois Vic had identified as roadman. A roll-up was a blem, trainers were kreps (best served fresh), the prospect of a party left him gassed. Everything was peng and peak and safe and gully.

"You don't think he's just a harmless idiot?" Justin said, when I relayed this to him.

"If he hadn't single handedly turned our son into a doper, I might," I said.

"I'm not sure about this ban on his coming to the house, Ellen. Maybe we should consider keeping our enemies closer?"

"I'd prefer to keep him as far away as possible," I said. "But I've spoken to Vic and we've agreed he'll relax things a bit."

"Really?" Justin was surprised. "How did he persuade you?"

"It was my idea. He was worried he wouldn't ever see Lucas if he wasn't allowed to bring Kieran with him."

"I think that's a good move. Better they're at his place than roaming the streets aimlessly, speaking in tongues. One of us needs to have a bit more . . ." He paused, finding the word. "*Access* to what's going on."

Well, our "access" would increase soon enough. Towards the end of the summer term, Lucas was off school with a cold one Monday when Vic rang me at my desk at home. "Have you seen this email from the school?"

"No, what?"

"It's from Friday, but I've been away and had my Out of Office on. You need to read it, El."

Checking, I found it in my junk folder, having come from an unrecognized address, FAST: Foxwell Academy Safeguarding Team. *Safeguarding?*

> Dear Mr. Gordon and Mrs. Saint,
> We are sorry to tell you that your son, Lucas, is suspended from school for one week . . .

"What the fuck? I'll phone you back." I disconnected Vic and hared upstairs, laptop in hand, to hammer on Lucas's bedroom door. When he didn't reply, I barged in and snapped on the light, ignoring both his protests and the appalling chaos within.

I thrust the laptop in his face. "When were you going to mention this?"

"What?" He scanned the email through eyes glued half-shut, his already high color deepening. His breath smelled foul.

"Is this cold of yours even real? What's going on?"

He let the laptop drop onto the bed, muttering, "It was just some stupid photo."

"What stupid photo? You haven't—" My hand flew to my mouth. "Oh, God, you haven't circulated a picture of Jade or one of the other girls? Something private?"

"No, I fuckin' haven't," he said, indignantly.

"Do not swear at me! What photo, Lucas?"

He glanced away, grunting. "Law it, bruv."

Law it, bruv? I felt my own anger unleashing. "What is *wrong* with you? Why are you acting like this? It's like you've been brainwashed!"

"It's like *you've* been brainwashed."

"I want your phone, now!"

"Too late. School's got it, innit."

"Get up," I ordered, tearing off his duvet. "We're going into school to sort this out."

"*You* can. I'm not, no fuckin' way."

The worst part was the scorn in that "you," the loathing. It was Kieran's scorn, Kieran's loathing. By now volcanic with fury, I slammed his door, making the windows rattle, and went in search of my phone to get Vic back on the line.

| | | | | | |

Is there any gloomier procession than the one taken by parents—
especially separated ones who have no other reason to come
together—down a strip-lit school corridor to the door marked
"Head"?

Actually, there is, but we'll come to that.

I'd always liked Mr. Avery. He had the buoyant energy of a young
cabinet minister and was flexible in his dealings, pragmatic, a quality
we hoped to appeal to now. As Vic and I settled in seats upholstered
in the flecked gray-brown of quicksand, he got straight to the point.

"Drugs were found in the sixth form changing rooms and a
routine phone check led us to Lucas."

He had confiscated Lucas's phone and now showed us the photo
of our son in what looked like a shower cubicle. Lucas had a spliff
between his fingers, a great shit-eating grin across his face.

"Couldn't that have been taken in any public facility? A gym or
somewhere?" I said, knowing that without a link to school premises,
the staff had no obligation to get involved.

"It's definitely the sixth form boys' changing room," Avery said.
"Lucas has admitted as much, so I'll spare you a site visit."

"Who took the picture?" Vic asked. "You can see both his hands,
so it can't be a selfie. Moaning Myrtle, was it?"

Avery chuckled, but I failed to crack a smile. "Do you really need
to ask? It will have been Kieran. He'll have put Lucas up to this."

Clearly disinclined to debate this, the head moved on. "Coming
so soon after the unauthorized absences, we were concerned enough
to decide on the suspension."

Not as concerned as they'd be if they knew what Lucas had been
doing during that truancy. Thank God I'd sanctioned a cover-up or

this would be his second school-related drugs offense this year and he'd be out on his ear.

On the other hand, if I'd been honest with the school then, Lucas might have thought twice about pulling the stunt that had brought us here now. I was furious with myself, with him, with Kieran, who once again appeared to have ducked trouble.

"Have you looked through all these photos?" I asked Avery.

"We have. But, as I say, we're only interested in the ones taken on the Foxwell site."

"How did you get the kids to give up their phones?"

"The threat of a call to the police did the trick." Seeing my expression, he hastened to reassure me that he had not involved them "on this occasion." "Since we're coming to the end of the school year, we thought the long holiday might be a good opportunity for Lucas to reflect on his time in the lower sixth. It's worked well before," he added.

He was softening the blow, suggesting this was unremarkable, fixable, but I wasn't giving up on justice quite yet. "None of this would be happening if you hadn't accepted Kieran Watts into the sixth form and made Lucas his buddy. We all know you choose the decent ones to buddy new kids—well, look how *that* worked out. Kieran's behind all of this, we all know he's brought drugs into the school, so why isn't *he* being suspended? Better still, excluded."

"Ellen," Vic said in a low tone and he gestured that the head should disregard this demand. He was right, of course. On the current evidence, if anyone had brought drugs into the school, if anyone was at risk of being excluded, it was Lucas.

"I'm sorry," I said. "I can't tell you what to do. But if your internal investigation begins and ends with Lucas, then we'd like it on record that we're not satisfied with its rigor."

God, I know I sounded like some lunatic disciplinarian, but we had a right to hold the school at least partly accountable. They'd thrown Lucas to the lions and now they were turning their heads to avoid looking at the wounds.

"Let's regroup after the holiday, shall we?" Avery handed me Lucas's phone. It was decent of him not to insist on the gratitude we all knew he was owed.

In the car, I thumbed through the rest of the photos. These days, there are pass codes and fingerprint recognition, not to mention the convenience of message apps with automatic deletion, but back then it was more basic and Lucas's phone didn't even require a code. The pictures were a record of his partying, basically. Some faces I recognized, others I didn't. There were a few of Jade, smiling at the camera, private and adoring—those made me gulp a little.

One image stood out: Lucas and a few other boys stared at the camera, blatantly stoned, while in the background Kieran was captured in profile, apparently mesmerized by something out of frame. There was a tension in his jaw, a tilt of his gaze, that made him look malevolent, scheming. Maybe even predatory.

I considered sending the picture to my own number, evidence to consult should I ever feel my conviction weakening, but decided against it. If Lucas somehow discovered I'd done that, it would be hard to explain.

It would look . . . well, not right.

nine

By now, Kieran had passed his driving test—I learned this from Vic, Lucas no longer daring to bring his name up in my presence. Anyway, the weekend after the suspension drama, I was driving Freya into Croydon when I saw Kieran at the wheel of Prisca's Corsa two cars ahead.

Without thinking, I tailed him as he slipped through an amber light on London Road and into the entrance of a multistory car park I'd never used but knew for its reputation as somewhere kids hung out, smoking. An upgrade to the site's CCTV was planned, I'd read, but for now security remained nonexistent. *What are you doing here?* I thought. *Meeting your connection to stock up on pills for your friends?*

The building was designed around a central spiral, cars directed one way up a narrow lane, with a central void just a few feet to their right beyond a curved wall. From the driver's seat of an SUV like mine, the wall appeared treacherously low and I found it all too easy to picture myself yanking the steering wheel in a moment of madness and smashing through it. Hurtling, nose-down, into that yawning emptiness.

"I don't like this," Freya said, voicing my own feelings as we followed the Corsa up level after level. "It's making me dizzy."

"It's fine," I said, hoping she hadn't noticed I was shaking.

At the top, crawling past the empty bays that lined the outer wall, I chose a spot in the center, while Kieran reversed with impressive skill into a tight corner space. He didn't appear to have noticed me, but had his head down, I guessed to look at his phone.

"That's Kieran's car!" Freya exclaimed.

"I know. That's why we're here."

"You mean you were *chasing* him?"

I flicked her a sideways glance and saw her shocked expression. "Not chasing. But I need to talk to him about something and there's no time like the present."

"Couldn't you just, like, phone him? This is *weird*, Mum."

I lost my patience. "Please stop questioning me, Freya. This is nothing to do with you." I released my belt and opened the door. "Stay here, I won't be a minute."

"Mum, *don't!*"

I shut the door on her protests. Trying not to think of the sheer drop beyond the perimeter wall, the concrete posts that looked like they were about to crumble, I marched across the empty bays and rapped on the window of Kieran's car. Brief surprise transformed into irritation and he shrugged at me—*What?* I gestured for him to roll the window down, which he did, sighing heavily.

"I want a word with you," I said.

He stared brazenly up at me with the same wrecked, bloodshot eyes as Lucas had. I'd never been this close to him before: his face was smeared with freckles and dotted with acne, his blond eyebrows flecked with red. "What 'bout?"

"Supplying drugs. Lucas was suspended from school because of you."

"For bunnin' a zoot, yeah." He snorted. "Respect."

"No, *not* respect. Why are you laughing?" I wanted to reach into the car and slap him. "This is serious, Kieran, he has university applications to think about next term!"

This earned only a smirk. He raised his near elbow and began plucking at his hair, his gaze drifting beyond me.

Wound-up practically to the point of pirouetting, I lost my temper. "Just because *you* don't have anyone who cares about you, it doesn't mean Lucas doesn't. We care about him very much and we won't allow you to ruin his future!"

I was breathing hard. The most unnerving thing was how unaffected he appeared to be by the cruel thing I'd said. His expression was quite empty, his eyes unseeing. "At least have the decency to answer me," I said.

He eased his chin forward in a weirdly reptilian movement and returned his focus to me. "You are cray cray, woman. Surprised you even up so high, real shit."

"What? Speak English, please."

He gestured towards the wall behind me. "There's a hundred-foot drop just there, you know that? Fucking scary. I've seen kids walking on the edge like it's a beam. Lucas, maybe, I don't remember."

As I gasped in horror, I could tell he was pleased with the effect his words—in grammatically perfect English—had. How on earth did he know about my phobia? The niche frailties of friends' parents were hardly everyday subject matter among teens. Then again, if you hated that parent, you might catch a passing reference and squirrel it away for future ammunition.

"No one's gonna survive that," he went on. "They'd go splat like a tomato. Why don't you go and take a look? Go on, lean right over, you know you're dying to."

I took a step back, feeling a tremble seize my body. "Just leave Lucas alone. *Please.*"

But my desperation only confirmed Kieran's power grab and I knew in my gut that approaching him had been a terrible mistake. Turning from me, he tossed his phone onto the passenger seat, started the engine, and pulled forward. I watched as he reparked in a spot near the doors to the stairs and then picked up his phone once more. Face burning, I scurried back to the Jeep.

Freya's window was open and she had obviously heard my part of the exchange. "Mum, that was so horrible, saying no one cares about him!"

"I shouldn't have said that," I told her, buckling my seat belt. But, seeing her face so stern with disapproval, I couldn't resist the urgent need to justify myself. "Did you hear what *he* said to *me?*"

"No, what?"

"He practically said I should throw myself over the wall! Do you know what incitement is?"

"No."

"It's when you encourage someone to do something they wouldn't have done on their own. If you incite someone to commit a crime, *that's* a crime as well." I started the car, released the handbrake. "It doesn't matter. Let's get out of here."

The route back to ground level did not involve the spiral, mercifully. I fed my unused ticket into the machine and sped through the barriers with nothing owed.

Nothing gained, either.

| | | | | |

It was telling, I suppose, that the only person I reported the episode to was Vic. I recounted it on the phone with a flush of the same heat I'd felt at the time, not sure if the emotion choking my voice was shame or pride.

"Freya thinks I'm a bully."

"You're not a bully," Vic said. "You're just concerned. You want to protect Lucas from danger and that's totally natural. I feel the same."

"I just hope I haven't made things worse."

He sighed in sympathy. "Someone had to warn Kieran off."

"That's the problem, I don't think he *was* warned. Maybe we should ring the police?" I suggested. "Tip them off about his dealing?"

"It's an idea," he agreed.

"Except that might lead back to Lucas . . ."

"Plus, we could be accused of slander," Vic said.

He had a point. Grumbling between ourselves was one thing, but maligning Kieran publicly might rank as more antisocial than any of his own antics.

Freya, meanwhile, must have said something to her father because the next time we were out on our own, Justin brought the incident up. This was—*is*—one of the admirable things about him, he knows how to bide his time. He's never jerked a knee in his life.

"I hear you had some sort of run-in with Kieran."

I dipped my head. "I'm sorry Freya had to witness it."

He eyed me with commiseration, but I wasn't insensitive to the undercurrent. When it came to Freya, he was a shade less tolerant of my spontaneities. "I don't think I realized just how bad it was, this personality clash of yours."

"It's not a personality clash, Justin, he's evil."

"Evil?" He was taken aback. "Come on. You must hear how that sounds."

"Yes, and I know it's hard to accept such a thing exists and I don't expect you to agree, but that's what I believe. And all I'm doing is trying to defend our family against it."

Bless him for leaning in when he could have recoiled. "Explain why you think he's evil, besides the possible drugs connection."

I answered him as honestly as I could. "He doesn't want other people to do what's best for them or have the good things they deserve. He wants to drag them down to his level. He's the opposite of the wind beneath your sails, he's sucking the sails back. He's trying to get you to capsize."

"By 'you,' you mean Lucas."

"Yes. And others as well, I would imagine. Jade, for one. They're all in thrall to him."

One of the side effects of banning the cult leader from Tanglewood Road was his disciples stayed away too—and, according to Vic, now reopened for business, Jade was as much of an adherent as Lucas. "Kieran makes them laugh," he'd said recently, in one of those devastatingly simple insights you simply cannot dispute.

"That isn't *their* perception, though?" Justin said.

"Of course it's not. All kids love a hedonist."

"He's had a tough childhood, don't forget. He's probably witnessed things we can't imagine. Shouldn't we cut him a bit of slack?"

"Not if it gives him a free pass to screw with whoever he likes. This is part of the problem, Jus, he knows the school doesn't dare punish him, he knows the parents don't feel they can criticize him. They're all too scared of looking like heartless rabid right-wingers. Well, I'm not—and nor is Vic."

There was a flicker of irritation in Justin's gaze. "You *really* think Kieran wouldn't swap his free pass—if that's really what it is, which

I personally doubt—for the kind of life Lucas has had? Come on, you're usually so kind, El."

"It's not *my* character that's in question here!" Did I really need to convince my own husband of my decency? Plainly, I did. Kieran had distorted me and I hated him for that almost as much as I hated him for leading Lucas astray. "What is it going to take for you to start believing me? When something *really* bad happens, will you believe me then?"

"It's not about belief, it's about interpretation," Justin argued. "And I'm obviously interpreting events slightly differently from you and Vic."

"Let's forget it," I told him, not unpleasantly. I wasn't naive. I had no doubt that if his and Vic's paternal statuses had been reversed, he would be the one backing me and Vic the one questioning. They had different degrees of exposure to my complaints and different roles in Lucas's upbringing. But neither of them had seen the look of malice in Kieran's eyes when he'd talked of that hundred-foot drop. Only I'd seen that.

It became my go-to daydream that he would crash that stupid little Corsa. He'd be driving—alone, of course, along pedestrian-free streets—and he'd veer off the road into a lamppost or a tree. The airbag would save him, because I didn't want him killed. Just injured.

Taken out of the game.

ten

WELL, THERE WAS ONE game I could take him out of, or, more ac-
curately, exclude him from signing up for, and that was our summer holiday to Crete. I invited Jade and Tom to join us—I know,
go ahead and slam me for rewarding Lucas for his bad behavior,
that's fair. Let me just say that I viewed the move as a necessary hy-
pocrisy. *Let's see how well the gang get on without their fire starter,*
I thought.

It helped that the villa had no broadband and poor mobile phone
coverage. The last thing I wanted was Kieran in constant contact, his
voice booming out on speakerphone, as it had been the day before we
left when I'd happened to pass Lucas's half-open door.

"To be fair, no one thinks their own sister is hot," he said.

"She's fucking *twelve*, K," Lucas protested and there was an
explosion of laughter, followed by a series of inaudible mumblings.

Then Kieran's voice rose again, crowing with amusement:
"Gonna forget you said that, bruv, real talk."

I wanted to go in and throw Lucas's phone at the wall. No, better still, I would take it from him and tell the boy on the other end that if he ever, *ever* laid a finger on Freya, I'd kill him.

| | | | | | | | | | |

Among other things, the holiday was an opportunity for us to get to know Jade, now Lucas's girlfriend of over six months. She was kind to Freya, that stands out in my memory. She'd make a point of including her as she and the boys arranged themselves in a dripping still life by the pool or, drunk with sun, colonized the terrace table with their music and beers and card games. "Come with us, Frey," she'd say, when they were heading into the village, and then, when the boys objected, "What? I need another girl, you guys!"

(The roadman dialect soon dissolved without Kieran there to drive it.)

Perhaps it was the Greek light, incomparably silky and translucent, but Jade was a standout beauty, even among the throngs of young on the beaches and in the village bars. Everyone was still in the white lacy dresses of the *Mamma Mia* trend and she had a whole wardrobe of them, looking like a beach bride with her seashell jewelry and brown bare feet.

She was one of the youngest in the year group and had her seventeenth birthday while we were away. After dinner in the port, as we relaxed in front of a lavender sea, she broke off from the boys and came to thank Justin and me.

"It's such a treat to be here. Thank you for everything."

"You're very welcome. It's lovely for us to have you here," I told her. "You're not missing your other friends too much? I know you spend a lot of time with Kieran."

I could never have asked Lucas this, nor been entitled to the flawless answer she gave about our wonderful hospitality making it impossible for her to miss anybody.

"I must admit I'm not his greatest fan," I said, cheerfully.

She was much too polite to contradict me. "He's a character," she said, as if settling on a compromise.

I gave up then—to recruit her as a collaborator was a stretch even by my standards. Instead, it was her mother who offered news of him:

Saw your arch enemy today . . .

Oh yes. How's he coping without his crew?

Bored out of his brain. He asked for your address there to send Jade a birthday pressie. Thought I'd better check with you first.

My pulse quickened. I had no doubt there was no gift, at least not one that couldn't wait, and that this was simply a ploy to find out our address so he could make his way out here and "bump into" us. Creep me out, put me in an impossible position. I replied with trembling hands:

Please don't! (It wouldn't get here in time, anyway.)

Understood. I'll say he should just drop it round to us.

A part of me marveled at the fact that Sheridan was able to interact with Kieran in this easy everyday way, while another rejoiced afresh in my having successfully isolated him from the pack. But a third part grew antsy every time a car drew up at the villa or a figure with his approximate build strolled towards us in the village. Might Sheridan have inadvertently given him enough intel to locate us? And he was some kind of computer prodigy, wasn't he, so might he have been able to hack into one of his friends' phones and discover our GPS coordinates? All too quickly it began to feel as likely that he would appear as not.

There was one particularly tense episode that has stayed with me. We'd arrived at the beach one afternoon and I was squinting into the mid-distance to judge how crowded it was and if there was any shade available, when I saw him. Kieran bloody Watts, here after all. He was in the water, standing waist-deep, his back to the shore. Without saying a word to the others, I dropped my bag at my feet, tore off my sarong and flip-flops, and waded out. As I reached him, a wave approached and we bobbed in unison, coming to land a couple of meters closer together. I'd never seen him unclothed, of course, but the breadth of his shoulders, pale and pimpled and with a chain of angry red insect bites, was an exact match. His wet hair was just the right shade of burnt orange.

Catching me looking, he plunged underwater and I half expected to feel my legs pulled from under me, my head held down—that encounter in the car park had left me in no doubt that he longed to be rid of me as intensely as I did him. Then he burst to the surface a distance away, shaking and laughing, great ropes of water flying from him. I couldn't see his face in the dazzle as he called out something to a couple nearby, but it sounded like German. He seemed, from this new perspective, too tall.

Seeing Justin peer quizzically from the shore, I returned, dripping. "I just had to cool off," I said. "Thanks for setting up."

"We're down here," he said, indicating the parasol he'd set up a respectable distance from the teens.

Freya, neither one nor the other, shuttled between the two camps. "No one will play beach tennis with me," she complained to her father, a bat in either hand.

"I will, darling." He took one of the bats and they found a section of smooth sand near the breaking waves.

I propped myself on my elbows and watched them for a while. Then, in one of those sudden changes of mood, the sea seemed to come alive and a figure came tumbling towards us with the surf, causing Justin and Freya to scatter. It was him, the redheaded boy. After he'd stood and shaken himself, he glanced blindly at them before ambling off with a gait entirely different from Kieran's.

"No need to apologize," Justin joked to Freya, and they giggled together before reclaiming their patch and starting a new rally.

Thank God I hadn't said anything to Justin. It would have been the nail in the coffin of my hopes that he'd keep an open mind to my suspicions of Kieran's activities—my "interpretation," as he'd called it. Soothed by the metronomic crack-crack of ball on bat, I sank into the sand and closed my eyes, a guard dog satisfied for the moment that her humans were safe.

| | | | | | |

Back home, I soon understood that that sense of security had been as false as it was brief. Lucas and his friends began in the upper sixth and picked up where they had left off, only now with more academic deadlines to disregard than before. Kieran, who seemed to have taken sole possession of Prisca's car, would pick Lucas up most evenings, waiting at the curb with his phone on his lap as I watched from the bedroom window. Sometimes there'd be others in the car with him and they'd be yelping and heaving with laughter, making the little car rock. Presumably to avoid the risk of cross-examination, Lucas would frequently leave without bothering to say goodbye and I'd spend futile hours worrying about Kieran being at the wheel drunk or stoned or just distracted by his own clowning.

Having decided not to apply to Oxford after all, Lucas now announced he wouldn't be troubling himself with open days, but would choose his unis on the basis of their websites. His predicted grades were both dismayingly low and—by the time mocks had come and gone—technically optimistic. It was not beyond the realms of possibility that he would miss his insurance choice, never mind his preferred one.

"How did we get from Oxbridge to being worried he won't be going anywhere at all?" I asked Vic, when I called at his flat one night to retrieve a forgotten textbook.

"I know." He ran his fingers across his forehead as if to wipe clean the frown lines. "Here's a personal statement for you: 'I've decided to put my future on the back burner while I smoke weed and take wonk with the town twat.' "

"What's wonk?" I asked.

"Ket. Ketamine. Horse tranquilizer." Seeing my expression, he backtracked. "Mind you, it's hard to know if they're taking it or just acting like they are."

And sometimes it was hard to know if Vic and I were having these conversations or just acting like we were. It felt surreal, as if I was one of those parents you read about in newspaper features, the last to know "the truth" about their offspring.

"It will suit Kieran if Lucas fails his A-levels and has to repeat the year," I said. "*He's* not going anywhere, is he? He never studies. I can't see him in any kind of career. There's no work ethic there at all, just total self-gratification."

Once more, I know this sounds unattractive. Poisonous, even. Then again, the advantage of presenting it in this form years after the event—and the reason I'm willing to cast myself in so unflattering a light—is that history attests to my being right. If you're not already aware that Kieran caused Lucas grievous harm, then it will take you ten seconds to google their names and find out what happened.

Or keep reading—because we're almost there.

eleven

THE FIRST THING I do the morning after seeing Kieran on the roof of The Heights is to buy a second phone, a cheap, prepaid one with rudimentary camera and audio recording functions. I can't risk storing anything on my registered phone that could later be construed as evidence of harassment.

Having slept on that conversation with Vic, I'm more convinced than ever that only photographic proof—or audio, if possible—will persuade him that the man I saw was Kieran. Only then can we proceed in whichever way we see fit.

I reschedule my morning meeting and take the commuter service to London Bridge. Standing in the crush of humanity, an inexperienced rider of the spurts and brakes of rush hour, I wonder if any of my fellow travelers is also a stalker?

I'm not proud to confess this, but I am more experienced in the art of tailing than a certain member of my family might realize—and I don't mean that long-ago low-speed car chase in a Croydon car park. Several times, when Freya was still at school, I shadowed her when she met friends. I'd linger out of sight or stroll by at a safe distance, satisfying myself that the person she was meeting was not some middle-aged scumbag trying to groom her or a drug lord type recruiting for a county lines gang.

Again, it had fallen to Justin to talk me down. "Think of all the variables that make a perfect storm, El. Don't make yourself the one element that causes something bad to happen."

"You mean, she spots me as she's crossing a road and gets run over by a bus because she's distracted? It wouldn't have happened if *I* hadn't been there?"

He blanched. "That kind of thing, yes."

And I thought, in silent protest, *What if the child you love is being led into danger, but it's the one time you* don't *believe it?* But, by then, the agony of yearning to turn back time had long since proved untenable and Justin and I had instigated a no what-ifs policy. We are where we are, we'd say.

And where I am now is striding along Tooley Street from London Bridge Station towards Shad Thames, scanning the faces of the oncoming pedestrians, cyclists, even motorists, all the way to The Heights. None belongs to Kieran, of course—that would be too easy.

I stab the bell for Flat 10, beanie-covered head dipped low to hide my face from the camera. I have no intention of going up again: this time, I want *him* to come down. In one hand I hold a small package brought from home, in the other my phone, set to "record."

"Hi?" It's a man's voice, but impossible to judge from that single syllable if it is *his*.

"Delivery for Mr. Watts. Needs a signature."

The hand holding the phone flies to my mouth: I should have said Mr. *Harding*—what a fool! Instantly, adrenaline surges through me.

"There's no one here by that name," the voice replies, and it's clear this isn't him, but someone decades older, with a commanding patrician accent. "I think you need to check the address with your dispatch team. Who is this, please?"

"GMB Deliveries," I improvise.

"Can I take a name?"

"What? No, sorry." *Fuck.*

I scurry away. There is a café across the road and I conceal myself in the unusually deep doorway just beyond it, trying to recover my composure. I am furious with myself, could hardly have been sloppier in my start to private detective work: I've given myself away and yet I have no idea who to. Then again, does it matter? If I'm lucky, the name Watts might mean nothing to this man, who evidently knows Kieran as S. Harding. Who is he? Flatmate? Friend? Lover?

A young couple, speaking English with heavy European accents and dressed outlandishly—fashion students perhaps, hadn't Selena said there was a local population of wealthy undergraduates?—enter the café, causing a second memory to surface from that same conversation. She'd seen Kieran in a café on Mill Street. This must be it: Bean Box. I could do worse than station myself inside for an hour or two and wait for him to arrive or depart of his own accord.

But just as I emerge from the shadows, the door to The Heights clicks open and a man steps into the street. He's in his late fifties or early sixties, about five ten, with silver-flecked hair and horn-rimmed glasses. Gray jeans, black sweater, expensive footwear, but no jacket or coat on this chilly late-October day. He pauses at the curb, frowning, before striding towards the café door on a collision course with me. Realizing this, I snatch off my black beanie, the only bit of me he will have seen on camera, but it's the wrong move because he's peering at me as he approaches and I can see from his face that he's making the connection.

"Hello? You didn't just ring the buzzer over here, did you? Flat 10."

I feel myself flush. "No, not me."

"Why did you ask for Mr. Watts?" He speaks as if I haven't just made the denial and, instinctively, I break into a run towards Tooley Street. "Hey!" he calls after me. "Wait! Tell me your name!"

On the corner of Tooley, I duck into a Co-op store. As I watch, motionless behind a shelf of throat pastilles and cold remedies near the tills, the man appears at the junction, glances either way, and enters the shop. Mercifully, he takes off down the first aisle, drawing him on a route through the store that includes a blind spot that allows me to slip into the street again. I zigzag back through Shad Thames to the bridge and down the steps to the riverside path, where I merge with the tourist throng. I've shaken him off—for now.

But that doesn't mean I'm safe. I can think of no reason for someone to descend ten floors to check on a messenger who'd got the wrong name, then hunt them down in the local streets, other than that he is a protector of Kieran's of some sort.

And that makes him no friend of mine.

Killing Time (cont)

Watching Ellen as she sits at her library desk, striving to impose order on her own chaotic history, I see very clearly the etchings of sorrow in her face. Of course, she's not the only one in the room who's grieving. Every single one of her fellow students has been through their own uniquely unforgiving mill. We have among us a victim of gang rape and another of domestic violence; one young woman's troubles began when her father was murdered by his own brother; two others had their childhoods blighted by poverty and abuse. There is an authenticity to the chain of events laid out in their life stories, before being stitched back together with Penney's guidance; a morbid pull. And yet, time and again, it is to Ellen's story that I keep returning.

Maybe it's because hers is the one that never quite ended when it should have.

How it should have.

Sunday Times magazine, December 2021

twelve

GOD ONLY KNOWS HOW we got through A-levels.

We, I know how that sounds. Like I was the one sitting them, or at least shadowing, heckling instructions ringside like a boxing coach. But it feels like a team effort, doesn't it? Not like when our gen was young and parents barely knew you had exams, only inquiring if you'd revised on the day the first one dawned, gray and dreadful no matter how blue that young summer sky.

With the kind of nagging I would once have thought myself incapable of, I exerted enough influence to keep Lucas indoors for most of study leave. Make no mistake, Kieran continued to arrive at our gate in his car, but Lucas would resist his bidding, hanging out only briefly in the street before sending him on his way.

"It's fucking lockdown here," I heard him grumble, one time.

And Kieran replied, sneering: "To be fair, no one gives a shit about A-levels once you start work, innit, bruv?"

You only get to start work if you give a shit about A-levels, I thought. Jade was revising hard, I knew from Sheridan. As for Tom, who'd had an offer from Cambridge, he'd scarcely been mentioned since the holiday.

Anyhow, I'll cut to the chase. Kieran, who was taking just two subjects, finished his last exam before Lucas and against strenuous advice Lucas broke out from jail to celebrate with him—even though he had a maths paper the following afternoon.

"You need to be in bed and asleep by midnight," I yelled after him on the doorstep, attracting a startled look from the neighbor across the road. By then, every interaction seemed to reflect badly on me, not him. Not Kieran.

Lucas came back far later than that, of course. I heard him bumping up the stairs and into the bathroom, laughing to himself. He was safe, I told myself, and so long as he was reasonably prepared, he could sleep late and still perform well in his exam.

In the morning, Justin and Freya already out the door, I gave him an hour's grace before going up. "Lucas? Time to think about getting up!"

There was no reply, so I nudged open the door and went in. The room was dark and stiflingly hot, so I drew back the curtains and opened the window. Lucas was immovable under his duvet, his face covered, and I shook his shoulder gently. There was no response. A blade of terror passed through me. Was he *breathing*? I shook him again and at last he groaned, as if from deep underground, and I felt his breath soft on my arm.

"Lucas? Wake up. Open your eyes."

He moaned again, his lids twitched, and finally he managed to wake. As I helped him sit up against the pillows and reminded him how to put a glass of water to his lips, it was obvious this was different from a standard hangover. I had to discover what he'd taken.

"If you don't tell me, we need to get you to A&E."

This drew a grunted protest—even with the water, he seemed not to be able to use his throat properly—and after several attempts to repeat himself, I caught the letters MD.

MDMA. Ecstasy in old money. I'd read a horrifying number of news articles about teenagers with bright futures overdosing on the drug.

Lucas slumped to the side, gently knocking his head against the wall, eyes closed. "Need to sleep," he pleaded, and began burrowing back into the bedding.

"No, Lucas, you need to stay awake. You've got an exam this afternoon!"

I fetched him a Coke, hoping the sugar and caffeine would have an effect, which they did—a little. Though crusty-eyed and dry-lipped, he had color in his cheeks and was sitting up in bed and breathing normally. It was by now eleven o'clock; the exam was at one. Satisfied he was in no real medical danger, I phoned the school and registered him sick. This was accepted without question, but we would need a doctor's note if he was to be eligible for the alternative exam date at the end of June.

By the time I'd dragged him to the doctor's, he was back to his customary self—uncommunicative by choice, not necessity—and in the car on the way home I let rip. "Are you completely insane? Doing drugs the night before an A-level exam! Why would you put your whole future at risk for a night out you could have had twenty-four hours later? Do you not realize they might not allow you the alternate date and neither of your unis will take you with-out three subjects? One night out and you might have to repeat everything!"

"I know," he said, weakly, turning his face from me. In the

glass, his reflection was of a young child, with a defeated, un-claimed quality to him, and I found myself thinking of the Lost Boys in *Peter Pan*.

At the next set of red lights, I caught sight of my own face in the rearview, eyes sunken, cheeks flushed, mouth a red-rimmed black hole. I looked like a banshee.

"No need to ask who supplied the pills," I said, bitterly.

| | | | | | |

Believe me, there's nothing you could suggest that I didn't consider over the next short, fraught period. The crisis I'd been fearing for almost two years had hit at exactly the wrong moment. Whether or not maths could be saved, there were also two further papers in biology.

Justin and Vic both read Lucas the riot act—or their versions thereof—and I even reached out to Prisca, who of course insisted Kieran was a normal teen who had approached his own exams with diligence and responsibility (what planet was she on?).

"Now wait a minute, Ellen," she said, when I raised the matter of Kieran dealing drugs. "You need to be very careful about making allegations like that."

"Why can no one see what's going on?" I snapped, which only strengthened her case, not mine. I felt like getting on the phone to the social services to complain, but I knew it would only make things worse, create a new reason for Lucas to hate me, the oppressor, and love Kieran, the oppressed.

My mother and several friends suggested involving the school counselor, but it seemed to me it wasn't therapy Lucas needed so much as a proper old-fashioned sense of perspective. His newly acquired taste for a short-term high had blinded him to the concept of a long-term future. "Could Danny have a go?" I asked Vic. "Give him a final pep talk, maybe a few stories about the mistakes *he* made at this age? That might scare him."

Danny was Vic's older cousin, a de facto brother and one of the reasons we'd landed in Sydenham after university: he'd lived there for years and still did. Though now making a good go of a painting and decorating business, he'd been in trouble with the police during a misspent youth and often voiced his regrets at having underperformed at school and missed out on college. No matter that he was still sometimes seen in South London pubs with an edgier crowd.

Vic obliged and the two of them arrived to take Lucas out for a stroll around the park. While we waited for Lucas to come downstairs, I chatted with them in the kitchen.

"Thanks for doing this," I said to Danny, keeping my voice low.

"No problem. I'm sure you've got nothing to worry about."

Unsure whether to interpret this as a platitude or a comment on my tendency to catastrophize, I just smiled. He and Vic, the sons of brothers, looked nothing alike—Danny was stocky and almost bald—but their humor was the same, the cadences of their accents. When Lucas was little, I'd identified him as a bit of an undesirable influence, luring Vic out to the pub, reminding him that he was young, with a life—dreams—of his own. But now that our paths rarely crossed, I saw the value in his loyalty, a loyalty that extended to his nephew, demonstrated in the bear hug he gave Lucas when he finally materialized.

On his return, Lucas said nothing, of course, and so I rang Vic. "How did it go? Did he engage?"

"Yes, a bit, but he seemed so exhausted, like he'd have crawled under a bush and slept if we'd let him. To be honest, I think we just have to get him through these last exams one day at a time and then hope that he'll lose touch with Kieran when he goes to uni."

"*If* he goes," I said, dispiritedly. "Thanks anyway, Vic."

"Come on, El, don't sound so glum. Some parents have it a lot worse than this. His timing is crap, but he's not doing heroin or anything *really* serious."

"Oh, well, in *that* case," I said. But I was grateful for his support. I didn't know what I'd do without him—and Justin, of course.

News arrived soon after that Lucas was allowed to take the missed maths exam on the alternative date.

"I bet I end up getting a harder paper," he moaned.

"I hope you do," I said.

"That's what Dad said."

"We're saying it because we love you," I said. "We want what's best for you and the best thing for you is to learn from your mistakes. I'm sure Prisca would say the same to Kieran if it was him who missed an exam. But it wasn't, was it?"

It was a dig along well-worn lines and Lucas didn't argue, surrendering to the demands of the final furlong with an attitude more disconsolate than resentful. There was a sense, too, that while we counted down to the end of exams, the end of school, he was counting down to the day he could get away from us. From me.

| | | | | | |

Summer passed with increasing unease. There'd be no Greek reprieve this year, for Lucas refused to come on holiday with us, and Justin and I took Freya to Italy on her own.

"One rule," Justin told me, as we buckled into our seats on the plane. "No one mentions the K word."

"Done," I said, and meant it. I simply could not stomach the stress of speculating where Kieran might lead Lucas in our absence, what altered chemical states the two of them might blunder into.

On our return, with exam results day approaching, we found Lucas fretful that he hadn't performed at his best (*finally!*), talking about resitting anything particularly disastrous and reapplying to uni for entry the following autumn. I began to dread the words "I thought I might go traveling with Kieran," dread them so intensely I crossed over into willing them. The sooner the worst happened, the sooner I could get on with surviving it.

I didn't know the meaning of "worst" then.

It was only when he went to pick up his results from the school that I understood just how anxious I'd become, too agitated to concentrate on the spreadsheet I was supposed to be working on, unable even to face a cup of tea.

Finally, he phoned with the news that he had the grades he needed for his first choice, Leeds. "We're all going out to celebrate," he added. "I don't know when I'll be back."

The moment we hung up I ran to the bathroom and began sobbing into a towel. When I emerged, I saw Freya watching from her bedroom door.

"Did he fail?"

"No. No, he did okay. He's going to Leeds."

As she looked up the exact distance between our postcode and her brother's new campus, I found myself feeling more joy-filled than most mothers would at the prospect of their firstborn living so far away. Because surely Kieran would not attempt to make the journey regularly, if at all, which meant Lucas could forget all about him in the flurry of freshers socializing.

We baked a cake for him, with his favorite chocolate fudge icing, and unveiled it the next afternoon when he'd slept off the night's partying. For once, he didn't slope off, mouth full, but lingered with us, nowhere better to be.

"So yeah, Mum, thanks for, you know . . ." he said.

I paused. "For what?"

"Just, you know, keeping the faith."

"Of course I kept the faith," I told him. "I always will."

And I gave him a proper hug, the one I felt he'd been resisting for so long but that he perhaps believed to have been withheld.

He's come back to us, I thought.

Just as he was leaving, he was back.

| | | | | | |

Not long after Lucas started at Leeds, we ran into Kieran at the shopping center in Croydon. I'd known he hadn't applied to uni and that vague plans for an apprenticeship had been shelved in favor of trying to start a business of some sort. ("He's already got one," I grumbled to Vic. "Pharmaceuticals.")

Though we greeted each other cordially enough, he didn't so much as glance in my direction after that, his gaze passing from Justin to Freya.

"Hey," he said to her, with a note of appreciation. "You got tall."

"Hi," she said.

She was wearing makeup, expertly applied, as makeup is by her generation. They watch YouTube tutorials by strange creatures who dedicate their entire waking day to the pursuit and then helpfully present it in time-lapse video for those with less time on their hands.

"What are you up to these days?" Justin asked, with professional good-naturedness.

Kieran scratched his right eyelid with his thumbnail. "Computer stuff."

Aka gaming.

"Looking for a job while I start my own thing," he added.

"Remind me what your A-levels were?" Justin said.

"Geography and computer science."

"I'll keep my ears open for you."

"Cool. What year're you in now, Frey?" Kieran asked her.

"Year eight."

"Enjoy it while you still can," he advised, and I had a tough time not rolling my eyes. As if he *really* thought sixth-form life had been tough. As if he hadn't spent his whole time in pursuit of anything *but* study.

His phone rang then and I watched as he smirked at the caller ID. I had an overpowering instinct that it was from Lucas and wanted to rip the thing from his hands and delete it, delete Lucas's details, scream at Kieran that the friendship was over.

"Hey." He turned from us to speak to his caller. "You here yet? Which entrance? Safe, bruv."

Safe, bruv: it all came back to me in a horrible toxic gush. And, knowing Lucas was over two hundred miles away in Leeds and could not on this occasion be the bruv in question, I felt the terrified relief of someone who'd been about to step into an empty lift shaft and pulled back just in time.

thirteen

IN NOVEMBER, THE WEEKEND before Lucas's nineteenth birthday, we went up to Leeds for a visit. Checked out the ransacked crime scene that was his room in halls, remarked on his paler-than-ever complexion and never-skinnier physique. Took him for the biggest steak he could eat.

"Has anyone from the old gang been to visit?" I asked, halfway through the main course—and I know you won't believe me, but I swear I was thinking of Jade, at Durham studying French. The two of them were still together, which I admit was a surprise. Justin and Sheridan agreed with me: two confident, good-looking arrivals in their respective spheres, they'd surely have received plenty of attention by now. Only Vic called it, insisting Lucas was properly in love—if such an antiquated term was still in use.

"Kieran came up," Lucas said, mouth full. "Everyone else is at their own unis. Jade's coming down for the Christmas ball."

"It's only an hour between you on the train, isn't it?" Justin said.

As Freya showed Lucas various Instagram posts of Jade's that she'd liked, and then Justin asked after Tom, now at Cambridge and naturally dismissed by Lucas as a sellout rather than the cause for admiration that he deserved to be, I watched them over my wineglass, waiting for a pause. "Kieran's been up, you said?"

Lucas shot me a cautious look. "Yeah, a couple of weekends ago."

"How can he afford to gad about if he isn't working?"

" 'Gad about'?" Justin and Freya snickered, and I recognized their instinct to try to divert the river surging their way.

"He *is* working," Lucas said, raising his chin in a self-consciously brazen way that was pure Kieran. "He's doing some freelance IT stuff and bar work to get the money together for a van. He wants to start his own delivery business."

"Well, that's great," Justin said, sounding genuinely impressed. "He's obviously made a lot of progress since we saw him a few weeks ago. It must be hard, with most of his friends at uni."

"Yeah." Lucas forked a mustard-smeared chunk of meat into his mouth and followed it with fries from his fingers.

"Wouldn't the insurance be astronomical for a van?" I said. I'd always presumed Prisca covered Kieran for her car, but a van in his name only? "Those points on his provisional license will have been carried over to his full one and at his age that'll push the premium through the roof."

"What points?" Lucas said, and he scratched his left eye, fork still in hand, almost stabbing Justin in the process.

"Careful! From the incident in Dover. Driving without super-vision, I think it's called." As if I hadn't looked it up and apprised myself of its minimum penalty at the time.

"What does that mean?" Freya asked, but before I could explain, Lucas was shaking his head.

"There never were any points from that. Prisca told the police *she* drove us down there."

I set down my glass. "I didn't know that. Did *you* know?" I asked Justin.

"I don't think so." With an air of blithe determination, he signaled to the waitress for another bottle of wine. "But even if she did, she wouldn't be the first parent to cover for their child, would she? If Kieran had admitted to driving himself, there might have been a court appearance, a massive fine. How would they have paid that?"

I gaped, outraged. Who were these adults colluding with their delinquent charges? But, hang on, I was one of them, wasn't I? I'd registered Lucas sick to get him out of his maths A-level, when the effects of a recreational drug binge likely didn't count as legitimate illness. I'd urged him to lie about the truancy too.

"You still thinking you'll learn to drive next summer?" Justin asked Lucas in a blatant change of subject, since Lucas had shared this plan with us only a few hours earlier. He'd bailed on his lessons earlier in the year after only two or three (the instructor's Saturday morning slot had been too early and Lucas's hangovers too heinous for the arrangement to be sustained).

"If they parked at the port, it would have been easy enough for the police to check CCTV and see who was at the wheel," I said.

"But they didn't," Justin said, more firmly now. "Thank you." He took the new bottle of wine from the waitress and smoothly filled our glasses.

I cleared my throat. "So now Kieran has a clean license and soon he's going to be driving a van around our streets day and night. Thanks for the heads-up, anyway."

Lucas glanced at Justin. "He's not a dangerous driver, Mum.

You make it sound like he's going to be deliberately mowing people down."

"Whatever he does, it's his business," Justin said. "He's an independent adult now. Freya, tell your brother about your netball match last week."

As I bit my tongue, my daughter's eyes lit up. "Olivia twisted her ankle so I got to play goal shooter for the second half. I scored four goals."

"One girl's tragedy is another's opportunity," Justin said, raising his glass.

| | | | | | |

Oh, God. Anyone reading this must think I thought about nothing but this one teenager who happened to be friends with my son. That I ignored my daughter and crushed any sign of dissent on the part of my husband. It wasn't like that, I swear. For the purposes of this project, Kieran's are the only relevant scenes: the encounters we had; the conversations in which his name came up. The rest of the time, I was doing what we all do. Earning a living, cooking dinner, loading the dishwasher, reading a novel, signing up for Pilates and giving up after the first session. Kieran wasn't mentioned from one week to the next.

Which brings me to early December, just before Lucas was due home for the Christmas break. That was when I ran into Prisca in W. H. Smith on the high street, having not seen her for months, certainly not since the boys left school. I'd heard she'd landed a part-time admin job at a local health clinic and I congratulated her on the move.

"Didn't Lucas do well in his exams?" she said. "You must be very proud of him."

"Yes, he got there in the end," I said, with exaggerated relief. We were clearly each as reluctant as the other to bring up that last brief row we'd had on the phone.

"Jade, as well, such a brainy girl. And so lovely, always helping Kieran with his geography, she was. Not that he needed any help with his computer science," Prisca added. "Got himself an A star in that. Knew more than the teachers, if you ask me."

The pride in her face acted as a stopper to the sudden rush of thoughts I had concerning her charge. "He's been up to visit Lucas, I hear?"

"That's right, but it's not the same as hanging out whenever you feel like it, is it?"

No, thank God. I remembered Justin's remark about Kieran being an independent adult and wondered if this were actually the case. "Is he still living with you, Prisca?"

"No, but he's just around the corner. He's got a room in a flat on Portland Road."

I assumed that was set up for him, perhaps even subsidized by social services. "But you're still in touch?" I said, warmly.

"'Course I am. He's my boy."

She looked offended and I hastened to make amends. "Well, I hope he doesn't miss Lucas too much. Maybe it's a good thing they're separated for a little while. They were a bit *too* committed to their nights out sometimes, weren't they?"

Prisca smiled. "I didn't like to say, but yeah, maybe it's for the best. Your Lucas will be happy up at Leeds. That's a big party uni, isn't it?"

It was only after we'd parted that I saw that what she'd meant was it was good for Kieran that Lucas had left town. *It's for the best.* I admit I was rocked by the thought that someone could misconstrue a situation so badly. It took willpower not to offload onto Justin that night, but I knew he liked Prisca and would put a positive spin on it. We are all the heroes of our own narratives, he'd say, and Kieran's had taken him from the depths of the care system to A-star exam success. *Undeniable, Ellen, right?*

Instead, I texted Vic:

> Prisca thinks Lucas was the bad guy, can you believe it?

Who cares? he replied. Let her. Water under the bridge.

But that night, I woke up in the early hours poleaxed with remorse. It was as if a stranger had taken possession of my mind, dictating thoughts sympathetic only to Kieran. However wrongly Kieran had influenced the Foxwell gang, Lucas had emerged from it just fine, hadn't he?

Lying there, Justin breathing gently next to me, I felt an unfathomable but very powerful instinct that Kieran was awake too. Just a few miles away in some featureless box room, right on the road, the traffic coughing below. Had Prisca told him she'd seen me? Had they talked about my attitude towards him in the past? ("Don't let her bother you, Kieran, she's just one of *those* mums.")

Oh, God. Was it possible that these last two years had been a needless exercise in overreaction? In obsession?

I reached for my phone and found Vic's message.

You're right, I texted back. It's nothing to do with us anymore.

fourteen

"A FLAT WHITE, PLEASE," I tell the girl on the counter at Bean Box.

"Can I take a name?"

"Prisca," I say, because I've just been thinking of her, wondering if she knows he's here. Her missing boy, alive and reconfigured. Elevated—in both senses of the word.

"Can you spell that?" the girl says, predictably.

I'm back in the shadow of The Heights. Of course I am—you must see by now how dogged I am. I know better than to try his flat again, not after leaving in a panic twice in a row, but have come straight to the café. He was a big coffee drinker, Kieran, I remember that now. In the early days, when he was still welcome at the house, he'd always have a giant takeout coffee from McDonald's or Starbucks in his hand. Later, he'd be slurping as he waited in the car for Lucas to come out. I remember watching him from the bedroom window once and seeing the careless way he tossed the empty cup through his window and into the road, cackling as Lucas slid into the passenger seat beside him.

The passenger seat. I feel a sharp puncture of grief and squeeze my eyes shut.

When I open them again, I focus on my immediate surroundings, as therapy has taught me to do. The café has the same aesthetic of sandblasted brick and black-painted ironwork as the warehouse flats that surround it. On the walls there are old *Illustrated London News* engravings of pedestrians in the Tower Subway that once ran below the river here.

"Do you know a man called Harding?" I ask the girl at the counter as I wait for my order. "He lives in the building over the road."

"That's his first name?"

"No, surname." I cannot yet supply a Christian name — or any information to do with *Harding*'s work or status. I've unearthed plenty of information about the flat, however, and from my discreet corner seat, with one eye on the door and the other on my secret new phone, I scroll through the pages I bookmarked last night. The building went up in 1991 and the land this side of the inlet is known as Jacob's Island (in case you're interested, the dock has a recorded maximum rise and fall of four meters). There is just one unit per floor, the living room overlooking the water and two bedrooms facing the street side. Pictures of Flat 10 show a stunning atrium-style variation on the standard, with a cool plywood spiral staircase leading up to the roof terrace. The flat last changed hands in 2016 for £1.7 million and was advertised for rental a year ago for £3,500 a month. If I'm right and Kieran is the tenant, that's a steep rent for someone in his early twenties.

Lost down the rabbit holes of my research, I've almost forgotten where I am when the hairs on my arms suddenly prickle. A man with a low-toned, estuary-accented voice is greeting the counter staff just a few feet from where I sit—and it's the same voice that plagues my vilest night terrors.

"White americano," he tells the girl at the till. "No sugar, thanks."

Kieran always used to say thanks instead of please. Can I get you a cup of tea, Kieran? *Yeah, thanks.*

Ignoring my breathlessness, the horrible commotion of my pulse, I swivel silently and check him out. He's much leaner than when we knew him, his silhouette triangular, with oversize shoulders and upper arms and a narrow lower body. I remind myself he'd already slimmed down when I last saw him, in Beckenham, almost two and a half years ago. He'd been working out, got himself in shape, and plainly, this has been maintained.

But whatever the transformation, it's him. No doubt about it. And now I need to get the proof I came for. Though I'm able to watch him in the mirrored panel on the wall behind the bar, it is instantly clear that in order to take a photo of him I'll have to angle my phone in such a way that will draw attention to me. Instead, hands shaking, I discreetly press "record."

"Can I interest you in a vegan brownie?" the girl says. "It's a fresh batch."

"Nah, I don't think so, thanks," Kieran says. "To be fair, the coffee's made with cow's milk, so it'd be a bit hypocritical."

To be fair, another innocuous tic that strikes a hammer blow to my ribs.

To be fair, Lukey, no one thinks their own sister is hot . . .

To be fair, no one gives a shit about A-levels once you're in work . . .

The A-levels that drove us to distraction, that I thought were so life-and-death. I'd trade every chivvy, every complaint, every tear of frustration for a second shot at my advice to Lucas the night I changed my mind and said go.

Go let off steam. Go do whatever that crazy friend of yours suggests.

Refocusing, I hear the barista calling out, "Large white americano for Sam!" and Kieran steps forward.

Sam. Sam Harding. So he *is* the tenant at the top of The Heights. He *has* changed his name. And seeing him again, tasting the bile that rises in my throat, I no longer view it as *possible* that he borrowed the name from me, but certain. It's some perverse tribute to our enmity, I'm sure of it.

He turns from the counter, coffee in fist. Is he heading back up to his flat or off to an office? Is my audio clip going to be enough to persuade Vic or should I try for a photo, after all? As Kieran pulls open the door, I spring up, staggering slightly in my haste and drawing the eye of a young woman at a table nearby. "Don't forget your coat!" she says, and when I reach for it, she smiles at me the way young folk do, kindly, because I am her mum's age. I think, fleetingly, of Freya, safe from harm. From him.

When I finally emerge into the street, I'm sure he must have gone. But when I survey left and right, I get a horrific fright: he is right there, standing on the pavement, a cornered animal with its hackles up, breath held.

I take a step towards him, my heart stabbing at my ribs. "Kieran?"

He stares me right in the eye, but there are no signs of recognition: no intake of breath, no heat to his complexion. His face is subtly different, more than the effect of that weight loss, but by cosmetic alteration. There is something different about his mouth, it's raised, misshapen—fillers, maybe—and his freckles have been either removed or concealed, his skin smooth and creamy. He feels as ephemeral as a hallucination, as if I've conjured him into being, my own, masochistic *Sixth Sense*. But he is here, in front of me, waiting for me to speak.

My instinct is to demand, *How are you here? How are you still breathing?* But I can't do that, of course, and I settle for a more direct opening: "Who was that man in your flat yesterday? Does he know who you really are?"

"Why should I tell you?" he answers. "Who *are* you?"

I snort. "You know who I am. You were in, weren't you, two days ago? I was outside your door and you were there. I know you were. And you knew I was there. We can smell each other, can't we, Kieran?"

An arriving customer walks between us, reaching for the door, and breaks the force field. As if released from a spell, Kieran growls, "You're fucked up. Keep away from me." And before I can respond he's pacing towards the entrance to The Heights, keying in the code, slipping through the door.

I rush after him. "Why are you using my maiden name? *That's* fucked up!" The doors shut in my face and I press my phone to the glass and take a series of photos as he waits for the lift. When I check, the images are next to useless, much of his face obscured by reflected light, but the audio is decent quality and I tuck the phone into my bag. Only now does my nervous system fully react: I double over and violently throw up, splashing my shoes with coffee-laced vomit. In the café window, the girl at the laptop looks thoroughly disgusted, turns her face away. And I feel like calling out, *What the hell do you expect?*

That man killed my son.

fifteen

When Lucas came back for Christmas, it was not quite the idyllic homecoming I had envisaged as I raced to finish the concepts I was drawing up for a new client in order to clear my schedule. As I sourced snowfall projector lights for the sitting room and decorated a twelve-foot tree with lights shaped as pinecones. Deep-cleaned his bedroom, bought a new bottle of the black pepper shower gel he liked, stocked the fridge with his favorite boyhood snacks.

Because, in the age-old tradition of freshmen navigating legacy sixth-form romances, he'd been dumped—Jade had done the deed over the phone just the night before. It was obvious from the moment he walked through the door that he'd been crying and my heart grieved for him.

"Oh, darling. I'm so sorry. Has she met someone at Durham?"

But he didn't want to talk about it, not with me or Justin, and it was a relief when I heard him on the phone to Vic, evidently freer with his confidences. "Pretty much. She wouldn't tell me, no. Yeah.

Yeah, I know. I just . . . I don't know, I just want to see her. No, she's staying up there till next weekend . . . Yeah, you're right."

Clearly, Vic was saying all the right things: best not to know who the new guy was or if there even was one; hard for any relationship to survive university; sensible to give her some space and make a virtue of having time with mutual friends while she was still out of town.

For most of the first week, Lucas remained glum, declining all offers to join the rest of the family for any festive activities and going out alone for walks, I guessed as much to smoke as to exercise or clear his head. Then, on the Friday—Friday, December 19—he told me Kieran had invited him over to his new place on Portland Road for a gaming session and I didn't hesitate to encourage him to accept.

"If you get tired of gaming, go into town, maybe," I said, passing him a fold of twenties. "Try and have some fun. Kieran's your man for that, isn't he?"

Was I influenced by that nocturnal crisis I'd suffered just weeks earlier after talking to Prisca? That sense of reckoning? Or was I simply leaping on anything that might stop my beloved boy from feeling *un*loved? Recasting Kieran's role for my own purposes? I can't say for sure, but what I do clearly recall is Lucas's pleasure in my approval. Everything that had been said about his friend over the last two years, everything that had not, seemed to pass across his face as we said our goodbyes, resetting him somehow.

"I'll text if I'm staying out," he promised.

"Great. Bye, darling."

A grin, a hand half-raised in farewell, and then the door closed and he was on the other side of the stained glass, a silhouette of many colors. As I listened to his footsteps receding on the path, I reflected on my new tolerance towards Kieran. It was a profound moment, I thought; a small step for me but a giant leap for parent-kind.

God, I thought I was so enlightened.

| | | | | |

Justin, Freya, and I ate together, as usual. Vegetable lasagna, with spinach and toasted pine nuts. Since Lucas had left for college, we'd got into the habit of a new seating arrangement, with Justin and Freya on one side of the table and me on the other, facing them. They looked alike, those symmetrical faces and noses so straight they might have been drawn with a ruler. The only difference was Freya's full face of makeup, which was becoming both a daily ritual and a passion. ("Don't hide your lovely face behind a mask," I'd advised her recently, from behind my own.)

"I know you've hardly seen Lucas since he's been back, but we'll have a really special Christmas together," I said. The school term had just finished that afternoon and she'd obviously been hoping to see her brother. "It will be a proper celebration." And, as if to back up this claim, there came the sound of fireworks exploding in a neighbor's garden, causing all three of us to chuckle.

| | | | | |

By midnight, Lucas still hadn't texted me, so I sent him a line checking he had his keys. Peering at the screen half an hour later, I saw my message had been delivered but not read.

"Should we be worried?" I asked Justin, putting on the polka-dot pajamas that Lucas and Freya had given me the previous Christmas and had become my favorites. "I mean, I know he's all grown up now, but he did say he'd text his ETA."

"I wouldn't worry. A week ago, when he was in Leeds, we wouldn't have known what time he was coming home," Justin reasoned. "He could have been sleeping on a park bench the whole term for all we know."

"You're not helping," I said, with a smile.

"Have you tried an old-fashioned phone call?"

This I now did, but the call went to voice mail. "Lucas, nothing urgent, just let me know if you're coming back tonight. Hope you're having a good time." Though my tone was breezy, I felt ill at ease. Perhaps it was the rain, which had started suddenly, a violent sideways assault on the windowpanes. Wet winter nights always made me want to know my loved ones were safe indoors.

"No luck?" Justin said, yawning. "He'll still be at Kieran's gaming. In the zone. I bet they haven't even left the flat."

Though this made perfect sense, I couldn't settle. In the dark, after Justin had dropped off, I texted Vic in case he'd heard from Lucas, but got no reply. Scanning my contacts, I saw I still had Prisca's number and my thumbs hovered over the keys before I abandoned the idea. Kieran lived independently now and she'd be unlikely to appreciate being alerted in the dead of night to an emergency that didn't exist. I had no number for Kieran himself; it had been, over the years, a firm policy of mine not to allow him in. Not to acknowledge him.

The unsettled feeling persisted and at 2 a.m. I began another round of efforts—Lucas, Vic, and then this time Prisca, after all—but each appeal went to voice mail. I slipped out of the bedroom and crossed the landing. The Christmas lights wound around the spindles of the balustrade were still on—we'd forgotten to hit the switch when we went to bed—but the house was otherwise in darkness. I opened Lucas's bedroom door, I suppose hoping he might have crept back in without my hearing, but, no, his bed hadn't been slept in. There was the usual scattering of clothes and books and devices across the carpet, and on his desk chair a towel from yesterday's shower, twisted and damp.

I went back to bed, but could do little more than snooze for the rest of the night. Then, at about 6:30 a.m., three noises sounded in close succession: the creaking of the radiators coming to life, the groan of an early plane, and the sound of a car pulling up.

It had stopped raining.

A car door smacked shut and my spirits leapt. It was a taxi bringing him home from wherever he and Kieran had ended up. I scrambled out of bed again. Closing the bedroom door behind me, I paused at the fairy-lit landing to look down at the hall and my ear caught a fragment of something in the dawn silence—a voice, far away, transmitted through a radio.

Then came a sharp rap on the front door.

Lucas wouldn't do that. Not this early. Years of experience told me that if he'd forgotten his keys, he'd go around the back first and check the kitchen door, hoping one of us had been absentminded and left it unlocked. Failing that, he'd text.

Now, a second rap.

Moving fast down the stairs, I felt my bare soles burn on the runner, before cooling on the hall tiles. Through the stained glass two figures were visible, but neither was the right height to be Lucas. I opened the door. A pair of uniformed police officers stood on the step. One man, one woman.

Never, before or since, have my heart and lungs reacted the way they did. It was as if there was a living creature in my chest, with huge strong wings and a beak, splitting my rib cage as it fought to get out.

"Are you Mrs. Gordon?" the woman asked.

"No," I said, so discombobulated that I offered my maiden name,

Harding, before hurriedly correcting myself. "I mean Saint. Mrs. Saint. Ellen."

"Are you Lucas Gordon's mother?" she clarified.

"Yes. Where is he? He went out yesterday afternoon and I haven't heard from him, but I'm sure he's at his friend's place in South Norwood. I can find out the address . . . ?" I was aware that I was delaying, extending by a few extra seconds this half of my life. This half that had been shifting and exhausting and complicated, but always the better for Lucas having been in it. Always.

"Would it be all right if we came in, Ellen?" they said, but it was only when they asked if I was on my own, or if my husband or another family member was home and could be called down to join us, that I finally demanded that they say what they'd come to say. After that, my voice got stuck, impaled on a single syllable of denial: "No, no, no, no."

No.

Killing Time (cont)

For those in need of a recap, Saint first appeared in the news following the tragic death of her nineteen-year-old son, Lucas, in December 2014. A first-year geography student at Leeds University, Lucas Gordon was home for the Christmas break and out with his old school friend, Kieran Watts, when, in the early hours of December 19, the Vauxhall Corsa the pair were traveling in plunged into Layham Hill reservoir near Purley.

The details that emerged were heartbreaking. The car sank front first and became wedged on its side. Watts, the driver, managed to escape through an open window but was unable to get help quickly enough to save his friend. Emergency services arrived at 3 a.m. and Gordon was pronounced dead at the scene.

In an echo of the infamous Chappaquiddick tragedy involving Ted Kennedy in 1969, the youngster was believed to have survived in an air pocket for several minutes before drowning. His seat belt had been disengaged, evidence that he was conscious for at least some of that time, but it is thought likely that his injuries made escape impossible.

Notoriously, Kennedy failed to call for help to rescue his passenger, Mary Jo Kopechne, in spite of there being a working telephone in a house close by. However, in this case, Kieran Watts, who repeatedly stated he "cannot recollect" events, may have had different reasons for failing to seek help in time. His mobile phone was lost in the accident and there was no public phone or accessible residence within half a mile of the reservoir. His own injuries, which included concussion and a broken shoulder, would likely have hampered his efforts. Both Watts and Gordon were found to have taken cannabis in the hours preceding the incident.

Many people will remember pictures published of Ellen with Lucas's father, Vic Gordon, in the aftermath of the tragedy, which caught the public imagination as Christmastime horror stories often do. For a brief time, the terrible, haunting quality of those photographs seemed to challenge every one of us to face what it was we feared the most.

Sunday Times magazine, December 2021

sixteen

I'VE LOST MOST OF my memory of those first days. There was a cata-strophic failure to process that he'd been taken from us, even before you allowed for the sedatives I freely consumed. Justin and Vic were always present, Freya absent. "Better for her" was the phrase we used; better for her not to see her mum catatonic. Oddly, I remember the taste sensations best: the permanent rustiness in my mouth, the vin-egary tears. Also, the ghastly, mesmerizing vision in the bathroom mirror, as if my face was not my own but that of an ancient ancestor who'd crossed time to visit, lacking the words to speak, able only to stare at me glassy-eyed. The mother of a drowned boy.

Is it helpful to excavate the details? To imagine every filthy, deathly drop of water as it replaced the air in Lucas's lungs, weighing them down, preventing oxygen from being delivered to his heart?

Well, the press thought it was, so the keener readers among you can search them out in seconds. Try "Festive Joy Ride Turns Tragic" or—in a cultural reference not immediately clear to younger readers—"Echoes of Chappaquiddick in Teen Horror Smash."

In less sensationalist English, Kieran abandoned Lucas in a car filling with freezing dark water and there was not a shred of evidence to suggest that he'd tried to help him escape the vehicle. The opposite: he left him to die. And once I'd emerged through the pharmaceutical cracks, I had some questions about that.

"They think he must have got out of the passenger window," Justin said. "The driver's side was blocked because of the way the car got wedged, so he couldn't escape that side."

"You mean he climbed over Lucas? In that tiny car?"

"Yes." Though Justin's tone was low and measured, the set of his face was grim. We were sitting in candlelight—or perhaps I just remember it that way. I certainly preferred dimness for a long time afterwards, the way it obscured the ravages in people's faces. The loss of faith in their eyes.

Police photos and diagrams proved the hypothesis: there wasn't much space between the driver's seat and the passenger window and Kieran couldn't have navigated it without physically struggling past Lucas, who was still strapped into his seat. In physical terms, a shove or a kick would have made little difference to Lucas's injuries, but that was not the point.

"How did Kieran get the window open?" I asked Justin. "Don't the electrics shut down underwater?"

"It was already open," Justin said. "They think Lucas must have been smoking before they went off the road. That very well might have saved Kieran's life."

I closed my eyes—as if *that* would prevent me from hearing, from imagining. "Why didn't Kieran help him, Jus? Even if Lucas was unconscious, he could have pulled him out with him, got him to safety."

"They think his instinct was to get himself to the surface as quickly as possible. Then when he got there, he'd lost his phone in the process, so he couldn't call 999."

"Then he should have gone back down!" I cried. "The reservoir isn't that deep."

"They think he collapsed, went into some sort of shock. He'd broken his shoulder, remember. By the time he thought to go back to the road and flag down a car, it was too late."

I frowned. "You keep saying 'they think.' Doesn't he know?"

"He doesn't remember, apparently. All he remembers is coming to and staggering to the road. He doesn't remember anything before that, the crash itself, escaping, swimming to safety. Nothing."

Including Lucas's last words on this earth.

If they'd been uttered in his presence, that was. The worst was to come, you see, and if there had been any way Justin could have kept it from me—not just then, but forever—I know he would have. Because at some point following Kieran's escape, Lucas had regained consciousness and found the strength to unbuckle the belt that had kept him alive. He had managed to twist himself so that his left shoulder and arm were positioned in the open passenger window, his head jammed inside in the upper corner.

"Was that . . . was that because that corner was where the last of the air was?"

"It's possible," Justin said. "They don't know for sure. But hypothermia would have been an issue by then."

All parents have it, at least that is my assumption: an empathy with their child so deep it is extrasensory. Their joy is your joy, their pain yours. And what inhabited me most deeply in the aftermath— and did for years afterwards—was that moment when Lucas came to. The dark, icy claustrophobia, the primitive terror he felt when he understood he didn't possess the strength to escape. Being aware, even for ten seconds, of his own hellish form of death: that's what haunts me.

If only he'd remained unconscious, he would never have known that terror.

Vic told me later that he'd tried and failed to find Kieran, both at the hospital—he was too late, Kieran had been discharged after receiving treatment for his shoulder—and at Prisca's home, which he'd found closed up, curtains drawn in every window.

Still, the police knew where to find him, which was the important thing. Because, by the time Lucas's body was released to us, it had been established that Kieran had had cannabis in his bloodstream at the time of driving and had been charged and remanded. The timing was important, because it meant he could not brazen out an appearance at Lucas's funeral.

Word reached us soon after that his claim not to be able to remember the circumstances of the crash had been authenticated by a police psychologist.

"Very convenient," Vic said.

"Isn't it?" I agreed, the taste of vinegar in my mouth.

| | | | | |

Unlike on the morning of Lucas's death, the day of the funeral started late for me, thanks to a sleeping pill. I'd just about conquered the daytime fog by then, but it would be a long time before I could do without chemical assistance at night. All I had to do was shower, get dressed, and climb into the car, because everything else had been done for me by Justin and Vic. They'd chosen the church, the plot in the cemetery, the coffin, the flowers, the music. The guests.

I don't know if you have ever been to the funeral of a young person, but it is usually a second tragedy to be endured by those who have not yet processed the first. What survives most clearly in my mind is the sheer mystification on Lucas's friends' faces, as if they'd found themselves in a dystopia. Some rallied and took photographs — of themselves, of each other — in the way that strikes my generation as unseemly but is inoffensive to theirs. They meant no harm. They were paying tribute to their friend, that was all.

Jade was there, of course, grief not quite subduing her prettiness. Expecting, when we came face-to-face, to exchange only the clichés of loss, she was clearly unnerved by my immediate and direct references to the circumstances of the accident. I'm not proud that I chose this occasion to interrogate her and, thinking of it now, I wonder if it was a defense mechanism. I was smothering my grief with a quest for understanding.

"Have you spoken to Kieran?" I asked her and her mouth opened in surprise. I smelled peppermint breath. "Do you have any idea why he didn't help Lucas?"

"It must have been impossible," she stammered. "Otherwise he would have."

"Is that what he's told you?" Though I had blocked all other voices, all glances, I could see she was distracted by those around us. She was probably shocked by my appearance, as well: owing to chest pain — a broken heart, what else could it have been? — I was a little bent in on myself, which brought my face closer to hers than was perhaps comfortable.

"I only know what I've read, honestly." She paused. "I wasn't there."

I saw it then, an electrical current through the muscles of her face: awe of the near miss. She was thinking how easily she *could* have been there. If she'd come back from uni when Lucas had, if she'd delayed breaking up with him till the New Year, she very likely *would* have been out with them, perhaps in the very seat where Lucas was trapped. Soon, a unique blend of elation and guilt would replace this awe, along with a way to rationalize it. She had a second chance at life and she would seize it. She would seize it in Lucas's honor.

"So he *hasn't* contacted you?" I persisted.

"He's been remanded in custody, I thought." The effort not to sob was clear in her eyes.

"But he can still make phone calls, can't he?" My voice was growing forceful amid the church murmurs. Beyond Jade, I glimpsed my husband and daughter standing with a group of Lucas's old school friends. The identical downwards turn of their mouths, their hopeless, leaden posture. "You need to tell me, Jade. This is our whole family that's been destroyed. You can't keep secrets about what happened!"

She turned from me and began weeping. Sheridan hurried over to rescue her. "What's going on? Are you all right, babe?"

"I'm just asking her about Kieran," I said as Jade clung to her. "I thought she might have had more of a handle on his state of mind that night. Why he did what he did."

"I don't think she knows anything," Sheridan said, her voice gently resistant. Nodding towards a cluster of mourners hovering to pay their respects to me, she steered her daughter away.

Speaking of mourners, I'd just like to say that people came to the service who have barely been mentioned in this story, people who were important to Lucas and our family: neighbors, teachers, colleagues, old family friends we saw once or twice a year. Most of them wouldn't have thought twice about diving into dark water to try to save Lucas's life and, if I could start this project again, maybe I would prefer to write about them.

Prisca was there. Vic must have invited her or perhaps she came of her own accord. I didn't mind, so long as the only person she represented was herself. She did not approach me and departed directly after the burial; I saw her walking down the lane to the bus stop, her arms limp by her sides. Her wrecked Corsa, having been dredged from the reservoir, resided now in a police garage in Croydon.

You know, even at the time, lacking in judgment and restraint though I was, it seemed remarkable that no one but me questioned Kieran's actions—or even mentioned his name. I suppose they feared sullying the occasion by invoking it, but I didn't like how this conjured a false narrative of solitary misfortune, the illusion that Lucas had driven *himself* into the reservoir.

Only Vic's cousin Danny broke the mold. "Pleased to hear the little bastard's being kept in on remand," he told me, at the wake, glass in hand. His suit was new, his face shiny and shaved with care. "Is that going to be right till the trial?"

"I think so," I said, adding that I hoped he was living in fear of the most menacing criminals his jailers could assemble.

"Oh, Kieran'll get what's coming to him, don't you worry," Danny said.

| | | | | | |

There was no trial. This is not a court drama—you are spared that. *He* spared us, technically, by pleading guilty, or rather his defense team spared us by convincing him to do so. For those who don't know, credit is given in the form of a discounted sentence for saving time and expense, as well as for saving victims and witnesses the anxiety of having to give evidence.

Of the various charges discussed with the CPS, the one that was eventually settled on was Causing Death by Careless Driving. *Careless.* The word offended me, with its sense of the throwaway, the extraneous. And yet it was perfect for that insolent, reckless individual who had arrived in Lucas's life on the first day of sixth form and taken so little care of it.

As for the sentencing, Kieran's team introduced all sorts of mitigating factors besides that humble guilty plea: the unsettled nature of his childhood years; his immaturity and impressionability; the academic success he'd achieved against all odds. Then there was the lack of definitive evidence about who had supplied whom with the cannabis and whose idea the joyride had been—the possibility could not be discounted that Lucas himself had been responsible for one or both. Indeed, it could be regarded as likely.

Disgusting lies, Vic and I agreed. Kieran's continuing memory loss was nothing more than a legal ploy. It was not even a mask for shame.

We had written an impact statement, which Vic delivered in court in a heartbreaking undertone, and the press quoted:

> "When a beautiful young man like Lucas is robbed of his
> life, a whole family is robbed of its power. Of its love."

I was watching Kieran as Vic spoke. He was blinking and twitching, displaying all the signs of distress you'd expect, and others in the room read his remorse as real, I could tell.

But Vic and I, we knew he was faking it.

Killing Time (cont)

After Kieran Watts was convicted of Causing Death by Careless Driving, Ellen and Vic launched a campaign to protest the brevity of his sentence. While not the first parent-led crusade for sterner prison tariffs, it must surely be a contender for the most vitriolic. No punishment was too extreme for Watts as far as they and their legions of followers were concerned.

"How often do we hear the cry 'Bring back hanging!' when there's a crime that shocks the nation?" the pair asked in one joint editorial for the *Mirror*. "Of course, most of us agree that's a barbaric measure, that the UK is a more civilized place without capital punishment. But we don't mind admitting there have been times since Lucas was taken from us that we've uttered the phrase ourselves—and meant it."

The piece ran alongside a photograph of their son's grave in a South London cemetery.

Like so many emotionally driven projects, the campaign blew itself out quickly enough, allowing the participants an opportunity for reflection one suspects they badly needed.

Sunday Times magazine, December 2021

seventeen

I'VE DECIDED TO DEVOTE only a single chapter to the years of Kieran's incarceration. There were not quite two of them once the sentencing discount and time served had been applied—insultingly short, as Vic and I would continue to argue until we went hoarse. As Kieran went on to reach the age of thirty, forty, and beyond—all the milestones Lucas would never see—his sentence would shrink in his memory, in time coming to seem as if it had never happened at all.

Because of his youth—just nineteen at the time of the trial—his term took place in its entirety in a young offender institute, YOI Danstone in Kent. The Prison Reform Trust document supplied to us made the place sound like a pared-down boarding school, with an emphasis on education and exercise, even socializing.

"It won't be like that in reality," Vic said, and we studied articles about new arrivals being stalked by the threat of violence, about kids having blades smuggled into the facility in the seams of clothing and the drug spice on the pages of books. "He might have a psychotic cellmate," he added, hopefully.

But it wasn't nearly enough to assuage the sense of injustice I felt, the duty to warn other parents of just how cheap their children's lives were to the courts and how crucial it was to follow those instincts about bad influences in the first place. At first, I could not speak without panicking; with every word, the loss of Lucas would swell until I felt I could no longer breathe. Over time, however, I could manage forty-five minutes or so, long enough to address audiences in libraries and other community spaces. Justin helped me put together a presentation, which began with a photo of Lucas on that holiday in Greece.

"This is my son, Lucas Gordon. He was nineteen years old when he was killed by his friend Kieran Watts . . ."

Lock Up Longer evolved from an introduction to a journalist from the *Mirror* after one of those talks. Roz Engleby's own daughter had suffered life-changing injuries in a careless driving incident several years ago in which the driver had walked away without punishment. Roz approached me for a short interview and, as we talked, we agreed that something larger and louder was needed to raise awareness.

A website was created, Twitter account launched. The *Mirror's* social media team got momentum going and a PR company represented us pro bono. Now our talks were supplemented with radio interviews and magazine features.

"Lay down the law with your teenagers, because you can't count on the law to do it for you," I exhorted parents in senior school workshops, and both the line and that photo of Lucas were widely published. The campaign took on a life of its own, until one day Vic and I were on the BBC News sofa, our own faces looking back at us from the monitors.

"Ellen, tell us what happened to your son, Lucas," the presenter said, her gaze at once theatrical and sincere.

And for a moment on that brightly lit set, before I could find my voice, my mind went quite blank. Blank and beautiful and painless.

| | | | | | | |

I learned a lot from the Lock Up Longer experience, including the lesson that there are no winners in fatal incidents. For every supporter of tougher sentencing there is a supporter of leniency. Rehabilitation. A second chance. There are the parents of the perpetrator who won't hear a word against them, partners and friends who insist that a miscarriage of justice has taken place. They suffer abuse, they field accusations, they stand at the far reaches of funerals, crying the same tears as the rest of us.

I do understand that, I really do.

Prisca was a case in point. Soon after the television appearance, she arrived at my door to appeal on Kieran's behalf—or, rather, her own. She was lucky I answered because I'd grown used to the doorbell going constantly and had long stopped bothering with it. (Not that I feared anything hateful, the opposite, in fact: at the height of the campaign, local supporters would leave gifts or flowers, cards containing outpourings of sympathy and love.) But this time, almost absentmindedly, I got to my feet and opened up.

Her face half-covered by a fleece hat and body enveloped in a huge puffer coat, she was scarcely recognizable as the Prisca I remembered. Her eyes brimmed and her voice, when she spoke, was congested with cold.

"Please don't do this, Ellen."

"Do what?" I said.

"This campaign with the papers. I've had hate mail, a brick through my window. Graffiti everywhere. I'm having to stay with a friend, I'm that scared."

Rumors of this nature had already reached me through friends. "It's nothing personal towards you," I said, in a neutral tone. Public speaking and media experience had equipped me with a steadiness I could draw on when ambushed like this. A loss of emotional control only obscured the message. "It's the principle."

"The principle of locking up boys?" she fired back.

"Kieran is not a boy, he's an adult. And taking another person's life is the same whether you're young or old. No one should be allowed to get away with it."

"He isn't getting away with it," she protested. "He's in that terrible place. I've visited him there and I can tell you he's as miserable as can be. They're fighting all the time, there's gangs, a boy in the next cell was beaten in his sleep—"

"But he'll be out before you know it," I cut in, coldly. "Time flies, right?"

"Not when every day is hell!"

I narrowed my gaze. "I'm afraid we might have different definitions of hell, Prisca."

And here we were, two minutes in, me occupying the moral high ground that no one else could access. Prisca took out a tissue to blow her nose and the sight of her ungloved hands, red and dry with cold, caused a stab of remorse for the way I'd treated her. After Lucas's death, she'd sent a card in which she shared a memory of him helping her fix a leak in her garden shed, "where the boys used to hole up." She would never have thought to ban Lucas from her house as I had Kieran from mine. She would not have tallied his faults the way I did Kieran's; she would not have called for their headteacher to expel him. Had the outcomes been reversed, she would not have blamed Lucas for surviving.

I remembered her presence at the funeral: I hadn't spoken to her. And here I was now, not even inviting her in, when she was obviously suffering with a heavy cold.

What was wrong with me?

As she regarded me with despairing pink-rimmed eyes, I gave a mental shake of the head, righting my brain. This woman was legally and morally responsible for the monster who killed my son.

I stepped towards her. "I'm glad you're here, actually. I wanted to ask you something."

"Okay," she said, warily.

"Those visits you've had with him, has he said anything new about what happened? On the night of the crash, I mean. I know the trauma affected his memory of the impact itself . . ."—I managed to say this without derision—". . . but does he remember how he came to lose control of the car? He'd never had an accident before, had he?" I remembered the tight spiral of the car park Kieran had navigated with ease; the drive to Dover before he was even qualified, illegal but without incident; and the plan to drive a van for a living. "It wasn't a mechanical failure, so to veer so suddenly like that, at such a steep angle, it was never explained."

Prisca looked puzzled. "The turning was tight and it was dark and raining. He lost concentration and misjudged it. That's what they all said, the police and the lawyers, didn't they?"

"They *guessed* it. But they never dug that deep, did they? They were happy with the lesser charge, the guilty plea. But I think *you* know more than we were ever told."

She stared at me, openmouthed. Her breath clouded in front of her.

"Come on, Prisca, he must have told you *something* new?" I paused, a choking sensation in my throat. "What was the last thing Lucas said? We don't even know that."

"I don't know, I'm sorry." Her eyes grew teary. "Kieran hasn't said anything."

I knew as well as she did that even if she *had* been party to incriminatory details either omitted in court or confessed since, she was hardly going to share them with a woman who'd just been on national television to whip up condemnation of him. But I had to ask. I had to keep on asking.

She shuffled back, drawing her collar to her throat with one hand and adjusting the strap of her bag with the other. "Don't do this to yourself, Ellen. You deserve peace, not all this torture. This hate."

I watched as she walked towards a silver Kia parked a few doors down. I went on watching until the car pulled away, stalking her words through my mind, seeking the smallest dropped clue but finding none.

"You know nothing about torture and hate," I said aloud, though I had no hope of being heard.

| | | | | | |

Our work with the *Mirror* was important but, by its nature, limited. Crime rolled on, injustices happened every day, and the time came when a new case caught Roz Engleby's imagination. It was a dangerous driving offense in Liverpool in which a fifteen-year-old girl was killed when her boyfriend of less than a week attempted to impress her with a ride in his brother's sports car. The passenger side crumpled on impact with a lamppost, ending the girl's life at a stroke, while the driver walked away with only a fractured collarbone and a suspended sentence.

I wrote to the victim's parents to express my condolences and as I positioned the stamp in the corner of the envelope, I felt a sense of symbolism deep within me. It was time to move my activism from the center of my vision to the periphery.

Not my thoughts of Kieran, however. Just a month after Vic and

I attended our last event, we had word that Kieran had been transferred to a wing at YOI Danstone that offered a special program of
group psychotherapy and "enhanced educational opportunity." Even
the food was better in this special unit: some celebrity chef, who'd
recently been cautioned after a brawl in one of his kitchens, wanted
to "give something back" and had created an experimental menu for
the participating inmates.

This was beyond the pale. I rang the family liaison officer who'd
been our contact during the original prosecution to ask if we could
influence the move in any way.

"As far as I know, the program isn't oversubscribed and it's certainly not a soft option," the officer explained. "He's there voluntarily
and that's considered progress. It's solid evidence that he wants to
understand his own actions."

"How can he understand them when he claims not to remember
them?" I asked.

"Maybe this will help him remember. It's a clear sign that he
wants to try."

I closed my eyes as she spoke of the undeniable results. Those
who took part in the program resettled better on release and were less
likely to reoffend—and the rest of it.

"He's even doing some advanced IT course sponsored by a
City bank," I ranted to Justin later. "Anyone would think he'd won
a prize, not been jailed for killing someone! I'm going to put something on the website, see if we can get this reversed somehow."
Though no longer featured in the *Mirror* or represented by their
PR, the Lock Up Longer website remained active and I still fielded
regular media inquiries. Vic, when he had time, moderated the
discussion forum.

"We need to focus on Freya," Justin told me, gently. He said everything gently during that period. As if the human voice, when raised, had the power to inflict bodily injury. To break us.

I know some of you will be wondering why on earth this lovely, reasonable man stayed with me, but I suppose love makes us do extraordinary things—and not always the bad kind.

| | | | | |

It's probably going to sound strange, but my father's death helped. It helped in that way self-harm is said to distract from the larger torment, to localize it, even, briefly, to cleanse.

Believe it or not, I didn't blame Kieran for indirectly causing it—this wasn't a case of collateral damage. If anything, the court proceedings and subsequent campaign had galvanized Dad. It was simply the natural order reasserting itself, with all its wistfulness and sorrow. He was in his early eighties by then, had never recovered from his hip surgery, and a second operation had led to an infection he couldn't fight.

I traveled down to Kent several times to help Mum sort through his clothes and personal things, decide what to donate and what to keep. Freya came with me on those visits. Even at the time, I was grateful that she had reacted to her brother's death and all the media activity by withdrawing. She was fourteen by then and could so easily have broken out, broken bad, punished the world by punishing herself. And I knew her grief was complicated by the fact that she'd liked Kieran—they all had, that was the truth of it. To know that her mother was focusing all her energy on his destruction—well, it must have been hard and I'm sorry for that.

When I remember that time now, I think of us driving down the M20, Freya in the passenger seat, choosing playlists from her phone for us to listen to. Sometimes a song would come on and she'd say, "Lucas really liked this one," and I'd ask her to repeat the name of the artist, as if by committing it to memory I'd be closer to him, though in truth, every minute lived, every mile driven, took us further from him.

Most of Dad's estate went to Mum, of course, but I found I had been left a lump sum of twenty thousand pounds. Though I had an idea I might donate it to a cause that honored Lucas's memory, a homeless charity, perhaps, I took no immediate action. The delay would prove fortuitous—from my perspective, at any rate.

eighteen

"I DON'T UNDERSTAND, ELLEN. How can this be true?"

The moment I play Vic the audio, he capitulates. I take no pleasure in the collapse of his facial muscles, the deathly pall that inches across his face — or the part of it not covered by the black and silver needles of his stubble. It doesn't help that whoever designed the lighting in the lobby of the chain hotel in Euston we're meeting in had the aesthetic of the interrogation chamber on her mood board.

Vic's just had a go-see with someone interested in trialing his lager in their new vending bar but, for now, the brewer in him is silenced. "Let me hear it again," he says.

I oblige. The line about cow's milk and brownies is hard to isolate from the hiss of the coffee machine, but the clip from outside the café is devastatingly clear. "Keep away from me," Kieran warns, his voice deep with malice.

"Did you hear that bit just before?" I say. " 'Who *are* you?' As if he didn't do time for killing my son!"

Vic is looking at me with a mix of apology and respect that I'd find satisfying if the cause were just about any other than this. As I told him on the phone, I don't *want* to be right. "I can't believe you were face-to-face with him, Ellen. I honestly don't know how I'd have reacted. I'd probably have decked him."

"It was weird," I admit. "I didn't handle it very well. I sort of froze."

"Can you forward this recording to me?"

"I'm not sure you want it on your phone. This is a pay-as-you-go I bought specially for this stuff. Maybe you need to get a burner as well, Vic."

As I speak, I have a sharp sense of history repeating. I had a secret prepaid phone once before, eventually disposing of it—along with the old iPad I'd been using to make all kinds of dodgy searches—in Regent's Canal on my way to an appointment in Little Venice. A young DJ's half-a-million-pound refurb and one of my first clients ("I want all my lights to be like meteors," he explained).

"What d'you mean, 'stuff'?" Vic says, warily. "What else have you got? Photos?"

"Only these through the glass doors." I find the images for him. "But you can't recognize him from them."

He studies them, frowning deeply. "Has he bleached his hair?"

"Yes, he's done something funny to his lips and eyebrows, as well. It's definitely him, though. No doubt about it."

"You don't have to convince me. I'd know that voice anywhere."

"His new name is Sam Harding," I say, and as Vic's gaze narrows, I give a half smile. "You think he was inspired by me?"

"Would he know that was your name before you got married?"

"He might. I remember us all talking one night on holiday about whether women of their gen would take their husbands' names." I falter as a vivid image arrives: teenagers with pink-streaked limbs and hair stiff with salt from the sea. Eruptions of laughter. Lucas at the center of it all, raucous and vital. "They might have mentioned that when they got back. Anyway, I'm his number one enemy, always have been. I wouldn't put it past him to have compiled some sort of dossier on me."

"Where does the Sam bit come from?" Vic asks.

"He probably just chose something you can google and get lost in a million alternatives. But once you add the address, it's a lot easier."

Which explains why it took me less than an hour to discover how "Sam Harding" comes to be living the life of Riley. "He designed an app called Moodsmart. It hasn't launched yet, from what I can tell, but the bastard struck gold and sold it to that big tech company, Saurus." I summarize what I know about the app. It has interactive functions that allow the user to dial up or down according to their mood or the occasion. (Set Your Own Mood, the brand urges. Be Kind to Yourself.) "He was backed by this trendy team of investors, let me find the website for you . . ."

If I'm right, the gray-haired man I fled from down Mill Street is James Ratcliffe, an angel investor specializing in ethical investment, whose company, Green Shoots, is based in Bermondsey Street, a five-minute walk from Shad Thames. The photo on his company website is dated from at least a decade ago, but it's the same guy, I'm sure of it. I pull up the image to show Vic. "I saw this man when I was there two days ago. He must be the one who helped Kieran do the deal with Saurus. He was in his flat, so they must still be working together or at least be friends. He struck me as very protective."

I don't mention the chase scene, my cowering behind shelves of cold and flu medication in the Co-op when I should have been engaging this Ratcliffe and learning all that was not so easily gleaned online. No, it is evidence only of my own tendency to overreact.

Vic zooms in on the image of the investor, a complicated expression passing across his face. Guilt is one component: it's clear he's regretting having doubted me. As he closes the screen and hands back the phone, there's silence between us, trepidation on both our parts as we wonder who will say first what cannot be put off any longer.

It is me, of course. I led before and I will lead again. "What do you think went wrong with our plan, Vic?"

"I have no fucking idea." He casts cautious glances in every direction, discreetly raises a finger to his lips. "But I do know we shouldn't say anything with cameras around. Police can lip-read this shit. Can we meet after work, somewhere outside?"

"Of course." I get to my feet. "Meet me at London Bridge Station at six and I'll show you where he's living."

Living: the word seems to cause an electric current between us, to connect us simultaneously with the central fact of our new reality.

The man we arranged to have murdered is still alive.

nineteen

NEVER IN MY WORST nightmares—and there were plenty of them—
did I think we'd actually have to see Kieran again after he was
released. That he would be free to come back to the community he'd
devastated and pick up where he left off.

But this was what he did. And, fate being the cruel mistress she is,
I must have been among the first to set eyes on him.

It was Easter, April 2017, and Justin and I had been to the
cinema—one of the few activities I was able to enjoy, thanks to its
obliterating impact on my emotions. It was just the two of us, Freya
having stayed at home to study for GCSEs, and we'd gone afterwards
to the pizza place on the high street. Sawing into my Fiorentina, I
became aware that Justin had frozen, almost comically, with his fork
halfway to his mouth, transfixed by something he'd seen through the
window.

"What is it?"

He lowered the fork, his eyes opaque, jaw tensed. "Over the road.
Outside the pub."

Following his line of vision, I saw for myself: a man who looked like Kieran, on the pavement outside the Crown, standing at the edge of a group of smokers.

"Is that *him?*"

"Yes, I think so."

Out of nowhere, I had a sore throat, a racing pulse, a terrible light-headedness, as if the mere proximity of Lucas's killer had infected me with some instant-acting virus. "I feel sick."

Justin placed a glass of iced water in my hand. "Drink this."

I was trembling and spilled a little before managing to take a gulp. I couldn't tear my eyes away from the figure across the road. He was thinner than when we'd last seen him, his jeans and sweatshirt too big, and his hair had been clipped short.

Strangely, once the shock had lifted, the first thought that surfaced was of the night of Freya's birthday at the sushi place. His face at the window, that gesture of contempt. What would he do this time to signal his hatred, now that so much had passed between us? He'd already made the gesture to end all others. There was nothing left.

"Better?" Justin had, by now, recovered. "I suppose it was only a matter of time, wasn't it?"

"Why's he allowed to come back here?" I whispered.

"There may not have been any other options. Do you know any of the people he's with?"

"I don't think so." How wounding it was that my eyes still searched for Lucas. Perhaps they always would, conditioned from the day of his birth to expect to find him right at the center of my world. I felt a shiver pass over me as a smiling young blond woman came into view and perched on the edge of a table close to Kieran. "Oh! Is that Jade?"

"I think it is. She must be home for the Easter holidays," Justin said.

I knew from sporadic meetings with Sheridan that Jade was doing well at uni. About to enter her final term and ambitious about a career in marketing, she'd secured an internship with a gaming company on graduation. Dressed in the hugging bodycon style all the girls were wearing these days, she had the same lean, eye-catching looks I remembered from Crete. Her bare legs gleamed white, almost pearlescent, in the pub's external lights.

"How can she bear to see him, Jus? I don't understand it." My voice shook. "And why didn't Sheridan tell me she was still in touch with him?"

His eyebrows lifted. "She probably doesn't know. Anyway, Jade might not have planned to meet him, they might have bumped into each other."

I took the napkin from my lap and placed it over my abandoned plate. Then I pushed back in my chair with a loud scrape.

"Don't," he said, putting out a restraining hand.

"Don't what?"

"Go over there. It won't help and you might even get in trouble."

I twisted my wrist from his grip. "*I'd* get in trouble?"

"If he feels harassed, yes. He could make a complaint. He'll know about the campaign, don't forget. Everything that went on while he was inside, he'll have seen it all."

Since Lucas's death, there had been the sense that Justin intended never again to make the mistake he'd made during Lucas's life, which was to give Kieran the benefit of the doubt. It was an indisputable fact now between us that Kieran was wicked and always had been, and Justin had supported every last sentiment of Lock Up Longer. But it had been easier when Kieran was absent, I supposed, and this gentle resistance in the face of his reappearance shouldn't have come as a surprise.

I sank back in my seat and picked up my wineglass.

After a minute or two, Jade went inside and Kieran remained with a handful of men I didn't recognize, laughing and chatting with his old ease. Far from appearing diminished by his spell inside, there was a new authority to him, almost a heroism, as if he'd returned from military service.

I tried to filter my kneejerk thoughts before speaking again. Could we restart Lock Up Longer with the *Mirror*, highlighting the harrowing effects of a premature release on the victim's family? Was Kieran legally protected in some way now he had served his time? Justin was right: deprived of internet access during his stretch, he had probably only recently been able to update himself on his own media coverage, his brief reign as a symbol of evil. It was unlikely he'd liked what he'd seen. Might he even feel justified in coming after *us*?

And, of course, I knew Justin would be against further media exposure, on Freya's behalf. I was against it for that reason myself.

Jade came back outside with a drink in either hand, handed one to Kieran, and I lip-read his "Cheers" as he took the glass. I wanted to tip back my head and roar.

There was a moment when he raised the glass to his mouth and stared over the top of it that I thought he'd caught sight of us, but the traffic was constant and he couldn't possibly see us through the headlights reflected in the pizzeria window.

At most, we'd be phantoms. And he probably hoped we'd stay that way.

| | | | | |

I called on Sheridan the next evening. She and her husband, Matt, lived in a Victorian semi on Blakeney Road and in all the years we'd known each other the front door had been the same strident yellow, as if reminding arrivals to check their mood before knocking. When she answered the door, her clothes—candy-pink tweed jacket, aquamarine trousers—reinforced the message that this was a zone of positive energy.

The sight of a black crow on her doorstep, I knew, would be dismaying.

"Ellen! Come in, I was just getting myself a G&T. Had a bit of a day at work."

I accepted a drink and we settled in her living room. There was more yellow here, with ill-advised accents of rust-red and ivy-green and a nod to Easter in the form of a bowl of egg-shaped LED lights on the coffee table. I didn't like going into the houses of Lucas's old friends. Seeing the paraphernalia of their continuing passage through young adulthood caused a deepening of the ache I carried in my chest, sometimes sudden enough to cause me to reel from the savageness of it. Graduation photos and birthday cards with numbers on them Lucas had not been allowed to reach. It wouldn't be long before there'd be talk of weddings and the arrival of grandchildren— I didn't expect to be invited to the former or encouraged to cast my bad fairy's spell on the latter.

"I can guess why you're here," Sheridan said, the glass in her hand trembling slightly. "Kieran?"

"I saw him at the Crown last night. He was with Jade."

"Ah, yes." The fingers of her free hand began to play with the edging of a velvet cushion. "I know she's seen him a few times since she came home for Easter."

"How long has he been out?"

"Just a couple of weeks, I think."

"Are he and Jade going out together?"

"No, of course not." She faltered, tipped her glass steeply and I watched her throat convulse as she swallowed. "At least not that I know of."

"Is she in?" I pictured Jade upstairs, cowering from the sound of my outrage in the room below.

Sheridan put down her glass. "No, she's out—not with him, before you ask."

"Why does she want to see him at all?" I said, more sharply now. "This is the man who killed her boyfriend. He took a life. Has everyone forgotten that?"

She looked at me with a mix of compassion and dread. Like Prisca, like *everyone*, she knew she couldn't win. Other parents, other mothers, could never prevail against a woman who'd lost her child. She was certainly not about to remind me that Lucas had been— just—Jade's ex. "They were close, as well," she ventured.

"Still are, evidently. Has he told her anything?"

"About what?"

"The night of the accident—assuming all that therapy he had inside loosened a memory or two. There are treatments for PTSD, aren't there?" I pressed. "Ways of releasing traumatic memory? Has he told her anything about *that*?"

Sheridan gazed unhappily at me. "I'm really not sure. I don't *think* so. I mean, if there was something to remember that cast a different light, something more sinister . . . Well, Jade wouldn't want anything to do with him, would she?" She gathered her confidence and spoke more firmly. "It was a terrible accident, Ellen. Kieran has admitted his mistakes. That's why he was put behind bars."

"Not for long enough." There was an edge to this that she would have known instantly how to interpret. It wasn't that she'd opposed Lock Up Longer, but she could have been more wholehearted in her support. She'd chosen to protect Jade from further anguish, I knew that. Families closed ranks, even on friends, it was natural. The flowers she sent when my father died had the scent of apology on them and I'd accepted it without rancor.

But her condoning a renewed friendship between Kieran and Jade, I couldn't accept. I put down my glass and stood. "I have to go."

"Ellen, wait!" Sheridan scurried after me to the door. "What can we do? Seriously, what's the alternative to just getting on with things?" When I failed to answer, her voice became thin with exasperation. "We can't force him to leave town, can we?"

Still I said nothing. The truth was I didn't have the answer. Yet.

| | | | | | |

The next morning, I rang Vic. "Did you know he's back?"

"Yes." His tone was bleak. "I just saw him in Bromley Shopping Centre. I thought about going and having a word, but it was too crowded and I lost him."

"Out and about in all his old haunts. We saw him drinking at the Crown." I didn't mention Jade, sparing him the hurt and indignation of *that*. "No doubt he's getting all kinds of help at the taxpayer's expense. Anyone would think *he* was the victim. It's a disgrace."

There was a pause before Vic murmured his agreement.

"I wish there was a way to make him suffer," I said.

"You and me both," Vic said, and a beat passed between us, a communion that had, it seemed to me, a natural link to that question of Sheridan's: *What's the alternative?*

Even then, I had faith that the answer would reveal itself.

| | | | | | |

Easter weekend passed and, after much persistence, I was able to identify and speak to Kieran's offender manager. He was called Marcus Flynn and sounded young and idealistic, with a tuneful West Midlands accent.

"How has he been allowed to come back to the neighborhood where his victim lived?" I demanded.

"He's not living in Beckenham, he's over in South Norwood, which was his home before his conviction."

"What, he's back with Prisca, is he?"

But Flynn would not confirm the address. "I know how hard this must be for you, but he will have friends from his old school neighborhood and there's nothing to stop him seeing them. In fact, it's encouraged that he should make contact with a supportive network."

"God forbid he should suffer," I said.

"He's not considered a high-risk person, Mrs. Saint. And he's on supervision, so rest assured we're here to make sure he settles in without incident. I'm sure there'll be no stepping out of line. Any meeting between you will be completely accidental."

"How long does the supervision last?"

He admitted it was only for three months, with three weeks already completed. It hardly mattered, because it wasn't *Kieran's* stepping out of line that I feared so much as my own. I imagined seeing him in the street and, without Justin there to restrain me, losing control of myself and shoving him in front of a car or assaulting him with my bare fists. Watching him bleed.

"We have to move," I told Justin that night in the bedroom. "I can't live like this, knowing I could bump into him at any time."

"Ellen," Justin said, with only the smallest hint of long-suffering, and there followed the inevitable discussion about Freya, the constancy provided by her school, her friends, and teachers. Forcing her to start again when she had just regained her strength was nothing short of cruel.

And yet, it was the same school Kieran himself had attended—Flynn had specifically mentioned the link. What if Kieran had had a good relationship with one of the teachers that he intended to resurrect? What if Freya ran into him in the very place she had a right to feel safe?

I sank onto the bed in silence, my arms wrapped tightly around myself.

"What are you thinking?" Justin asked.

"I'm thinking about that bloody school. Imagine if there had been a way of stopping Kieran getting a place there. Then all of this would be happening to another family, somewhere miles away, and Lucas would still be here with us. We were forced by Foxwell into knowing him. We were never consulted."

Though this infringed forbidden what-if territory—not least because we'd agreed not to demonize the school for Freya's sake—Justin recognized the need for it and pondered his answer. "Without a crystal ball, we would have said yes, though, wouldn't we? And so would Vic."

I didn't answer, knowing this was true.

"You know, I sat in on a seminar the other day and they were talking about the ancient Greeks, how they used to eliminate the threat of bad people in advance. A kind of preemptive ostracization. Now *that* would have been useful."

"Really?" I glanced up. "How did they punish murder?"

"Lots of ways." He hesitated. "Sometimes it was left to be settled by the victim's family."

I held his gaze. "If it was Freya who'd died, would you want to settle it yourself?"

"I would." His eyes shone. "And I also want to because it was Lucas, you must know that. I loved him very much."

"Yes. I'm sorry."

"But I'm going to rise above it—we all are. No one's going to settle anything." He flashed me a mirthless smile. "Whatever that's a euphemism for."

Killing Time (cont)

Spend any time with Felix Penney and you will become aware of the stress he places on angles. "Even within the context of autobiography, our understanding of crime must come from multiple points of view," he says.

Ah, the vaunted POV. It was only a matter of time before that turned up in a story about storytelling. Consider, for a moment, the POV of Ellen Saint's bête noir, Kieran Watts. In the school portrait of him favored by editors at the time of his conviction, he looks guileless enough, all hastily flattened hair, snub nose, and acne scarring. But those juvenile features are said to have belied a magnetism to which other students responded—Lucas Gordon included. This was a boy with a powerful voice.

Following his stretch at HM YOI Danstone, Watts's re-entry into society was well supported: he benefited from funding raised by the Friends of Danstone and had, by all accounts, a good relationship with both his offender manager and his former foster mother, Prisca Evans. He lodged with the latter on release and appeared to manage his three-month supervision period without controversy. But just a week after it ended, in July 2017, he was reported missing. He was twenty-one years old.

How fascinating it would be to hear his side of the story, I suggest to Penney. To discover if any memories of the accident that killed Lucas Gordon had been loosened before he disappeared from view.

"Yes," Penney agrees. "That would be fascinating. Just so long as the memories were true."

Sunday Times magazine, December 2021

twenty

I CAN TELL YOU the exact moment I knew I had to get rid of him.

It was early one Sunday morning in the first week of May, when I pulled aside the curtain at our bedroom window to check the weather, and I saw him standing right there at our gate. He was in running gear and my first instinct was to imagine the joy of sprinting through open spaces after a stretch of restricted freedom. Rain would be as pleasurable to the skin as sunshine.

What the hell was he doing here? His face was sufficiently puce to suggest he was well into his run; had he strayed into Tanglewood Road accidentally or was this his intended destination? Either way, it was hard to tell precisely where his attention was directed. The tilt of his head suggested our living room window.

Just as I was about to summon Justin, still half-asleep in the bed behind me, Kieran pushed open the gate. I held my breath as he walked down the path with that familiar loathsome spring of his. I hissed over my shoulder—"Justin?"—but he groaned and rolled to face the other way.

Downstairs, the letter box rattled. Next thing, Kieran was bouncing back down the path, through the gate, and off out of range.

I tore down to the front door. On the mat lay an envelope, facedown. I knew immediately what it was—to an extent, I'd been expecting it for years—but now it was here I didn't think I had the stomach for it. A written apology. Dared I hope there'd be answers too? If not a full confession of the events of the night of the accident, then at least a less sketchy version than the one that persisted.

But when I picked it up, it felt thin between my fingers, no more than a single sheet of paper, I judged. I turned it over and frowned. The name on the envelope was not mine, but Freya's.

Without thinking—and certainly without consulting her or her father—I ripped it open.

> Dear Frey,
>
> I hope you are well. I know life must have been very sad for you since Lucas died. I don't know if you hate me like your mum and dad do. All that stuff on the internet was brutal. If you would like to meet, here is my number. We can talk about Lucas or anything you like.
>
> Love Kieran

Maybe because it was early, the house still silent, or perhaps because I was standing right up at the front door, I had a sudden and acute sensory memory of the day the police came and I doubled over, clutching the note to my abdomen. We'd all changed since that morning, a part of each of us had been extinguished, and Freya was no exception. Well, I was damned if I was going to stand by and watch her be robbed of more.

Straightening, I moved to the kitchen and read the note a second time—*Frey . . . very sad . . . love*—before ripping both it and the envelope into small pieces and sprinkling them in the kitchen bin. After standing doing nothing for a minute, I put on rubber gloves, went back to the bin, and stirred the shreds deeper into the rubbish.

I said nothing to Freya of her stolen mail. To Justin I served up a reduced account with a cup of tea in bed.

"I just saw Kieran. He was at the gate."

"*Our* gate?" Justin sat up at the news. "What was he doing?"

"Running."

"*Running?* That doesn't sound like him."

"He's a changed man. You saw how much thinner he is. He probably came from Prisca's through South Norwood Country Park. It's not a crazy distance if you're in shape."

Justin rapped his fingertips on the mug. They made no sound. "If it *was* him—"

I interrupted: "It was. There's no if."

"Okay, well, I'm sure it was a one-off and he won't come again. If he does, we'll talk to the police and see what can be done."

Nothing can be done, I thought. *At least not by them.*

| | | | | |

The following morning, as soon as I was alone in the house, I phoned the Foxwell Academy safeguarding officer. "You may not know that the man who caused the death of Freya's brother has recently been released from jail and has come back to the area. It's possible he may try to contact Freya, which is something we would very much like to prevent. Can I ask you to keep an eye on her?"

"Of course, Mrs. Saint. We're grateful to you for alerting us." She was a relatively new member of staff and I had no idea how much she knew about the school's role in bringing victim and killer together, but she duly took notes and promised to brief Freya's teachers.

"Have you considered monitoring her social media?" she asked, but I only half listened to her suggestions. Kieran's first approach had been quaintly old-fashioned, but sooner or later he'd have a fully functioning smartphone and his tech skills would quickly surpass any that Foxwell's safeguarding team could offer. As for me, even if I were to demand to know Freya's pass codes and the right to scrutinize her friends and followers, I had a cat's chance in hell of identifying an avatar or username as his.

Next, I phoned Vic at work. Through the window, the garden was drenched with color, but I thought only of that old Stones song "Paint It Black." I'm sure you know it. Melancholic, but not without elegance. The feeling that grief might have some kind of grace wrought from it.

"I've got something to say," I began. "And I think you're the only person I can say it to."

"Okay."

"You don't have to get involved, obviously, but I want to give you the option."

"Ellen," Vic said. "What are you talking about? Get involved in what?"

"I warn you, it's going to sound like something out of a bad TV show."

"Just say it."

I sucked in my breath. "I want to deal with Kieran once and for all."

"'Deal with' him?"

"Yes." I turned my face from the window, from the glorious, sinless colors of the natural world. "I want him gone for good."

twenty-one

THE FOLLOWING DAY, VIC and I met at the cemetery. It was early evening, the light weakening as we stood facing each other across Lucas's grave, and I could feel the intensity of my own gaze as I searched his face for shadows of our son. But the older Vic got, the fewer there were.

"Has something happened?" he said. "Something new, I mean?"

"Yes." It was obvious to me that I could only involve Vic in this if I was going to be completely honest. There could be no deception between us, no withholding of information. "He tried to contact Freya. She doesn't know, nothing came of it, but he won't stop. He won't keep away. He'll groom her, he'll take her, he'll destroy her."

Vic's eyes flared. "Jesus."

"Even without that, I can't bear it, Vic. I want an end to this, this *condition*." That was how I thought of it, this thing that blended my long-standing hunger for revenge with the fresher emergency of protecting my daughter. A condition with no medical name. "I fantasize about attacking him. Beating him, seeing his blood."

He raised a hand to his ear and scratched. "I can certainly identify with that."

"Can you identify with what I said on the phone?"

We locked eyes. "About wanting him gone? I assume you mean—?"

"Dead," I said. "I mean dead."

He dropped his hand to his side. "That's the dream, sure."

"But if there were a way to make it a reality, would you be on board?" I took his silence as permission to continue. "We wouldn't do it ourselves, obviously. It wouldn't help anyone if we ended up being put away. It would have to be completely untraceable, which means it would cost us."

"I would have thought so. To be honest, I think this could be out of our budget, Ellen. Out of our league." Vic hesitated and I knew this was a prompt for me to laugh the idea off, to say, *You're right. I'm talking crap. Forget it.*

"I've already done the research," I said. "The going rate is fifteen thousand and I've got the money."

He gave a single heavy blink. "Tell me you haven't googled 'contract killer' on your phone?"

"No, an old iPad. I taped over the camera and I'm only using it in public places where hundreds of people are connected to the Wi-Fi. I'm going to get one of those burner phones as well. Completely untraceable. I'll ditch them both the moment it's done."

"Right." Vic's gaze narrowed and I found myself speaking slightly beyond him, into the dipping sun.

"I've read all about these people. They usually use a gun, shoot the person point blank, but they can also make it look like an accident or natural causes. Maybe that's better in this case. And nothing too similar to how Lucas died or it would look like an eye for an eye."

"Wow, Ellen." A siren started up in the street and he waited for it to fade before continuing. "Look, if we *do* try to sort something out, you know, along professional lines, I think Danny might be able to help us."

"Danny? Do you trust him?"

"I trust him. One hundred percent. I'm not saying he'd want to take an active part, but he's got the contacts, might be able to recommend someone."

Like we needed a roofer or a piano teacher. Someone to clear the gutters.

"He'll need to be paid, as well," I said. "That's fine, of course. I'll find the money."

Vic made a quick dismissive gesture. "Danny won't want paying. He loved Lucas."

As I fought a suffocating feeling in my throat, Vic moved a foot back and forth over the grit. "He shouldn't be here," he said, watching the cloud of dust he'd kicked up. "He should be living his life—whatever that turned out to be."

"That's why I have to do this," I said. "I can't *not*."

He raised his eyes to mine. "I'm seeing Danny at the weekend, so I'll sound him out. Meanwhile, don't go making any contact with these people you've researched. If we do use one of them, let me and Danny be the go-betweens. You keep out of it. You've got Freya to think about."

"All right."

We parted with a peck on the cheek and I watched as he made his way past the rest of the dead to the main gates. Idling a moment or two, I summoned Lucas's face in front of mine, that heartbreaking blend of adult and child, of tough and tender. *We love you*, I swore. *Dad and I will prove to you we have not forgotten.*

But could I count on that plural? Instinctive agreement was one thing, but after he'd slept on it would Vic really want to unite with me in this the ultimate, the most extreme act of parenting?

I had my answer late on Saturday night, when he texted me in the concise, nonspecific style that would characterize our ongoing communications:

Spoken to D. He will help us.

| | | | | | |

And so it was agreed: I would supply the money and Vic—with Danny's help—would make it happen. A reasonable division of labor. When we met again, by then almost a week after that graveyard conference, Vic suggested as our target date the Wednesday of the week after Kieran's supervision period ended: July 3. He'd be subject to less nannying then; plus, it gave me time to liquidate the fee.

Using the secret iPad, I'd researched how to amass fifteen thousand pounds in cash without triggering the interest of HMRC or the police. I'd need to withdraw it in smaller amounts over the course of several weeks, get a bit creative with my personal and business accounts. Helpfully, I had almost two thousand already, withdrawn to pay a supplier who'd asked for cash and then changed his mind.

"That amount is bang on, according to Danny," Vic said.

"Good. So tell me what else he said."

"At the risk of sounding like a line in a soap, he said he knows someone who knows someone."

"Who are they?"

"I don't have a name. I've deliberately kept us in the dark, because if it does end up looking like suspicious death and not an accident, we're sure to be questioned." He gave me a rueful smile. "It's not like it hasn't been in a national newspaper that we hate Kieran's guts. It's an Albanian outfit, though, Danny says."

"Right." I experienced a wash of disbelief. Organized crime. Contract killers. And not to have stumbled into it by accident like a character in a novel in the wrong place at the wrong time, but to have sought it out! To be a paying client.

Vic sensed my hesitation. "I haven't confirmed yet, so we can still change our minds. We need to be totally sure."

"I'm sure." I bit down on a fingernail, felt the stickiness of my lipstick on my fingertips.

"Has he tried to make contact with Freya again?"

"I don't think so. Certainly not by post." I'd been watching my daughter more closely this last week and nothing about her demeanor had suggested a fundamental change of mood. My guess was that Kieran would give her time to respond to the letter before trying an alternative form of communication.

Vic lowered his voice, causing me to move closer. "Okay, so listen. I've been keeping a bit of an eye on him since we spoke. These people will want to see where he goes and if he's got any routines, that kind of thing."

I felt a gathering of nerves. "Oh, yes?"

"He's got a job at a takeout chicken place in Penge, but it's part-time and seems to be a different shift every day. He's not allowed to drive, obviously, and so far he's had a lift with Prisca twice, got the bus once, and walked once, so it's impossible to anticipate. But there is one constant: he goes for a run almost every morning."

"In the streets?" I thought of him at my gate, striding down the path. The Lycra gear, the newly honed physique.

"Partly. Every time I've seen so far, he's taken the most direct route to South Norwood Country Park and then he runs laps there. He uses the entrance on Albert Road, a few streets over from Prisca's place. And I've only ever seen him running alone. That might be useful information for our new colleagues, wouldn't you say?"

"Definitely," I said.

He pulled back a fraction, looked me in the eye. "I need your word that you will never tell anyone about this. Not even Justin."

"You have my word." My sincerity was profoundly real and not without regret. This would be my sacrifice: the frankness I took for granted with the man I loved. The knowledge that he could never again fully know me. My daughter too. As for the changed status between Vic and me, the increased codependency, it was a calculated risk. Neither of us had anything to gain from breaking the pact, but plenty to lose.

"Anything else to report?" I asked.

"No," he said.

"Then let's do it."

twenty-two

I'VE NEVER TOLD VIC this, but there was a heart-stopping moment in the process of my putting together the fee. Getting dressed one morning, Justin discovered part of the stash in a box in my wardrobe. (There was another in a rarely touched cupboard in the utility room—I'll leave you to make your own puns about laundry.)

"Is this your running away money?" he said, with a trace of real concern.

"Why are you looking through my things?" I countered.

"I need a belt. The buckle on this one's just snapped."

Thinking furiously, I found a belt looped over a hanger and handed it to him.

"Thanks. So what *is* the cash for?"

I shook my head, acted a little sheepish. "I didn't want to tell you in case you thought I was mad."

"Go on." He began feeding the new belt through the loopholes of his waistband, helpfully focusing on that and not on me.

"You know how Lucas started giving cash to rough sleepers after doing that geography coursework? Well, I thought I'd use some of the money Dad left me to do the same. Basically, I've been carrying cash with me everywhere I go and handing it out. Every time I take money out of the cashpoint, I think of both of them. It really helps."

This was both wholly true and shamefully false.

"Is that not a bit labor-intensive?" Justin queried. "Wouldn't it be easier just to give a lump sum to a homeless charity?"

"It doesn't always reach the people on the street. That was the whole point of Lucas's project, arguing the case for direct action."

"True." He checked himself in the mirror before heading down. "Well, don't let anyone see you getting wads of cash out, okay? You don't want to be mugged."

"Of course." It was shockingly easy to lie, and not only because I knew the truth would appall him (not to mention end our marriage), but also because my commitment was unwavering. Far from getting cold feet, I had begun to feel the fanaticism of someone whose mission is absolutely—almost divinely—right.

| | | | | |

At his own request, Vic had received no details of the planned method, only the agreed date: necessary for us to be able to provide ourselves with an alibi.

"They know about his jogging regimen," he said, when we next met. He'd made no remark when I handed him a small knapsack containing fifteen thousand pounds in fifty- and twenty-pound notes. It didn't look like a whole lot, but it was all there, down to the last twenty, and my fingers carried the repellent odor of used banknotes for hours after I'd done the final count. "The Albert Road gate to the park is pretty quiet, so maybe they'll run him over in a van or snatch him when he's out of range of any CCTV. I don't know. I don't want to know."

"Just tell me this," I said, "so I can prepare myself: will there be a body to find?"

"I don't think so, no. I've made it clear I'd prefer the other way."

What did *that* mean? Kieran's remains at the bottom of the river, weights on his wrists and ankles? Buried in concrete on a building site? Put through some sort of meat mincer and fed to pigs? I'd seen all and worse on screen and often in the form of documentary. Real life, not fiction.

"Will they send us proof? A picture or something?"

"I'm not sure it's a good idea for us to have something like that," Vic said, "even on the unregistered phones. The proof will be that he's no longer here."

I tasted the phrase. Kieran Watts *no longer here.*

Vic continued: "If it plays out the way I expect it to, Prisca or a friend will report him missing the next day. Or maybe the day after that. It's not like when a young child disappears. They give adults a bit more time."

"We might find they get in touch with his offender manager rather than the police?" I suggested. "It's probably not that unusual for ex-convicts to take off just after their supervision period ends. It might not even be escalated into a missing persons inquiry."

"Exactly," Vic said. "That would be the best-case scenario. But we can't count on it, so on the day—and the ones before and after— we need to make sure we're accounted for every minute of it. Just in case a body does turn up."

"I understand."

"And don't go anywhere near that park, okay? Not even in the car, and definitely not alone."

"You too." It occurred to me that, with two housemates, I was going to have an easier time being accounted for than he was.

"I've got someone staying with me at the moment," Vic said. "Just temporarily."

I struggled for a name. "Chloë?"

"No, we split up a few weeks ago."

A new woman then. They came and went. I didn't like to ask if he'd recruited this new one simply to cover for him, but it was certainly convenient.

He continued: "Now listen, this is important: if you run into Danny, don't say a thing. It's too risky, you never know who might be listening or what cameras might pick up. It's not a secret we can even whisper about, okay?"

"Absolutely. How are you communicating with him?"

"We meet at the pub near his place—always have, so nothing different there. We know where to sit to be completely safe from security cameras and eavesdroppers."

"Excellent."

"So, if and when the police come, just tell the truth about when you last saw Kieran. It's natural you should've been upset by him being back in town, even pleased that something bad might have happened to him."

Throughout this final briefing, Vic sounded pragmatic, even cool, but I knew he must be as devoured by nerves as I was. There'd be no MI5 glamour to this assassination, we both knew that. This faceless killer doing our bidding might even feel some degree of the primal terror Kieran did himself—and that Lucas had the night he died.

I wondered if I'd have an instinct when it took place, if the moment would be marked by some visitation to the soul, a sudden sense of justice or release. But the day passed with no noticeable disturbance.

| | | | | | | | | | | |

There was no way of accelerating the process of discovery. From July 3 onwards, I regularly checked the local missing persons website on the iPad, but Kieran's profile wasn't there.

And then, early the following week, his name was suddenly everywhere: in the local paper, on my Facebook feed, even the BBC News:

RESERVOIR HORROR SURVIVOR REPORTED MISSING

The circumstances of Kieran's disappearance were described exactly as Vic had predicted. He'd gone out for a run at 7 a.m. on July 3 and Prisca had left for work soon after. He'd had a shift starting at the chicken place at 11 a.m. and had told her he intended to take the bus to work. His manager, who was aware of Kieran's circumstances, had called her on her mobile at 12:30 and said he hadn't turned up. They agreed he must have not been feeling well and stayed home. But, returning from work, Prisca found there was no evidence that Kieran had come back from his run. He hadn't showered or changed, the running kit and trainers were nowhere to be seen. No documents were missing that she could tell. His phone went straight to voice mail.

Each report included a recap of the reservoir accident, the sentence dealt to Watts for his careless driving conviction, and the campaign it had inspired, with some also alluding to continued ill feeling. His manager at the chicken shop was quoted as saying Kieran had been recognized by customers a few times and, on at least one occasion, verbally abused. "We didn't put him on the counter after that," he said. "We kept him out back in the kitchen."

Reservoir horror. Seeing the phrase again in media headlines punctured the delicate membrane that had at last grown over my grief. Once the main focus of the story, or at least an equal to Kieran, Lucas was in this second act only an adjunct, reduced to a few short lines, sometimes not even given a name but written off as the "tragic victim."

Well, not by us, my friends. Not by us.

Killing Time (cont)

It is a matter of record that both Ellen Saint and Vic Gordon were interviewed by the police in the weeks following Watts's disappearance. Neither was asked to make a formal statement.

Sunday Times magazine, December 2021

twenty-three

IT WAS SEVERAL DAYS — PERHAPS even a week — before the police came, and I took this to be an excellent sign. Perhaps they were delayed by responses to the appeal; posters had appeared on supermarket notice-boards, pasted on bus stops, or pinned to trees. *Have You Seen Kieran Watts?* On one, in Sainsbury's, someone had scrawled "Murderer" in red felt tip. Another, pasted to a lamppost on Beckenham High Street, I tore off, screwed into a ball, and deposited in the nearest bin.

In any case, there were clearly more plausible theories surrounding Kieran's disappearance than any that involved the criminal activity of two grieving middle-aged parents.

Freya had just left for school and Justin and I were still home when the officer arrived. He was an approachable, old-hand sort, who accepted tea and made an admiring comment about the garden — lush, almost tropical, following weeks of heavy rain — before setting out his questions.

"You're aware, I'm sure, that Kieran Watts has been reported missing?"

"We've seen the news," Justin said, his tone as politely earnest as you'd expect. He had nothing to hide, after all. "We were just talking about it last night, actually. Wondering what could've happened to him."

This was true. Freya had seen a poster and heard chatter at school, and so we'd discussed it as a family. Or, rather, *they* discussed it as a family, while I discussed it as a murderer and a liar.

"What's your theory?" the officer asked.

"Maybe he realized he wasn't very popular around here and decided to move on before anything too unpleasant happened," Justin suggested. "Had his supervision period ended?"

"Yes, just the week before."

"There you go then. That can't be a coincidence, can it? He probably wasn't allowed to change his address before that. Don't you risk being sent back inside if you break the conditions of your release?"

I suppressed a smile as Justin made exactly the point I'd hoped he would, though of course the theory didn't explain why Kieran should up sticks without taking any of his possessions and without uttering a word about his plans to Prisca or his employer. This was a detail that had been in the press: neither had received so much as a texted goodbye. I'd kept on top of the news, memorizing reports, knowing that in even the most casual exchanges with the police I could allude only to facts in the public domain.

"You're well informed," the officer told Justin, appreciatively.

"Oh, believe me, it doesn't feel like it," he replied, drily, and glanced at me. "We've had to second-guess a lot of what went on with his release. A bit more information would have been welcome, I can tell you."

"It certainly would," I agreed.

The officer's attention turned to me. If anything, his affability was even more marked, but I knew not to trust that. "Have *you* seen him since his release, Mrs. Saint?"

"Yes, back in April, when we went to the cinema." I picked up my diary. "Let's see, it was just before Easter . . . Wednesday the twelfth of April. We were in the pizza place on the high street and we saw him having a drink at the Crown. He was outside, where the smokers go."

"This was what prompted you to call Kieran's offender manager, was it? Marcus Flynn."

"You know about that?" It was hardly surprising, I supposed. As Vic had anticipated, we would be most people's first choice of those whose feathers had been ruffled by Kieran's return. Of course Flynn had mentioned my call.

"Yes, I spoke to him the next week. He will have logged the exact date and time if you need it. I expect he told you I was very upset, which is true." Seeing the officer's doubtful expression, I spelled out the reasons in a tone of controlled outrage. "This man killed our son. I didn't like the idea that he could just come here and behave as if nothing had happened, as if he hadn't had a devastating impact on the community. Lucas's friends and their families are still here, our daughter is still at Foxwell Academy. As I told Mr. Flynn, I would have preferred Kieran to settle somewhere else, but he explained that he wasn't considered a risk to anyone. I'm not sure I agree, but you'll know better than me the stats for reoffending."

Under my foundation my face burned. Ever since Kieran's disappearance, I'd applied thick makeup for just this occasion, to conceal any errant guilty flushes. I ran a hand through my hair—it felt cool and synthetic, as if not a part of me—and waited.

"What's *your* theory about his disappearance?" the officer pressed me. "The same as your husband's?"

"Yes. Like Justin said, he must have decided to make a fresh start somewhere no one knows him. Escape all the negative comments."

"Do you know of anyone specifically who would wish to make those comments?"

I paused. Either he knew less about the history of this than he ought to or he was playing dumb to try to trick me. "Not specifically, no, just anyone who followed the case and thought he got off too lightly. You must be familiar with our campaign, Lock Up Longer? We had almost a hundred thousand signatures on our petition to review his sentence, people from all over the UK. Don't forget, this is someone who murdered an innocent boy."

He didn't correct my language, just as he had not when I'd used the word "killer": officially, Kieran caused the death of a man.

I continued: "I can give you admin access to the website, if you like? There was a lot of new activity when he was released and there'll probably be more now he's back in the news. I don't know where you'd begin, to be honest."

As he gave me the email address to forward the details to, I tried not to think about the waste of time involved if the police were to pursue this red herring. "Maybe he killed himself?" I added. "The guilt was too much for him?"

There was a pause, a sideways look from Justin, and I wondered if I'd spoken with a little too much relish. We sipped our tea, by now tepid enough for me to note that the "couple of routine questions" were taking a lot longer than we might have expected.

"What about his life inside?" Justin said, presently. "Have you checked if he made any enemies there? Someone who came out at the same time or just after him and had a reason to track him down? He's a strong personality, Kieran, quite charismatic. I can imagine him rubbing people up the wrong way."

"That's certainly an angle we're considering," the officer agreed, but, again, seemed to prefer to focus on me. Behind his tolerant gaze there was something more complex than objective investigation. "So you saw him in April outside the Crown. Did you see him again after that?"

Justin and I exchanged a look.

"I saw him outside here one morning," I admitted, reluctantly. "At the front gate. He was just standing there, looking at the house."

"He didn't ring the bell?"

"No," I said, truthfully. "And I didn't open the door." Also true. "After a couple of minutes, he just left."

"Any idea why he was here?"

For the first time, I had to lie outright. I kept my eye contact steady, my hands motionless. "I'm not sure, but it's possible he was thinking of apologizing to us. Criminals do that sometimes, don't they? Maybe he saw me at the window and lost his nerve." I didn't mention that he'd been wearing running gear. I didn't need the police to know that I was aware of this element of his lifestyle. I hoped Justin wouldn't add the detail—or even remember.

Justin surprised me with his next comment. "I saw him a week or two later, as well. He was outside that chicken place on Penge High Street, talking on his phone. He was in kitchen overalls, so I guessed he must be working there."

"You didn't tell me that." I felt myself flush with the shock of this unscripted information.

"I didn't want to upset you," Justin said, gently placing his hand on mine.

Didn't want me confronting Kieran at his workplace, more like. Was it suspicious that I *hadn't* tracked him down there myself? Or, at the very least, torn around to Prisca's to lay into him—or her? Had Vic and I misjudged the psychology?

No. Our plan was flawless, I was sure of it. I'd even been careful to continue to fret about Kieran and his whereabouts as frequently and vocally as I knew would be expected of me. A phone call to Sheridan, questions about what she and Jade knew (nothing, she swore). Silence on my part would have been a remarkable change of behavior.

"Did you speak to him at the chicken shop?" the officer asked Justin.

"No. I was driving. But it was definitely him. I saw in the papers he had some sort of placement there after his release."

We were both able to share our full schedules for July 3, neither taking us to the vicinity of Prisca's home or South Norwood Country Park at any time.

Only then did the officer divulge something I didn't already know. "The day before he disappeared, he bought a security bolt at B&Q in Penge and fitted it to the front door of his foster mother's house. Any idea why he might have done that?"

"It's fairly obvious he must have been feeling unsafe," Justin said. "Wanted to up his home security. Wouldn't Prisca be the one to ask about that? Did *she* not question it?" He checked his phone and shifted in his seat. "I'm really very sorry, but I need to leave for work in a minute if you don't mind? I have an appointment I can't reschedule."

"Of course." The officer stood and smiled. "I'm sorry to have had to interrupt your morning and to bring up difficult memories."

"That's fine." Justin smiled back. "I hope you find him safe and well. We don't wish him any harm."

Speak for yourself, I thought, willing him to leave it there. Both his tone and body language had relaxed and our visitor was looking at him with the masked eagerness of one who knew the most significant details can be extracted on departure, in nice unguarded postscripts.

"I just think . . ." Justin said, shaking his head.

"Just think what, Mr. Saint?"

"I just think I'd like my family to have nothing more to do with this search, if that's all right. Nothing personal, I know you're just doing your job, but we feel very, very unlucky to have crossed paths with that boy and we'd prefer them never to cross again."

Very, very unlucky. They talk about stabs of pain, but the simple truth of Justin's statement struck me like a ten-foot wave breaking on my back. Blowing me off my feet and depositing me, bruised and disorientated, twenty feet closer to the shore.

As soon as Justin and the officer left, I crumpled onto the sofa and wept.

| | | | | | |

Vic's interview proceeded in a more spirited vein, he reported, when we had a coffee in a busy Caffè Nero, a meeting I was careful to put in my phone calendar and mention to Justin. While we were under even the lightest surveillance, there could be no secret liaisons to come back to haunt us.

"I told them I was happy he'd disappeared," he said. "I told them they shouldn't waste their time looking for him, that rats like him will come out of the woodwork when they're hungry."

I felt a deep thrill. "What did they say?"

He shrugged. "Not a lot, but I could tell they agreed."

"They accepted your alibi?"

"Yep. The day he went missing, I was in the office early, working all day, then I had team drinks in the evening."

Vic had by then been working for the same tool hire business he'd joined over two decades ago when we were still together and had several colleagues who'd known him for much if not all of that time. His was as rock solid a cover story as any that could be devised.

"What about Danny?"

"They've got no reason to talk to him, but if they ever decide to, he dropped the kids at school first, then went straight to a job in

Forest Hill where the owner of the house was working from home. He didn't even nip out for his lunch, she made him a sandwich and they ate together in the garden."

"Good," I said. "The last thing we want is to put him in the firing line."

"Agreed."

We drank our coffees, watching with wonder those coming and going with only mundane cares, issues not even worth voicing. Extraordinary to think that Vic and I sat here, to all appearances an ordinary pair of friends, having arranged a death.

"There's no chance these people will come back and make trouble for us? Like trying to blackmail us or something?" I asked.

Vic's dismissal was unequivocal. "No, they're not connected to us in any way, Danny made sure of that. Anyway, they're professionals. We paid for a job and the job's been done. You don't fix someone's heating and go back and blackmail them after the event." He leaned in and lowered his voice. "Remember what I said about not talking about this—and not just with Danny, but between us, as well. From now on, unless something catastrophic goes down, none of it ever happened."

I wondered what the catastrophic event could be. A return of that officer with his complicated gaze. Arrest and interrogation, I supposed. Prosecution.

Vic seemed to read my thoughts. "*Even if* something catastrophic happens," he corrected himself. "Total denial from start to finish, that's the deal."

"Total denial," I repeated. "As long as I know he's gone, *really* gone, I'll never breathe a word as long as I live."

"He's gone," Vic said grimly.

We hugged goodbye. Feeling the shape of Lucas in his body, I gripped him tighter, and tighter again, and there was a breathless moment or two when I think he worried I'd never let him go.

twenty-four

In the dark, from the Butler's Wharf side of the St Saviour's footbridge, The Heights stands out more sharply than in the day. Those wide, curved windows are foreshortened, gleaming buttery yellow; a cut diamond of light glows on the roof.

"He lives in the top flat," I tell Vic. "I've looked at the plans and there's an atrium roof just behind the terrace. Pretty smart, eh?"

"Unbelievable," he mutters.

"That's the word all right. How is he living anywhere, Vic?"

Glancing, I see the bleakness in his eyes. Confirmation of Kieran's survival has obviously blindsided him, just as it did me.

"I don't know," he says, finally. "I wasn't ever told how they actually did it."

"Or actually *didn't.*" I remember querying at the time whether we'd be sent proof of death. Why didn't I insist? Because it sounded like something from a thriller, the sinister trophy that only succeeds in getting the client nailed. And because we trusted these contacts of Danny's to get the job done. "Do you think maybe he saw the guy coming and grabbed the weapon somehow and killed *him*? Then disappeared, got himself a new ID?" Picturing Kieran standing face-to-face with his killer, some huge brickhouse of a hoodlum, I find it unlikely that he could have overwhelmed such an adversary. But everyone has a first day at the office, don't they? Perhaps mistakes were made or circumstances intervened—and who knows what self-defense skills Kieran learned inside. It is often quoted that first-time convicts come out of prison knowing more about crime than they did when they went in.

I say all of this to Vic, who listens closely, clearly impressed by the flow of ideas. But of course I've had longer than he has to consider the variables that might have facilitated Kieran's survival. "But there was nothing in the local papers about a body being found near the park, was there?" I add. "I remember checking constantly."

"Me too." Vic nods. "I suppose the other guy's disappearance might not've been reported if he was an unregistered foreign national."

"You mean Albanian?"

"That's what we thought, yeah." There is a note of defensiveness in his tone. He fears perhaps that I'll blame him for this catastrophe, but how can I, when we were equally quick to trust?

"The other possibility is he begged for his life and convinced them somehow?" I consider Kieran's fabled powers of persuasion. "Maybe he promised them money and negotiated the time to earn it—or steal it?"

Vic's eyes widen. "God, I just don't know, Ellen. This is a fucking nightmare." His gaze returns to the roof of The Heights, where the strip of balustrade gleams silver. "He's really up there, in that flat?"

"He really is."

A trio of tourists join us on the bridge and we fall silent while selfies are taken, first with the dock behind them and then the river, the lights of St Katharine's Dock glittering on the opposite bank. A restaurant boat glides by, its diners in conversation, waiters bearing trays of wineglasses, as if there is nothing remarkable about drifting downriver in a glass lightbox, and the tourists take videos of that too. Satisfied, they move on.

"Whatever went wrong," I say to Vic, "we need to get back in touch with those guys."

He looks taken aback. "How're we meant to do that?"

"The same way we did before. Through Danny."

"Danny won't remember the names, if he ever knew them in the first place. It's not like there was ever an actual contract. It was cash, you know that." His face darkens. "There's no way back, Ellen."

Defensiveness is one thing, but this sounds a lot like defeatism to me and I lose my patience. "Well, there has to be! They screwed up the job and I want my money back. Then I want to find someone who'll do it properly. And if the price has gone up since then, I'll find the extra."

Vic flinches. The singular was a mistake, I realize. *My money. I want. I'll find.* He feels cut out. "We're not going to be able to get the money back," he says levelly. "It's been almost two and a half years."

"I know how long it's been, Vic." Two years and four months. Two years and four months of veering between the elation of knowing that justice has been served and the dread of being discovered to have been the one responsible for it. They'd just about canceled each other out, creating a sufferable sense of acceptance, when this happened. "Do you really not feel the same?" I demand. "You can't be pleased he's come back from the dead like this?"

"Of course I'm not pleased. I'm fucking gutted." Vic's hand grips the handrail of the bridge as his right foot kicks gently against the steel post. Overhead, an air ambulance thunders into range, heading south. "But time's passed, hasn't it? What good would it do us to pursue it now?"

"The same good it would have done then! Stop him from ruining more lives. He's still the same person, the same heartless sociopath, he'll do it again."

"How? He had a lifetime driving ban, remember."

"When has that ever stopped people like him from driving? Anyway, I don't mean he'll do it exactly the same way. But you watch, there'll be a story of how someone fell from that terrace after some drugs binge. Someone else's son or daughter. And when that happens, it will be on us, Vic, because we stood here today and made the decision to let it go. Let *him* go."

"It's not 'on us,' that's insane." Suddenly Vic's frustration matches mine and we're clashing in a way we haven't for decades, and in public, too, in range of the enemy himself. "What we did back then, *tried* to do, we weren't some crime-fighting double act. It was private revenge. It was *murder*."

"It was what he deserved." I gape at him. Just hours ago, in that hotel lobby, we listened to the audio clips together and felt an identical sense of betrayal and pain—I am sure of it. "Has something happened since we met earlier?" I ask.

"Yes." He throws up his arms. "I've had time to get my priorities straight. To think it through. And what I think is if you hadn't seen him again, if you were none the wiser about this, you'd be quite content, wouldn't you?"

"I was never *content*," I say icily. "Our son is dead."

"I know he is." There's a spasm, a single twist of pain, in his face. "And I know you miss him. I do as well. But this isn't the right way to deal with our grief. We were crazy to think it was. If you want my advice, you finish your business with your client here and never come back. The last thing we need is for Kieran to report us to the police. He's got money now, which means he can protect himself. His complaints will be taken seriously." Vic adjusts the strap of his laptop bag, tugs his collar closer to his throat. "Look, I have to get home."

"Will you at least ask Danny?" I plead. "Where's the harm in that?"

"Where's the harm? That's the question you should be asking yourself, Ellen, because that's exactly what you're unleashing here. Harm. You need to promise me you won't hassle Danny about this, yeah? There won't be anything he can do after all this time. Let him get on with his life. Let *me*."

He strides off into Butler's Wharf and I stare after him, openmouthed. I would have put money on his desire to avenge our son's murder being as true as mine, as enduring. What's changed in the two and a half years between then and now? What are the priorities he's citing? His new business is one factor, and his relationship with India. I accept that he doesn't wish to jeopardize the success of either, but come on, this is *Lucas*.

I make my way back to the station, still half expecting to see Vic in the street in front of me, his step faltering before he turns back to say he is sorry and of course he is still my comrade in arms. But there is no sign of him. Before I go to my platform, I find a cashpoint and withdraw the maximum permitted on my card. It's only hundreds, not the thousands I'll need.

But it's a start.

twenty-five

THE POLICE DIDN'T COME again. In the absence of physical evidence and the brick walls of our alibis, they had no cause to. In any case, they presumably had an instinct for these things and, to them, as to the rest of the world — even our own loved ones — we were mourners, not murderers, Vic and I. People like us read about contract killings in crime novels on holiday by the pool; we didn't know the first thing about setting one in motion.

Speculation about Kieran's disappearance continued, of course, both online and in real life, and I knew it was important to maintain a realistic engagement, not least with Justin, who soon noticed how I startled every time the doorbell rang.

"Relax, Ellen. I really don't think he's coming back any time soon."

He certainly isn't, I thought. "How can you be so sure?"

"Just the psychology of it, from his point of view."

"His point of view?" Sensing reluctance in him, I pressed for more. "Go on, what's his point of view?"

Justin grimaced. "Okay, well it's not easy, that's for sure. You come out of prison and you go back to your old haunts, see who's hanging out. Maybe it feels like a laugh at first, like nothing's changed, but then you realize you can't escape the comments and the looks. Maybe you spot your victim's family, see the grief on their faces, the permanent, physical impact of what you did. You try your best to reconnect with your friends, one of whom happens to be your victim's ex-girlfriend, but it's too hard for both of you because she's changed too. Her mother knows your victim's mother, your foster mum's getting grief, it's all interlinked and everyone still blames you. Even people who've never met you before recognize you from the papers. You're abused at your new place of work. There's no way you can stick around and expect to stay even half-sane. Your supervision is the only thing keeping you where you are—you're counting down the days for it to end."

All of this was said in one seamless gush, and I could only stare at Justin in surprise. My belief that he would never again defend Kieran had clearly been naive. He'd put himself in Kieran's shoes and stretched his toes while he was at it.

"Anyway, what I think doesn't matter," he said, seeing my face. "The way our society works, he gets a second chance, and we should just be grateful he's chosen to take it somewhere else, somewhere *we* don't have to meet him."

"Well, I agree with *that*," I said, and the subject was dropped. What in God's name would Justin say if he knew the truth?

Sheridan was among those brave enough to phone me in the aftermath of Kieran's disappearance. "I saw Prisca over in Elmers End," she said, after pleasantries had been exchanged. "She was putting up more posters."

"Oh, yes."

"She's convinced someone must have seen something that day. If he made it as far as the park, he wouldn't have been the only one running, would he? And what about dogwalkers? They're always out at the crack of dawn. It's quite the mystery, isn't it?"

There was a trace of exhilaration in her tone, as if she'd momentarily forgotten she was talking to someone whose life had been blown to pieces by this missing man. "At the risk of sounding rude, I'm afraid I really don't share Prisca's concern," I said coolly. "From my point of view, it's just a relief to know he's moved on and I'm not going to come face-to-face with him when I walk down the street. I hope this 'mystery' keeps him away forever and I'm sorry if that sounds callous."

"No, of course it doesn't sound callous. I completely understand. I feel the same, to be honest, but . . ." She broke off, presumably thinking of Jade. She couldn't possibly have actively approved of him as a boyfriend to her daughter. How long before Jade gave up on him? If her mourning for Lucas was anything to go by, not long.

Believe it or not, I did feel for Prisca, however. Putting up her posters and praying that someone would come forward with an explanation, something to help her sleep at night. I knew that, like every mother, she had no choice but to cling to the last fibers of hope that he would return.

| | | | | |

Vic had been smart to predict I would run into Danny. Though I'd rarely attended family events at his Sydenham home since Vic and I split, our neighborhoods were close enough for there to have been accidental meetings now and then.

It was about three months after we'd got rid of Kieran and I was on the tram to East Croydon when Danny got on a few stops down. We made eye contact straightaway in the half-empty carriage.

"You're normally in your van," I said.

"It's in the garage. MOT."

"Day off then?"

"It happens—once in a while." He smiled, causing lines to ripple outwards from his mouth and eyes. He looked much older than the version I'd held in my imagination these last years. It was a phenomenon I'd grown used to: just as Lucas remained always nineteen, so did those I associated with him remain the age they'd been when he died.

I asked after Jo and the kids, answered questions about Justin and Freya. I told him about the holiday we'd booked to the States at half term. New York and Washington, something absorbing for Freya. The opportunity to forget her ravaged life in South London.

As ever, even with Danny, I knew to introduce Lucas's name first to save the other person from the excruciating awkwardness of deciding whether to avoid the subject or not. "When Lucas was younger, he and his friends witnessed a knife fight on this line. Two guys were fighting over a girl. The oldest story in the book."

"I remember Vic telling me about that," Danny said. "Lucas and his mates rang the emergency alarm, didn't they?"

"That's right. I had to go and collect him from Sandilands station. I was far more upset about it than he was."

Danny started to say something, but cut himself off as if thinking better of it and there was a strange charged moment between us. I glanced either side of me. We were approaching East Croydon and the other passengers had congregated at the doors, waiting to be released. "What were you going to say, Danny? No one can hear us."

His eyes, fixed on mine, were ambivalent, unsure. "I was just going to say . . . I still think of him as alive."

"Kieran?" I whispered.

His cheeks flooded with color. "No, no. Lucas."

Of course he meant Lucas! I floundered, my face reddening deeper than his—fifteen minutes together and I'd already breached our sacred rule. I had no choice but to act as if nothing had happened. "Well, he always will be, in a way. In our hearts, that's the cliché, but it's more than that. He's . . . he's everywhere."

Danny nodded in that exaggerated way people do to convince themselves. "Yeah. That's the way to think of it, isn't it?"

I felt such deep gratitude for him then, for ignoring my blunder, for keeping Lucas at the center of our secret and not Kieran, for agreeing to help us in the first place. *You saved my life*, I thought, looking at his careworn face and seeing Vic's and my own reflected in it.

"It's the only way," I said.

twenty-six

I AM AT JACOB'S Wharf supervising the rewiring, when Selena says, "You know that guy you were asking me about, in the building opposite?"

I almost blurt out Kieran's name, catching myself just in time. "Oh, yes? You've seen him again, have you?"

"No, but I met one of his neighbors at a drinks thing the other night. A woman called Asha. We had a really good chat."

My gaze follows hers to the portion of The Heights visible through the nearest window. It is a building designed for after dark, I think. Unlit, empty of its worker occupants, it looks innocuous, even drab. "Does she know him then?" I ask, casually.

"I asked her that, and she said only to say hello to. He works from home, apparently, is a software designer or something. He's known in the building as a bit of a recluse. I've been keeping an eye out and he comes onto the roof terrace every morning to do these tai chi moves. Sun salutations, you know?"

Sun salutations, *seriously?*

"Anyway, she said she wants to redo the lighting in her kitchen and bathroom. She's still got these original nineties fittings that she hates. I said I'd give you her number, I hope that's okay? I wasn't sure how busy you are, but it'd be fun to have a poke around one of those flats, wouldn't it?"

"Yes," I tell Selena. "Thank you. That *would* be fun."

| | | | | | |

With time to spare before heading to my next appointment, I pick up a coffee and pastry from Bean Box, lingering a few minutes to survey the entrance to The Heights—it's about the same time of day Kieran picked up his white americano last time. Lightning doesn't strike twice, however, not when a "recluse" is involved, and I decide to get some exercise and walk east along the river to Bermondsey Beach.

The tide is low, the river lapping the foreshore in foam-edged waves. I tuck my coat under me and settle on the stones. The autumn sun, filtered by thin cloud, is pleasant on my face. Gulls skim the water. In a garden downstream, a man jerks back and forth on a rowing machine, moving in and out of my peripheral vision. I wonder, does Kieran still run? Has he ever rested in this spot? These years I've presumed him dead, how many times have we been in the same street, even the same building?

It's a while before I become aware of someone watching me from the path. Just as he addresses me—"Excuse me? I wondered if I might introduce myself?"—I recognize him as the older man from Kieran's flat.

Quelling the automatic flurry of panic connected with our previous encounter, I answer him smoothly. "I already know who you are."

"You do?" He moves towards me, squinting into the light. He

has warm amber eyes behind the kind of horn frames Gregory Peck might have worn.

"You're James Ratcliffe." At closer proximity I can easily match his features with those of the face in the old photo. His skin has the kind of gloss that speaks of a professional shave and other indulgences. Is that how Kieran lives now too? Lackeys to take care of his personal hygiene. Cosmetic enhancements on tap. "I take it this meeting isn't a coincidence?"

"Partly. I was leaving The Heights and happened to see you coming out of the café opposite. So I thought I'd take a walk this way myself. May I?"

He wants to sit next to me. He's followed me for ten minutes without making himself known, but, hey, *there's nothing to be scared of.* Even stalkers get stalked sometimes. He's in good shape, far less creaky when he lowers himself to the ground than I was a few minutes ago.

Sighing softly, I fold the paper bag with the last of the pastry and slip it into my bag. "So you're the one who invested in Kieran Watts's app and made him rich?"

"Sam Harding's app," he corrects me, but I ignore this.

"And you were at his flat last week. You chased after me."

"You ran from me. I was intrigued as to why you should do that." His grammar is extremely correct, his accent cultured, and I imagine that usually impresses people, perhaps even intimidates them.

"You scared me," I say. "And when you chased me, I knew I was right to be scared."

"There was nothing to be scared of," he says, baring excellent teeth in a smile. "You're not scared now, are you?"

This kind of banter right out of the blocks might look flirtatious on the page, but, believe me, it is anything but. "Do you live with Kieran?" I ask tonelessly.

"Sam. No, but not far away and my office is down on Bermondsey Street. You probably know that already."

"Green Shoots."

"Right. And you're a lighting designer, with a client in Jacob's Wharf."

"Correct." I drain the last inch of coffee. It tastes suddenly briny.

"You work with Habitus Architects, I gather. But I couldn't find you on their staff list."

"I'm freelance. There are a few of us they use on rotation. Why? Are you interested in investing in my business? Want to build me into a lighting giant? We could call it Edison Ellen."

His answering smile is a little tighter this time. "Actually, my interest is more in how your presence in the neighborhood might affect Sam."

"I don't know any Sam, Mr. Ratcliffe. You'll have to use his real name if you want to discuss him with me."

He exhales. "Kieran."

I cock my head a little to consider him. There's the softness of compassion in his face, but something hard and metallic behind the eyes. "What about *his* presence in the neighborhood, how did *that* happen? He approached you with his genius idea, did he?" Disgusted though I am by Kieran's success, this is too good an opportunity to fill in the gaps of his lost years for me to pass up, especially as Ratcliffe seems all too willing to oblige.

"I met him for the first time at Danstone. A contact of mine is a fundraiser there and she got me involved with a computer science initiative they were doing. Kieran was a part of that. He won a lot of fans there, he was quite the whiz."

"I'm sure he was," I say, sarcastically. "Last I heard, he was working in a fried chicken shop."

"So I understand. But he'd already had the idea for Moodsmart when we first met. He reached out to me about six months after his release. He was based in Glasgow then and it was a while before we met again face-to-face. But I made an investment, connected him with a few people. His hard work and talent did the rest."

So he was in Glasgow, I note. There are more expensive cities to hole up in, but still, how did he fund that? And has he confided in Ratcliffe about the circumstances of his Houdini act? "Why up there? Who was he staying with?"

"That I don't know," Ratcliffe says.

"So it only took you, what, eighteen months to make all that money together? That's got to be unusually fast, even for tech?"

"It was the IP they paid for. The valuation was fair." Ratcliffe flicks me a conspiratorial look. "It didn't hurt that the social media companies were actively looking for something with a mental health angle."

"Given they've played such a key part in wrecking it?"

"You said it." His gaze lingers with new significance and I guess he's thinking of Lock Up Longer, its website forum flowing with vitriol.

"Why change his name? Wouldn't it have helped with PR that he's an ex-con? Isn't that your whole angle?"

"Not my whole angle, no." He tilts his head, patient with my errors. "I'm interested in social and entrepreneurial mobility in general. To answer your question, we could have made it work had his conviction been basically unknown to the public, but it was widely known, as you're well aware. An extensive community had already engaged with it. We decided too many people would remember his story the way it was originally told."

The way it was originally told. Fury rampages through me. Who the fuck is this guy, reducing my son's death to a matter of narrative approach? But he *is* thinking of Lock Up Longer, that's clear. He's worried I'm going to expose Sam Harding for who he is—I've whipped up hate once and I can do it again.

"In any case, he'd already changed his name when we reconnected," Ratcliffe added. "He became Sam the moment he had to leave London."

Is he implying anything by this? His easy gaze does not alter and nor does his body language. "Why did you say you didn't know him?" I ask. "When I rang at the flat and said I had a delivery?"

"Because he's Harding now and I knew that if someone calling him Watts turned up out of the blue, we needed to pay attention. It could only be the wrong sort of inquiry."

"From the wrong sort of parent," I snap. "The kind whose child was left by him to die in agony."

This stark comment seems to galvanize Ratcliffe. He drops his equanimity for a more combative stance. "Why are you involving yourself in his affairs, Ellen? Are you planning something with the *Mirror* again? Because if you are, I can't stress how bad an idea I think that would be, now of all times."

So this *is* about the app, exactly as I supposed. No doubt there's a massive launch planned by his Saurus overlords, who won't be best pleased if eleventh-hour bad publicity comes raining down on them. The finance might even be structured so that there's still a substantial payment outstanding.

I let him chafe for a moment or two, before saying, "I'm not interested in rekindling my relationship with the media, no. I prefer a quiet life these days."

"I'm relieved to hear it." Ratcliffe doesn't look relieved, however. Rather he seems to be battling some internal dilemma. "If I can be frank with you, PR is not my only concern here."

"So what is?"

He leans a fraction closer. "This is confidential, but the reason Kieran relocated to Scotland and changed his name was he was tipped off that someone wanted to hurt him. I'm not talking about local abuse or internet trolling, he expected all of that, but a real threat. A death threat."

I jerk upright, shocked. This man knows not only about Kieran's escape but also the crucial elements of it that Vic and I have only been able to guess at. A *tip-off*? This must mean that Kieran staged his own disappearance out of some preemptive fear for his safety. And since Ratcliffe is the one sharing this secret, his camp clearly has no suspicion that the threat originated with Vic and me.

"I can see this is news to you," he says.

"It is. I don't understand. Who tipped him off? How did he know the threat was real?"

"Only Sam knows that. I trust his instinct, though." There is something in his tone that makes my nerves flare. Am I being too quick to assume an absence of suspicion on his part? Is it possible that as he sits here, with his gracious manners and smarmy talk of reaching out, he knows exactly what Vic and I tried to do?

"Why are you telling me this?" I ask.

"To let you know that any noise you decide to make, even just a bit of casual gossip with a client in Shad Thames, could have serious repercussions for Sam."

"And I should care because . . . ?"

There's a twist of irritation in his face, followed by a look of pleading. "Throw me a bone here, Ellen. I'm trying to solve this situation, not make it worse."

Throw *him* a bone? He's got to be joking. "We came face-to-face last week, did Kieran tell you that? He pretended he didn't know me. That was disrespectful."

The implication is that if he'd only acknowledged me to my satisfaction, then I'd have been on my way. *Right.*

"He did tell me that, yes, and I don't think he intended disrespect. You caught him unawares." Ratcliffe makes a show of preparing for another revelation and I feel my pulse accelerate. "Ellen, he feels an enormous sense of guilt about what happened with your son. His inability to overcome that is crippling him. He's really suffering."

"*He's* suffering?" This is so laughable I hardly know where to start. "If he felt enormous guilt why did he start going out with Lucas's girlfriend the moment he was released from Danstone? Did he tell you that?"

Ratcliffe gives a sympathetic nod. "Sometimes, after a tragedy, those left behind grow close. They understand how the other one feels. But he hasn't seen the girl since leaving the area. That was a tough sacrifice for him."

"Not as tough as the one Lucas made," I bark. "*He* hasn't seen her for a while, either." I've had enough of his "poor-Kieran" stance, applying the language of the victim to the perpetrator. "Look, Mr. Ratcliffe, maybe your charity work makes it possible for you to see these criminals as normal, and maybe most of them are, but I can tell you that the Kieran we knew was not normal. He was reckless and malicious and the fact that he's now changed his mind and wants to make the world a kinder place makes me feel worse, not better. He denied my son the future *he's* now living."

I'm breathing heavily, perilously close to lashing out physically.

"Ellen, please, I know you're hurting, but—"

I interrupt: "Stop. You know nothing about me. Just say what you came to say."

"All right." He straightens, clearly as tired of my hostility as I am of his evangelical sincerity. "He wants no further contact with you. It's a reasonable request, and I think you should think of it as an unofficial restraining order."

"I'll do nothing of the sort."

He sighs. "Fine. But please know that if we think there is any threat to his welfare, we will take measures to protect him."

I meet his gaze. "His welfare or his reputation?"

"They are one and the same," Ratcliffe says, and he at least admits that, not without a certain sorrow. If I had to guess, I'd say he had his own history of delinquency, that Kieran's second chance is a reliving of his own.

The problem is their victims have fallen by the wayside in the process.

I scramble to my feet, blinking into the sun, and walk away without even saying goodbye.

twenty-seven

ROBUSTLY EXPRESSED THOUGH VIC'S wishes are on the matter of Kieran, I consider them for all of five minutes before calling him. The encounter with Kieran's mentor is too crucial not to share, the nuggets of information mined too valuable. "Can you meet? I've got a lot to update you on. You know that guy I told you about? James Ratcliffe? He's Kieran's mentor—"

"No!" Vic's voice cuts across mine, sharp and angry. "I don't want to know, Ellen, I told you that the other day."

"I thought you just needed a few days to process it."

"What I need is to put what we did behind us. For fuck's sake!"

It is a long time since he has sworn at me. Before we split up, I would say, when Lucas was small. When I could scoop him up and squeeze him, carry him around on my hip before groaning and protesting, "You're getting too big for this. You're not a baby anymore."

Vic's apologies vibrate in my ear: "I didn't mean to have a go. I'm a bit stressed out."

"It doesn't matter," I say. "I suppose I can tell you on Thursday. I will see you, won't I?"

There is a silence. The twenty-first of November is Lucas's birthday. On the last four, Vic and I have visited his grave together.

"I'm really sorry," he says, "but I have a work thing I can't change."

"What thing? Can't one of the others cover for you?"

"No, they can't, sorry. Look, let's keep in touch," he adds, but I'm not stupid, I know what that means.

You're on your own, Ellen.

| | | | | | |

I ask Justin if he's free to remember Lucas with me on his birthday and he agrees to take the afternoon off work.

I drive. It doesn't take long for him to question the route. "We're not going to the cemetery?"

"No, I thought I'd do that later. I want to go somewhere else."

"Ah," Justin said, as I take the turn signed for Purley. "I see." Then, "Are you sure about this?"

"Yes." It's natural that he should ask. I haven't returned to the reservoir since the week of the accident almost five years ago and I don't know how I will react. I don't know how Justin will, either. As I drive, I think of all the times—both before and since Vic and I pledged an undying secrecy that excluded all others—I have expected him to call time on our marriage. Perhaps even willed it, for his sake, not mine. Freya has glued us, of course. Her grief. Her longing. These last two years, *I've* known (albeit mistakenly) that her brother's murderer has been neutralized, but *she* hasn't. To her, Kieran has remained living; not a malign spirit, but a flesh-and-blood threat with the potential to come back to town. She's needed her parents to shore up their marriage, not allow it to fracture.

But now she is at university, independent and resilient. Will this be it? Will this be the time Justin says *I can't take any more of this*?

We're almost there. The turn from the B road is steeply angled and you need to slow right down, take it with a little extra looseness. Easy to imagine joyriders shrieking and swearing as the car turns too tightly. A momentary loss of control that thrills, a close call that feels euphoric. The sign is the same as it was then: "Layham Hill Reservoir—Do Not Enter." At least I *think* it's the same. It's hard now to know what was my personal experience of that time and what has been grafted into my memory by media images. The blue-and-white police tape, the basin of black ink beyond. The car being hauled out, sheets of water flowing from its windows.

We park and climb over the fencing, past the "Keep Out" signs, to get as close to the spot as we can. There is a tremor in my arms and legs, a tightening of my lungs, as I survey the innocent flatness of the water, silvery and reflective in the afternoon light.

I turn to Justin. "If it had been daylight, would there have been light in the car?"

He considers this as if I haven't asked it before. As if he hasn't borne witness to a thousand individual collapses as question follows question, no answer getting us any closer to acceptance than the one before. "There would have been some, yes. There would have been more of a chance of a witness, as well. Busier roads. A passing driver who saw them and stopped to call for help."

They'd have to have seen the crash; the car was not visible for long.

"Do you feel like this overshadows everything?" I say. "I mean, us? Freya?"

His gaze narrows. "How can it not? When you lose a child, you make your life in that shadow. You're never going to be cured. You're managing a condition." He reaches for my hand. "We've survived this far, we'll keep on surviving."

"I've got something to tell you," I say, abruptly.

"What?"

"I've known about it for a while, but I wanted to be sure. Kieran Watts has come out of the woodwork. He lives near Tower Bridge."

"What?" A bolt of alarm crosses Justin's face. "After all this time? How do you know?"

"I saw him. I've seen him twice, actually."

"When?"

"The first time was about a month ago, completely by chance. I spotted him from a client's window." I pause. "I've told Vic. I had to." Seeing the tic, light as a moth's wing, by his right eye, I feel a reciprocal flutter. It has never been clearer to me than in this moment that Justin was as much a father to Lucas as Vic and yet he never behaved as if he were entitled to the same status.

"And?" he says.

"And he wants nothing to do with it."

"With what?"

"With . . ." And I can't say any more, I can't confess, not to that. "Just with the fact of it."

"That explains it," Justin says, and his brow actually clears. "You've been so preoccupied. Glum. I knew it was more than the time of year."

The annual year-end deterioration of my spirits. The approach first of Lucas's birthday, and then the anniversary of his death.

"It is," I agree. "I suppose I'd got used to the idea that Kieran was dead."

Paid good money to be sure of it. I feel so angry with myself. And angrier still with Vic for cutting himself off. I shouldn't have to burden Justin right now—not when I don't know if I can trust myself. *"He was supposed to be dead!"*

I've said it before I can think it through, feel my face flush in horror. In two and a half years, I haven't come this close to confessing.

Fortunately, Justin misinterprets my outburst. "That was never confirmed," he points out. "Personally, I always assumed he'd run off somewhere and kept a low profile."

"Really?" I stutter.

"I know you wanted to think it was something more permanent, but there was never any evidence, was there? That police investigation, they were only ever guessing."

I press my lips tightly together, avert my eyes.

"Wherever he's been hiding since he left, he's obviously been keeping out of trouble."

"More than that, he's made a lot of money." I give him a concise update. The app, the change of name, the friends in high places. The flat in the sky with the view of Tower Bridge.

"Have you told the police any of this?" Justin asks. "Their file might still be open for all we know."

My answer is a tricky one to get right. Of course I haven't told the police. I haven't for the same reason I bought the second phone, currently zipped in my handbag with the power turned off: I need to keep myself under the radar for what might come next. A second attempt, if I can arrange it. "I wanted to tell you first, see what you think. Anyway, they might already know." A cold feeling presses down on me as I realize I have no idea whether or not Vic might have contacted the police, for exactly the reasons Justin states. But no, he wouldn't want the police reconnecting with Kieran again. Wrapping things up, interviewing him about the details of that tip-off Ratcliffe knows about. Asking who he thinks might have issued that death threat.

Justin has his phone out. "When did you last check the Missing People site?"

"I don't remember." This is true. When Kieran was first reported missing, I googled his name constantly, the Missing People listing even claiming a spot on my most-visited list. Then, confident we'd successfully got rid of him, I'd had no need to continue with the ritual. After a month or so, I took a walk along Regent's Canal and threw my iPad and second phone into the water (Lord knows I never imagined I'd one day be buying another). On the few occasions since that I've tortured myself by revisiting original reports of the car accident, I've passed over the old links to scan for fresh references.

"Here it is." Justin shades the screen with his hand so I can read the message: "'Page no longer available.' And look, when you put his name into the search box, it doesn't come up. He's no longer missing."

"Does it say when the page was taken down?"

"No. Could've been any time."

He hands me his phone and I examine the matrix of faces, so many of them tragically young. Many of the "missing since" dates predate that of Kieran's case. "So the police *do* already know. Why didn't they tell us?"

"None of our business, I suppose."

"It's totally our business!" I cry. "Do you think Kieran asked them to keep this from us? To protect his new identity? Every step of the way, they've put his needs before ours."

"You want me to phone them and find out?" Justin offers.

"No, leave it." I'm trembling as I pass back the phone. I need to calm down. "So long as he stays away, it will be fine."

And the look Justin gives me then—like he's proud of me, of how far I've come in my grief—is a new, terrible kind of heartbreaking.

"Where was it you said he lives?" he asks.

"Shad Thames."

"Okay, so it's not like it's Oxford Street. I can't remember the last time I went there. I think you should make a point of not taking new clients in that area. Finish the one you've got, then keep well away."

"Yes." I think fleetingly of the prospective client in The Heights with whom Selena has shared my number. I know that if I do not hear from her, I will follow it up myself.

I *should* stay away, but I will not.

We fall silent and I look out across the reservoir. I imagine stepping away from Justin and dropping into the water, sinking in the same spot Kieran's car went under. Drawing my last breath exactly where Lucas drew his, scream for him as he did for me. Know the utter bleakness of death.

I step back, seasick, heartsick, my vision blurring. "Let's go."

Killing Time (cont)

"I'm staggered by how courageous some of the women in my class are in confronting pain—theirs and other people's," says Felix Penney, and it is true that Ellen Saint exhibits a forensic understanding of her own agony.

"Since Lucas died, I've lived with pain every waking second of every single day," she tells me. "My life has mostly been an exercise in managing it. Right now, writing is a big part of that."

I ask her if she thinks men would gain as much from the course as she and her fellow female students have?

"For me, this isn't about being a woman," she says. "It's about being a parent." She is pensive for a moment, before adding, "Actually, maybe it is about being a woman."

Sunday Times magazine, December 2021

twenty-eight

IN THE END, A work emergency keeps Justin at his laptop and so I visit Lucas's grave alone.

Though the light is almost gone, it's the best time to come, I've found, not because dusk mutes the emotions, but because it frees them. It lets them breathe. Exposing your suffering in broad daylight can be . . . Well, that can be frightening for others.

That Vic is not here with me feels grievous, even in spite of the forewarning. For the first time—perhaps inspired by that episode of death wish at the reservoir—I question whether I will survive this second round with Kieran Watts.

"Ellen?"

I'm so deep in thought, she has to repeat my name before I turn.

"Prisca. Oh."

I haven't spoken to her since the height of the campaign, when she appealed to me on my doorstep (*"Don't do this to yourself, Ellen . . ."*). She looks considerably better groomed. Her hair, a rich chestnut, is swept forward over made-up eyes. Her coat is well cut, suede boots pristine. It's hard not to wonder if Kieran is back in touch, sending her funds from his Moodsmart windfall.

"Did you know it's his birthday?" I say, and she turns to the headstone. Only the years are marked: 1995–2014.

"I didn't. But I come sometimes, I pass by on my way home from work. I hope you don't mind."

"Of course not." I swallow. "Does *he* come here, as well?"

She looks startled. "Who?"

"Kieran, of course. I know he's living in London. I assume you do too?"

There's an ambivalence to her expression that suggests she's more shocked by my raising this than the fact of it. "I didn't know he was in London, no. We're not in touch anymore," she says, finally. But her fingers stray to the lovely fabric of her coat, an unconscious association that confirms my previous assumption. Let him help her out, I think. It's not my concern.

"But you've known he's alive and well?" I press. "You were the one who reported him missing back then, weren't you?"

"Yes." She lowers her eyes. "And yes, I knew he was safe."

"How? Who told you? The police?"

"I had a call from Kieran's old supervision manager."

"Marcus Flynn?"

"That's right. He told me Kieran had made contact and asked them to let the missing persons unit know he was fine."

"But you didn't hear from Kieran personally?"

She hesitates. "An email came. It wasn't signed or from his address, but it was him."

Creating an untraceable email address would have been child's play for Kieran. "What did he say?"

"Just that it was better for us not to be in touch because there was a risk it would put him in danger."

"What danger?"

"I assumed he meant from all the haters. Your lot, the ones who couldn't let go. He must have been worried they would track him down through me. He wouldn't have wanted me to be in any danger, either. That really upset him." She cups her elbows and hugs herself in a defensive gesture and yet her expression is open, her words flowing. Perhaps it's the setting, the bodies under our feet, but it's as if she's on the witness stand, telling the whole truth. "Before he went missing, when he was back living with me again, I sometimes felt like the house was being watched. I told the police that. Anyway, I thought he had a right to privacy, to a life without abuse, so I did as he asked and didn't reply or try to track him down."

"You didn't think to tell Vic and me?"

"I didn't have the authority to do that. Maybe if we'd been . . ." She falters. On the same side, she means. "Maybe if we'd stayed in touch, but we've never really communicated, have we?"

There's a depth to the regret in her tone that stirs something reciprocal in me. I see now that there could have been a way for communication between us, maybe even for mutual consolation. I rejected it because I knew, subconsciously at first, then consciously, that getting close to Prisca meant compromising my commitment to revenge.

And just as it would have then, so it would now. "When did you get this call from Flynn?" I say. Exactly how long were Vic and I kept ignorant of Kieran's survival?

"I don't remember the date, but it was a good few months after Kieran went missing," she says. "The posters were still up though. I took them down right after I heard."

I remember noticing they'd been removed and assuming this was standard practice after a certain period of appeal. "I wish you'd let me know," I repeat. "I've only just found out in the last few weeks."

She brushes her hair from her eyes, revealing deep lines of uncertainty in her brow. "You're not going to . . . ?"

"What?"

Make a fuss, she means. Demand some sort of investigation into the oversight or the lack of transparency towards victims' families or whatever the hell other label crazy Ellen Saint chooses to give this.

"Complain," she says, settling on the safer word. "To the police. The probation people."

I stare at her. The simplicity of her assumption shifts something in my reasoning of the situation: ever since rediscovering Kieran, I've been resolute in avoiding the risk of drawing attention to myself by contacting the police. But now I'm known to Kieran himself, not to mention his protectors old and new, isn't it potentially more suspicious if I *don't*? I helped build a campaign on moral outrage, so isn't it peculiar if I don't display a single shred of it now? It breaks the pattern of my behavior and the police are interested when patterns are broken.

I need to call them and complain, do exactly what they'd expect of *the ones who couldn't let go.*

After all, no one matches that description as fully as I do.

twenty-nine

I GUESS IF YOU were kind enough to give me the benefit of the doubt, you *could* believe that, with time, I might have come to view the game as the rest of the players thought I should. James Ratcliffe and Vic; Justin and Freya; Sheridan and Jade; Prisca. And Kieran himself, of course, sending word of his "tremendous guilt" through his mentor and trusting that the accompanying veiled threat would be the end of it.

But I think you've followed my account for enough pages already to know that was *never* going to happen.

I do not consult Justin or Vic before I phone the police the next morning. I do it after my only client appointment and right before I set off for an overnight trip to my mum's on the coast. Since Dad died, I've visited weekly—until my detective work regarding Kieran interrupted my routine, that is. This afternoon's trip feels overdue.

The police officer I speak to is either genuinely unable to access the original notes or unusually eager to pass the buck, because I am referred to the Prison and Probation Service before I can even suggest it myself. They, in turn, insist that only Marcus Flynn can handle the query. Fine. He must have worked on dozens, maybe hundreds, of cases since Kieran, but I have no doubt he'll remember his famous killer. He's not available, so I leave a voice mail for him and hit the road. It makes little difference to me if my call is logged today or after the weekend. The point is only that it is done. I am acting in character.

He surprises me with a prompt call back. I'm on the M20, about twenty minutes from Mum's place, clear skies ahead. I settle in the inside lane to take the call hands-free.

"You want to talk about Kieran Watts? I've got a couple of minutes before a meeting." He sounds as if he can think of pleasanter ways to spend his Friday afternoon, but, then again, they all sound like that when they speak to me. They all cite a meeting they're late for, another caller on the line. Vic, too, now. Even Justin. The only person who's leveled with me, shown no fear, is James Ratcliffe.

"Yes," I say. "I've been made aware that he's back in London and living under a new name." *Made aware*: a nice passive form. No need to point out that I've been staking out his building and gathering intel of my own. "The last I heard, he was missing, so I'm wondering when it was that he reestablished contact with you?"

There's a pause and I sense Marcus weighing up the pros and cons of engaging with me, a known agitator. Might it be easier to pass me on to the press office, with whom Roz Engleby, Vic, and I liaised satisfactorily during Lock Up Longer? On the other hand, what harm can it do to cooperate, given that I now know what they've been keeping from me?

"I don't have the notes in front of me, Mrs. Saint, but I remember he made contact with us about three or months after he left. He'd seen himself on a missing persons site, he said, and wanted his foster carer to know he hadn't come to any harm and we should close any investigation."

"So that was, what, October or November 2017?"

"It would have been around then, yes."

Which tallies with Prisca's "a good few months" and with James Ratcliffe's having established himself in Kieran's life soon after as a force for good. An angel investor in more ways than one.

In the distance, the traffic is bunching, and I ease off the accelerator. "He was up in Scotland for a while, I know that much, but when was he actually back in London? In the same city as his victim's family, walking around with a new name, a new identity, when all the time we thought he was missing. My family should have been given the opportunity to take measures to avoid him." I allow my tone to grow more forceful. "Maybe it's best if you just let me know the process for making an official complaint, please."

Flynn is rattled by the threat. "Hang on a minute, let's talk this through. First off, I don't know anything about a new name. That's a private matter and nothing to do with us. The same goes for his current address. But we certainly let you know he was no longer a missing person."

"You certainly did not, that's the reason I'm calling!" There's a choke in my voice. I'm starting to feel real emotions now. When it comes to Kieran Watts, I seem incapable of fraud; it is all true.

Flynn takes pity on me and asks me to wait while he digs out the notes, after all. I hold for two or three minutes, trying to focus on driving safely, and then he returns. "Here we are. I've got a note here that my colleague Dina phoned you in late October 2017."

"That's nonsense. No one phoned. I've never spoken to anyone called Dina."

"It was Vic she contacted. Vic Gordon. He was the primary

contact by then. Actually, there's a note that you were out of the country. Were you on holiday, perhaps? Late October is half term, isn't it?"

He's right, that must have been when Justin and I took Freya to the States. "Maybe," I concede. "But why was Vic your primary contact? I thought *I* was."

Flynn politely insists his facts are correct and the note is dated and initialed by this Dina. "There's really nothing else I can add. But I hope that helps. It's been good to speak to you again, Mrs. Saint. My regards to your husband and daughter."

After he hangs up, I try unsuccessfully to steady my breathing. Mum's turn is coming up on the left, but I ignore it and keep going towards Dover. Then I swing east to the car park for the Cliffs.

I get out of the car and step into the unforgiving November wind that rises from the sea. The air tastes almost grainy with salt. I cross the cliff path, my body braced against the buffeting air, until I'm as close to the edge as my legs will allow.

I have not done this since I was a small child.

I lift my chin and open my eyes wide to the cold winter blue. I allow my vision to blur as I summon the ghost of Lucas: he's a young boy again, in my parents' garden, spraying a water pistol and laughing wildly. He loved spinning, I remember that suddenly. He'd spin and spin until he made himself dizzy and crumpled to the ground groaning, his arm already reaching out for one of us to pull him back up.

"Don't do that too near the edge, you might fall off into the sea," my father would warn, playfully, for the coast was over a mile away and the "edge" of the garden in fact a gentle bank, with robust hedging beyond.

In spite of the wind, my blood is fever-hot, angry tears burning my eyes. Two years. Two years Vic has known that Kieran Watts is alive, that our plan to rid the world of him failed. *So why the hell didn't he tell me?* Weeks, *days*, ago we stood together on St Saviour's footbridge and looked up at The Heights, cursing Kieran, agonizing over his survival, and *still* he said nothing.

Slowly, I allow my gaze to fall to the ground, to my own feet. I allow myself to visualize the short running jump that would launch me into the abyss of blue. I think of all the poor souls who've sailed through the void before me and I am one keen, deviant impulse from going after them.

And then, recharged by my own terror, I walk back to my car and prepare to start my story again.

part two

Killing Time (cont)

As you will probably have gathered, it is not possible to talk about Ellen Saint without also talking about Vic Gordon. Though frequently by her side in the aftermath of their son's death and a partner in their Lock Up Longer campaign, he is said to no longer be in touch with her in any meaningful way.

Theirs is an intriguing yin and yang: just as her fortunes have declined, so his have improved. While she has made questionable choices in handling the devastation of losing a child, so he has modeled best practice. Friends say he has redirected his energies into a craft microbrewery business with enough green credentials to satisfy the toughest eco warrior, and is rumored to have found happiness with a new partner.

"The media campaign was very much Ellen's passion project," says a friend who knows them both well. "This book is a new way for her to make her point and express her grief.

Everyone respects that and Vic is never not going to support her, not when it comes to Lucas. But if he'd been given any choice in the matter, I suspect he would have preferred to grieve in private."

Outside of the pages of her book, Ellen is reluctant to discuss the status of their relationship. "Vic and I will always be bonded," is all she will say.

When I ask her if she can imagine him reading her finished memoir, she considers the question carefully before saying, "Yes, there are some details he won't know. He might be curious."

Mr. Gordon declined to be interviewed for this article.

Sunday Times magazine, December 2021

Vic

NOW

It is a Saturday morning, the one weekend in an age that he isn't on duty in the taproom or out at a market or festival, when her text comes:

Need to see you URGENTLY.

She knows, he thinks, straightaway. It's a guttural thing, just as he's always guessed it will be. (Nothing to do with those crazy, shouty capitals—that's normal communication for Ellen.)

His reaction, though, is less predictable. He expected to be panic-stricken, to drop everything to ready himself for his Waterloo (the acquisition of a bulletproof vest is not the stretch you might think). But, in the event, it is more like how he supposes it must feel when you've been on the run for years and finally feel the helicopter searchlight on you. Hear the megaphone-loud instruction to remain where you are, there is nowhere left to hide.

Because the terrible truth is that there is no such thing as a relaxed fugitive. There is no such thing as the enjoyable deception of a loved one—and Ellen is and always will be a loved one. So he is, now they're here, relieved. Released.

By the time he's thought all of this, she has sent a second message:

> Vic????

Clearly, she is not going to be ignored. This will have to be done today. He responds:

> Meet me in Beckenham Place Park at 2

She agrees at once and he knows she'll be there before him. Even if he gets there early, she'll be waiting.

| | | | | |

He leaves it till the last minute to tell India.

"I have to nip over to Beckenham and see Ellen. I'll just be an hour or two."

Having been facedown on her yoga mat in a pool of sunlight by the balcony doors, his girlfriend rolls onto her haunches to face him. Her skin has that attractive rosy glow of the olive-complexioned (he, on the other hand, looks in need of hospitalization when he exercises). "Right now? You said you'd be here for the John Lewis delivery. You know they won't leave it in the lobby."

"You won't be in either?"

"I told you, I'm meeting Coco in town."

He's forgotten. In the hours since receiving the text, he's forgotten most things. "I'll arrange for Li to take it in, then as soon as I get back from seeing Ellen, I'll go and collect it." Never mind that Li, in the flat next door, is usually gaming with headphones on, oblivious to the sound of the buzzer.

India points this out. "Can't Ellen come here?"

"You know she can't." Vic's eyes stray past her to the view over the rooftops towards the hazy skyline of Central London. Was it conscious or subconscious, his decision to live somewhere so high? Knowing Ellen wouldn't come marching up here whenever she liked? His flat is on the fifteenth floor, nothing to a high-rise city like New York or Hong Kong but *Blade Runner* living in East Croydon. And anyone imagining those sleek oatmeal interiors you always see in show flats would be way off because the place has got a whole lot more colorful since India moved in last month—a riot of exotic color to befit her name if not the home counties reality of her upbringing. A lot more chaotic, as well, now they are setting about reorganizing the space and redecorating the second bedroom.

"What does she want to talk to you about, anyway?" she says, mildly, and he marvels for the hundredth time how nothing is unacceptable to her, because everything—every flare of anger, every error of judgment—has a psychological reason that merits compassion.

They're all like this, the younger millennials, a cohort obsessed with well-being (maybe it's a disorder in its own right? Obsessive compulsive well-being?). Mild anxiety or full-blown psychosis, both are regarded with the same sincerity by his twenty-eight-year-old girlfriend. His thirty-one-year-old head brewer, George, is the same. They are what Vic's gen used to call "precious."

Sure, there are days when he misses that cynicism, the sheer grit of his own age group's commitment to mockery. But he has his friends, his cousin Danny, and Danny's partner, Jo, for that. Ellen, too, in her own way.

"It will be to do with Lucas," he says. "Maybe because I missed his birthday on Thursday."

"You didn't miss it, babe. You just didn't spend it with her. You were away, growing the brand." India gets to her feet and comes to him. She is a woman who expresses her sadness—all emotions, really—through touch.

He draws her to him and buries his nose in her hair, damp at the nape. "Sorry about the delivery. If Li takes it in, I'll start putting it all together as soon as I get back."

"Are you going to tell Ellen our news?"

"Yes, at some point. But not today."

"Okay, but don't let her find out from someone else, Vic. That's not right."

"Don't worry. I know how to handle her." Well, he *thought* he did, but they're in uncharted waters now, aren't they?

India pulls away and they both look down at her abdomen, the faint curve of which is clear through the second skin of her yoga gear. In normal clothes it's not yet evident.

The day she told him she was pregnant was the same day Ellen told him Kieran Watts had rematerialized. Seriously, what were the chances?

He'd listened to their messages one after the other:

"Vic, babe, I need to tell you something. Something crazy." (India, sounding giddy.)

"Call me as soon as you get this. I mean it, Vic, it's urgent!" (Ellen, sounding tearful, paranoid.)

He'd played them both a second time before deciding which call to return first.

Ellen's, of course.

Like there'd ever been any real alternative.

Vic

THEN

IT SEEMED TO VIC that only someone who had looked mania directly in the eye could appreciate the full, unstoppable force of it.

Okay, mania might not be the clinical word for Ellen's case. She'd had counseling, that kind of thing, in her teenage years, but not been given any psychiatric diagnosis. *Highly strung*, that was the label society reached for back then, and he'd known she was this right from the time they met at Bristol University in the early nineties (improbably, given their career paths later, they were both studying anthropology). In a world of long-haired, blissed-out girls emerging from the second summer of love, Ellen was punky with her sharp-boned face, cropped platinum hair, and wine-red lipstick. Like a young Annie Lennox.

Not so rock 'n' roll in her habits, he discovered, when they'd been out a few times. She was a moderate drinker, never touched cigarettes or drugs, unlike Vic himself.

"I have to be careful about mixing booze with my medication," she explained.

"You're on medication?"

"On and off. On at the moment."

There was panic involved, he learned. Phobias, the kind of irrational stuff that was often passed off in that era as eccentricity. That high place phenomenon thing, for instance: she made it sound so artistic, so chic, especially when she used the French term, *l'appel du vide*. She'd been raised by the Dover cliffs—a childhood with a view of France, no less—and yet couldn't walk the celebrated coastal path. When Vic first visited the family home, he'd explored the clifftops and experienced those immense, lung-filling vistas with her parents, while Ellen remained in the visitor's center with a pot of tea.

"No one *likes* heights, El," he told her. "No one *wants* to fall. Just stay away from the edge and you should be fine." That was his position on the matter, presented with his trademark guffaw.

Yes, it was all very charming at first, but, once they'd left the security of the college pack and lived as a couple in the real world, it rapidly came to grate on his nerves. It wasn't like he had the patience of a trained professional; he was just an ordinary guy!

An ordinary guy who depended on his girlfriend to take the pill and know whether or not its efficacy would be affected by any other medication.

Efficacy: he didn't think he'd ever used that word in relation to his own circumstances before the day Ellen told him, at twenty-two and both of them recklessly in debt following a postuniversity trip to Bali, that she was pregnant.

| | | | | | |

Parenthood made him view her through a new lens (and she him, presumably, given that she was the one who would do the ditching, a few years in). It made him see that those kooky fears of hers might be transferable.

For starters, it wasn't just cliffs that stirred her peculiar thoughts of jumping, but also ledges and balconies and roof terraces. Even bridges, for heaven's sake. He remembered one time, when Lucas was about nine months old, and they'd taken him into Central London to show him the sights. Vic had unstrapped him from the buggy and was carrying him when they reached Westminster Bridge and Ellen drew to a halt.

"Let's put him back in the buggy," she said.

"Why?" He loved walking with the baby in his arms, their faces pressing together, cheek to cheek, as they looked at the world from the same height, the same angle.

"Just while we cross the bridge," she said, with the earnest pleading that had come to irritate him.

"Why?" he repeated.

"You know how I get that feeling?"

"But this is a *bridge*."

"I know, but I'm worried I'll get it with him."

He gave a disbelieving laugh. "No one in their right mind would want to jump off a bridge with their baby. Besides, *I'm* holding him, not you. Come on, let's go. You push the buggy."

People were starting to eye them as they clogged the pavement. At last Ellen moved, marching ahead with the foot of the buggy angled upwards, her rigid arms an extension of the handles. Some distance behind her, Vic felt that phrase ring in his ears: *No one in their right mind*.

They reached the other side. "See," he said, cheerfully. "He's still here. He had a lovely time looking at Big Ben."

Ellen's face was pale, her jaw tensed. There was a stripe of red on her lower lip where she'd chewed a fiber from it. "I saw you walking backwards at one point."

"Yeah, so we could look back at the clock face, like everyone else!"

"Someone could have knocked into you, Vic. They could have sent Lucas flying!"

Overhearing this last exclamation, a passerby pulled a face at Vic that made it clear what he thought of this dynamic. That Ellen was deranged, basically, and Vic the unlucky bugger who had to deal with her.

"Well, they didn't," he said, more acidly than might have been advisable.

| | | | | | |

She was an overprotective mother, no doubt about it. That was unusual among the younger mums, according to Danny's new girlfriend, Jo, who had a preschooler of her own from a previous relationship, so she knew what she was talking about. It was generally the older ones who were the control freaks, she said, used to the cause-and-effect certainties of a career-driven universe (not Jo's exact words, but that was the gist). Young mums still thought they were immortal and that this gift extended automatically to their babies.

Jo swore by childminders, but Ellen wouldn't have anyone caring for Lucas but her, which meant that for the foreseeable future she wouldn't be earning any money. She'd worked a little over a year in her entry-level role at a heart health foundation before making her exit.

"What about doing something part-time?" Vic suggested. Although he had by now secured a junior position in the leasings team of a big tool hire company, he considered it temporary, if not beneath him.

"Maybe." Maybe meant no in Ellen-speak.

Living on one junior salary meant they couldn't upgrade their one-bed rental in Sydenham, where they'd settled to be close to Danny, and so they put Lucas in the bedroom and made do with a studio arrangement for themselves. While Vic worked, Ellen roamed South London's better neighborhoods, compiling a wish list of the streets she'd far rather live on than their own. They didn't have a car and she'd travel by bus, complaining about the rude treatment she'd received by drivers and, sometimes, other passengers.

Frighteningly quickly, Vic found himself in a three-person catch-22. He couldn't go on in the relationship with someone so tense and inflexible and *weird*, but it was his duty to be available to offer Lucas an alternative model to tense, inflexible, and weird. He made a deal with himself: get his son to senior school—he'd be eleven, strong and fearless and able to stand up for himself—and then ease out of the relationship with Ellen.

"You could always have an affair," Danny suggested, one night in the pub. He had a talent for simplistic solutions.

"No," Vic said. "If she ever found out, she'd want revenge."

"Looks like you're fucked then," said Danny.

| | | | | | |

When Lucas was a year from starting school, Ellen at last loosened the reins a little and enrolled him in a local kindergarten. At about the same time, she announced that she wanted to work in interior design and signed up for an evening class in electrical installation at Beckenham Technical College.

Not long after the course had finished, she came to Vic and said, "I'm sorry, but I've met someone."

"What do you mean?" he said, unsure why she should want to apologize for making a new friend.

"I mean, I've fallen in love with someone else. We want to be together. He's already met Lucas."

"He has?" Vic was stunned. "Who is this guy?"

His name was Justin Saint and they'd literally met in a corridor at the college. He wasn't very senior at work then, still in his late twenties, but seemed to be able to fund the deposit needed for a large Edwardian villa on one of Ellen's dream streets, Tanglewood Road in Beckenham. With Lucas, of course. Vic moved from the Sydenham flat to a scarcely less poky two-bedroom place on an estate on Shannon Way by Beckenham Place Park. (It wasn't all bad: the housing had been built in the eighties on the site previously occupied by Haddon Hall, where his hero David Bowie had once resided.)

He was invited to Tanglewood Road to admire the swing that had been strung from a creaky old oak in the garden and the huge climbing frame with monkey bars high off the ground. There was even a trampoline. When Lucas started at the primary school at the end of the road, Ellen sometimes let him walk to school with a group of other neighborhood kids, led by an older girl she trusted.

Within a year, the lovebirds had married and had a baby girl. Vic didn't ever get to know Freya particularly well, but the mere fact that Lucas had a sister was a cause for jubilation—someone else in the mix to take the pressure off the boy. Because these outward signs that Ellen had relaxed her parenting style couldn't possibly be the true picture. Vic knew she must watch Lucas on that swing and climbing frame and trampoline like a close protection bodyguard. She couldn't possibly now be trusting a young schoolgirl where once she hadn't felt able to trust a qualified childminder. Perhaps she tailed that gaggle of kids to the school gate in the new 4x4 Justin had bought her.

No one just *suddenly* got better, did they? Even if rogue impulses were being better managed, they were still there. Starter flames waiting for their oxygen supply.

| | | | | | |

In the blink of an eye, Freya had started primary school, Lucas was about to move up to Foxwell Academy, and Ellen was telling Vic she had taken a part-time job working for a lighting shop in the West End. "I want to get a few years' experience, make some contacts, then start up on my own as a lighting consultant."

She stuck at the low-paid retail job for three years and Vic had to admit he was impressed. He'd assumed those dreams of hers were just that. Conversely, he considered himself rather more than a dreamer. While continuing to work full-time at the tool hire company (he'd been promoted to manager by now), he'd taken his own evening class in running a small business, done exhaustive research into micro-breweries, and put together a business plan for his own craft beer brand.

He talked his boss into funding presentation skills training at work, before honing his pitch to investors and mentors ("I've always wanted to organize a piss-up in a brewery"). As time went on, the cold calls were replaced by an online submission process, but the out-come never varied: thanks, but no thanks. In the age of the hipster, microbreweries were two a penny and he had neither the image the trade—or consumer—expected nor a story that made him in any way PR-worthy. As for the name, Common or Gordon, would millennials get it? "Doesn't it give the impression the product's bog standard, not premium?" one asked.

Not if they don't get it in the first place, Vic pointed out.

He recalled one pitch with the special pain of the near hit. It was a collective of investors in an übercool Bermondsey factory conversion and though his contact was junior—gatekeeper to the real decision-makers—there was real enthusiasm in his eyes. "Common or Gordon: I like that. We could do something with that."

But when the knockback came, it was a variation on the usual theme. "We're finding the brands that break through are the ones that have more of a personal story behind them. A lifestyle to buy into."

"Can't I get the product out there and then *add* the lifestyle?"

"The lifestyle *is* the product. Look at the guy from Blur."

Alex James and his artisan cheese business had cropped up several times in meetings like this one, but it was the first time Vic felt like ordering a great wheel of the stuff and crushing someone's face in it.

"Thank you for your time," he told the whippersnapper, and closed his laptop with a defeated little click.

Vic

HE HARDLY EVER COMES to Beckenham Place Park these days.

They used to come all the time, Lucas and him, when he lived in the flat on Shannon Way and saw his son most weekends. They'd ride their bikes or hurdle fallen trees, fence with sticks and roar and yell together till their throats were sore. And, sometimes, they'd get on the bus to the Bowie Bandstand and caterwaul "Life on Mars" with the other pilgrims.

Vic supposes it was because of Ellen's caution that his own parenting style was so committed to chaos and noise, but, God, did he really use to have all that energy? Of course, it wasn't a constant riot. Sometimes, he and Lucas would just sit on a log and eat apples and crisps and look for mini beasts, as the schools had taken to calling insects. Lucas particularly liked finding something stuck and setting it free.

He was the best, their boy. Not a mean bone in his body. How is it going to feel, Vic wonders (well, *fears*), when his second child arrives? What if he and India have a boy who looks just like Lucas?

Might Vic's life turn sadder, not happier? Did he have the skills, the stamina, to put on the required brave face?

"Vic!"

He breaks from his reverie and sees Ellen, already at the meeting point by the mansion, waving at him. One look at her striding down the path to intercept him and he sees he was on the money.

She knows.

Her forehead is puckered with outrage and her eyes burn. She is a woman who finds it hard to conceal her feelings, which worried him a lot when they hatched their plan to kill Kieran. It was obvious to Vic that the police would come calling—Jesus, a rookie on his first day in the job would've put their names near the top of any list of people with an axe to grind against the kid—and he wasn't at all confident she'd be able to mask her guilt.

What he hadn't appreciated was that she felt no guilt.

"Hi, Ellen." They go through the motions of hugging and cheek-kissing. "Are you all right?" He doesn't leave time for her to answer, before saying, "I'm sorry I couldn't be there on Thursday. I went yesterday when I got back. Nice to see all the flowers."

She waves off the apology. "That isn't why I wanted to talk."

Oh, God. They begin to follow the path towards the new swimming lake, its waters undisturbed, of course, on this sharp November afternoon. Her furious energy makes her march so fast she's almost shaking him off.

"Ellen, slow down. Talk to me."

With an air of concession, she slackens her stride to match his steadier one, and then she begins. "I rang the police about Kieran resurfacing and guess what they said?"

I don't need to guess.

"They said you already knew." Her tone hardens. "You've known for two years."

"That's nonsense." It seems to Vic that it's only sensible to at least go through the motions of denial — just in case she doesn't have the appetite for full discovery, might be willing to hear what she wants to hear. That's always been her way, after all. Decide your own truth.

But not this time.

"They said they told you as a courtesy, to let us know he'd turned up again and was no longer living in the area. I checked the date and we were on holiday in New York. We didn't take our phones, so fair enough that they might not've been able to get hold of me. But they got hold of *you*."

Vic protests, but she cuts him off. "Don't do this, Vic. It's bad enough you lied to me then, but don't do it now." She grasps his arm with sharp fingers and they come to a standstill. "I've spoken to Prisca and she obviously found out at the same sort of time. I appreciate *she* would have her reasons for keeping the news from me, but it's hard to see what *yours* were." Her voice lowers. "Given what we'd done. *Thought* we'd done?"

"Give me a chance to explain. That's hurting, Ellen." He gently removes her fingers from his arm. "I *did* get the message that he was alive and well, yes. I *was* told he had settled somewhere else. But I didn't tell you because I didn't want to turn your life upside down." How grave he suddenly sounds, suddenly *feels*. "I thought if you carried on believing he was dead, you'd have a better chance of moving on and being happy again."

"Oh, come on!" Incredulity drips from her voice. Her glare is pure outrage. "I didn't just *believe* he was dead, Vic! *We arranged it*, remember?"

He swallows his impatience. How could he possibly not remember?

"Weren't you desperate to know what went wrong?" she demands. "That conversation we had the other night, why weren't we having it back then? Why weren't you shocked and confused and terrified there might be repercussions? *I* would have been."

"I *was*. Obviously, I was. And had you been around I'd probably have told you straightaway. But I had time to get over my shock and come to the conclusion that it was best to keep the news to myself."

She snorts. "I don't believe you. I don't think you were shocked at all. You were probably expecting the call. Praying it would come to you and not me. Or maybe you phoned *them*, is that it? I know you'd already told them you were the primary contact, not me. You were covering your tracks, Vic, admit it. You did a damn good job of it, as well."

He stares at her, horrified. "What are you talking about? This is madness."

"Don't you dare." She is almost snarling now. "Don't you dare gaslight me. As I tried to tell you on the phone before you swore at me, I met that investor guy, James Ratcliffe. He told me Kieran had to disappear because he was tipped off that someone was planning to kill him."

Though the sun now emerges from cloud, turning the path a dazzling white, there is a chill on Vic's skin.

"And you know who I think tipped him off, Vic? *You*."

"Fuck off!" Fear makes him coarse. "Why the hell would I do that?"

"You tell me! But if I had to guess, I'd say you lost your nerve. I think right at the last minute you got cold feet and it was too late to call it off and so you somehow sent word to him. Please, just tell me the truth. It's despicable to treat me like this."

To his disgust, he feels tears rising, as if he is a child getting a dressing-down from a teacher. Because she is so terribly, profoundly *disappointed* in him. "Can we sit down?" he says, blinking, and Ellen gestures to an unoccupied bench on the hill above the lake.

They climb up in silence and sit far enough apart that a third person could fit between them. Who is the third person, he thinks? Lucas? Or Kieran?

Below, the reflection of the tree line in the still, silvery water is looking-glass-perfect.

"Why did you change your mind?" she says at last, very quietly, and he exhales a long stream of fear and regret, guilt and relief.

"Because I couldn't live with it. I couldn't eat or sleep or work. I talked to Danny and—"

She interrupts: "Hang on, you said we couldn't speak to Danny about it. You said once it was in motion, we had to act like it had never happened, even with each other. You made me swear!"

She's right, he remembers it clearly. Her face wrung with passion as he extracted her vow. "I know. But I had to talk to him, I was having a massive fucking crisis, Ellen. I needed to see if it was too late to back out."

"And it was, I assume."

"Yes, so I tipped Kieran off instead. I told him there was some crazy person who wanted him dead." Vic groans. "He was supposed to leave London. He was supposed to fuck off to Scotland or somewhere—for good. Anywhere but here."

Only as he watches her absorb this—the idea that if Kieran *had* settled somewhere far-flung, she might have lived a lie to the end— does he recognize the immensity of his actions. The full extent of his fraud. Ignorance is bliss: people trot out that maxim all the time, but that doesn't make it true. Sometimes, keeping someone in the dark is plain cruel.

"He did go to Scotland," Ellen says. "Glasgow. But only for a while. Then he got in touch with this Ratcliffe guy and came back. I got the impression they don't suspect us of having anything to do with the death threat, but maybe you know differently?"

"I have no way of knowing," Vic says, "but I would doubt it."

"So who *did* he think was after him? What did you say to him, exactly? What crazy person did he think you were talking about?"

Vic shrugs. "Take your pick, just one of those weirdos who came out of the woodwork during the campaign and then got obsessed. All that 'bring back hanging' stuff. I made it clear there was no personal connection to us, obviously. To be honest, I was lucky he believed me. I really wasn't sure he would."

"*Lucky?*"

The word is hissed and scornful, stirring indignation beneath his guilt. Though her fury is predictable, it confounds him that she can't see the fundamental reality of the situation: plotting to kill a man is the crime here, not calling it off! He wants to shake her and make her listen, listen properly, but how would that look to the woman with the retriever who's just drifted into range? A man abusing his wife? She'd pocket that tennis ball and call 999.

He sits on his hands and addresses her in a level tone. "Yes, Ellen, lucky. You need to see this as good news for you. It means you didn't commit a horrific crime, you're not a monster. Now you can get on with your life with your lovely family and be grateful you're the decent, law-abiding person they always thought you were."

It's too much to expect the miracle of agreement and he braces himself for the lashing he deserves for applying the word "monster" to anyone except Kieran Watts. But that isn't what happens.

Instead, she is silent, seeming to harness her emotions, intensify her focus.

"The contract is still live then," she says, finally.

He is taken aback. "What do you mean?"

"I *mean*, all my theories about them botching the job were wrong. He disappeared before they could do it, and they would probably still honor it if we told them where to find him." There is a flush of color on her exposed collarbone as inspiration strikes. "Think how easy it would be, much easier than before. They'd just need to trick their way into his building and he'd be right there, a sitting duck."

Vic gapes at her, appalled.

"I take it you didn't get onto Danny when I asked you to?" she continues, suddenly all business. "About the money?"

He finds his tongue again. "No. I told you, we're not going to be able to get hold of them now. It's been way too long."

"Two and a half years isn't that long."

"Of course it is! People like that change their phone numbers constantly, probably even their center of operations, as well. We thought they were Albanian, didn't we? I bet they've upped sticks and gone home, what with Brexit and everything."

"Albania isn't in the EU," she says and sighs as if he's being deliberately obstructive over petty details. As if this isn't murder they're talking about. Seriously, he's in awe of his previous self, the Vic who humored this lunacy. And yet . . . And yet, he understands. Lucas was the love of her life. The love of his. He knows that what she wants is not for Kieran to be dead but for Lucas to be alive.

"I don't know what else to say," he says, truthfully.

"Fine, it doesn't matter. If you don't want to be involved, I would never force you. I'll ask Danny myself." She springs to her feet, her bag slapping against her hip. "It goes without saying that if you tell anyone about this conversation, or anything to do with this, I'll deny it. I'll deny everything, just like we always agreed."

"Of course." Determined not to call after her as she hurries away, Vic concentrates on a pair of spaniels circling an ancient oak in the distance, heads raised to whatever they've detected above. A squirrel, probably.

Lucas could never spell "squirrel," he remembers.

When the dogs and their owner have moved on, he continues to sit there, scratching his neck, kicking the toe of one boot against the heel of the other. Trying to figure out what just happened and what might happen next. What did she say? *He'd be right there, a sitting duck . . .* If he has been in any doubt before that her passion for vengeance has been reignited, he isn't now. *There was some crazy person who wanted him dead.* It pains him to say it, but there still is.

He digs in his pocket for his phone. He needs to get to Danny before she does.

Vic

THEN

IT WASN'T UNTIL LUCAS started in the sixth form and Kieran Watts announced himself on the scene that Vic found himself implicated in the micro-parenting approach that Ellen had long subscribed to. Though he said so himself, he thought he'd done a pretty good job of managing her since their split, honing a strategy that had come to work so well he was tempted to put it in a document and email it to Justin.

Then again, it was a lot easier to humor someone's neuroses from afar than it was from the same room.

The basic premise was this: collude to win. Whatever Lucas's or anyone else's failing, however spurious it struck you, you had to be sure to agree with her—and agree with heart. Never challenge when the outrage was at its hottest. Meanwhile, offer a safe place for Lucas to let off steam and wait for her to be the one to make the compromise or the concession you'd had in mind from the start.

Because she always did. Ellen was, fundamentally, a good

person. A fine one, even. Only when it came to Kieran did she have the ability to disengage from mercy, from the humane and enlightened part of her that most people were more accustomed to. Which meant, when she began phoning Vic every other day to consult, update, complain—mainly complain—he needed to pay more attention.

"He was supposed to be finishing his history essay, but he went out with that Kieran . . ."

"He came back from the party with that Kieran and I could tell he'd been smoking weed . . ."

Somewhere along the line, "that Kieran" became "that druggie," "that wastrel," "that delinquent," and, eventually, "that monster." (She was a one-woman thesaurus, Ellen.) But what set this challenge apart from others involving undesirable influence on her firstborn was how quickly the focus widened to include Ellen herself:

"The way he looks at me, it's unsettling . . ."

"I really think if we were on our own, just me and him, he could turn violent . . ."

"Don't say anything to Lucas, but I'm going to have a word with . . ."

There were dozens of people she hoped to appeal to: the staff at Foxwell, the police, the social services, the foster mum ("She's very nice, Prisca, but she obviously doesn't have a clue what a monster he is"), even a friend of a friend whose son was hopelessly addicted to skunk and now languished in a room above the garage, his brain wrecked and useless.

What Justin made of it, Vic could only guess, but Vic's girlfriend at the time, Yazmin, was unambiguous in her view. "If you're going to spend the whole night on the phone to her about Kierangate, I might as well just fuck off home," she told him, scowling.

| | | | | | | | | | |

For what it was worth, Vic didn't share Ellen's view that the boy had been born evil, only that his life circumstances had produced a uniquely careless individual. Kieran was as impressionable as he was influential, in Vic's opinion. For instance, he had a stupid gangster way of speaking that you'd expect from a much younger kid—roadman, they called it. "Thought they wuz gunna G-check me, I was shook," he would say, as if arriving from some notorious sink estate and not the cozy semi provided for him by the caring and sensible Prisca.

But it didn't matter how juvenile Vic judged his act to be, Lucas still thought this particular "homie" in his "mandem" was wonderful. A policy to ban him from both homes was soon instituted.

"Fine with me," Vic said to Ellen. "Good call." Collude to win.

Sure enough, following discussions about the dangers of driving Lucas deeper into Kieran's orbit, Vic was once again free to welcome the devil to Shannon Way. Lucas's girlfriend Jade would be there too and the three of them would sit on the sofa with the rolling heads and stupid eyes of kids newly committed to drinking and smoking. Vic would make them something to eat, tell them to keep it real (*that* dated him), and then go and meet Danny or a mate in the pub. Give them space, basically.

"Thank you *so* much, Vic," Jade would say, as he bade them goodbye. Her voice was rough-grained, as if she had a permanent sore throat (Kieran had an unexpected voice too, a rumbling baritone. By contrast, Lucas's was as sweet and clear as a choirboy's).

Meanwhile, Ellen tried hard to pitch the two friends against each other, and none too subtly at that. Where Jade got invited on the Saints' three-week holiday to Crete, it went without saying that

Ellen would sooner lie naked on the runway than take *Kieran*. It rained relentlessly in England while they were away and Vic imagined the kid with Prisca in a rain-lashed caravan park in Margate—if that—and felt bad for him.

As the dynamic ripened, Vic's impression was less of Jade and Kieran competing for Lucas as of Lucas and Kieran competing for Jade. There was one night he remembered particularly. It was after the holiday and they were back at school—that was right, it was around the time Lucas was doing his uni applications. The Oxbridge deadline had come and gone and though Ellen claimed it was for the best, Vic knew she was crushed. Not only was Lucas naturally academic, but he also had the pretty-boy looks that photographed so well in an ancient quad or on the emerald-green banks of the River Cam.

When Vic had left the flat that night, it had just been Lucas and Jade, sitting in front of the TV with beers, laughing and taking the piss, but when he returned the tableau had altered. R&B pulsed through the rooms, its lyrics egotistical and, frankly, illegal. Lucas was nowhere to be seen (it transpired he had passed out in the bedroom), and Kieran and Jade were on the floor by the sofa. At first, Vic thought they were just mucking around, but one glimpse of Kieran's body grinding away on top of Jade's and he quickly upgraded the observation to their having sex—entirely consensual, judging by the female groans he now identified as being distinct from those layered into the music. Unsure of the right course of action, he hung back, feeling like some sordid voyeur. Then he remembered that trick of reopening and closing the front door, which he duly did, as noisily as he could, before heading straight into the kitchen and swinging open the fridge violently enough to make all the lager bottles chink together. Such stage antics must have broken the pair's illicit rapture, because when he went back into the living room, the music had been cut and they were in their coats, saying a mini cab was waiting outside.

"Make sure you drop Jade first," Vic said to Kieran.

"Thanks for having us," Jade said, remembering her manners even when thwarted or embarrassed or whatever her primary emotion was. Had Vic been asked to come up with an adjective it would have been exhilarated—there was wildfire in those hazel eyes.

He said nothing of the incident to Lucas, but asked, in passing, "How's it all going with Jade, mate?"

Lucas shrugged. "Yeah, good."

"D'you think you'll stick together when you all go off to uni?"

"Might do. That's ages away, Dad. We haven't even sent off our applications yet."

"True. You might be on girlfriend number ten by then."

As Lucas protested Vic's lazy sexism, Vic noticed a faint flush rise in his son's cheeks. He really liked Jade.

And so, evidently, did Kieran.

But hey, perhaps what he'd seen had been a one-off. At seventeen and eighteen, they were old enough to sort things out for themselves and too young to be expected to observe the rules of fidelity *his* gen had been bound by.

One thing was certain: this was one piece of evidence he was not about to share with the prosecution. Why make Kierangate even more of a scandal than it already was?

| | | | | | |

You'd have to have been insensitive to the point of being in a medically induced coma not to notice that tensions ran especially high as A-level season approached. There were a few times during the spring term when Vic seriously considered pressing the case for Lucas to come and live with him full-time—not that Ellen would ever have allowed it.

He had a suspicion of how bad it had got at home one day in late April when he swung by to deliver a biology folder Lucas had left at his place. Tanglewood Road was almost achingly English in summer, with its beautiful old trees, their foliage buzzing with insects, and those blue mop-head hydrangeas in every garden.

No one was at home, so he left the folder on the doorstep (who would want to steal the notes of an underperforming student?) and was just returning to his car when a voice called out from the garden opposite the Saints':

"Excuse me, are you Lucas's dad?"

"I am," he said, approaching. "We've met before, I think. I'm Vic."

"Meg." She was a type typical of Ellen's upscale neighborhood, the thick-waisted figure of middle age counteracted by the ageless face of the cosmetically preserved. Strands of soft, stripy hair lifted in the breeze.

"Look, I don't mean to interfere," she began and Vic's spirits sank. No one but people who meant to interfere ever said that. "But is everything okay with Ellen and Lucas?"

"How do you mean?"

"Well, she was really shouting at him the other day."

Frowning, Vic slipped his car key in his pocket. "You heard them from all the way over here?" It was a wide road, with luxuriously deep front gardens and driveways.

"No, they weren't inside, it was in the street. Just a bit further down from here."

"What happened, exactly?"

"Well, Lucas came out, he *really* banged the door after him—that's what made me look up—and then she came running after him. 'If you don't take this seriously, then you can find somewhere else to live! Live on the street for all I care!' That kind of thing, with swearing," Meg added.

"Sounds like a typical interaction with a teenager," Vic said, but his lightheartedness was feigned. He had never said anything like that to Lucas. There were rough sleepers in the area, many of them young, and Lucas himself was so concerned he'd chosen to do his geography coursework on the homeless problem. "Was Justin not around to referee?"

"He was at work. It wasn't *that* serious. No violence. Just the usual."

Violence? The usual? Vic was taken aback. "Lucas has got this friend Ellen doesn't approve of, so I would guess it was about that. I don't approve of him either, to be honest with you," he added, making a stab at presenting a united front.

"They're a pack at that age, aren't they?" she agreed. "They'd jump off a cliff if their mates were doing it."

"I suspect that's what Ellen's worried about," Vic agreed. "Thank you for keeping me in the loop. I'll have a subtle word."

But, sitting in the car afterwards, he was aware of his mind scanning for ways to procrastinate. It would be more strategic, perhaps, to approach Lucas not Ellen.

He phoned him that evening. "You and your mum getting on okay?"

"Fine," Lucas said and Vic could hear the sounds of his video game in the background.

"Look, mate, if she's a bit tough about A-levels it's only because she wants you to fulfill your potential." God, he almost gagged on the cliché. "There must be some other way of saying that, eh?"

But Lucas wasn't in the mood to riff and Vic deserved the cliché that came back. "It's my life," he said. "Not hers."

Not yours, either.

Vic

IT IS JUST AS he expected: within half an hour, Ellen has hunted down Danny and demanded to see him. Thanks to Vic's warning and an excuse involving a child's football tournament, Danny has been able to delay her till Monday morning.

"Well done," Vic says, though a twenty-four-hour delay is nothing to Ellen. Twenty-four *years* and she'd still be there.

Throughout Sunday, nerves devour him from the inside out. He has a regular pitch at a posh farmers' market in Chiswick and it's just as well India is with him to win hearts and minds because he is about as animated as—God, he can't even think of a simile. A three-toed sloth, maybe. Algae growing on its fur.

Danny has arranged that Ellen should visit him at the house he's working on in Crystal Palace. It's on one of those streets where keeping up with the Joneses has been raised to an art form—you'd be forgiven for thinking you were in Hampstead—but luckily these particular Joneses are away, which means Vic can also gain admission to the event. Arriving twenty minutes before Ellen is due, he finds plastic runners on the floors and dust sheets draped over the furniture, paint-smeared tools collected on a foldout table. The living room walls are a peculiar lacquered green, like something from a gypsy caravan.

He greets his cousin with a hug. "I can see why they'd want to paint over *this*."

Danny splutters with laughter. "This is the *new* color."

They could be shit brown for all Vic cares. The only thing that matters is that the layout works, with the kitchen connected to the living room via glass doors he can wedge open and with a nook behind the fridge where he can conceal himself. "Whatever you do, don't let her come in here," he briefs Danny. "She's nosy about houses, it's her work." But somehow, he doubts that inspecting a stranger's light fittings will be on Ellen's mind this morning. This business with Kieran must be playing havoc with her work sched-ule—God knows it's disrupting *his*.

"What if she wants a glass of water?" Danny asks.

"Get it for her. Or say the water's turned off, I don't know. The main thing is to play dumb, yeah? You know what she's like." Vic turns off the ringer on his phone. "Right, I'm going in. See you on the other side."

Danny slaps his shoulder. "You're a fucking loon."

A tense five minutes later, the doorbell rings. There's an ex-change of greetings Vic can't quite make out and then their voices grow clearer as Danny leads his visitor into the living room.

"Thanks for seeing me. I'm sorry to bother you at work, I'll only be a couple of minutes." Ellen's voice is gravelly, like she's been crying, and Vic feels a plucking sensation deep inside him.

"What's this about, Ellen? You all right?"

"Fine, yes. Well, no, actually. There's stuff going on." She pauses. "Have you spoken to Vic recently?"

"Yeah, I rang him last week on Lucas's birthday."

Danny and Jo always remember. It is sad how few people do.

"But not since I rang on Saturday night?"

"No. I mean, he's left a couple of messages, yeah, but I haven't had a chance to get back to him. I was gonna call him later. Why?"

The line is rehearsed and Danny doesn't sound altogether convincing to Vic, but he must look sincere enough because Ellen replies with relief. "Good. If he knows about this, he'll try to contradict everything I say."

"Contradict what?" Danny says. "I'm in the dark here."

There's the sound of Ellen clearing her throat. "I want to get back in touch with your contact."

"What contact?"

"I think you know who I mean. From 2017." Vic can hear the effort it takes for her to curb her impatience. "Vic says it's too late, they'll have moved on, but can you at least try? It's a hell of a lot of money to just write off." Clearly, Danny is looking doubtful, because she rushes to reassure him. "I don't mean I want you to put yourself in any danger, please don't think that. But you must still have a mobile number I can try?"

"Put me in danger?" Danny repeats, and Vic pictures their expressions, Ellen's rigid with determination, Danny's slack with confusion. "Try who?"

"The Albanians. The ones who walked off with our fifteen grand."

Vic holds his breath. Maybe it's the setting, the suburban kitchen, his immediate view of a wine rack, a vintage tea caddy, a glossy-leaved cheese plant in a terra-cotta pot, but Ellen's statement sounds about as preposterous as can be. Like someone having a delusional episode.

Danny says, "Look, I don't know what you and Vic've got your-selves into, but it's nothing to do with me. I'm just making a living here." Then, with deeper concern: "You're not in trouble, either of you? I mean, all the Albanians I've come across . . . You *really* don't want to mess with them, El."

Bless him, Vic thinks.

Ellen's voice sharpens: "You don't have to pretend anymore, Danny. Vic must have told you he's not dead?" There is an awful pause, then, "Oh, God, he hasn't, has he?"

"Who's not dead?"

"Kieran Watts, of course!"

"That cunt," Danny says, with casual disgust. "Excuse my French. Where's he popped up, then?"

"Shad Thames, up near Tower Bridge. He lives in a very nice flat overlooking the dock."

Danny, now sounding as offended as he is puzzled, says, "Vic hasn't said a word about this to me."

"Okay, well, *I'm* telling you. Take my word for it, I saw him with my own eyes."

There is a silence, broken a second later by a strimmer whining in a neighboring garden, and Vic has to ease forward to continue to hear.

"To be honest," Danny says, "I'm not sure why you needed to come here in person when—"

"Please," Ellen interrupts, more urgent now. "All I need is the phone number. I'm begging you!"

Danny isn't good with needy women, Vic knows. They embar-rass him, stress him out. And he's always found Ellen unpredictable. He'll be gawping at her, trying to think how to placate her before she starts screaming and crying and potentially breaking objects that don't belong to him.

But she doesn't do those things. She just sighs—an exhalation of defeat that is audible even to Vic.

"Fine, I can see you're not going to help. I can't force you." The same words she used with Vic, the same profound dismay that he should fall short. "But if you *are* able to find it in your heart to dig out the contact details, don't text me on my normal number. Use this one, all right?"

Next thing, the front door is closing with a flimsy little click. Vic emerges from his hiding place in time to peek down the length of the hall and catch a glimpse of Ellen through the ridged glass of the front door. She's in black, as ever, but for a splash of scarlet, a collar or a scarf.

Danny appears in the kitchen, his face flushed. "What the hell was that all about?" He holds up the torn page of a notebook. "What's this number, is it her old man's? Maybe you ought to have a word with him, yeah? She can't go around spouting conspiracy theories about Albanians."

Vic takes the paper from him, recognizes the number as the one for Ellen's second phone. Her *second* second phone—is this *really* happening all over again? "Forget it," he tells Danny. "You did great. I wasn't entirely sure what she was going to say."

"Is it true you've seen Kieran Watts?"

"*She* has. I have no desire to. I don't want anything to do with him."

Danny frowns, fiddles with his right earlobe. "I thought she was all right now? Getting on with her life?"

"She's had a shock, seeing him again. It will pass." Vic leans against the worktop, feels its sharp edge cutting into his spine. "But thanks for this. I needed to hear for myself what's on her mind."

Danny looks dispirited. They've thrown his morning off-kilter, he and Ellen, and Vic feels bad. He searches for something to redress the balance. "Since I'm here, I've got some news—for your ears only for now, okay? India's pregnant."

Danny's face lifts. "Oh, mate. That's amazing. Boy or girl?"

"Too early for that," Vic says. "Next scan, hopefully."

They say their goodbyes. As he lets himself out, Danny turns on the ancient transistor radio he takes to all his jobs. They're playing "Live Forever" by Oasis, a song that, every time Vic hears it, sends his insides into free fall, makes him think he's about to collapse to the ground.

Prisca's Corsa was a decade old and wasn't fitted with a digital sound system, so if Kieran and his mates wanted music in the car, they had only her stock of CDs to choose from. The classics of her heyday, eighties and nineties, mainly. The night Lucas died, *Definitely Maybe* was in the CD player, the volume turned up high. It wasn't possible to determine after the event which track had been playing as the vehicle spun off the road, but Vic believes so ferociously it was "Live Forever" it has come to feel like fact.

He has to clutch the gatepost to steady himself, to wait for his nervous system to right itself, before he can put one foot in front of the other and walk to his van. He supposes it must look peculiar to a passerby, but he is used to that.

Vic

THEN

WHEN LUCAS DIED, IT was Justin who phoned Vic with the news.
Ellen was incapacitated and sedatives had been prescribed as an
emergency. By cruel coincidence, her father's health was ailing and
her mother tied to the south coast nursing him, so Justin's family
stepped in to take Freya for whatever passed as Christmas and New
Year among the shell-shocked.

It was Justin, too, who suggested Vic stay in the spare room at
Tanglewood Road for a few days. He gave the impression he wel-
comed help with looking after Ellen, but Vic knew what he was
really doing was making sure Vic got looked after too. He'd somehow
got wind of Vic having passed a manic afternoon hunting Kieran,
rampaging through the hospital and Prisca's street demanding to
know where the little bastard was hiding, and thought it best to reel
him in.

For two weeks, Justin cooked meals for the three of them, removing the untouched plates without comment and dispensing
glasses of brandy (it was the only time in his life Vic had drunk

brandy and he would forever associate its rich afterburn with loss). He answered the door, dealt with the deluge of messages to their various mobile phones, and handled their liaison with the police and the undertaker.

Vic remembered little of it now, but he retained a general image of them passing one another in darkened rooms. At first, he had thought no one was bothering to turn on the lights, until one afternoon, when they were all in the living room, he noticed Justin get up to switch them on. Ellen, who had been dozing on the sofa next to him, woke suddenly as if *she* had been switched on, and got up from her seat to turn them off again. As she did so, she kept her eyes averted from Justin and Vic, as if seeing their faces would turn her to stone. Justin said nothing about this bizarre behavior and made no retaliatory move. When working on the forms and papers needed by the authorities, he'd retreat to his desk in the study, where he had a little anglepoise lamp he could use without interference. Vic realized this lights-on-and-off routine must have happened before, perhaps often. He grew to suspect that Ellen had banished light not because she couldn't stand to see his and Justin's faces, but because she couldn't bear to not see Lucas's.

She hardly spoke on account of the tranquilizers, though Justin's murmur was often in evidence, only growing animated when he spoke to his daughter on the phone. As for Vic, he could not risk words, not at first. Words were fearsome things, fogging his mind and crushing his chest. Instead, a recurring memory played of Lucas's seventeenth birthday party, when, at Ellen's behest, Vic had driven by the house to check on things. It had been a moonless night, that dense, granular darkness of late November, and the streetlamps streamed yellow. He'd rolled down the car window and heard first the bassline of the music and then, through an open upstairs window, the sweetest melody in the world, the laughter of young people who no longer laughed like that with their parents. Had he detected Lucas's cackle in the mix? If not at the time, he did now. He did now.

Only two more birthdays had passed since then. Eighteen, nineteen. Nineteen years old and already gone. There'd been that song, hadn't there, back in the day? N-n-n-n-nineteen. They used to sing along to it in the union bar at uni. More of an elegy, really, than a pop song.

| | | | | | |

The court proceedings provided a focus, albeit a grim one. Ellen was energized again by then, unwavering in her disbelief in Kieran's claims of memory loss and relentless in her insistence that he must be concealing a truth even more terrible than the one pieced together by investigators. Vic despaired of so ardent a longing for an account that could neither improve on nor reverse the outcome, but what she was doing, he was told on good authority, was a common form of displacement. A kind of deferred pain.

It was that same obsessive yearning that fueled Lock Up Longer. To have refused to take part would have been to expose himself to the accusation that he cared less deeply for Lucas's memory than she did and so he went along to as many of those talks and interviews and support groups as he could bear. And it grew to be quite the roadshow, with guest appearances by police officers and paramedics and driving instructors—Vic lost count.

"All these people care about our boy," Ellen would exclaim, filling herself up on the collective energy. But Vic had learned to distinguish at a glance between those attendees who'd suffered comparably and those who were seduced by the there-but-for-the-grace-of-God frisson that came from having left one's own children safely tucked up in bed.

He was secretly pleased when the *Mirror* modified the campaign to include other types of driving offenses, in effect retiring their grievance from view. He felt they'd made their point to hundreds of thousands more people than they'd had any right to expect to reach, even if the sentencing guidelines remained, for now, unchanged.

And, if he was honest, he wasn't sure he wanted to be associated with some of those thousands. String 'em up, they demanded. An eye for an eye. There were even slurs regarding Kieran's hair color. "No wonder sperm banks don't accept donations from redheaded men," one woman posted. Women were more vicious than men, Vic noted, though he didn't say that to Ellen.

"It makes sense to quit while we're ahead," he told her, when they drove back to South London after a talk in Tunbridge Wells, one of the last in their diary. "We're lucky no one's delved a bit deeper and challenged us."

"What are you talking about?" Ellen said. In the gloom of the passenger seat, she was almost invisible in his peripheral vision, until oncoming headlights flooded the car and her fine, tragic profile would suddenly be aglow.

"About Lucas, I mean. Say there'd been a full trial, with witnesses . . . they'd have testified to *his* habits and behavior, not just Kieran's. Put him on trial as well. We knew he was doing a lot of drugs, didn't we?"

"Thanks to that dealer, Kieran," Ellen said, and Vic glanced warily at her before returning his attention to the road.

"It was never really established he was dealing, was it?"

"I caught him in that car park on London Road!" she snapped. "I told you."

"Did you actually witness a transaction, though?"

"No, because we drove off after I confronted him. I should have hung around, got a photo of him doing the deal."

"Right," Vic said, as if agreeing. "But remember how the school singled out Lucas, not him. That photo they got from his phone, that's the kind of thing I mean. We're lucky no one's published that or others like it. How many more might there be on all these sites and apps we've never heard of?" He indicated right and sped past a van. "All I'm saying is it could all have looked very different."

"This is about careless driving," Ellen said, with cold fury. "We're not fronting an antidrugs campaign. Though we *could*."

He said nothing more. It was still too unkind—perhaps always would be—to ask her to question the account she'd not only publicly given but also wholeheartedly believed. That Lucas had been blameless, an innocent with no agency of his own possessed by a malign force.

Often in media interviews, Ellen would invoke her memory of seeing Lucas handing out cash to the homeless living under a local bridge.

"Which bridge?" Danny had asked, when Vic had mentioned this practice at the time. It was early in Kierangate then. Good times (relatively).

"The one under the railway on Queens Road."

Danny chuckled. "He'll be getting something in return for his donations, know what I mean? It's notorious down there—and not just weed, by the way." He grew serious, remembering Lucas's youth, perhaps. "You need to tell him there's dodgy stuff on sale there. He shouldn't trust it."

Vic *had* told him. He'd laid down the law. "Wait for university for all this stuff," he advised, in a spirit of compromise, and had known, before being told, that Leeds would be his son's first choice. It was the party uni of the day.

| | | | | | |

God, work was a shitshow by then. He was not so much phoning it in as communicating it telepathically. He was in his midforties and had given up on his craft brewery ambitions, not least because his three most recent applications to join someone else's launch team had not even merited a reply.

By then, he was drinking way too much of the type of product he'd once dreamed of making. Friends fell away—he could hardly blame them. Danny and Jo still came around, proposing all kinds of changes: that he move in with them, say, or that they help him make over the flat he'd rented for over fifteen years and not once asked the landlord to redecorate. That he cut down on the booze. When they visited, they no longer brought the bottle of wine or the six-pack they used to, but a low-maintenance house plant or satsumas in a net sack. He'd tear the netting open with his teeth a week later and eat the dried-out fruit one after the other.

Jade's mother, Sheridan, was welcome, therefore, when she turned up one evening with not one but two bottles of cheap Tesco Bordeaux. She'd made a point of keeping in touch since Lucas's death. (Okay, so she fell plum into the there-but-for-the-grace-of-God category, but, in her case, it was actually true.)

"I've just discovered Jade's been getting letters from Kieran," she said, drinking so urgently her glass chinked against her front teeth. Dressed in monochrome gray and not her usual gerbera shades, she seemed to be wallowing in a darker mood than usual.

"From inside? Wow. Don't tell Ellen that, will you?"

"Don't worry, I'm not stupid."

Jade was at the end of her second year at university by then. Vic had seen her in the street in college holidays, looking morose, though it was hard to know if the melancholy was really hers or if he was projecting it on her. She'd gained a little weight and he found himself fantasizing about her being pregnant with Lucas's child, even though the dates were wildly impossible. But in movies and novels, that was always what revived the hearts of the bereft, wasn't it? New life equaled new hope.

"So what's he been saying to her in these letters?"

Sheridan raised an eyebrow. "That, I don't know. But when she was home last week, I noticed two envelopes on her desk with that prison service stamp on them. Like, who else writes actual letters?"

It sounded to Vic as if Sheridan had been snooping. "I used to wonder if they had a thing going," he said, experimentally. "Kieran and her. Back when she was with Lucas."

The look Sheridan returned was considerably less surprised than it might have been. "I think they didn't know what they had going. They were kids, all three of them." She paused. "Not that we get any better at knowing, do we?"

And, suddenly, her face was coming towards Vic's and her mouth was on his, bloody with wine. He eased back, embarrassed. "I don't think so, Sheridan."

She flushed and shrank away. "I'm so sorry, I thought . . ."

He couldn't bear to hear what she thought. "It's fine. Forget it. You've had a tough time."

"No," she exclaimed, "*you've* had a tough time!"

"The thing is, I have a girlfriend," he said, in belated—and bogus—explanation.

"And I have a husband," Sheridan countered, and they mustered a laugh before she remembered she needed to get home to said spouse, and left.

Vic finished the wine on his own and fretted that he could have handled the situation better. He felt sorry for her, he really did. Confused by her daughter's choice of pen pal and so disconnected from her husband that she'd had to remind Vic she still had one, she had her share of stresses, no doubt about it. But sleeping with her daughter's dead boyfriend's alcoholic father was hardly likely to improve matters.

What were they like, these older women? Even those who hadn't been shipwrecked with grief were ill-equipped for the high seas they seemed so determined to sail into.

Vic

THEN

AFTER LOCK UP LONGER wound down, he might have been entitled to think that the rest of Kieran's time inside—there was about a year of it still to be served—would offer a period of welcome reprieve. That he and Ellen would return to their careers and set about the painful rebalancing of priorities that was required, eventually, of the bereaved.

But Ellen was not yet ready to rebalance. She transferred her work ethic to a lower-profile endeavor: tracking the inmate's progress. Vic began to dread her calls; even her voice mails agitated him. She'd discovered this and that from Kieran's key worker or from digging online, infiltrating forums where the parents of young offenders exchanged tips about visits or sending parcels.

Her greatest hope seemed to be that Kieran would take his own life, though, like a birthday wish, this was not explicitly declared. Instead, she talked about suicide more generally. "The rate is really high in these places," she reported to Vic.

"That's tragic. They throw themselves off those landings, I

suppose?" He guessed that she, of all people, must find it quite natural to picture Kieran meeting his end by plunging from a height.
Exiting his cell and diving over the rail towards the central rec hall far
below, other inmates watching in horror from the rungs of identical
walkways.

But evidently not. Those voids had safety nets these days, she
said, and anyway, didn't he remember her telling him YOI Danstone
was a modern, low-rise building?

Other, viler ideas were discussed on the Lock Up Longer forum,
which remained open, if no longer formally monitored. The use of
razor blades and showerheads was invoked, or shoelaces by which
Kieran might hang himself from a light fitting or bunk. Vic made
occasional efforts to delete these comments and block those posting,
but the venom kept coming.

This was their world now. It hardly mattered that they'd helped
create it.

| | | | | | |

Whether by obligation or courtesy, the police surely ought to have
alerted them to Kieran's release date, but in the event Vic only knew
the boy was out when he spotted him in Bromley Shopping Centre.
It was April 2017, a Saturday afternoon.

He wasn't even supposed to be there himself. His new girlfriend
Chloë had dragged him along at the last minute to help her choose
a gift for someone or other. As she browsed a homewares sale, Vic
idled on his phone in the entrance to the store, and that was when
he saw him. He was directly across from Vic on the other side of
the escalator void, apparently alone, his elbows propped on the top
of the balustrade as he looked down at the teeming throngs on the
concourse below. His expression was one of mild disdain. Boredom.

After years of considering himself the moderate to Ellen's zealot, Vic surprised himself by wanting to march over and kill the bastard. No prison landings needed, just a standard design shopping center: one shove and the punishment would finally fit the crime. Kieran would be out of their hair forever. But he found he couldn't move. It was like when your muscles go into paralysis when you dream to stop you from hurting yourself. By the time he'd mobilized, Kieran had covered his head with a low hood and moved onto the escalator, gliding rapidly downwards.

"Wait a minute," Vic yelled over the barrier. "Hey, Kieran!"

But none of the faces that turned his way was the one he was after and by the time he'd made the descent himself he couldn't place Kieran in the crowd in front of him. He drew to a halt, breathing heavily. The pounding of his heart was so agonizing he put a hand to his chest, causing a security guard to approach and check he wasn't having a heart attack.

He didn't go back to find Chloë and when she tracked him down by phone later that day, he didn't tell her about Kieran. She dumped him soon after. "It's not like there's anything really to finish," she told him, with exactly the sense of impotent sorrow the circumstances called for.

| | | | | |

After that, every conversation he had with anyone either began with the words "Kieran's back" or else fizzed with the tension of the subject being self-consciously withheld.

Ellen called to say she'd had a sighting too and already taken the opportunity to harangue Kieran's probation officer. "The way they try to protect him, anyone would think *he* was the victim," she said, with bitterness.

Not long after, Vic ran into Justin at the train station and they had a pint at the Farmers Arms. It was, remarkably, the first time they'd drunk alone together and both scanned the bar on entering with a wariness that would have been redundant a few months ago. It was a Monday, pretty quiet, no trouble to be found.

"So he was living it up at the Crown, I hear," Vic said, after sharing news of his own near miss.

"Yes. Ellen was pretty upset." Typical Justin understatement.

Vic no longer thought of Lucas's stepfather as the poor bastard who hadn't signed up for this drama, this *tragedy*, but had come to appreciate that he was one of life's natural carers and caring for Ellen was his calling. What troubled Vic was the suspicion that, in tending to her pain, Justin had subjugated his own. He had no doubt that Justin had felt the loss of Lucas just as they had. They'd been three equal parents.

Three of them and still not enough to protect the boy!

"She says she saw him outside the house yesterday morning, as well," Justin added. The clue was in the "says." She probably *did* see him, but there was just the smallest chance that she hadn't.

"What was he doing?" Vic said, curious.

"Nothing, apparently. Just standing there watching."

Vic glanced down at his pint. God, he drank so quickly these days. He had become one of those middle-aged men he'd secretly admired as a fifteen-year-old, when Danny had taken him to his local boozer. Men who had drunk with a no-nonsense suction Vic aspired to emulate one day. Well, here he was, emulating. "That's a thing, isn't it? Revisiting the scene of the crime—or in this case the locations linked to the victim. I can imagine getting something out of that psychologically."

"Has he turned up at yours?" Justin asked.

"Not that I'm aware of, but he certainly knows where to find me if he has the urge. He was over often enough back in the day." Vic gave a bleak chuckle. "Talking like Ice Cube, telling the others about the strap he was going to get."

"Strap?"

"Gun. Wonder if he met any real gangsters inside, eh."

Justin's guilty smirk made Vic see how unused he was to joking in this way. Not about Kieran. "The thing is, should we be worried he might be planning some sort of revenge?"

The thought had crossed Vic's mind, of course. He'd known from Ellen that a limited selection of newspapers was available to the Danstone residents, but had assumed any reference to a current inmate's crime would be redacted. Besides, the worst of it had been online and free access to the internet was definitely not part of Her Majesty's offering. He'd also assumed that the first thing ex-cons did when freed was to google themselves. Pump themselves full of the accumulated hatred of those they'd strewn in their wake — and those who'd just piled on for the hell of it. Well, Kieran must have had more reading material than most.

"I don't think he'd risk getting into any trouble, at least not during his supervision," he told Justin.

"Ellen's talking about wanting to move, but I think, why the hell should we? We lived here long before he came along." Justin took a swallow of lager. "I'm not sure what the alternative is, though. I get the feeling she wants me to go round there and threaten him." He gave Vic a wry half smile. "Maybe I should take Freya's old rounders bat with me?"

"I wouldn't go anywhere near him," Vic advised. "He'll have all kinds of social worker types looking out for him right now and they'd be sure to escalate it."

"I wasn't serious." Justin sighed deeply. "To be honest, I'm hoping he'll slink back into his video game hole and Ellen will forget he's even back."

"That's pretty much my best hope, as well," Vic said.

"It doesn't help that he seems to be hanging out with Jade, does it? Did Ellen tell you that?"

"No, but if he is then it's definitely not going to help his cause." Deciding not to mention the love letters sent to Jade from the clink, Vic eyed his companion's empty glass. "Fancy another?"

"No, I'd better get back," Justin said.

See if Ellen might be in the mood to forgive, Vic thought. Maybe they could watch the pigs fly past the window together.

He had two more pints on his own and then walked home. Having begun the evening in a comfortably neutral mood, he now felt his spirits decline with every step. Perhaps Ellen was right and removing themselves from the area was the only solution here. Because the idea that that feckless wastrel was free to enjoy all of the places—and people—Lucas once had, but never would again, was diabolical. And what if this connection with Jade continued? Deepened into something serious, with ghastly mini Kierans tearing around the neighborhood?

He expected to feel better in the morning, but the malaise was still there and he called in sick, spending the day on the sofa drinking and lamenting. Ulcerating. Looking through the few photos and drawings he had from Lucas's childhood (Ellen kept most of them at Tanglewood Road), he came across a printout of the impact statement he'd read out at Kieran's sentencing. He'd forgotten those statements were edited by the court, to remove biases—you couldn't start ranting vitriol at the killer or speculating on alternative outcomes, you could only say how you had been impacted—and the sentiment that had always felt the most profound had never actually been read out:

Had the roles been reversed that night, Lucas would have rescued his friend. He would have dived back in, over and over, he would have stood in the road and flagged down cars, he would have done everything in his power to save that life.

Reading it again, it had never been clearer to Vic that the universe had taken the wrong boy that night. It had failed every one of them.

Which was when, just at the right moment—or was it the *wrong* moment?—Ellen came at him with her plan.

Vic

NOW

THE DAY AFTER THE scene at Danny's client's weird green house, Ellen phones Vic, asking to meet again.

Well, at least the agony isn't drawn out.

It is Tuesday evening and he's in the spare bedroom, finishing constructing the baby furniture that came flat-packed from John Lewis at the weekend (Li came through, after all). There is a painted white cot and a matching changing unit, a nursing chair with supportive cushions patterned with pineapples. All the things he and Ellen lacked when Lucas was born. He remembers only a Moses basket by their bed and towers of nappies stored in a cardboard box, feels a lurch of remorse. Did they fail Lucas with the start they gave him? They were unprepared, low-spirited, and, within months, divided. Was there enough laughter in that tiny flat?

India is having a snooze on the sofa. When he last checked on her, her bare feet were poking out from beneath a fur throw. She has neat feet, with smooth heels and pale unvarnished toenails.

"Can you come here?" Ellen says in his ear.

But he no longer likes going to her house. The moment he sets foot inside he feels his breath shorten at the thought of that empty bedroom above his head. The urge to hare upstairs and fling open his son's door is no less strong now that Ellen has finally redecorated. Not for her the creation of a shrine—her sacred place is internal, of the soul, as if she and Lucas were twins, not mother and son.

"I can't keep coming to Beckenham. You need to come here. Call me when you arrive and we'll talk downstairs."

Because she won't come up, of course.

She arrives forty-five minutes later, dressed, as usual, in black. They sit together on the backless beam that passes for seating in the lobby. It's tipping it down outside and rainwater from her umbrella puddles at their feet.

"I went to see Danny yesterday," she begins. Her lipstick is flame red and clearly an excellent match for her mood.

"I know, he called me." Vic sinks his front teeth into his lip. He honestly doesn't know if he has the strength for another clash. His upper body aches from the DIY. "Did you get the information you wanted?"

"No. The opposite. He acted like he didn't know what the hell I was on about."

"Like we always said we would." But Vic is nervous beneath his affability and knows she will smell it.

"But there's really no need now, is there? Since we know Kieran's alive?" She eyes him with scorn. On her lap, her hands are balled tight, the knuckles sharp and white. "Of course, at the time I thought Danny was just playing dumb, in case I'd dreamed the whole thing up. But when I played it back, I could tell it wasn't that at all."

"Played it back?" He frowns. "You mean you recorded your

conversation with Danny? You can't go around doing that without people's consent."

"Can't you?" She shrugs, as if to say, *Whatever. It's hardly the worst crime being discussed here.* (This is true.) "Don't worry, I've deleted it now. Not that he said anything that could possibly incriminate him or anyone else."

Playing for time, Vic scans her slim-fitting coat for phone-shaped lumps. "Are you recording us now?"

"No. You can check if you like." She unzips her handbag, plucks out her two phones and lights the screens to show him. "My point is, when I listened again, I could tell he wasn't faking. He genuinely didn't know what I was talking about."

There is a silence. Vic knows from the way her eyes are moving that she is calculating what he might admit freely and what she is going to have to forcibly extract.

"Because you didn't ever arrange to have him killed, did you, Vic? You lied to me the other day about Danny saying it was too late to stop. You didn't ask him in the first place."

Vic's heart is a pitched bass drum pedaled by a maniac. Still, he does not speak. What is he so scared of? Not Ellen per se, but the power of her hatred of Kieran. The fact that it is escalating when it should be waning.

"What did you say to him, Vic? If that mad bitch of an ex of mine ever says anything about professional criminals being hired to take out Kieran Watts, just deny it, yeah? Just laugh it off."

"It wasn't like that," he says, feeling heat creep up his collarbone onto his neck.

She gives a twisted little laugh. "He was worried we'd got ourselves mixed up with Albanians! Which is exactly what I thought myself, strangely enough. So what happened to the money? Did you keep it for yourself? Use it for this?" She gestures to the space around them, the salvaged industrial chic that doesn't come cheap.

"For fuck's sake, I can pay my own rent," Vic says.

"What then? You used it for the business?"

He swallows. This is the part she obviously hasn't guessed. How he wishes he could just say yes—and there is a moment when he thinks he actually might. But there is a difference between lying to protect her and outright gaslighting her. She called him out on that last time, didn't she?

"I gave it to him," he says, quietly.

"Who, Danny? You mean he just kept it?" The crisscross of frown lines on her forehead deepens above disbelieving eyes.

"No, not Danny." He pauses. "Kieran."

She flushes the pink of a camellia. He can feel the heat of her anguish coming off her. "You gave it to *him*? You mean when you told him about the nonexistent hit, you paid him off while you were at it?"

Vic closes his eyes. "Basically, yes."

"Why the hell would you do that?"

How many times has he rehearsed this? Whichever way he phrases it, it won't convince her. So little ever has, even before they lost Lucas. "I did what I thought would suit all of us. *You*, first of all. You were happy thinking he was getting a bullet through his skull. You didn't need to actually see bits of his brain on the roadside to believe it." Glancing, he sees she is unruffled by the violence of the image. "And *he* had a chance to make a start somewhere else, out of our sight, which by the way he wouldn't have done if I hadn't managed to convince him he was in serious danger. And he couldn't possibly have done it without a pile of cash to help him on his way."

"I can't believe you're twisting this to make it sound like you did the right thing," Ellen says, revulsion on her face. "You paid our son's killer. You *rewarded* him."

"I fucking did *not* reward him!" Vic is more explosive than he intended to be and, to his shame, she cringes from him. But he must defend himself, he must, finally, stand up to her. "I paid him to get out of our lives and that's what he did. *You* might not think that was the right thing to do, but *I* did, and I'm sick of you behaving as if your opinion is the only one that counts."

He stops at the sight of her eyes leaking tears. He's not so naive as to believe she's crying because he is challenging her; she's crying because he betrayed her. He was the one person she trusted to share her faith in avenging Lucas's death and now it turns out those brave and dangerous decisions they made were never joint, after all, but hers alone. And, thanks to his cowardice, never set in motion.

The register of her voice drops very low. "Why didn't you just tell me at the time you didn't want to do it?"

"Because I wanted to stop you from doing it on your own. You were completely out of your depth, talking about hiring killers on the dark web. It wasn't that long since your dad died, you were in a bad way. I wanted to help you. I still do."

She gives a derisive little jeer. "You haven't helped me. You've deceived me. You stole from me and then you lied to me."

The accusations wound, of course they do, but he holds his nerve. "Again, that's your perspective. I'm an unfeeling twat who did the wrong thing. But that is not *my* perspective. *I* thought I was doing the right thing by all of us."

Her fingers are playing with the chain of her handbag. As long as he can remember she's used this bag; the links of its chain are her worry beads. "You paid him the whole lot, did you?"

"Yes."

"That was my inheritance from my dad. Kieran Watts was the last person on the planet he would have wanted that money to go to."

"I know. But he would have wanted his only daughter sent to jail even less. For life, Ellen. You'd have got far longer than Kieran did, did you ever think about that? It was premeditation." He exhales his next breath in an audible blast. Now that he has confessed, he longs to escape her, to get up, slam his palm against the button for the lift, shoot up to his new life with India and the baby furniture. But the questions keep coming, as he's always known they would, once the genie was out of the bottle.

"How did you do it? I don't understand how you convinced the police that you didn't see him that day when you obviously did. How did your alibi check out?"

"I *didn't* see him that day," Vic says. "I'm not stupid. I planned it all out."

She touches him then, for the first time since her arrival, using her hand to turn his face towards hers and bring him so close he can see the tiny broken veins in that camellia flush. He can smell the rain on her hair.

"Tell me the whole thing, Vic. You owe me that much."

Vic

THEN

I WANT TO DEAL with Kieran once and for all. I want him gone for good. Those were her words: a proposal to murder a man. And she meant it.

Retribution was the key motive, of course. Measure for measure. But there was also a secondary one, a catalyst. Kieran had made an overture to Freya and, in Ellen's mind, her younger child was in as grave a danger as her elder one had been. She wanted to act immediately and had unearthed God knew what dodgy outfits on the dark web, but Vic proposed involving Danny, which won himself some breathing space to consider his options.

Which were *what*?

Okay, he could refuse point blank to be involved in her scheme, but that ran the risk of her going ahead solo, getting caught, and condemning herself and her family to a future of abject misery—not to mention implicating *him* in her activities regardless.

He could appeal to Justin—by anyone's standards the last person who deserved to be deceived—but that smacked of some

Victorian plot in which men conspired to have women confined to asylums.

Or he could use his tried-and-tested tactic of calling her bluff. Go along with her scheme and give her the time to talk herself out of it, to wake up one morning and see this wasn't what middle-aged, middle-class mothers from Beckenham did when angered or threatened or grieving. (*I'm going to get one of those burner phones . . .* Like this was *Breaking Bad,* for Christ's sake.)

And if she didn't, well, Vic was just going to have to keep on pretending while he thought of a solution.

| | | | | | |

It was easy enough to feed her information, cryptically, quasi-gangster-style. And he had time: there were two months between her first talk of a contract killing and Kieran's supervision period elapsing. Not that it mattered to her whether he was bumped off before then, but it certainly did to Vic. Because the alternative plan taking shape in his mind involved Kieran bolting and this could only be done if he was completely free, otherwise he risked being pursued and sent back inside—and he wasn't going to do *that,* no matter how badly Vic frightened him.

The Tuesday after the three months had elapsed and the day before the date he'd supplied to Ellen for the killing, Vic ambushed Kieran on his morning run. He'd followed him several times by then and knew he always ran in South Norwood Country Park, setting off from Prisca's house at 7 a.m. and entering the park from Albert Road. He'd scoped out a good spot, an overgrown clearing off the main path and opposite the visitor center, with a half-hidden disused electric station just beyond.

He intercepted Kieran on the path at 7:10 a.m. "I need to talk to you."

"What the fuck?" Kieran backed away a few steps, breathing heavily. His fair skin was stained a rich pink.

"Come in here. I don't want anyone to see us," Vic said, and Kieran took a few wary paces after him into the clearing. "Listen to me. You need to get out of town."

"Piss off, I live here," Kieran protested.

"No, I mean it. This isn't a threat, it's a warning."

"What warning?" Then, as if interrupting his own train of thought: "Wait, is this about Jade?"

"Jade? No." Vic didn't have time for red herrings. "Someone's after you. I'm serious, Kieran. They want you gone, as in six feet under."

Kieran was breathing normally already, must've been pretty fit to recover so quickly. He cast a glance at the sign on the door of the electric station: "Danger of Death." "How do you know?"

"We saw something in the Lock Up Longer forum—you know about that, I assume?"

Kieran's eyes narrowed.

"There was a death threat against you that was flagged, and it looked pretty credible to me. *After next week, he'll have checked out for good*, that was the wording and the thread led to some pretty unnerving places. They've been watching you, Kieran. They know your address, they know where you work. I seriously think you should get yourself into hiding."

Kieran digested this. His gaze was level, even brave, but fear showed in the chewing motion on the inside of his cheek. "Send me a screenshot. I'll show the police."

"I can't. By the time our tech people tried to trace it, it'd been deleted. Whoever it is seems to know how to cover their tracks." Vic kept this vague, knowing that to fake technological know-how would be to give himself away—Kieran had aced his computer science A-level, if he remembered, and been a champion gamer. Better to present himself as the obsolete middle-aged geezer he actually was. "Go, Kieran. I'm serious. I'll make sure you've got the cash you need to make a new start."

Undeterred by the other man's obvious doubt, Vic outlined the plan. Kieran would come back to the same place the next morning and he'd find a bag with cash, a dark anorak, a baseball cap. "Wear the cap. Keep your head down. Don't bring anything, except maybe your passport. Prisca won't notice that's missing, will she?"

"I haven't got a passport," Kieran said.

"Okay. You obviously know the quickest way from here to Elmers End station? Good. Don't talk to anyone. Don't show your face to any cameras. It'll be rush hour so you should be able to hide in the crowd. Go to Euston or King's Cross and get yourself as far away as you can. Glasgow, Aberdeen, somewhere like that."

"Scotland?" Kieran's face clouded, as if suddenly seeing he'd been cornered by a fantasist. "*Then* what would I do?"

"Change your name. Use the cash to sort out a flat. Think of it as witness protection."

"How much cash are we talking?" Kieran asked.

"Fifteen thousand."

"What the fuck?" Amazed, Kieran began pulling a tuft of hair on his crown, as if teasing it straight, an old habit Vic had forgotten he had. "How do I know this isn't a scam?"

"You don't." Vic had anticipated that he might suspect a bluff, that this was a ruse to guarantee his presence so a killer could get the job done in this place of perfect tranquility. "You have to take my word for it."

"Yeah, but why would *you* want to help me?"

As he sensed the beginnings of a conversion, Vic felt his pulse accelerate. "Because this isn't right. Whoever these crazies are, killing someone is not the solution. It never is."

There was a moment of silent accord. "What am I meant to do today then?" Kieran said.

"Just carry on like you normally would. Go to work, go home, have dinner. Whatever you already have planned. But don't say a word about this, not even to Prisca. You'll need to be reported missing and she's the obvious person to do that." Vic remembered that reference to Jade. "Don't trust anyone from your old life, understand? If you want to stay safe long term, you have to cut off from everyone you know. Don't be tempted to think the problem's gone away. These people who hate you will know who you've been close to."

"I need to think about this," Kieran said.

"Think about it, then do it. It's the only way you're going to survive. So, same time tomorrow, got it? The bag will be behind this building under a bit of tarpaulin." He showed Kieran the exact spot. They were close enough to touch. Either could attack the other in this unseen place, leave him for dead.

As they drew apart again a look passed between them then that Vic couldn't begin to process in the moment but would think of often afterwards with a feeling of revulsion. Some sort of mutual pleading. Understanding, if not quite apology. Trust. Because Vic had to trust Kieran too. Trust that he wouldn't decide to take the money and remain exactly where he was. Or, worse, take the money to the police.

He gestured for him to go and watched him sprint off down the main path, gravel crunching underfoot, the man who had no passport. The man whose tethers to the judicial system had only in the last few days been loosened for the first time since the night in

December 2014 when he'd driven his car into a freezing reservoir and left his friend there to die.

| | | | | | |

Scotland, he'd said, and that was where Vic pictured him when he returned in the late evening to stow a waterproof backpack with Ellen's fifteen thousand pounds, along with the outer garments he'd promised. The clothes were oversize, which would help mask the fugitive's identity if anyone decided to check CCTV footage from the local streets and train stations.

If he did as Vic prayed. *If* he took the money and ran.

Vic didn't know for sure until, forty-eight hours later, he judged it safe to return. He felt woozy with relief to find the bag gone. In its place, under the tarpaulin, lay a sheet of paper with the scrawled message:

I WILL PAY YOU BACK

"Don't," he said under his breath. "It doesn't matter."

He stood in the clearing for ten minutes or so, breathing the air, exorcizing himself of Kieran Watts. He honestly never expected to see him again.

And, if the rest of his own life was to proceed along an even vaguely peaceful course, Ellen absolutely, categorically, must not be allowed to either.

Vic

NOW

ELLEN IS AGHAST. THOUGH her fingers have stopped playing with the bag chain, her feet fidget and the umbrella gets kicked over, lying sopping and ignored on the lobby floor. In the street outside, headlights streak by.

"You mean you left a bag with all that cash in a public place? What if an engineer came and found it?"

"It was completely hidden. And, anyway, the station looked abandoned." Vic's tone is defensive. Even in his hour of discovery, he feels a certain pride in the technicalities of his plan. He'd spent most of his waking—and working—hours combing it for loose strands. He'd even transported the bag meant for Kieran inside a second identical one, so that—in case of a camera he'd failed to note—he could walk out of that park looking exactly as he did when he walked in.

"You were lucky the police didn't decide to launch a manhunt and search the park," Ellen says. "They might have found his note before you did."

"It was a risk. It paid off," Vic says.

"It did *not* pay off!" Her voice rises, shrill enough to make him wince. "How can you say that? I wanted him dead and I thought you did as well!"

The lobby is empty, but Vic can't help glancing around. Anyone could have come out of the lift or in through the main doors and heard what she just said. "Let's keep our voices down." He's had enough of this, he really has. He visualizes his pregnant girlfriend upstairs—she'll be awake from her nap and wondering where he is—but try as he might, he can't invest enough power in the image to conquer the one in front of him.

"Sorry." Ellen seems to notice for the first time where she is. "Does India know any of this?"

"No, she wasn't on the scene then."

"What about other girlfriends?"

Vic scoffs. "Funnily enough, it's not something you tend to introduce into the conversation. 'Me and my ex had this revenge fantasy—wanna hear how crazy it got?' "

"Revenge fantasy." She repeats the words with distaste. "So everything I thought, everything that made it possible to carry on, it wasn't actually true. You've made me keep a secret that didn't actually exist. You've wrecked my life."

Vic looks narrowly at her. "No, Ellen, I've *saved* your life—and I've saved his, as well." He draws air deep into his lungs, like a man about to tombstone from a sea cliff. "You know what? Maybe Kieran deserves a bit of consideration here. A tiny shred of sympathy. Maybe it's time for us to accept that he couldn't do anything to help that night."

"*What?*"

He feels the electrification of her shock. She hasn't expected them to rove into this territory, and he didn't either when he came down to meet her. But, if he's formed any conclusion these last few years, it is that she needs to hear this from someone—from him—just once. "Think how his mind might've worked down there. It's pitch black, icy cold, he's thrown forward, not sure which way is up, and he's badly injured and in pain. He's a teenage deadbeat, not a trained SAS operative, there would have been a survival instinct, literally nothing more. Get out of the car, get out of the water, get onto dry land. It was a miracle he got himself to safety. Easily the most likely outcome was that they were both going to die down there."

"*Don't.*" Ellen puts her hands to her ears, palms flat. "Change your mind about everything else, but not about that night. I can't bear it." She drops her hands and gives her head a little shake, as if ridding it of the words he's forced her to consume. "If he could get himself out of the car, he could have got Lucas out with him. He chose not to, Vic. He *chose* not to."

Vic does not argue. She may be right, she may be wrong, but either way he is done. "Just so you know, I'll pay you back the money. I always intended to, the moment you found out."

"For God's sake, this isn't about the money, it's about justice, justice for Lucas." She makes a desperate gesture to the doors, the world beyond, as if their son is out there somewhere, judging their efforts. "I can never forgive you for this, Vic. Never."

She's on her feet, gathering her bag and brolly, buttoning her coat. Looking down at him with a blend of martyrdom and fury. "And don't get me wrong, I *do* want my money back. I want it as soon as possible. In cash."

| | | | | |

The lift delivers him to the fifteenth floor with mute efficiency. The thought of screwing together the last piece of furniture—a chest of drawers, he's left the hardest till last—makes him want to pluck his own eyes out.

In the flat, some crap meditative music is playing, all harp strings and—what is it called?—glockenspiel. He craves something with screaming metal guitars, music to throw TVs through the windows to. The immersion heater is whining, which means India is in the shower. He pours himself a Coke, though he'd prefer a beer. But since launching Common or Gordon, he has a strict rule for himself: no stock at home. He can't risk plunging back into the near alcoholism of the years directly after Lucas's death.

Taking his glass with him, he slides open the balcony door. The downpour has ceased, but the air is still greasy with drizzle. He steps out and pulls the door shut behind him. They are mean with space, these developers, and you couldn't swing a cat out here. He hasn't put on a coat and his skin begins to stiffen with cold. The Coke is flat but he gulps it anyway. He imagines throwing his glass—it could kill someone from this height. What if Ellen's still down there and it hit *her*?

He resents her for putting him in this mood and yet, come on, did he *really* think he was going to get away with it? For*ever*? She has every right to despise him for his deception, and nothing in the way she's behaved in the past suggested she would pass up that right.

Presently, the door grinds open behind him. India, dressed in a pink toweling robe, her hair damp and tangled. "What are you doing out here? It's freezing."

"I needed some air," Vic mutters.

"Why? What did she say?"

"Nothing. Go back in."

She frowns. "You're scaring me, Vic."

He loses his cool. "I said, go back in. It's nothing to do with you, for fuck's sake!"

He doesn't wait to see the hurt in her face, but pivots back to face the night. The brisk crack of the door closing says it all. Some women would lock it for good measure, leave him out here to teach him a lesson, but he knows the thought wouldn't occur to India.

He's unaware of how long he stands out there, but when he finally goes back in, she is cooking dinner. The music is off, TV on, and the room smells of garlic and tomato and basil.

"Sorry," he says.

She doesn't turn, but continues to prod a pan of boiling vegetables with a utensil too short for the job. "I don't appreciate being barked at like that," she says.

"I know. Mind you don't scald yourself there."

She puts the utensil aside. "What's going on, Vic? You've been weird ever since I told you about the baby."

Ah, of course. Thanks to the dreadful coincidence of Ellen's news arriving at the same time as hers, she's naturally made the connection to her own.

"I've always been weird," he says, mustering a laugh. "You just didn't notice before." There is a thawing sensation in his muscles and he feels his mood warm along with it. "Chances are the baby will be too. Sorry about that."

She smiles. She doesn't hold grudges, India (not like you know who). In her worldview an apology is a gift to be accepted, not a springboard for further recrimination. She adjusts the heat under her pans and goes over to check he's locked the balcony doors.

"Should we move?" she says.

"What? Why?"

"Because we're having a baby and I don't want it to fall from a fifteenth-floor balcony."

There is a nightmarish moment when it could be Ellen

speaking to him. *Not that swing, Vic. Watch him on the steps, Vic. Careful, Vic!*

He gropes his way back to reality. "Plenty of kids live in high-rise flats," he says. "We've talked about this: we'll childproof the doors and windows to within an inch of their lives. She'll love bringing her friends up in the lift." By unspoken consent, they always refer to the baby as female. "When I was a boy I lived in a bungalow, so going in a lift was like Thunder Mountain to me."

India giggles. "I suppose she might like the views. She could stick stars on her bedroom window."

"She won't need to. She'll have the sky."

"Aw," India says, moving towards him. Her breath is soft. Her mind is reasonable. He is forgiven.

Which means he can stop worrying about her and go back to worrying about Ellen and the money. Where the hell is he going to find fifteen grand? He has no property to mortgage. Every penny of investment funding has been committed to the business—not that he'd ever consider siphoning any off for personal expenses. You don't try for decades to get something off the ground only to sabotage it when you finally succeed.

More troubling still is what Ellen plans to do with the cash if and when he returns it to her. The same thing she tried to do the first time, it would seem.

If so, and if that money were traced back to him, it means he'll remain embroiled in this nightmare whether he likes it or not.

Fuck.

Killing Time (cont)

I suspect that many readers of *Saint or Sinner* may ask themselves the same question I asked Felix Penney when I'd read the finished manuscript: doesn't some of the content—notably Ellen's attempt to arrange the killing of Kieran Watts in the summer of 2017—expose her to the risk of prosecution for conspiracy to murder?

"There was never a conspiracy to murder," Penney responds. "It was only ever a fantasy."

A criminal barrister I consult confirms the extreme unlikelihood of any charges being brought at this stage. "The Crown doesn't have unlimited funds," she points out. "The police may even choose to interpret Mr. Gordon's feigned cooperation as a form of crime prevention."

Whichever way you look at it, Vic Gordon does appear to be the only one to emerge from this mindboggling plot twist with his honor intact.

Sunday Times magazine, December 2021

Vic

NOW

"VIC GORDON?" REPEATS THE receptionist, with several degrees' less warmth than she's just extended to the fashionably muscled and bearded young man ahead of him. How blissfully untroubled the guy appears as he waits for the lift, whereas Vic, with his knotted shoulders and repeated glances to the street, must look as skittish, as hunted, as he feels.

Before he can state his business, the receptionist's screen has identified him. "You must be here to see Cam? I haven't got your name down, but let me give him a buzz and see how his schedule's looking."

"Actually, it's James I'm hoping to see," Vic says. "James Ratcliffe."

Her fingers pause on the keyboard. The big boss. "Do you have an appointment?"

"Not exactly, but would you mind trying?"

"Of course," she says, with the kind of proper politeness that telegraphs her full confidence of failure.

So urgent are the circumstances that Vic hasn't given much thought to what he will do if Ratcliffe declines to see him. Slink away and pick up his thinking cap from the dusty South London streets where he'd left it, he supposes. He can feel spasms above his left eyebrow and hopes they are not visible.

After a brief phone exchange, the receptionist turns back to him with new respect. "James will be down in a few minutes. Take a seat, Vic."

The seating in the offices of Green Shoots is spongy-looking and pouf-style, too low to get back up from easily, Vic judges (God, he's old), and so he remains standing. The offices upstairs are, he knows, just like those start-ups you see photographed in the *Standard*—an old rickshaw repurposed as a coffee stand; a tubular slide linking the floors (again, hard to get up from), a bank of retro arcade games—nicely ironic given all the tech services and products the firm invests in. The address is a ten-minute walk from Shad Thames, and though he didn't say it to Ellen when they stood on St Saviour's footbridge craning for a glimpse of The Heights, Vic knew exactly how Kieran Watts had come to land in this part of town: James Ratcliffe.

Of course, Ellen had already discovered the great man for herself by then and would meet him face-to-face soon after. Vic is not proud that he swore at her when she tried to tell him about the encounter (*For fuck's sake, Ellen, I don't want to hear it!*). As for the one element she *has* managed to share—Ratcliffe telling her about the tip-off to Kieran, now revealed to have been made by her own coconspirator—well, that's only the start of the deductions she might make. The intelligence she might put to use.

They can't go on like this.

He is watching the lift doors when the man himself approaches in his peripheral vision, having taken the stairs. Dressed in black jeans and a daffodil-yellow button-down shirt, he is lithe, with scarcely a spare ounce at the waistline, despite being over a decade older than Vic.

"Vic!" Ratcliffe offers his hand. Loose on his wrist is some vintage watch Vic couldn't begin to identify but which no doubt cost more than his own van. "Good of you to come in." He is absurdly at ease. Really, it's as if he's arranged this meeting, not been surprised by it, which is helpful because Vic already knows he is not going to be able to do what he's come here to do. Which is to ask for the money. No, what presented itself as an ingenious solution during last night's attack of insomnia now strikes him as embarrassingly naive. How could Ratcliffe *not* link such a request to the renewed hostilities between Ellen and Kieran? And yet . . . he *is* making time to see Vic. Perhaps he's come up with a fix of his own to their Ellen problem.

Oh, God. Vic feels a deep and grinding shame as he remembers their last parting. *I can never forgive you for this. Never.*

"Thanks for sparing the time," he says, summoning a smile.

"Not at all. I had a feeling you might be in touch," Ratcliffe says. "Let's walk up to the river, shall we? Get some air."

The short walk takes them past Tanner Street Park and under the railway bridge up Tower Bridge Road, and they talk only of what passes before their eyes: the traffic, the road works, the pubs and the many products they serve that aren't but absolutely should be brewed by Common or Gordon. Cutting down Queen Elizabeth Street, they pause at a beautifully maintained historic building where Ratcliffe says he lives in the penthouse apartment. An interesting intimacy, Vic thinks—or just a crass display of wealth? For a moment, he thinks he is going to be invited in, but, no, Ratcliffe begins moving again and presently they are turning up Shad Thames and past the entrance to Jacob's Wharf, where Ellen's client lives, and from whose window she first saw Kieran on his roof terrace.

He can only hope Ellen is not prowling the neighborhood this morning, tracking Kieran, plotting logistics. If she really does still want him dead and can't get someone else to do it, will she . . . will she try to do it herself?

They reach the river. The tide is high, the currents making harlequin patterns of silver and gold, and the beauty of it fills Vic with sudden optimism. The Thames, the City with its commanding new towers, the thousands of people bustling back and forth, up and down, the billions of pounds they earn and spend: the scale of it all makes his own troubles less significant, less disastrous.

"Where shall we start?" Ratcliffe says, affably. "With Ellen, I'm guessing?"

"Yes, I gather you've met her," Vic says. "What did she say to you?"

Ratcliffe eyes him with mild surprise. *That's why you're here?* "She didn't tell you herself?"

No point pretending, Vic thinks. "We're not exactly bosom buddies right now. Nothing major." (Well, maybe he'll pretend a *bit*.)

"Ah." There's a flicker of sympathy behind those costly looking frames. "She's found out you have a separate connection to me?"

"No, not that." Nor would she consider it separate, Vic thinks. Just as he did not. There were no coincidences in this sordid little circle of theirs. "I just meant we don't see eye to eye on a lot these days."

"That's a shame," Ratcliffe says, with a tolerance honed, no doubt, over decades of difficult conversations. "I'll level with you, Vic. I'm concerned about her. When we talked, she didn't strike me as someone who will listen to reason, even after all this time."

"It's not that long," Vic says. "Not to her." It feels like a betrayal, that "her." He should have said "us"—*It's not that long to us.* Because it is not. Five years ago, Lucas was still alive. He steadies himself, tries to focus. "I wondered, maybe, could Kieran be persuaded to move on?"

"You mean move out of his apartment? Out of London?" Ratcliffe pulls a doubtful face. "You can't get much more discreet than the top floor of The Heights. That's why we chose it." He sighs, his eyebrows lifting. "You know, there must be only a handful of flats with a view of his terrace and she happened to be in one of them."

"It's unfortunate," Vic agrees, as if he hasn't had this thought a thousand times already.

A Thames Clipper sails towards Tower Bridge and he thinks suddenly of that trip to the river when Lucas was a baby. Ellen marching an empty buggy across Westminster Bridge, Lucas reaching out to try to touch the clock face of Big Ben with his fingers. He remembers suddenly what he said to his baby boy: "Look, it's as big as the moon!" And Lucas mimicked his excitement, his little body going rigid.

Pain spreads inside him as if from a ruptured organ and it is all he can do to stop himself from doubling over.

As if aware that something terrible and internal is taking place, Ratcliffe gives him a moment before going on. "To answer your question, no, I don't think he can be persuaded to move, and I don't think it would help, even if he did. There's a link with me now, isn't there? Your ex-wife can get to him now as long as she can get to me."

Vic doesn't bother correcting him on the wife. "Leave Ellen to me," he says firmly. "I'll keep an eye on her. She won't get to either of you."

As Ratcliffe sizes him up, Vic gets the distinct sense that his strength of conviction compares unfavorably with that previously observed of Ellen. Hating Kieran is a form of religious extremism to Ellen. Her passion is matchless. "Who's holding the fort this morning, Vic?"

He is slightly thrown by this. "George. I'll be in the taproom later."

"But you have an hour or so?"

"Yes."

"Good. Then you know what I think we should do? Go and see Sam."

"Sam?"

"Kieran. I know he's in—I spoke to him earlier. Let's talk this through, the three of us. Make sure we're all on the same page."

Inside Vic's chest, his heart thrashes in protest. "I'm not sure I'm ready for that," he says, and Ratcliffe surprises him by giving his arm a reassuring squeeze.

"It will be fine, trust me. And it's long overdue. On his part, I mean. I know he's wanted to reach out to you for a long time."

Vic feels snookered. He's just said his work is being covered by George and, in any case, if a man as important and powerful as Ratcliffe is willing to make the time, *he* has no excuse. Except . . . except he is Lucas's father, and Kieran is Lucas's killer. He doesn't want to be "on the same page" as him. He doesn't want to be "reached out" to.

As Ratcliffe taps out a message on his phone, Vic sees what must have taken place half an hour ago when he checked in with the Green Shoots receptionist. Ratcliffe alerted Kieran at once and a strategy was agreed: Ratcliffe would warm Vic up and then bring him on over.

It is a fait accompli.

He casts a last look over the river wall at the shifting metallic waters and feels his earlier optimism vanish. He is about to see Kieran for the first time since that morning in the woods, when he promised him a way out—on the naive understanding that there could be no way back. Well, *this* doesn't feel much like no way back, does it?

Ratcliffe pockets his phone and extends an arm eastward. "Shall we?"

Vic

THEN

IN THE LAST WEEK of 2018, almost eighteen months after Kieran took Vic's offer and fled, and over a year since Vic took a call from a probation officer named Dina about the runaway being safely accounted for in a location far from South London, Vic received an interesting email.

It was from an investor he'd drawn a blank with when he'd pitched Common or Gordon to him years ago, Cam Goodfellow. He said he'd been watching the craft beer sector carefully in the years since their meeting and that quirky, ironic brand names had been proving increasingly marketable. Common or Gordon had been a bit of an earworm for him ("never not a good sign") and if Vic was still looking for investment, he was keen to have another chat.

Vic googled Goodfellow to remind himself of his company. He'd been in the Lifestyle department, that was right, but had since moved across to work with the director of Mobility, a man whose specialism was investing in entrepreneurs from disadvantaged backgrounds, particularly projects with an ethical or ecological flavor.

Vic couldn't see how *he* fell within this new remit, but maybe these departmental labels operated with a certain fluidity—and it wasn't as if he was in any way *privileged* (other than being white and male, of course, which, if he was allowed to say, hadn't always felt so much of a bonus). In any case, he wasn't about to turn down what might be his last chance to get Common or Gordon bottled and down the throats of a thirsty nation.

He met Cam in his office near Tanner Street Park, where the young and affluent played tennis and slurped flat whites in the shadow of the Shard. A little piece of the East Village in South London. Vic's spiritual home.

The meeting was successful—it seemed to Vic that Cam had already made up his mind, with or without Vic's hastily tacked-on ideas about compressed wood pulp packaging and donations to well builders in Africa—and was followed by a brief introduction to the director, who expressed his pleasure in bringing Vic "into the family."

"This is so exciting," Vic said, as they returned him to the lift via the staff coffee kiosk, which was a customized vintage rickshaw. Once inside the lift, he hardly recognized his own flushed and jubilant face in the mirrored panel. He took his coffee to the park, where he sat on the grass, alone but finally a part of the tribe he'd long ago identified as his own.

But, come on. The whole thing was too good to be true—any fool could see that.

| | | | | | |

By the time the papers arrived for his signature, he had dug a little deeper. Cam Goodfellow was not quite thirty, an Instagrammer with little traditional media to his name, and tagged to within an inch of his life as he worked and played with a millennial vengeance. Vic gazed quickly at the images of the genetically blessed young man gallivanting in Costa Rican eco lodges with a tanned and teeth-baring girlfriend and posse of identikit chums.

The boss was older, his history less curated, and there were years of local press coverage on his visits to schools, community centers, and prisons, where he'd spoken inspirationally about opportunity and ambition. He'd made countless appearances at corporate events and political summits, attending receptions and having his photo taken with government ministers, at all times emphasizing his outreach philosophy.

This was summarized to stirring effect on the company website:

> It's not talent that is the prerogative of the wealthy, but ac-
> cess. Wherever I find talent, I'll create access, regardless of a
> person's background or social standing. Past mistakes do not
> make a person's brain wave ineligible; on the contrary, they
> make it remarkable.

In the last few months, he had been mentioned in the financial press in relation to one particular investment from which he had profited with spectacular speed. Within just a year of investing in one of his disadvantaged young talents, he'd brokered the sale of the IP and early development work to one of the tech giants in a multimillion-pound deal. It was just the sort of news story Vic might have mentioned to Ellen back in the day, sharing a grumble about some undeserving scally getting the nod from senior investors at the expense of someone like him.

But he didn't mention it now. He didn't want to get anywhere near telling Ellen or anyone connected with her about the source of his unexpected investment offer. The money he was going to take.

Blood money, he was quite clear about that.

Because the phrase "past mistakes" had leapt out at him, leading him via a series of clicks to an article in *Inside Time*, the newspaper for prisoners, in which Kieran's name had been listed among those who'd attended a talk by this illustrious speaker. Kieran, who had an A* computer science A-level under his belt and who had continued to hone his IT skills inside, now had an idea for a mental health app and had many questions for the visiting VIP about how it might be developed.

It was the only time their two names were linked in the press. After that, a new name cropped up alongside the investor's, Sam Harding, and *his* app had a name: Moodsmart. Early meetings with several European national health services had gone very promisingly, and then there was that lucrative deal with Saurus.

In all the coverage, Vic couldn't find a single picture of Sam Harding, but there were plenty of the investor, who was, of course, James Ratcliffe, cofounder of Green Shoots and head of its award-winning Mobility unit.

I'll pay you back, Kieran's note had said, and Vic had replayed the line many times over the years. It could so easily be made to sound menacing if you knew the context. *Pay you back* for the misery they had subjected him to with Lock Up Longer, for instance. The army of haters they'd marshaled.

Pay you back for having forced him to leave behind Jade and Prisca and who knew which other loved ones.

But it turned out he'd meant the money, after all.

Vic never questioned Cam Goodfellow directly about the timing of his renewal of interest in Common or Gordon. He didn't need to.

Of course it was at Ratcliffe's and Kieran's behest. *Of course* it was Kieran's cash (and massively in excess of what he owed, at that). *Of course* it represented Kieran's attempt to buy atonement for his sin.

Kieran Watts was Magwitch to Vic's Pip—as perverse a pairing as the original ever was. And the moment Vic signed the contract, he signed away any right to challenge his investors' motives.

Only his own.

| | | | | |

He came out of the trap like a champion greyhound. Rented a huge unit in East Croydon and watched it shrink as he installed the kit he'd been mentally acquiring for years: the kettles and tanks, coolers and refrigeration units; the modest bottling and labeling plant. He hired George as his head brewer and India as general manager and sales support. The plan was for a taproom to open on the premises within nine months.

He had always suspected that the more you had the more you got and this turned out to be quite true. The rent on a two-bedroom flat in Skylark Apartments near East Croydon station was readily negotiated now he was a business owner with the backing of a trendy investment team in Bermondsey. Just the kind of tenant the building's management had hoped to attract. He'd been in there three months when he and India went for dinner to debrief a fantastic meeting with the team at Boxpark, ending up drinking more than was strictly necessary and going back to his place.

Would a woman like her have looked at him twice if he was in his old job, his old flat? He chose to believe that it didn't really matter. As Ellen and Justin liked to say to each other, *We are where we are*.

And so, suddenly, where *he* was was in a cool flat with a much younger woman who expected to live her best life with him, meaning he got to live his best with her.

And the sex. What was it the young'uns said? *I'm not going to lie,* that was it. Well, he wasn't going to lie: the sex was great. And not always as careful as it could have been.

Hence his second family.

His second chance.

Vic

THE ENTRY SYSTEM TO The Heights involves an old-school keypad and code. Inside, when Ratcliffe calls the lift, he has to press the button three times before it lights up and draws a reluctant groan from high in the shaft. These details strike Vic as incongruous; you'd have thought an app-designing whiz kid would want to be in one of those buildings with smart everything. Sleek and silent and operated by fingerprint or iris recognition or whatever.

Still, it's a long way from a foster home in South Norwood. Or a car wreck in a disused reservoir.

"The Heights," he says, in an effort to appear at ease, as nausea creeps through his stomach and up towards his throat. "My building in Croydon has more height than this."

Ratcliffe flashes him an expensive smile. "It's a relative claim. Most of the buildings around here are no higher than six floors. You wait, Vic. When you're up there, you'll feel like you're on top of the world."

Vic doubts this. The lift is one of the smallest he's ever been in and since he and Ratcliffe are about the same height their faces are closer than is comfortable. It would be just his luck if the thing broke and they were trapped together, dependent on Kieran to rescue them.

"The penthouse," he mutters, eyeing the lit button for the top floor. "He's certainly done all right for himself."

Ratcliffe nods, earnest, appreciative, as if Vic has said something exceptional. "I genuinely believe it's possible for everyone to start again. If someone like me linked up with every young person leaving an institute like Danstone, the reoffender rates would plummet. It's about faith, Vic. Doesn't everyone deserve a bit of faith?"

Only if they have an idea you can make money out of, Vic thinks, though Ratcliffe's plea is scarcely different from the one he himself made to Ellen the previous night. (*Maybe Kieran deserves a bit of consideration here* . . . did he really say that to her?) He can't imagine her being won over by this sort of messianic set piece. It's no surprise Ratcliffe didn't bring *her* up here that day.

The lift rocks to a halt and the doors part, but Ratcliffe makes it impossible for Vic to exit without shouldering past him. "Don't they?" he repeats, and Vic knows what he wants. Before they see "Sam," he wants Vic to acknowledge that he is as responsible as Ratcliffe himself for the reinvention of Kieran Watts. That fateful fifteen thousand pounds made him, in his way, Kieran's earliest investor.

"No," he answers. "Not everyone deserves it. Some people should be left with nothing. No future, no luck. Definitely no faith."

"Oh, Vic." With a look of stately resignation, Ratcliffe steps from the lift and Vic tails him onto a carpeted strip of landing. Directly ahead there is a skinny full-height window with a splintered glimpse of Tower Bridge and the City. He is reluctantly impressed.

They approach the door. Just as he prays Kieran won't hear their knock, Ratcliffe produces a key. "Ready?"

Vic wants to throw up as he is steered into the hallway, which is painted the unsettling yellow of bruised skin. The door shuts behind them and he almost expects Ratcliffe to lock it, to incarcerate him in this vaunted lair, but that's ridiculous, Vic is one of his clients—not an important one, like Kieran, but still part of the Green Shoots "family."

He turns instinctively to his left, towards the bland white walls and gray carpeting of the living room. It is a simple, high-ceilinged space, with a wide-screen version of the skyline he glimpsed from the landing, the curved window giving it the feel of a spaceship hovering above the rooftops and preparing to land on the rooftop of Butler's Wharf. What a view! What a place to hide!

Speaking of which, there is neither sight nor sound of Kieran. Is there to be a reprieve, after all? Has he given Ratcliffe the slip, deciding he wants this reunion even less than Vic does?

"He must be up top," Ratcliffe says, and now Vic sees that the rear of the room is split by a shallow mezzanine, accessed by a pale-wood spiral staircase. Above that, an impressive expanse of glazed roof showcases a cool sunlit sky.

Ratcliffe strides to the foot of the stairs and raises his voice: "Sam? You up there? Let's go," he says, and the sensation Vic has of having been brought up here with a gun to his back only intensifies.

Their footsteps on the spiral are silent, the air odorless. From the mezzanine, the space below looks even starker. Sofa, TV, neatly kept bookshelves. A desk with a single laptop. Where are the banks of terminals and devices you'd expect of an app-designing genius? In a room on the street side, presumably. Vic is guessing he won't be offered a guided tour.

Glass doors open onto the terrace and he finds himself emerging into the winter light, sound (traffic, sirens, the horn of a boat) and odor (fumes, dirt, brine) restored. From the doorway, local rooftops aren't visible, only a figure at the balustrade, his back to them, outlined by a stretch of empty celluloid sky. He is clothed in black and has a powerful upper body, with an exposed strip of muscular neck and a bleached buzz cut.

Ratcliffe strides towards him—"Sam, how are you?"—and Kieran turns to accept his embrace, the fatherly slap between the shoulder blades. Only when they part does Kieran look Vic's way, and Vic sees at once what Ellen meant about cosmetic surgery. There is something different about his jawline and mouth and perhaps his nose too. His eyebrows have been darkened and reshaped into oddly flawless twin lines.

"Kieran," he says, and the other man cringes.

"Sam, please," Ratcliffe prompts.

"Sam. Right. Congratulations on your app. It all sounds very cool." Vic speaks in the level tone he hopes to maintain throughout this ordeal.

Unexpectedly, Kieran glances away with a trace of humility. "Wasn't me." His voice is exactly the rumbling exaggeration of maleness Vic remembers.

"He's a bit disappointed he had to sell," Ratcliffe explains. "It's never an easy decision to give up your pet project."

"Had to?" Vic queries.

"Yes. If we'd taken Moodsmart to market with him front and center, it was likely he'd have got too much of the wrong kind of attention."

"Ah." No need to spell out why: the faint note of reproach is enough for Vic to understand. The product, the commercial value, would have been compromised the moment someone made the link between Sam Harding and Kieran Watts. Even with its expertise in making a virtue of the disadvantaged or downright dodgy, Green

Shoots' PR team would have struggled to neutralize the legacy of Lock Up Longer (*Crash Horror Monster Cashes In!* anyone?). On the contrary, they've done such an immaculate job of keeping Kieran's real name out of the press Vic suspects they've employed one of those scrubbing services. "Looks like you played it right, whatever you did," he says.

"Shall we sit?" Ratcliffe suggests and they gather at a white bistro table at the river end of the terrace. A jug of water and three beakers sit between them on a chrome tray. Kieran the gracious host, who would have thought it? The boy who only took and never gave, that was how Vic remembered him. Arriving at the flat one weekend after the next, empty-handed but full of shit.

Feeling fractionally steadier now he is seated, he tries not to stare too curiously at Kieran's weird new face.

"Right." Ratcliffe is pouring water for them all, preparing to launch this little confab. He wears the tolerant expression of the seasoned mediator. "Why don't I kick off by saying I feel very strongly that it's in both your interests to keep Ellen out of Sam's business. Her reappearance is at the very least an unnecessary headache for all concerned. Starting with you, Vic, I imagine you can do without her knowing the full extent of your continued involvement with Sam?"

"There's no continued involvement," Vic corrects him.

"Not directly, that's true, but you share an investor team and when she finds out, which she almost certainly will, she's unlikely to consider that a quirk of fate."

"Because it's not." Vic can't stop blinking—the light is sharp up here and he wishes he'd brought sunglasses. Neither of the other two appears as troubled by it as he is.

Ratcliffe's gaze sweeps to his protégé. "And, Sam, you found her somewhat unnerving when you came face-to-face with her recently.

She's since assured me she has no desire to share your new identity either with the press or those who supported the smear campaign against you, but I'm not convinced she won't change her mind."

"It wasn't a 'smear' campaign," Vic protests. "It was a campaign for sentencing reform." He speaks directly to Kieran because it feels important to break down this dynamic of Ratcliffe as simultaneous interpreter. "Look, she's just in shock. She assumed you were dead and she's discovered you're alive. She needs time to adjust all over again."

All over again. Would that shame Kieran, that last phrase? He doesn't *look* ashamed. He looks detached, as if all of this has little to do with him.

Ratcliffe says, "So your position is that she poses no physical threat to Sam, either?"

"She's a middle-aged woman living in a South London suburb," Vic retorts. "She may dress like a ninja, but she doesn't pose a physical threat to anyone." He sounds a lot surer than he feels, tries not to picture Ellen at their last meeting, her face so close to his he could feel the heat of her outrage.

"All right," Ratcliffe says. "Perhaps not *personally*." Suddenly changing gears with the vim of a drinker responding to the bell for last orders, he places his hands palms-down on the table. "Vic, in the interests of efficiency, and because we all have jobs to get on with, I should tell you that we strongly suspect it was Ellen who tried to pay someone to kill Sam when he was released from Danstone in 2017. We have to assume you already know this."

Shocked, Vic swings to face him. "What did you say?"

"You heard me. She was the one you protected him from, wasn't she?"

Vic stares, speechless.

"Come on, it's not that hard to work out. You weren't exactly flush back then, so how else would you have come by that cash, if not from her?"

Vic tries to process what is happening here. Though he's always known that Kieran must have confided in Ratcliffe about Vic's part in his escape (hence Vic's reward), not once, in any interaction with Cam or other personnel at Green Shoots, has this, or even Kieran's name, actually been mentioned. As for any suspicion on their part that Ellen was involved . . . Wow. How long have they had *that* theory? Only since she popped up in the neighborhood acting like a crazy woman, he suspects. *Oh, Ellen.* She really has gone about this the wrong way.

"I'm not sure you're in a position to know how much money I did or didn't have back then," he says, finally.

"Except for the business plan and financial statements you'd supplied to Cam when you pitched to him a few years earlier. And, when he went over your updated financials, there was no new debt for fifteen thousand pounds, so we know you didn't fund Sam from your own income." Ratcliffe's smile tightens a fraction. "Has she worked out you deceived her? Is that why you're not seeing eye to eye at the moment?" When Vic struggles to respond, he continues, "That's not good news for us, Vic. It makes us wonder how much influence you have with her now. If you have any at all?"

Vic feels completely outmaneuvered. Is there any point denying what is true, on both his and Ellen's parts? Except . . . one of them might be recording this meeting. It is best, perhaps, to avoid overt admissions of guilt. "She was out of her mind with grief back then," he says, carefully. "She wasn't the first bereaved parent to fantasize about revenge and I doubt she'll be the last. But that's all it was. She's in a different place now."

"She looked out of her mind when I saw her," Kieran says, addressing Ratcliffe.

"I would have to agree, Sam. She didn't seem stable to me. Hence this conference."

It couldn't be clearer that they were expecting Vic's visit and, had it not come soon enough, would have scheduled it themselves.

"I'll keep an eye on her, okay?" Again, he tries to engage Kieran. "I'll do my best to influence her—and, yes, I *do* still have some." Then, at the sight of the other man's expression, not so much remote now as bleak, he adds, with a touch of impatience, "What else do you want me to do?"

"There's nothing you *can* do," Kieran says, his tone fatalistic.

Vic is taken aback. What is going on here? Did Ellen actually threaten him when they met? He heard the audio from their skirmish, but only what she chose to share with him. He thinks of his debt, the reason he made this expedition in the first place. How easily Kieran could spare the sum and yet the way he and Ratcliffe are talking about her, taking as read her part in the 2017 "attempt" on Kieran's life, they'd as soon throw a bag of cash into St Saviour's Dock as advance the funds to subsidize a second. It would be like turkeys voting for Christmas.

He doesn't know how he could have been so stupid, coming here today; he wants to throw back his head and roar into this expensive air space. The mood is already unsalvageable and perhaps this is why he finds himself glaring at Kieran with open hostility and demanding, "It was all about Jade, wasn't it? Back then. She was the reason everything happened that night, wasn't she? Are you ever going to come clean about it? That's what torments Ellen, you know. That's all she wants, in the end. To understand the background of what happened. What was going on before you drove off the road. Not how, *why*."

"Vic, is this relevant?" Ratcliffe chastises gently, but Vic has lost control of the words coming from his mouth.

"Relevant? I'd say my son's death is highly relevant, yes." He leans closer to Kieran, whose upper body stiffens. "I saw you together, you know, you and Jade. When she was going out with Lucas. I saw you fucking in my flat."

Kieran gapes, flicks a look at his protector.

"Vic, please," Ratcliffe says, sharper now. "We need to focus on the present dilemma."

Vic continues to ignore him. "Was it worth it? Everything that's happened, all these lives destroyed, the fact that you're still feeling like a prisoner in your own home . . . Was it worth it for a fling that didn't go anywhere?"

"That's enough!" Ratcliffe exclaims. He removes his glasses, the better to display the censure in his glare. "Can we get back to the point, please. Because, if not, I suggest we wrap this up right now."

"Okay." Vic isn't about to apologize, but he at least manages to reset, holding the older man's eye with all the strength he can harness. It won't do him any good to disrespect the boss. He has to think of his brewery, his finances, his second child.

"Is there decent security here?" he asks Kieran. "Cameras in the common parts?"

"Just the video entry phone. An alarm in the lift, but no camera." Kieran shrugs and Vic remembers a detail the police mentioned at the time of his disappearance: he'd fitted a new bolt to Prisca's front door. But almost two and a half years on, he knows that bolts and cameras and other strategies discussed in meetings like this don't deter zealots like Ellen. Zealots and mothers. It's all too easy for Vic to imagine her barging her way into the building and . . . and what? It's the same question he asked himself half an hour ago but only now does an image surface. Ellen standing at Kieran's door with a knife in her hand.

Feeling his face convulse in horror, he averts his eyes from the two men and looks out at the bridge, the Tower of London beyond. Ratcliffe was right, they *are* on top of the world up here, or at least their square mile of it. Squint and the lines of that clear glass balustrade disappear, leaving nothing between you and the city beyond.

"Well, as long as you're out here, you're safe, aren't you?" he says, with a sudden note of triumph. "You know Ellen's terrified of heights?" He can see from the expression that breaks over Kieran's face that he does know, or did once. "So, if she breaks in with a machete or whatever it is you both seem to think she's capable of, then just get yourself out here. I guarantee she won't follow. You could ring the police then, couldn't you?"

There is a moment when he thinks he's done enough to convince them, but another, more meaningful look between Kieran and Ratcliffe makes him fear otherwise. They've invited him here with the expectation of solid intelligence, if not a concrete plan to foil Ellen then at least some disgrace of hers that could be used as leverage. Not talk of phobias.

"Forget it," Kieran says, with an air of finality. "I'll think of a way to warn her off."

And it is not so much the sentiment that chills Vic as the realization that in this entire conversation Kieran has not once acknowledged Lucas. Far from wanting to reach out, as Ratcliffe claimed, he has, it would appear, arrived at a position in which Lucas's death is incidental to his battle with Ellen.

Just as it had a life of its own before so it does again.

"Fine," Ratcliffe says. "Just make sure it's legal."

Vic

THEN

THE DAY HE MOVED out of the Beckenham flat, working alone as he loaded his possessions into his newly acquired work van, Vic became aware of a young woman in a pretty blue summer dress watching him from down the street. At first, he thought she was curious about the van's graphics. His new hire, India, had helped with the branding and the words "Common or Gordon, am I right?" were emblazoned across the van in the scripted capitals of a Lichtenstein speech bubble from the mouth of a friendly hipster barfly.

Then he recognized her, raised a hand in greeting. "Jade! Long time, no see."

"Vic." She walked up to join him and he remembered how, sometimes, when he came home from the station or the pub, he would suddenly see his flat through Lucas's friends' eyes. How ordinary it was compared to the Tanglewood Road pile. He hadn't ever set foot in Jade's or Tom's houses, but he guessed they were similarly well-appointed. Only Kieran would have walked the cracked paving stones of the approach to Vic's flat and thought it worth coveting.

The stones never had been repaired.

"I like the van," Jade said. "You started the business then?"

He'd forgotten her sore-throat voice. Like she'd been singing karaoke through the night and chain-smoking with every spare breath. Did they still do drugs, Lucas's old circle, or had his death scared them into clean living? Her eyes and skin were clear, her previously smooth blond hair tinted pink and arranged in those fashionable corrugated waves Vic had seen a lot of lately. She looked healthy, beautiful. "Yes," he said, trying to ignore the familiar pain that came with encounters like this. Lucas's circle growing up, leaving their friend behind. "Looks pretty cool, doesn't it?"

"Wait, you're moving out of the flat?" she said, clocking the contents of the van—not stock but personal possessions. Clothes and books and his old vinyl collection.

"Yep. Going down the road to East Croydon," he said. "I've been in this flat almost twenty years, believe it or not."

"I used to come here all the time with Lucas. You were so nice to us, you used to go out, give us a bit of privacy." She chuckled. "You probably didn't even *want* to go out half the time."

Vic smiled. "Maybe there were a couple of cold winter nights when I just went to the Odeon on my own, but hey. You were thick as thieves, you, Lucas, and Kieran. The three musketeers and all that." It was progress, speaking about Lucas in this nostalgic, almost folk way, fondly emphasizing the good times, the cute stories. Then again, there *had* been good times, hadn't there? There *had* been cute stories. Even with Kieran in the mix. His eye fell on a crate of old albums. "Remember when you went to that fancy-dress party as different incarnations of David Bowie? Lucas was the Thin White Duke . . ."

"I was Ziggy with the eye patch," she chipped in, smiling.

"Kieran was Aladdin Sane. He looked the best, actually."

"It suited him," she agreed.

"You started seeing him when he came out of prison, didn't you?" Vic said and could tell she was startled by his directness, tried to cover it with a shrug.

"For a couple of months, yes. Before he went missing."

It was interesting that she used that term. She believed the official line then. He decided a little tentative speculation wouldn't do any harm. "That moonlight flit of his was odd, wasn't it?"

She looked puzzled. Did they not say "moonlight flit" anymore? Flit was probably something else now. It probably meant nice, but only when applied to eyebrows, perhaps.

"I take it you haven't heard from him since?" he added.

"No." She hesitated. "Well, he did send me one message."

Vic's pulse accelerated. "Did he? When?"

"Ages ago. Right after he went. Just to let me know he was safe. Made me swear not to tell anyone—not that I would've dared. I thought it might be a witness protection thing, you know?"

Swear not to tell: she'd obviously decided the statute of limitations had run out on that, then, Vic thought. Why had he not thought sooner that Jade could be a loose cannon? (Because he'd trusted Kieran not to make contact, that was why. The fucking idiot.) If she was being this open with him—and five minutes into a roadside conversation—might she also have shared this information with others? Her mother, for instance, who was still a friend of Ellen's, albeit not as close as she'd once been. But, seeing the twist of anxiety in her brow, he decided not. He was the first to be hearing this, he was sure of it.

"Witness protection?" he said, just lighthearted enough. "Wow.

Mind you, he always did have delusions of the gangster lifestyle, didn't he?"

Jade's shoulders straightened and her chin lifted in protest. "No, it wasn't, like, a delusion. He must've been really worried. He wouldn't have done it otherwise. He wouldn't have . . . Unless . . ." Her voice petered away, but Vic tracked her train of thought easily enough. *He wouldn't have given up on me unless he had no choice.* "He was different after his release," she said, rallying. "He had all these plans. Positive ones, you know? To help people struggling with life. Maybe through a phone app or something."

Vic took a long look at her. Unless she was an excellent actress, she clearly had no idea that her former beau's fortunes had changed with his name. "Yes, well, the road to hell is paved with good intentions," he said, his tone short. He was no Ellen, but even so, there was only so much balance he could bring to his own position. It occurred to him that Jade might still be pining, even *waiting.* "Don't waste your time, Jade. Make your own way in life, don't hitch your star to some boy. Definitely not to the memory of him."

She met his gaze. "That's what my mum says," she said.

"How is she?" He had seen little of Sheridan since the night of the Tesco Bordeaux.

"Same as ever." Jade's easy dismissal of the one who loved her the most was heartbreaking, truly. Did Lucas use to be like this about Ellen and him? But Jade's mind was already on more important concerns. "Can I ask you something, Vic?"

"Sure."

"Does Ellen hate me?" Her voice gave on the last syllable as she struggled to stifle her emotions.

"Of course not. Mind you, I wouldn't tell her you heard from Kieran, even just that once." Vic had an unwelcome image of Jade presenting herself at the house on Tanglewood Road in some belated attempt to atone. "It suits her to think he's . . ." He paused. "Gone for good. She can get on with her life, if you know what I mean?"

"Of course. There's no way I'd say anything," she assured him. "Not to anyone."

"Thank you." There was a sense that the conversation was over and they should part, until a loop snagged in Vic's mind. "Why would she hate you, Jade? You mean because you and Lucas had just split up? You mustn't worry about that. She always understood the boys were still great mates and if it hadn't been that night it would have been another."

Jade's throat convulsed. "No, I meant because I told her I didn't know what they were arguing about in the car. I didn't want to upset her. But sometimes I think I upset her more by *not* telling her."

Vic's senses stood to attention. *Arguing?* He was pretty sure that, even though he and Ellen had speculated ad nauseam, it had never actually been established what Lucas and Kieran were talking about—if anything—when they drove off the road. He slammed shut the van doors and looked at her. "To be honest, I'm not sure we knew they were arguing at all, let alone what it was about." His gaze tapered. "What is it we don't know, Jade?"

"Nothing really. I'm sure you don't have time . . ." She had the look of a child now, a girl with a secret she needed to spill before it ate her alive. It made no difference to her if she saved him from misery or caused it.

"I've got time," he said.

part three

SAINT OR SINNER

by Ellen Saint (cont)

thirty

Vic betrayed me—well, you knew that.

When you write your history, you find that you identify—and scatter—clues you couldn't possibly have seen when you were living events in the present. Which means what's blindingly obvious to you reading this now was unfathomable to me at the time.

Until, finally, it was not. When I stepped back from the cliff edge that Friday afternoon in late November, I already had an instinct that his deception concealed another—and then another—and so it proved. It was a set of matryoshka dolls. Not telling me he'd been informed that Kieran was still alive was the outermost, the one I saw first, but inside it others nested, the innermost being that he'd never wanted Kieran dead, not like I had.

He'd never craved justice.

I won't detail the showdowns. There was one in the park, when he hoped he could get away with a half confession. It pains me to recall the nub of his defense: *Be grateful I stopped this.*

Be glad you are not a monster.

I knew then that he had allowed himself to forget who the real monster was.

Then there was a meeting with Danny, who—I know, you got there first—knew nothing about the contract killing I'd been so profoundly grateful to him for having facilitated.

Albanians, my ass.

Then, our final clash, in the lobby of Vic's building, a shiny and soulless tower in East Croydon. That was when he confessed fully. "I want my money back," I told him and he recoiled at the animal urgency in my voice. "As soon as possible. In cash."

I was crying as I traveled home, but at least I knew the truth by then. I knew what I had to process. Make no mistake, it takes courage to come to terms with the knowledge that the person you thought you were bound to—by love, by grief, by crime—is scarcely more than an actor. It takes time.

But you know what? After my pride healed and my blood cooled, I saw that none of what I'd discovered in those distressing confrontations actually put me in a different place from where I already was. I already knew Kieran had survived. I already knew I would be acting alone in getting the job done a second time.

Because this story has always been about me versus Kieran Watts. The others—Vic, Justin, Freya, even my precious Lucas—they are all minor characters.

| | | | | | |

I am a great believer in the saying that when one door closes, another door opens. It was Alexander Graham Bell who said that, did you know? People usually forget the second part of his statement—that we spend too long looking at the closed door to notice the open one—but I, for one, have no intention of doing that.

Especially when the door in question is in The Heights itself.

Selena's contact Asha lives on the fifth floor. Having been caught in Vic's avalanche, I've almost forgotten about her when she phones and asks when I'm free for a consultation.

"I'm free now," I say.

When I arrive at the building it's as if I've known it all my life. The carved stone panel with its elegant lettering, the antique brass plates, the glass doors that kiss shut behind you as your heels clack across the marble lobby. Lift on the right, stairs on the left. Heart in my mouth.

Asha is a sleek and fashionable mid-thirtysomething, one half of a high-earning young couple. She is very sure of her ideas, which exceed the updating of kitchen and bathroom and amount to the creation of a space for entertaining that will require planning and building work. As I outline the process, I cast a wary look at the half-open main window—I hadn't realized they are designed to slide open to reveal a Juliet balcony over the water. Directly opposite, Jacob's Wharf obscures the view of Tower Bridge, but the top of the Shard is visible, a switchblade catching the light. "Do all the flats in this building have the same layout?" I ask, though I know the answer.

"All except the top floor. That has a massive skylight over part of the living room and a spiral staircase up to the roof terrace."

"Have you ever been up there?"

"A few times, when the owner lived there himself. He knew what a space like that was for, he had these epic parties. But the new guy's a bit of a hermit. Has everything delivered, groceries and takeaways— not that that's unusual, there are people round here who've never once used their kitchen."

"Does he not have any friends?"

"The only person we've ever seen going up is this older guy, maybe his father?"

James Ratcliffe.

"You should ask him if he'll swap," I joke. "Then *you* can have the parties."

"I wish." Asha laughs. "But, listen, Ellen, we *are* having a party, a Christmas party. I've just sent out the invites. You should come. Bring your architect, see the space when lots of people are here and get a sense of what we need. Then we can talk time frames in the New Year."

This is not the first client party I've been invited to—there's a certain cachet in having "your" interior designer or architect on the guest list—but it's the first in a building that houses a man I once hated enough to plot his murder.

"When is it?" I ask.

"December the nineteenth. It's a Thursday. I know, it's not great, but everyone leaves town on the Friday."

I accept her invitation without hesitation.

I'm not sure I believed in signs before, but I do now. The nineteenth of December is, of course, the anniversary of Lucas's death.

|　|　|　|　|　|　|

A day or two later, I receive a package through the door containing twenty fifty-pound notes. A scrawled message is enclosed: *This is all I can get for now. I'm sorry.*

Believe it or not, this is Vic's first apology to me in this whole crisis, and I'm not sure I'm inclined to accept it. The money, yes. I add his contribution to the £1,500 I've amassed from cashpoint runs, kept in an unused drawer in the bedroom that used to be Lucas's, and then I phone him.

"Is that really all you can scrape together? After everything you've done?"

Everything you *haven't* done.

"I'll pay you back, Ellen, I told you that." How utterly sincere he sounds. Almost sheepish. "But you need to realize it will take me months, maybe years. You know what small businesses are like, they don't turn a profit for ages."

He's right, I do know that. But I'm feeling spiteful (can you blame me?). "That's not good enough. You've already had this loan for two and a half years. Maybe I should add interest, eh?"

An edge of impatience enters his tone. "If you need money fast, can't you get it from Justin?"

"Of course I can't. He'll want to know what it's for."

"What *is* it for?" There's a pause. I can tell he half wishes he hadn't asked, but can't help himself. "Is it what I think it is?"

"Why? You said you're not interested anymore."

"You called me," he shoots back. "I assumed you wouldn't want to speak to me again after everything."

Everything. The word, all that it encompasses in our shared lives, drives a spear right through me. For all my grand pronouncements when we parted, calling Vic, talking to him, however briefly, is part of the rhythm of my world. I might not be able to forgive him, but I won't silence him. I will never expel him. "I phoned about the money," I say. "That's all."

Maybe he hears the concession in my tone, because he responds by making a sudden confession—yes, a *new* one. "Look, Ellen, since we met, something's happened. I've seen him. Kieran. I've been up to his flat and spoken to him. James Ratcliffe was there as well."

I feel blood flood my face. "How did you arrange that? He just let you in?"

"That doesn't matter. But he's scared of you, that was obvious.

He's defensive—and defense can turn to attack very quickly. I think you need to watch out for yourself."

"What do you mean?" I demand. "What did he say, exactly?"

Vic lowers his voice and I have to strain to catch what follows. "He said he had his suspicions about your part in the threat to his life when he came out of prison and he's worried what you'll do now you know where he's living. He seems to think you might turn up at his flat and assault him."

I inhale sharply, try to process this. "'Had his suspicions'? What did you say?"

"I said you had no intention of harming him and never have."

I exhale. "Thank you. The last thing we need is him going to the police about what happened back then."

"He won't do that," Vic says. "Ratcliffe wouldn't let him. He won't do anything that jeopardizes this deal they've done with Saurus. There's sure to be a big launch and they won't risk Sam Harding being connected to Kieran Watts. We might be the only people who know besides Ratcliffe."

"When I met Ratcliffe, that was definitely his concern. He was worried I was going to blow the whistle in some way, expose Kieran's identity. I told him I have no interest in doing that."

"I said exactly the same."

There's a silence as if we've startled ourselves by being in agreement. To a point, anyway. What I haven't added is that I wouldn't waste my time damaging Kieran's reputation, not when it will only draw attention to me later.

But Vic doesn't want to know about later.

"I'd better go," he says. "Be careful, Ellen, okay? And don't be surprised if Kieran sends you some sort of warning."

thirty-one

FREYA COMES HOME FROM university in early December. It is exactly two months since I saw Kieran on the roof of The Heights and exactly five years since Lucas came home after *his* first term at college.

Once a home bird, my daughter is sociable now, out most nights seeing old school friends and new college ones, going to pubs and clubs and house parties. Like all parents of new students, I'm relieved she's survived the first term, thrilled to see she's popular, busy, motivated. Justin's done a good job. While I've been distracted by tragedy, he's raised a fantastic young woman.

But a week or so in, I notice a trace of artifice in her farewell as she heads out for another evening with friends, a greater eagerness to get out of the door.

"Where're you off to tonight?" I ask. It's obvious she's dressed with care, a fitted black dress visible under the long mustard suede coat she found the day before in a vintage shop in Crystal Palace— whoever she's seeing warrants more than her standard jeans and puffer. Proper knee boots with zips and heels, too, not her go-to ankle flats. I thought she'd given up on her adolescent ritual of full-face makeup, but it is back for the occasion, glamorous and eye-catching, her hair blow-dried.

I compliment her as she checks she has her keys. "Is this a date?"

"No, just a drink with a friend," she says, shrugging.

"From round here?"

"No, in town. Near Tower Bridge."

"Oh, I've got a client in that area. What street?"

"I don't remember, but it's on the water, apparently. One of the docks in Shad Thames."

My hackles rise. I've never heard her mention any friend living in that part of town before. A coincidence? Or the malevolent, black-hearted opposite? Since her return for the holidays, Justin and I have made no reference to Kieran's unwelcome reappearance in our lives. "Lucky them," I say. "Cool area."

She lingers, sensing my trepidation, trying to read my face. "You're not going to follow me, Mum, are you?"

I feel myself flush. "What?"

"I know you used to and I understand why." Her smile is forgiving, but conditional. "But don't, not anymore. I can look after myself."

"I know you can, sweetheart. Don't be silly."

Justin interrupts then, from the top of the stairs, and I realize he has been listening. "You heading out, Frey? Have fun. Just let us know if you're going to be late."

After she's gone, I can tell he is waiting for me to say it, and so I do. "Did you hear where she said she was going? Shad Thames, on the water. You don't think . . . ?"

"No," he says. "I don't think. And nor should you." He moves past me, ignoring my expression, which states, very clearly, that I find his trust dangerously misguided. "Come on, let's get dinner started."

| | | | | |

We eat griddled tuna and asparagus and wedges of sweet potato roasted with Cornish salt. I have a glass of Picpoul. To an outsider, we look like empty nesters focusing on the finer things, on ourselves.

Afterwards, leaving Justin to trawl Netflix for a half-decent movie, I take my phone to the bathroom to make a call. My finger hovers over "Asha"—no, I mustn't jeopardize my party invitation—before selecting "Selena."

"Do you happen to be at home?" Work has continued on her apartment (I told you right at the start she'd have a beautifully lit flat and so she will) and I know she often decamps to her boyfriend's place in North London.

"I do happen to be, yes. And I'm thinking, oh God, will this *ever* be finished?"

After I've gone through the motions of assuring her of our excellent progress, I say, "This is very unprofessional of me, but can I ask you a favor? Could you just look out of your window and see if that guy's in? The one we were talking about who lives in The Heights."

"The top flat? Sure."

I hear the seesaw of her breathing as she moves from wherever she is to the waterside window, followed by the creak of a window opening.

"I think he's home. The skylight's all lit up."

"Can you tell if he's on his own or with someone?"

"Sorry, unless he comes right up to the window or onto the roof, I can't see him at all."

"Okay, thank you. Sorry, Selena, you must think I'm deranged."

"I think we're all deranged," she says, which makes me smile.

I end the call. Justin and I settle on the sofa with our drinks and a comedy he's chosen that I know I won't be able to laugh at. I'm aware that I'm rationing my wine in case I need to drive, to pick up Freya from a crime scene.

"You all right?" Justin asks. If he could read my mind he would despair.

An hour in, my phone rings. It's Selena. "I have to take this," I tell him. "It's a client." I move out of earshot. "Yes?"

Her voice pours excitedly into my ear. "I thought I'd tell you he's come out onto the roof."

"Oh!" My pulse stutters. "Is he alone?"

"No, he's with a girl. He's got the terrace lights on so I can see them quite well up there—I've zoomed in on them on my phone." She laughs. "You've got me acting like I'm on a stakeout here! Anyway, they've been outside a while now, they must be freezing."

"What does she look like, this girl?"

"Tallish. Dark hair."

"Is she wearing a coat? A long, yellow coat?"

"She is, actually." As I grapple with the sensation of a boot stamping on my chest, Selena gives another cackle of laughter. "How the hell did you know that, Ellen?"

"I used to know him," I say, illogically, my throat constricted.

"Well, I'd worked that much out. And he only dates girls in yellow coats, does he? That's quite a fetish."

The assumption that they are dating is so repugnant I almost heave. "What are they doing?" I blurt. "Are they—"

"Just talking, by the looks. Enjoying the view. Oh wait, you won't like this bit: they're leaning right over the barrier and looking down at the water."

She's right, I don't like it. I picture Kieran making a sudden lunge and tipping Freya off her feet—already pitched forward in those high-heeled boots. Her lovely unsuspecting face contorting with terror as she makes her last ever eye contact . . . with *him*.

Just like Lucas.

"Now they're smoking—or he is. Want me to send you a shot?" Selena asks.

I think of Justin in the next room, the movie paused. "No, don't take any pictures. I'm sorry to rope you into it, it's nothing sinister, I promise."

But it bloody well *is* sinister, of that I am certain. Kieran was the one to initiate this meeting with Freya, I'm certain of that too. This claim on her is the warning Vic told me to expect, the warning I now realize I've been anticipating ever since that encounter with James Ratcliffe when I basically declared war.

She's still not back when Justin and I go up to bed—our latest night in a long time—but just as I'm turning off the fairy lights on the landing a text arrives. Our daughter is in an Uber, homeward bound.

thirty-two

FREYA IS NOT YET up when I leave for a morning appointment and so I have to wait till the afternoon to confront her—

No, not confront. Consult. Advise.

I find her in her bedroom, lying on the bed and staring at her phone. Her blinds are down and her bedside table is crammed with mugs and Diet Coke cans. I have a sudden, acute memory of that morning years ago, when I tried to rouse Lucas for his maths exam, and feel bile rise through my gullet.

"Frey, I need to talk to you." It's a long time since I've been this nervous around her. She's all I have; I can't risk getting it wrong.

"What about?" She glances up. Her face is bare, every scrap of last night's makeup removed, the better to express that uneasy blend of wariness and solicitude she reserves for me. There is a pink mark like a scar down one cheek where she's been resting her face on the pillow.

I sit on the edge of her bed and lightly place a hand on her long jeaned calves. I can feel a tremble rising; I mustn't let her see how distressed I am.

"I know who you saw last night," I say.

"What?" Her expression clouds. "Who?"

"Sam. Sam Harding. I assume you know who he really is?"

She stares at me, horror-struck. "How am I supposed to unpack *that?*"

Unpack. They speak differently, this generation. What would Lucas have made of his grown-up sister, I wonder? They were five years apart, but a different breed in language, in spirit. "Let me re-phrase. This man who calls himself Sam, you do know he's actually Kieran Watts?" It may sound ridiculous that I ask this, but she was only thirteen or so when she last had any contact with Kieran and, given his new name and altered appearance, I can't discount the pos-sibility that she's been duped.

"Whoa," Freya says and puts down her phone.

"What does that mean?"

"It just means whoa. *Of course* I know it's him, Mum. I don't have amnesia." Noticing my hand on her calf, she shakes it off, tuck-ing her feet to the side of her.

"Okay," I say. "He looks a bit different, that's all, and it's been a few years. I just wanted to be sure."

"You followed me," she accuses. "I *told* you not to. It's a complete invasion of privacy."

"I didn't follow you," I say.

"Well, my Find My Phone's turned off, so you couldn't have tracked me that way. How *did* you know?"

"Someone who knows us saw you going into his building," I say.

"Who?"

"I'd prefer not to say. Please trust me when I say that's not what's important here."

She chews a thumbnail, her brow creased. She's calmer now,

thinking like her father, finding the rational path through this. "Why don't you tell me what *is* important?"

"Keeping you safe is important," I say simply. "Nothing matters as much as that. How long have you been in touch with him?"

"I don't know, not long." I'm heartened by her eye contact, her basic willingness to engage.

"Months? Weeks? Days? Try and think, Frey."

"It was ten days ago, maybe."

Ten days, and yet already she is prepared to cover for him. First Vic and now her. Why are they so ready to collude with Lucas's killer? I feel a stinging behind my eyes. "Did he contact you or the other way around?"

She sighs. "He contacted me. He found me on Instagram. Don't ask me for his socials, Mum. I'm not going to tell you. It's weird enough you know his address."

I nod, as if in the spirit of compromise. I've searched at length for accounts in the name of Sam Harding and found nothing I believe to be connected with him. I glance at her phone, facedown on the duvet. Was she communicating with him when I walked in? *Great to see you, Frey. You free again tonight?*

"He tried to get in touch with me before," she says, watching me. "He told me last night. He sent me a letter, years ago, after he was released, but I never got it. Do you know anything about that?"

I try not to flinch. "I don't, no. Maybe it got lost in the post."

Her mouth tightens. "He posted it through the door, Mum."

I gaze at her, reining in my fear. I can't let a foiled attempt to insinuate himself in the past overshadow a charm offensive gathering pace in the present. "Freya, you were a child. He was a convicted criminal."

"Stealing mail is a crime, as well," she points out.

I exhale heavily. I am not about to debate the relative merits of intercepting a single piece of post and leaving a man to drown. "Please, tell me what happened when you were in his flat last night."

She groans, obviously sensing I'm not going to give this up. She'll be willing her father to come home early from work and appear in the doorway to save her from my inquisition, like he did when she was leaving last night, like he always does. "Nothing. We had a few beers. Had a good talk."

"A good talk? What about?"

"I don't know. Everything."

Nothing, everything: which is it?

"It was just the two of you, was it?"

She looks down, as if there really *is* something to hide, and I feel my fear slip its lead and rear up in front of me. "Why, Freya? I don't understand! Why did you want to be alone in the same room as your brother's killer?"

"Mum!"

"Please, just try to explain to me."

Her eyes meet mine again. Wide, gray, full of compassion—for *him*. "Maybe because it helps. Like the counselors told us, you feel better if you forgive."

Ah, forgiveness. You may find it stunning that I've reached this late stage in my account without having introduced the notion, at least not where *he* is concerned. And Freya is right, it *has* been proposed, both by professionals and amateurs. *Only when you forgive can you move on* . . .

Absolute bullshit.

"I will never forgive him," I tell her.

"That's not healthy," she replies.

"Maybe, but it's the way it is."

"Well, it shouldn't be! Lucas's death was an accident, but you still act like Kieran deliberately murdered him."

He did! As good as!

"It wasn't like the internet said," she continues. "I hated it, you know, your horrible campaign. I know you made sure the papers weren't ever in the house, you put parental controls on my phone, but everything was still out there. I could read it on a computer at school, at friends' houses. It was vile."

Horrible? Vile? I'm winded by this, just as she is warming up, her eyes firing. "It was supposed to be about justice, but it was malicious, all those things people said about him. It was bullying."

I gape. I didn't give enough thought to her, clearly, as I traveled around the southeast with Vic warning strangers of the perils of their teenagers' inadequate road sense, the systemic failings that added insult to injury when tragedy struck. *When*, not if. I put the fear of God into those audiences when I could have been urging them to love, to trust, to live.

"People are bullied for far less online, Freya. That's why we've always advised you to keep off social media. It's one big kangaroo court. Anyway, when all that was going on, Kieran wasn't allowed online. He was in prison." Seeing her expression grow more resolute, I continue, "You have to understand that if people took a hard line during the campaign, it was because they thought what he did deserved a more severe punishment than he got."

"They were whipped into a frenzy, Mum. By you and Vic and that journalist. What if it was me driving a friend?" she demands, straightening her back as she changes tack. "What if I was the one who crashed a car? Would you say *I* needed to be punished? Or would you say it's only natural to fight your way out of a submerged vehicle, that I was right to save myself no matter what?"

I grip her hand, pulling air into my lungs. "He should have gone back down. Once he realized Lucas hadn't come out after him, he should have gone back down and dragged him out. At the very least he should have called 999 the second he knew he couldn't attempt the rescue himself."

"He didn't have his phone, though, did he? And he was in shock. It was so bad he had PTSD."

"Yes, very convenient," I say.

"PTSD is not 'convenient,' Mum, it's a psychological disorder. This is 2019, you can't say things like that anymore."

Freya tears her hand from mine, disgusted by me. I don't know how to make this right. Maybe we will never agree. But I can't bring an end to this conversation until I know exactly what is being set up here. What Kieran's limits are in using my remaining child as his pawn. I think of Jade, there for him when he came out of Danstone. He spun his lies with her and now he is doing the same with Freya.

"He's actually doing great things now," she says, on cue. "He's not allowed to talk about it, but he started something that's going to help a lot of people, maybe millions."

"Yes, I know about that," I say. I also know that he is not supposed to discuss his part in it. How did Ratcliffe put it? Even "casual gossip" could be dangerous. Which means either Kieran's keenness to impress her led him to be indiscreet or—I breathe in sharply as the possibility takes shape—he *intended* us to have this conversation. It's developing just as he scripted it, with himself right at its center.

Freya is looking encouraged. "Then how can you not be impressed by how he's turned his life around?"

Like he did when he joined Foxwell, I think? A troubled youngster worth supporting, worth nurturing. *Let's buddy him up with one of our best.* "I'm glad his work will help people. It definitely sounds like something worthwhile." And although it takes all of my mental strength to make this statement, my reward is a form of settlement between us.

"You can't stop me seeing him again," Freya says finally.

"I know I can't."

It would only put her in the position of having to choose and I would never do that.

All I can do is take the choice away.

Killing Time (cont)

There is a memorable scene in *Saint or Sinner* in which Ellen visits a notorious South London housing estate with the aim of obtaining a firearm. It's an episode that is both excruciating and compelling: a sometimes pompous-sounding suburban housewife doing business with the criminal underclass. (Can't you just see the scene in the movie? Some national treasure with RADA training code-switching with the best of them.)

One of Ellen's recurring criticisms of Kieran Watts—besides the obvious and justifiable—is his habit as a teenager of speaking like a gangster, and yet the chilling taciturnity of the real-life estate juveniles she encounters only accentuates the fallacy at the heart of her loathing of him. In this respect, and possibly others besides, Watts was never anything more than a pretender.

The scene also raises further questions about the author's exposure to a potential review of criminal charges.

"Something easy to use," she briefs the gang apparatchiks, showing them a photo of her preferred model, and if that is not an expression of intent to cause bodily harm, then I don't know what is.

Sunday Times magazine, December 2021

thirty-three

I KNOW YOU'LL WANT to hear about the gun.

You'll want to be scandalized by how easy it was for me to get hold of one—I would be exactly the same if I were reading this. We like to think it's so hard to obtain weapons here in the UK; we like to think we're so civilized compared to our trigger-happy friends across the Atlantic.

Well, let me tell you, some of us are a lot less civilized than others.

But first, to be strictly chronological, there is a call from Asha at The Heights.

My immediate guess is she's been talking with her partner about her new plans to spend an awful lot of money on *light* of all things— it's common once the initial excitement has blown over to be advised that budgets are out of reach after all—and so I'm amazed when she says, "You know my neighbor upstairs, the one I told you about when you were here?"

"Oh, yes, the hermit," I say as if groping for the memory.

"That's him, though maybe he's a bit more sociable than I thought. We got talking in the lobby this morning and I mentioned the work I'm thinking of having done and he asked for your details for some advice about his place. I thought I'd better ask first before just handing over your number to a random male. He looks—how can I put it?—a bit strange, but I think he's harmless."

My heart drums painfully. Kieran must have been monitoring the entry-phone video and seen me arrive or leave. Did he linger outside Asha's flat as I once did his? There is no reason for her to wonder why this neighbor she's barely exchanged two words with before is suddenly being so friendly, but every reason for me to. He could have found my details in a couple of clicks, but this way he makes his point. He's planning something, even if I don't yet know what. "Thank you, I appreciate that, Asha. I'm sure he's perfectly trustworthy. I'll pop by when I next come in."

"That will be the day of my party, so why don't I ask him if he wants to drop in and meet you then? I need to invite the neighbors, anyway."

"Great idea," I tell her.

| | | | | | |

So, the gun. An investigative piece in the *South London Press* sends me to the Whitley Estate on the outskirts of Bromley. It's both brutalist and brutal, set up on a hill, low-rise but for a grim trio of towers at its center. It's a scary place, of course it is—we've all read about gangs and county lines, these places where the savage few rule and everyone else is classified as "vulnerable." As I cross from safe postcode to unsafe, my body brims with the strange tension between instinctive fear and a kind of learned abandon.

I haven't thought it through, no, especially where Freya is

concerned. I'm not thinking of how it might feel for her years from now, should her mother choose to make use of that gun. How long the scandal and the shame would last. I'm only thinking I have to put a stop to the horror of Kieran being in her life, inhabiting her brain as he did Lucas's. Contaminating, destroying.

What did my darling Justin say that time to the detective? *Our family was very, very unlucky to have crossed paths with this boy* . . .

A narrow street of low-rise housing opens onto a so-called plaza, the concrete lobbies of the towers on three sides and a parade of shops on the fourth. At its center is an area of bench seating and a small children's playground. There is a smell of burning, but no obvious source. As if entering the compound of a jail, I'm surrounded immediately by guards. Kids, really. Lads. (It is, by the way, a school day.) All black kit and baseball caps and trainers in brands that presumably signify something to them and their kind but nothing to me and mine. Three of them are on bikes and another rides a scooter meant for an infant. Some have smooth skin and gentle features, others skinny, undeveloped physiques, but they all eyeball me with the same empty, inhospitable glare of adults with decades of wrongdoing under their belts.

I identify the leader and hold out my phone to display a photo of a Smith & Wesson revolver I've researched online. My pitch is rehearsed right down to the last word: "Listen to me, I am not police. I am a private citizen and I need to get hold of something like this. Something easy to use. Please go and tell whoever your decision-maker is. Your boss." My tone is clipped and commanding and though the boy mutters a string of insults about me to the group, he snatches my phone out of my hand and peels away on his bike.

I wait, my heart hammering. Why did I let him take my phone like that? It's not worth anything, but it contains texts to Vic, as well as that audio clip of Kieran. Worse, I didn't bring my regular phone, which means that if this feral pack comes at me, I can't even call 999.

More optimistically, at least any plans to search me for valuables are on hold until the boss returns and I'm too old for these boys to want to sexually harass me. They remain close by, only half watching me as they scroll on their phones. Loud music starts up in a flat overhead, with menacing bassline and nasty vocals. It is soon opposed by a second stream from a floor in the same tower and the kids react with a brief show of excitement that feels routine. It's as if I've arrived midway through a war.

My nose runs and I wipe it with the back of my hand, feel the liquid drying on my skin. *Just get through this. Think of Freya.*

Think of Lucas.

Finally, the leader spins back into view on his bike, comes at me so fast I cringe, before swerving and stopping with real skill, like a skier. Not powder, but dust. "Three G," he says.

Three thousand pounds is almost certainly above market rate, and, if I pay it, these kids—or more likely their overlords—will be partying on my stupidity. But what do I care? I think of my cash at home. A little over two and a half; I can top up the rest. "Fine. I'll bring cash. When?"

He indicates my phone. "This clean?"

"Yes."

He thumbs a message, presumably to himself, then hands it back. There is no question of our exchanging names.

"When?" I repeat, then, when he still declines to answer, "I need it by next Wednesday at the latest." The day before Asha's party.

He just sneers. "Christmas present, innit?"

I harden my tone. "Seriously. If you can't get it by then, forget it. Text me and let me know. I'm going now, okay?"

A trio of younglings accompany me back to the main street, baying and buoyant. They're suddenly like real kids, not a million miles from Lucas and his pals when they were this age.

There's a lump in my throat so big I can't swallow.

| | | | | | |

The message arrives on Wednesday morning.

Leave $ in fone box Mare St 3pm

I noticed the kiosk on my first foray. It's right on the corner of the street leading to the square, disused, of course, as they all are now. It's been burned out and pissed in and generally abused, so classically a PO box for gangs. I wonder if the police might have put a camera in it. But criminals would sweep any devices, surely.

As I drop the cash, zipped in a small knapsack, I think of Vic and the story he gave me of leaving my fifteen thousand pounds for Kieran—*It was a risk. It paid off*—and feel a fresh surge of rage. Why, Vic? If you'd only followed the plan first time around, this could all be over now, long since finished. I could be up in town today, Christmas shopping with Freya. We could have our noses at the window of Fortnum & Mason, before cutting through to Regent Street to gasp in delight at this year's lights. Thinking life is worth living, after all.

Not that there aren't Christmas lights on the Whitley Estate. The house nearest the phone box is practically sheathed in them, an oversize fake snowman by the door. I linger by it for ten minutes or so. The pavements are empty, but I know I'm being watched. I've never been so aware of my own nervous system: my stomach is eating itself, my heart is speeding. At last, a child I recognize from my first visit bikes up and enters the box. He's in there for a minute or two and

I picture him thumbing through the notes, checking it's all there. When he leaves, he shoves his foot in the door, and gestures in my direction. As I step forward, he lets the door bang shut, throws a leg over his bike, and pedals away.

I pull open the door. Inside, the stench of urine is even more overpowering than before and makes me gag. On the floor, there's a brown bag like the kind takeout comes in. I open it to look, but I don't touch the contents, not directly. I shove the package in my bag, not my usual one, but one selected for its combination of zip, studded flap, and buckle that no pickpocket could hope to crack in less than half a minute. Only when I've secured it do I exit the kiosk. I can taste the odor on my lips, smell it on my scarf at my throat.

As I walk home, my bag feels oddly *living*, as if I've taken possession of an exotic pet and startled it into stillness. Maybe one of those venom-secreting lizards.

Silent and deadly and indiscriminate.

thirty-four

ON THE DAY OF the party, my nerves are complicated at the eleventh hour by interference from Justin.

"I know you've had this client thing in the diary for a while, but are you sure you want to go? Freya will be expecting us to be together. We always are on the nineteenth."

This is true. We mourn together on the anniversary of Lucas's death and I'm the one who insists on it. "I was thinking, maybe we should approach it differently from now on. Now that she's at college, I don't want her to feel like she has to sit around moping when she's back, not for my sake. It might put her off coming home. We need to find joy in Lucas's life, not dwell on his death."

"I think that's a great idea," Justin says, but it is quite a leap from my customary seasonal doldrums and I can tell he is doubtful. "What's Vic doing tonight?"

"I don't know."

"You've heard from him, though?"

"We exchanged texts this morning. He sent me a photo." I show him the picture: Lucas aged seven or eight, school sports day. Pale legs, pink cheeks, a trace of *Lord of the Flies* in his eyes. "I need to get ready, Jus. Don't worry about Freya, she's with you tonight and we both know that's the best thing."

"What does that mean?" he says, perplexed. "Why are you speaking like this, El?"

"Like what?"

"Like you're about to go and, I don't know, throw yourself off the top of the Shard."

"I'm not." I smile. "You have my word I will never knowingly go to the top of the Shard. Don't overthink it, Jus. Let me do what I have to do, which is show my face for half an hour and paint a little picture of how much prettier next year's party will be with the lighting fixed. Then I'll be back and we can have a drink together before we go to bed."

I kiss him then. Soon after, I seek out Freya and hug her. There are too few hugs and kisses in this book, I know. It's an unfortunate consequence of choosing to tell a story about hate.

| | | | | | |

I dress with care. I want to be blandly glamorous, to blend in, but not so restrictively that I can't make a run for it if I need to. Instead of a party dress, I choose a jumpsuit in a glittery black fabric with a bit of give in it. Boots with a chunky heel and a proper tread. A jacket I can keep on and not risk abandoning in a heap in the spare bedroom. In the same buckled bag that I took to the estate, sitting alongside my purse, house keys, and two phones, is the gun.

Weirdly, now that I've held it, it feels less real, not more. Though I'm confident I'll need it at most to threaten, *definitely* not to shoot, I'm of course aware that I'm already a criminal. I've checked online and the mandatory minimum sentence for possession of an illegal firearm is five years.

Justin and Freya are watching TV when I leave, a sushi takeaway on order. Justin has a can of Common or Gordon on the go, Freya a Coke. Grateful for the earlier affection, I forbid myself any thoughts of when I will see them again and cheerfully call goodbye.

"Love you, Mum," Freya calls, half-distracted by the TV, and it's impossible not to think of this same night five years ago when Lucas walked out of the door for the last time. I handed him money, I said the right things, but I didn't hold him. I should have done, I would have done, but he was gone before I could.

Closing the front door behind me, I startle at the sight of Vic's van at the curb, the zany Pop Art livery incongruous in our street of black Volvos and 4x4s. My first thought is, God, has Justin contacted him? Told him I'm acting strangely? No, it's more likely he's here because I didn't reply to his text with the sports day picture, my mind elsewhere.

His window is wound down and he watches me as I approach. His breath hangs visibly in the cold air. "Ellen."

"What are you doing here?"

"I just wanted to see how you are. I thought we might go for a quick drink."

"I can't, sorry. I'm off out. But I'm fine. You?"

"Not bad." He offers a half shrug. "Where are you going? Christmas party?" He's noticed the way I'm dressed. The hair and makeup. I probably look unusually glamorous, though when I checked my face in the mirror, all I saw was the violence in my eyes, the shake of my hand as I tried to apply mascara.

"Yes. A work thing."

"Oh, one of your rich clients. Where? In town?"

"Yep, just off Marylebone High Street." The same lie I told Justin, just in case.

Vic eyes the wine bag hanging from my arm. "I hope there's the family brand in there." The humor is a little galling—he's acting as if he never betrayed me and we're still buddies—but I'll let it go. I don't have time for another difference of opinion.

"Sorry, but I need to get going," I tell him. "Justin is home, though, if you want to go in and have a drink with him?"

"No, I'm good. I'll drop you at the station," he offers.

"Don't be silly, it's just a couple of minutes' walk."

"Humor me."

"Why, Vic?"

"Because I need to tell you something," he says, smiling in defeat. "Please, just get in."

Grumbling, I do as he says. The van has the malty, toasty aroma of a pub at opening time. I place my handbag in the footwell and keep the wine on my lap. Vic indicates to an empty street and pulls away. Soon, Tanglewood Road becomes a cozy blur of amber rectangles and blinking Christmas lights.

"Have you had any more contact with Kieran since we spoke?" he asks.

"No. And if I had, I wouldn't tell you."

There's an uneasy pause. "You haven't . . . You haven't done anything careless, have you, Ellen?"

"*Careless?* You mean like driving a car into a reservoir with him in the passenger seat?"

He blanches and I apologize.

"No, my fault," he says. "I shouldn't have used that word."

"Just tell me what it is you want to tell me, Vic."

"Okay." He doesn't like my mood, I can tell, but he must assume he's at least partly responsible for it. "India is pregnant," he says.

There is a stretched-out moment of pain. The world outside the window shimmers like a migraine. "Congratulations," I say, at last. One word, but the ache in my chest makes it hard to say it. "You could have told me that over the phone, you know."

It's bad news that needs to be given in person. A faraway voice over the police radio. Officers at the door.

"I know I could." He pauses to brake at the junction. His expression is rueful, as if one unenviable job has been completed, but another remains.

"What?" I say.

"We just had the second scan. It's a boy."

The world goes still. Suddenly, the van smells turn my stomach. I see the two of us at Lucas's scan. I'm smiling, asking the technician if she can see if it's a boy or a girl. She says, "Do you both want to know?"

"Yes!"

How many times must she have taken part in that exchange and yet her delight was sincere, I was sure of it.

"Well, that's wonderful," I say, and I blink into sudden oncoming headlights, grateful for the dazzle. For a terrible moment I think I won't be able to move from my seat. I won't be able to get on the train and go to The Heights. "I'm happy for you both. Really."

"Thank you," Vic says. "That means a lot."

We're on the move again, already slowing for a red light before the turn into the station. Vic's concerns do not seem to have been entirely eased. "Like I said on the phone, Kieran's on his guard. You should be on yours too."

The lights turn green. "Vic, this is nothing to do with you now. We agreed."

"That doesn't mean I don't care." He's pulling over by the station entrance. The next train is in six minutes. It is not a fast service, but will snake through Crystal Palace and Dulwich, delivering me to London Bridge in thirty-five minutes.

"You want some company at this party?" he says impulsively. "I can easily park and come with you if you like?"

"No. I said this is nothing to do with you." I open the door. The woven handles of the wine bag dig into my wrist where the glove ends. "Go back home to India. She's the one who needs you now, not me. Thank you for the lift."

"You're welcome."

I'm halfway to the barriers when I hear him calling after me and I turn, frowning. He's wound down the passenger window. "What?"

"You forgot your bag."

Trying not to gasp, I scurry back, reach through the open window, and tear it from his hands. Was there time for him to un-buckle, unzip, look inside, then zip and buckle it up again? While keeping control of a car?

No. No way. His face, when I glance at him, is impassive, his attention on the rearview and the car behind that's agitating for his spot.

I head into the station a second time.

thirty-five

THE HOSTESS IS WEARING a dress covered in those huge silver sequins that look like scales. A mermaid of the night. Her boyfriend is a classic financial services type: conceited gaze, alcoholic flush, box-fresh party shirt. The flat is rammed with others from the same tribe — affluent, international, and, I'm guessing, unaccustomed to having their fun spoiled. They can't possibly know they have a cuckoo in their nest and, for Asha's sake, I hope that whatever unfolds tonight no feathers will fly here on the fifth floor.

May she only benefit from her brush with notoriety.

The music is, inevitably, Christmassy. "Jingle Bell Rock" plays as I arrive and "Santa Baby" will follow, I expect. (*All I Want for Christmas Is You, Kieran.*) Asha has solved the lighting issue by turning them all off, but for several hundred meters of string lights and an enormous neon reindeer head mounted on the living room wall. There are a dangerous number of candles, too, and I'm presuming these are the source of the rich plum-pudding miasma that envelops the throng.

"This is our lighting designer," she tells her already pie-eyed partner—Sebastian? Anthony? A *Brideshead* kind of name—who quips about always being the last to know while making it clear he's entitled to be the first.

He presses a glass of champagne into my hand and I raise it to my lips. I need to be careful not to drink more than a couple of mouthfuls, but it is gloriously icy and I long to suck it down in one.

"Did you bring your architect?" Asha asks. "The one from Habitus you work with?"

"No, he couldn't make it, I'm afraid. We'll set up a proper meeting in the New Year." I haven't asked any architect, of course. Chances are I'll be in no position to take on the work. In my mind's eye, I see myself in the New Year in a police interview room or even in a cell, sleeping on the same standard-issue mattress Kieran Watts did years ago.

"I told you the guy in the top flat is coming, didn't I?" she says, on cue. "In case I get sidetracked, you can't miss him. He's got bleached hair—a bit like yours, actually. Maybe you've got the same hairdresser."

A polite smile conceals my sharp intake of breath.

"Oh, *he* won't show up," Asha's man says. "He's a total recluse. He barely answers the door."

"He will. I told you, he's trying to poach Ellen."

"She's not a wild animal, Ash!"

I laugh, wondering if they will repeat all of this later when the police come. Asha's remembered the name of the architects, obviously has excellent recall. One dilemma is resolved, in any case. I am easily going to be able to slip away without being seen. It's going to be impossible for people to account for others in this crush, especially someone they were never introduced to.

As my hosts are claimed by other guests, I find Selena in front of me, leaning in to kiss first one cheek and then the other. It startles me to see her here, though I should have guessed since she's our connection in the first place. That call I made to her the night Freya went to Kieran's place: if she were to mention that to the police, would that suggest premeditation? But watching and planning are two separate activities, aren't they?

(You may well scoff at all this—there's the small matter of the gun in my bag, right?)

"Careful of the window," she says, steering me through the moving crowd and away from the opening, that dark hungry drop. With a little polite struggling, I'm in the corner of the room, with a view across the entire assembly. "Oh, did I tell you, Ellen, I remembered something weird that *I* did once? I was at the zoo and I totally had the urge to throw my bag into one of the enclosures. Is that the same as your thing?"

I try to engage, to be normal. "Kind of. You wouldn't have got your bag back, so it does sound like an urge to self-sabotage."

"Definitely. They were African hunting dogs, they'd have torn it to pieces. I didn't do it, though. Like you said, you don't act on it, you just feel deranged for a couple of seconds and then you come to your senses." As she laughs, her teeth flawless, breath sweet, I lay my hand on my own bag, protecting it like a pregnant belly.

"I *have* to tell you what happened today with the builders . . ." As she segues into a new anecdote, I feel the hairs on my arms rise and I search over her shoulder for the cause. There it is, in the doorway: a bleached-blond top of a head, a fragment of wax-smooth forehead. Kieran. I can't see his eyes, but I can tell from the way his head is angled he's looking in my direction and I give an involuntary shudder.

"What?" Selena swivels to follow my gaze, but she's shorter than me and her view is obscured. She turns back, continuing to prattle, and in doing so creates the gap needed for Kieran and me to lock eyes. Again, I shudder and again she turns, mid-flow, still unable to catch a glimpse of what's spooked me. It's as if I'm the only one who can see him, the only one to identify his cold-blooded presence in this hot-blooded crowd.

Should I point him out to her? Would that harm my defense or somehow help protect me? Before I can decide, there's another adjustment within the throng as a couple arrives with what must be a dozen balloons, huge and shiny and shaped like Christmas trees. By the time the shrieks of delight have faded, the balloons set loose to bob above our heads, Kieran is gone. I doubt he even bothered to make himself known to Asha or her man. He just did what he came to do and left.

"I must use the bathroom," I tell Selena. "Do you know other people here?"

"No, but when has *that* ever stopped me," she says conspiratori-ally, as if I've known her for years. I touch her arm and smile, then slip through the swarm and out of the front door.

On the landing, the temperature dips by about five degrees. I can hear the lift rumbling and I know it is delivering Kieran to the top floor. I take my gloves from my pocket and put them on. A wild, heightened feeling rips through me as I push open the door to the stairs, a visceral recognition of the momentousness of the occasion. I'm as certain as I've ever been that what happens next will come to be questioned, recounted, reconstructed.

In half an hour's time—less than that—one of us could be dead.

thirty-six

Do I HAVE YOUR sympathy at all, dear reader? It's so hard to judge. How proper writers do it, I really don't know. Invest their hearts and souls in their work with no guarantee that it will be liked—or even interpreted as they intend it to be.

One thing I can be sure of: if I don't have your sympathy now, then what I tell you next is definitely not going to help.

I take the stairs quickly. Up that featureless well, with its portholes onto the lightless brick wall of the building next door. The creaks from the lift shaft, the odor of cleaning products blending with that of the cloying spiced pudding that has attached itself to me. I arrive at the top out of breath, but the absence of pain in my thigh muscles tells me just how much adrenaline is swamping my system. All sensation is centered in my stomach; it's as if the flesh has been scooped out and the hollow crammed with nerves.

When I knock on his door, the sound blunted by gloved knuckles, it gives way. He's left it ajar—of course he has. He knows I'm in the building for him, he knows my attendance at Asha's party is for his benefit. He is as prepared for me as I am him.

I step inside, scanning jaundiced walls for cameras, finding none. Exactly as in Asha's flat five floors below, a narrow hallway leads left to the living room and right to the bathroom and bedrooms. I turn left. Music is playing, not the festive anthems of five floors below, but the soundtrack to a wake, a female voice lamenting in dark, mournful tones. At first, I think she's singing a language I don't know, but then I realize these are not words, but something invented, and the strange melodies snake around me.

Through the curved window, Tower Bridge glows white and blue and, as I move forward, the top of the Shard comes into range, a festive silver steeple for the godless. I imagine Freya standing up against this glass, Red Riding Hood in a mustard-yellow coat, the wolf right beside her with a paw on the small of her back. That gruff voice saying, "The view's even better from the roof."

And then I realize the voice is in the room, coming from behind me, speaking not to my precious daughter but to me. I swivel, lift my gaze to the double-height skylight, the jewel in the crown of the building, and then to the mezzanine walkway built under it.

He is standing at its center, up against the rail, a sphere of light on the wall behind accentuating the broad beam of his shoulders, the taut muscles of his neck. It is impossible not to register this time what eluded me when we met outside the café: his grotesque impersonation of me—the black clothing and bleached hair, perhaps even those alterations to his features. And yet, he is no admirer of mine. When he speaks, loathing drips from every syllable.

"Come to pay me off, have you? Like last time?"

"That was Vic, not me." My tone is hard and flat. "I had no interest in saving your life, so please don't flatter yourself. Could you come down?" I don't like the backlit effect that is suddenly making me think of the angel Gabriel, when this man is the spiritual opposite.

He doesn't move. "What do you want?" he asks, and it occurs to me he's nervous. He feels safer with the extra height, the vertical separation. His large pale hands grip the rail and I picture them on the steering wheel that night five years ago. I hear the sound of Lucas screaming.

"I want you to stop seeing my daughter," I say and my fingers graze my bag.

"Why?"

"*Why?* Because I know you're using her to torment me. You don't care about her. You'd happily destroy her."

His chest rises. "I *do* care about her."

"Come on, you were released over two and a half years ago, but suddenly you want to reconnect? At the exact moment you think I could make life difficult for you?"

"It's not suddenly. I've tried before."

He must mean the letter, but I have no intention of discussing that. "Look, I know you're using her to warn me off, just like Ratcliffe tried to—and even Vic. I'm not stupid."

He appears to puzzle over this, his head tilting, brow furrowing, but I can tell he's play-acting. "Why would me and Frey being back in touch be warning you off?"

Me and Frey. The insolence of him. "Because you know she's all I've got left. You stuck the knife in five years ago and now you want to twist it and watch me writhe in agony."

The image pleases him. There's a twitch of a smile on those surgically bloated lips. "Why would I want you to writhe in agony, Ellen?" He says my name almost tenderly, before adding, coldly:

"Oh, wait, because you orchestrated a massive hate campaign against me? Or maybe because you tried to have me killed?"

I swallow. I will not waste time denying this last claim or discovering how he knows—since Vic's heads-up, I've come to the conclusion that it makes no difference, not in practical terms. All that matters is I failed, otherwise he wouldn't be standing in front of me now. "No. Because you're a psycho," I say. "You were then and you are now. You couldn't bear to see a happy person, a happy family, and you made it your business to destroy us."

He dips his head a fraction, his gaze darkening. "You're wrong. *You're* the psycho. You flaunted your perfect family and deliberately excluded me. You were a snob and a crazy, obsessed mother and, when the accident happened, you had a ready-made villain."

At this, his first reference to Lucas's death, grief stampedes through me. "You made yourself the villain when you left Lucas to die," I gasp. "Vic should never have set you free."

"Set me free?" He gestures with both hands. "This is what I'm talking about, you act like I'm an animal—you always did."

"Okay, if you prefer, he should never have paid you off. It wasn't his money to give away."

"You'll have to take that up with him. I'm satisfied I've paid him back." As surprise registers on my face, he gives a tight bark of laughter. "He still hasn't told you, has he? Why d'you think James decided to invest?"

"James?" I feel my cheeks flame under my party makeup. "You mean James Ratcliffe?"

Now he really does laugh, that big rattling sound of old, taking genuine pleasure in my ignorance and confusion. "You're a pretty pathetic detective, aren't you? Vic got the backing for his business because *I* made it happen."

"I don't believe you." I've never had any reason to investigate the source of Vic's capital, but have taken at face value his account of having made a successful pitch to an investor. He'd been shopping his business plan around town since long before Kieran entered our lives. "I've googled Ratcliffe, the company, his clients, all of it. There's no way I would've missed Vic's name."

He shrugs. "So his brand isn't featured on their website. Must've been someone he didn't want to find out, huh?"

"Well, I don't care," I say. "If he wants to take Ratcliffe's money, let him. He has completely different priorities from me." A new son. A new Lucas. I see Vic in his tower, in the flat I've never set foot in, high above the gray, rain-slicked streets. His lovely young girlfriend, their baby in her arms. And I'm glad he's there and not here. This is *my* war.

The song ends and another starts. The same singer, the same gibberish, but with an urgent mood that acts on me, galvanizes me. Funny, I thought I'd want to talk to Kieran long and hard, extract the details I've sought for years, but it isn't unfolding like that. Already I've had enough of his posturing from on high. Already I want this over with.

I unbuckle my bag and open the zip, take out the revolver. I position the grip in the heel of my hand, finger on the trigger guard, as I practiced at home. Kieran cries out in shock, though I'm pointing it at the floor. "If you won't come down, I'll come up. One of us has to end this. It's the only way. You know that as well as I do, Kieran."

I'm aware of him moving to his right as I pace towards the spiral stairs, the weapon knocking my thigh as I climb. When I emerge onto the mezzanine, the space is empty, a bitter cold spreading through open terrace doors, the night gloom beyond. As I step onto the threshold, the darkness causes a momentary loss of vision and I hold my breath in my lungs, feeling the frigid air deep inside me. I can, at least, hear: the pulse of music from Asha's open window, the din of party chatter. The horn of a boat on the river. Those keening vocals from Kieran's living room have been silenced.

I start to get my bearings. The roof lights are off, but a little of the lamplight from below glows through the skylight, weakly, as if the glass is smoked. Kieran is directly in front of me at the balustrade. There are perhaps five paces between us, but I can't take them. Not yet.

"Come out and join me," he invites, his breath a gray cloud in the black night. "What, too scared? Oh, of course, you don't like heights, do you? You're going to have to get over that. Just this once, Ellen. Just this once."

Still, I can't move. I can do nothing but stare, both attracted and repelled by the sight of him, by the illusion that the balustrade is edgeless, invisible, as if one backwards step, one tiny readjustment of a heel, will send him plunging out of sight.

He speaks again, something more complex in his voice now, something that seems to conjure those teenage years, all the joy and sorrow of lost times:

"Here's the deal, Ellen. And you don't need your gun."

Killing Time (cont)

Autobiography is a slippery form at the best of times, and this is never more evident than when Saint's account of her cat and mouse game with Kieran Watts reaches its final maneuvers. How can we know what really happened the night they faced off for the last time when only one of them survived to tell the tale?

Here, then, are two legally proven facts:

One: exactly five years after the incident that claimed Lucas Gordon's life, a second incident put an end to Kieran Watts's.

Two: Ellen Saint was arrested at the scene.

Sunday Times magazine, December 2021

thirty-seven

THEY SAY YOU HAVE to remember catastrophe in all its detail before you have a hope in hell of forgetting it. (Don't ask me who "they" are. Bankers? Premier league managers?) Well, there can't be too many catastrophes where a reconstruction feels as appropriate as mine does—no, make that a *resurrection*. After all, this whole monstrous situation began with one, didn't it? The resurrection of Kieran Watts on a rooftop in Shad Thames.

And justice being the elegant creature she is, it ends in the same place.

"Here's the deal, Ellen," he says. "And you don't need your gun."

My eyes have adjusted and I see his face better now, the strange and mesmerizing glow of his eyes. "What deal?"

"I'll give you exactly what you want. But you have to come here. You have to come to the edge."

His manner is more seductive than threatening and I'm confused, mistrustful. "What do you mean?"

"I mean push me. You can tell everyone I jumped, obviously. Or don't say anything at all. No one even knows you're here, do they?"

No one knows you're here: why would he say that? I cast about for the blinking eyes of a camera, but all I find are the red dots of cranes in construction sites over the river.

He continues, his tone different again, regretful now and conciliatory: "I know what you're thinking. I'm not messing with you, I promise. I've wanted to do this for a long time. I can't go on, not remembering, not knowing. It was all lost, Ellen. Lost with Lucas."

I can't bear him to say my son's name. I swallow my pain. "Please, if you really want to do it, do it. Jump."

But he shakes his head. "That's not the deal. I need *you*. I need to feel your hand on my back when I go . . ."

"Why?" This is crazy, wrong-footing trickery. It is—

Oh! *Now* I see. Now it is clear. It's his final revenge. To make me the very thing he was, the thing all men despise. A killer. A thief of life—a young person's life. Yes, the world will say it is suicide, but I will know. I'll always know and it will be his way of preying on me forever.

"You understand," he says gently. "But you have to be brave. You have to face your fear."

I drop both my bag and the gun. My foot lifts, but does not step. *Just this once, Ellen. Just this once.*

And I do it. Finally released from my paralysis, I leave the safety of the terrace doors to walk across the roof towards him, towards the huge gaping space between the cliff face of The Heights and the twinkling city beyond. His expression now grotesquely jubilant, Kieran turns his back on me and leans forward over the barrier, folding so steeply his head hangs towards the ground. My stomach flips as if I too have been turned upside down. His left foot springs off the ground and then the right, his upper body lowering, fraction by fraction, until he is holding himself in perfect balance between life and death.

His voice comes from far away now, from a separate place, one word repeated: "Push," he says. "Push." And it is what I've dreaded and desired for as long as I can remember. I place my right palm on his back. He is already tipping when I do it.

The push and the jump are one.

I clap my hands to my ears so I cannot hear him land—one, two, three, all the way to ten—and then I look down. And when I say look down, I mean I press against that barrier with my full body weight and double right over it, exactly as he did moments ago. I have to: it's the only way I can see what's happening below.

I see the tops of heads of people on the fifth floor leaning from the window. A dress of silver scales. Bangles glinting on wrists. Phone screens lighting up and then turning downwards. In a sudden flare of flashlight, I glimpse a splayed, broken shape on the walkway.

Something feels different within me then. Something incurable has been cured. And I can't help smiling to myself when I understand what it is.

I am standing right at the edge of the highest building in range and yet I feel no urge to jump. No urge at all.

Which is, I think you'll agree, the only acceptable ending.

Killing Time (cont)

I began by describing a typical library and so it is—except for one thing. You can't just walk into it off the street. You need the correct authority and an official escort. You need— if I counted correctly—seven doors to be unlocked for you to pass through and then locked again behind you. Because, in an attempt to follow Felix Penney's "rules of revelation" (his term, not mine), I have willfully delayed mentioning that Ellen Saint and her fellow students are not free citizens but prisoners. Their residence, HMP Langton, Berkshire, has been rehabilitating female offenders since 1961. Or attempting to.

Penney's memoir-writing course is just one of a range of intensive self-analysis exercises offered by Langton's controversial therapeutic unit, designed in the 2000s to overturn stubborn reoffender rates. I say controversial, because, inevitably, it attracts its share of detractors. It is a matter of public record that the program, which includes art, theater, and a host of other creative activities, costs almost ten thousand pounds a year more than a standard prison stretch.

"I would question whether this is legitimate therapy and not simply an expensive and indulgent treat for some of the least deserving people in our society," says former shadow home secretary Gareth Symonds.

Penney begs to differ. He points out that much of the extra cost is met by the Langton Trust, a charitable body with a formidable fundraising record, and adds that his own fee is waived. "There is no way a convicted criminal like Ellen could have reached this level of rehabilitation—and atonement—in a conventional prison," he argues.

Might "atonement" be overstating it, I suggest?

But Penney isn't backing down. Langton's memoir course is his baby and Ellen Saint is the baby's shiny new rattle.

Sunday Times magazine, December 2021

thirty-eight

I FEEL STRANGELY COMFORTABLE in the aftermath—I mean, it isn't like we haven't been here before, is it? A shocking incident involving two people, only one of whom comes out of it alive. A sequence of events that is hard to prove and easy to doubt. Press interest—a *lot* of press interest.

After a period of legal negotiation as process-driven and emotionless as Kieran's ever was, I plead guilty to Encouraging or Assisting Suicide. It is an unusual charge and prosecutions are rare; where my sentence will land between minimum and maximum, my team prefers not to predict.

James Ratcliffe is an unlikely ally, giving evidence of Kieran's depression, which dated from well before my reentry into his life. According to the investor, the inescapable guilt of having failed to save his best friend had left him staggering from one antianxiety medication to the next. He has several times threatened to throw himself from his terrace.

The Moodsmart app is not mentioned; business interests

protected to the last. I wouldn't be at all surprised to hear that the launch has been delayed (maybe, thanks to accounts like this, it will be given a new name).

But the historical link between Kieran and me has to be explored—of course it does. Ratcliffe testifies that Kieran's new surname *was* inspired by my maiden name, which he'd learned years ago from Lucas. He also had a photo of me, taken without my knowledge, and later shared it with the cosmetic surgeon who worked on his face. Body dysmorphic disorder is mentioned, as is borderline personality disorder, but neither quite defines the obsessive way he came to regard me following his release from Danstone.

Still, if anyone understands obsession it is me.

Asha gives a statement confirming that the encounter between her neighbor "Sam" and her new lighting designer was engineered by him, and that I had expressed only casual interest in returning his overtures. Neither his brief attendance at the party nor my premature departure was noticed by any of the partygoers who gave statements.

Selena is not among those asked to give one.

As for my second phone, I surrendered it to the police willingly on arrest. What was there to hide, in the end? An audio file, a photograph, the search history of a bereaved mother getting herself up to date on the upgraded lifestyle of the criminal who wrecked her life. The very fact that I procured it is argued to be evidence of a paranoid mind. Unstable thinking. And maybe it was. Certainly, the record of Kieran's trial, the stress of Lock Up Longer, the years of medical notes I've accrued, it all works in my favor. The sentence, when it comes, is right at the best-case-scenario end of the scale. Just two years, the same as Kieran's.

But, wait, what about the gun, you ask? That five-year minimum term I mentioned. Well, I am extremely fortunate to have the firearm charge dropped after the item is found to be a replica, the type used in historical reenactments—perfectly legal and with a market value of about £150. I now know that an imitation firearm is only treated as a firearm in law if it can be "readily convertible into a weapon" and my convincing little toy was not. I owe more to those kids on the Whitley Estate than they could ever know, though I'm not so naive as to think they would gain an ounce of satisfaction from that debt of gratitude.

Of course, there will always be those who think I got away with murder. I understand that. But, as the judge said herself after pronouncing my fate, there are no winners in this case.

| | | | | | |

Early in my stretch, I am told of a prison unit to which I might request a transfer, a therapeutic facility that I'm convinced must be oversubscribed, but, it transpires, is not. The prospect presents barriers to the majority of the prison population, it seems. The unluckiest of lives have left most lacking any desire to express themselves in psychotherapy, let alone memoir or art or theater.

I get the transfer—obviously.

If there are any of you yet to make the link between this program and the one Kieran himself undertook, I'm sure you will now. Just as he met James Ratcliffe inside, so I now meet Felix Penney. I'm following in his footsteps, how about that? Poetic justice, dramatic irony, double tragedy?

Take your pick.

Killing Time (cont)

There were grumblings in some quarters about the leniency of Saint's sentencing—more of that anon. But lenient it was. Among those to give a character reference for her was Vic Gordon, the last time he has gone on record in discussion of his infamous ex-partner. He judged her "anxious" and "emotional," but "in no way harmful." "The only thing she ever wanted from Kieran Watts was the truth," he said.

With good behavior—and her behavior, according to the prison governor, has been exemplary—Ellen Saint will be a free woman again in time to enjoy the fanfare surrounding publication of *Saint or Sinner*. The initial print run is "bullish," according to her publisher, though sceptics will be pleased to know that UK law prohibits convicts from profiting from their crimes. Proceeds will instead be donated to a charity of the family's choice.

Sunday Times magazine, December 2021

thirty-nine

I AM ADDING THIS short final chapter just before my book goes to press. It has a title now—*Saint or Sinner*—an editor, a publisher, even a publicist. I have approved the image that will grace the cover: mugshot me—I suppose *that* was inevitable. Taken on the night of Kieran's death, I look like an aging punk mildly inconvenienced by having been booked. (Justin told me that Vic said it reminded him of that famous mugshot of David Bowie from the 1970s. He had a poster of it on his wall when we met as students.)

Release day is coming soon, in both senses of the word.

According to my publisher, the media are interested in meeting with me, even shadowing me on the day itself and documenting my return to society. There's been a call from the journalist from the *Sunday Times* magazine who sat in on our group months ago. Michaela Ross, she's called. She's read the full manuscript now and wants to schedule a big feature, maybe even a cover story, with photographs taken in the library. Imagine that!

To be honest, I didn't sense that Ms. Ross liked me much the first time we met, so I don't hold out much hope for a sympathetic portrayal. But who am I to talk about sympathetic portrayals? I doubt that Prisca will recognize mine of Kieran—or of herself, for that matter. Nor will James Ratcliffe or Jade or Sheridan, maybe not even Justin and Freya, who have visited me regularly here and support this project. Support *me*. And, believe me, I know just how lucky I am that they have not disassociated themselves from me and hidden themselves away. Instead, they consider me altered by my crime, cured by the act of retelling.

I have not seen Vic. Through Justin, I asked that he not try to see me or contact me. As I told him the last time we were alone together, he needs to forget about me and focus on his new family.

When the book comes out, the publisher is going to donate copies to prison libraries across the UK and Felix and I are scheduled to give a series of talks to women prisoners. I've been to those sorts of events myself while I've been here. They usually hold them in the sports hall. An outside speaker comes in and for a blessed hour you could be anywhere in England where educated people like to gather. The only difference is there's no glass of wine, no bowl of crisps. No handbag on your lap or car key in your pocket. Only a faint guarded fascination in the speaker's eye when it comes to rest on you. *I wonder what* she *did.*

I will try my best not to look like *that*.

And, then, after it all dies down, what next?

Felix wants me to write fiction. "In many ways, it's much easier than memoir," he tells me.

Yes, I say. I imagine it is.

part four

Killing Time (cont)

If there is one certainty to take from our society's long history of crime and punishment, it is that we humans have a habit of repeating the actions of those who came before us. Sometimes, very recently indeed.

On the two occasions I meet Ellen in HMP Langton, she gives no indication of knowing that while she has been busy writing a campaign has been launched outside to review the sentencing for her offense. Lock Ellen Up for Longer, in other words. There is no national newspaper partner, no army of supporters—it is progressing, in fact, in a style that is discreet to the point of covert—and yet its instigator, Prisca Evans, is no less tireless a warrior than Ellen herself ever was.

"Encouraging or assisting suicide is a serious offense," she tells me in an email sent just before this piece went to press. "Let's be honest, it's the difference between life and death, isn't it?" A couple of recent cases in the US have given her hope that lawmakers in the UK will take a new look at the tariffs recommended for this highly unusual crime.

"Meanwhile, I'm here to remind people that there's a woman about to be released who directly and intentionally caused a man's death," she says. "If Ellen Saint hadn't involved herself in Kieran's life, my boy would still be alive and getting the mental health support he obviously needed."

A fascinating parallel, I'm sure you agree. And just imagine if we were to follow this to its logical conclusion: Ms. Evans might one day close her emails, seek out her nemesis and take the law into her own hands. She might even find herself jailed as a consequence, doing her time perhaps in the very unit Saint now occupies. Writing the story of her crime.

But, no. That would be too incredible an ending, even for Felix Penney.

Wouldn't it?

Sunday Times magazine, December 2021

Vic

DECEMBER 2021

HE'S ALREADY TURNING THE pages when he gets back to Skylark Apartments and waits for the lift, shamelessly scanning the print for his own name. Having torn open the plastic wrapper in the street outside the newsagent's, he had the surreal experience of clapping eyes on Ellen on the cover of the *Sunday Times* magazine while treading on a discarded box of chicken bones. They've photographed her at her desk in the prison library, which looks pretty much like any other library in the land, and she's not dressed in one of those prison jumpsuits you see on TV but in drab garments any civilian of limited means might wear.

All in all, she looks okay, he thinks. There is none of her old glamour, of course, but she's lost that terrible haunted quality he remembers. She looks earthly again, even at peace.

The coverline reads, "Killing Time: The Sins of Ellen Saint."

Clever. But, then, the name's a gift, isn't it?

| | | | | | |

"Hey, you got it," India remarks, when he lets himself into the flat. Through their son's open bedroom door, he can see Milo on the floor with his Noah's ark shape sorter. He's much too busy to call out to Daddy and is mercifully uncomprehending of any conversation involving words of more than one syllable. "Remind me when Justin said she gets out?"

"Three days before publication, apparently," Vic says. "So that's a week tomorrow. He's bracing himself for all the publicity."

"What about their daughter?"

"He's shielding her from it as much as possible, but she sounds pretty strong. She's coming home for Ellen's release, but he thinks once she's had some time with her mum, she'll go and stay with her boyfriend for a while. Lie low there until the new term restarts. She's in her final year at Warwick now."

"Sounds sensible." India has half an eye on the shape sorting. The wrong shape is being smashed into the wrong hole, causing volcanic frustration. She makes an encouraging noise and turns back to Vic. "Two years. It seems like no time, does it?"

"It's gone by really quickly." Though perhaps not so for Ellen.

"Do they mention Common or Gordon in the article?" Though technically only part-time now, India is always thinking about the business. It—and Milo's future—is shaping up nicely.

"I haven't read it yet," Vic says, "but I don't think so. I'm not really in it, thank God."

She nods. "I've just made a new pot of coffee. You have some time, read it properly."

She closes Milo's door behind her and Vic hears her enthusiastic cry as she joins the fun. He does as he's told and pours himself a coffee, sits down to read. It's not a long feature, but the photographs and an extract from the book mean it extends to six pages.

The final argument is a bit of a stretch, in his opinion. A little flight of fantasy on the part of the journalist, who plainly didn't warm to Ellen. Whatever Prisca hopes to achieve, the crime is surely too rare for her campaign to gain traction in the mainstream media and, in any case, it is far too late to have an impact on Ellen herself. As for the notion of her following in Ellen's footsteps and coming after the enemy vigilante-style . . . No, he can't see it. Ellen is a one-off, all heart and soul, all intensity.

He turns the page to the extract—they've chosen the night of Lucas's death, when a sleepless Ellen has a premonition that something terrible has happened, hours before the knock on the door confirms it. But Vic doesn't need to read that because he's already consumed *Saint or Sinner* in its entirety, having been sent an advance copy by Ellen's publisher several weeks ago.

He took the day off work for the task, reading the last few chapters three times to check he hadn't missed any clue regarding his own role. His final appearance comes on the evening of Kieran's death, when he gives Ellen a lift to the station in his van and breaks the news about the baby. His final line is nicely prosaic: "You forgot your bag." Then, the very last reference to him comes in the closing chapter, about how Ellen wants him to forget her and concentrate on his new family.

Which is exactly what he has done.

Her account of Kieran's death is immaculately handled. It is not only consistent with the official record but also quite poetic in its way—what was that line Vic liked? *Something incurable has been cured*, that's right. She's managed to construct an outcome of perfectly balanced justice, of symmetry—*It is what I've dreaded and desired for as long as I can remember . . . The push and the jump are one*—that doesn't often occur in real life.

It certainly didn't occur in *this* one.

Because, whatever else is true in Ellen's soon-to-be-bestselling memoir, he knows for certain that Chapter 37, her account of Kieran's death, is nothing more than a beautiful lie. Everything after Kieran tells her, "You don't need your gun" is pure fantasy. A deliberate, self-sacrificing cover-up of the truth.

And Vic is its only beneficiary.

Vic

DECEMBER 19, 2019

FROM THE FOOTBRIDGE, THE Heights is a natural focal point thanks to the window halfway up thickly draped with lights, the oblique glimpse beyond of a seething Christmas party. Through its opening, the bells are ringing out—it's "Fairytale of New York," everyone's favorite—overlaid with human shrieks and cackles. The stories above and below are dark, but for the very top, where pale light from both window and skylight suggests the occupant is at home.

Of course he is, Vic thinks. The flat is a mousetrap, but whether Kieran or Ellen is the one operating that trap, he does not know.

He zigzags through the passageways to reach the top of Mill Street, then spends a moment at the main doors examining the entry-phone keypad. He is counting on the code remaining unchanged from the day he watched James Ratcliffe key it in and committed it to memory. Presumably, it's an easy enough task to change it and inform the other residents, but the fatalism in Kieran's manner that day makes Vic think he will not have done so. His dilemma these last weeks has not been if Ellen will come for him but how he will overcome her when she does.

Well, tonight's the night. Vic knows this not only because of the significance of the date—to Ellen, that will make her actions feel predestined—but because she as good as gave the game away herself in the car. *I said this is nothing to do with you*, she told him, in clear reference to Kieran, and yet Vic had only offered to go to a client's party with her. Then there was the ferocity with which she snatched her bag from him, a different bag from the one she's used for as long as he can remember. She has something in that bag that matters to her. Something that could harm Kieran.

The code works! The door releases and he makes straight for the stairs; there is no time to lose waiting for the lift. He prays he is not too late. Once he'd ditched his car near the station and waited for the next direct train to London Bridge, he calculated that Ellen had only a half-hour head start on him. But then his train stalled owing to a signaling fault and put her lead at closer to an hour.

As he climbs, the music from the party grows louder and then begins to fade. He reaches the top landing. His legs ache and his chest burns, but he can't afford to rest. Ahead is that narrow window, with its glimpse of Tower Bridge, all lit up for its photo op. He raps on Kieran's door. It opens at a push and he knows he was right. She's here. She must have forced her way in and driven Kieran back before he could shut his own door properly. As he moves noiselessly into the main room, he half expects to see blood spattered on the walls, Kieran's mutilated body slumped in a corner. But it is unoccupied and, as far as he can tell, undisturbed.

At first, he hears only the thud of the party below and perhaps the hum of an appliance of some sort, but then he picks out voices from above. As he creeps silently up the spiral to the mezzanine, he remembers his own advice to Kieran: *Just get yourself out here. I guarantee she won't follow.* It seems he may have been wrong, however, because here she is, her slim black-clad figure poised on the threshold, her back to Vic.

He prefers to stay unnoticed for now, to get a sense of her intentions, but Kieran's voice drifts in—"Here's the deal, Ellen. And you don't need your gun"—and Vic cries out without thinking:

"*What gun?*"

Ellen pivots to face him, her features twisting with confusion and annoyance. Her bag is over her shoulder, resting at hip height, with her right hand obscured. Does she really have a weapon? She must for Kieran to have said that. It is both surreal and frightening to know his instinct at the station was correct. *She has come here to kill.*

"What the hell are you doing here, Vic?" She answers her own question: "You followed me."

He swallows his panic and steps towards her. "No, but I guessed. Where is he? Is he all right?" He can't see beyond her from where he stands and she now widens her stance to block his path out to the terrace. He pictures Kieran hanging off the balustrade by his fingertips like one of those free climbers. "What gun?" he repeats. "Show me, Ellen."

As if it were nothing, she twitches her right wrist to give him a glimpse, stepping adroitly aside when he tries—and fails—to reach for it. This at least allows him access to the terrace. As the sharp air hits his face, he registers Kieran in the unlit space, pressed dangerously backwards against the balustrade, as if he cannot support his own weight—

Oh, God, has she already used that gun? Vic feels a clench of terror in his chest. *But no, impossible.* He'd have heard the shot, and so would everyone in the building. All those partygoers in the flat down there, they'd be screaming and fleeing, but, instead, the music plays on and their revelry is audible above the beat.

"Well, you're just in time," Ellen tells him, her voice pitiless. "He's going to do us all a favor and fall." Addressing Kieran, she snarls, "Did you hear that? I've got no interest in any deal. *I'm* in charge here."

Vic gapes. He's going to *fall*? She's forcing him to jump at gunpoint? Ignoring Ellen's protests, he strides over and grabs the young man by the shoulders, manhandling him a few feet forward and away from the drop. It is the first time he's touched Kieran since—when? A slap on the shoulder as he exited his flat with Lucas in the summer after sixth form? Under his hoodie Kieran's body is solid. He's made himself muscle-bound, a new version of himself. With this strength and youth, he should be able overpower the two of them—if he weren't being threatened with a gun.

Where the *fuck* did she get hold of it? The same place she once looked for a contract killer, he supposes. It figures that she's cut out the middleman this time.

He and Kieran stand facing each other, both breathing heavily. There is wary gratitude in the younger man's face, a throwback to the ambush in the woods, when he understood that the rope Vic was throwing was to save him, not to hang him. It's obvious he regards Vic as *his* ally in this crisis, not Ellen's. It's the two of them against the crazy lady. "Thank you," he mumbles.

"Don't thank me," Vic tells him curtly. He wants to save him, but that doesn't mean he has to like him. He'll never *like* him. He addresses Ellen. "Why don't we all go inside and talk about this?"

"I don't want to talk." The hand holding the gun jerks. "If he doesn't jump, if I let him live, he'll hurt her, he'll do to her what he did to Lucas."

"Who?" Vic says.

"Freya, of course."

What is she talking about? She can't mean Kieran is back behind the wheel—and why would he be in a car with Freya Saint, anyway? Cries rise from the open window below and a few seconds later a helium balloon in the shape of a Christmas tree drifts past, trailing a silver ribbon. Glancing down, Vic sees the water far below, shivering in the lights of the dock.

"What deal?" he says to Kieran. "You said, 'Here's the deal.' What is it?" He prays it wasn't just some desperate tactic of Kieran's to create an opportunity to save himself, that the bastard really does have something to trade.

"I meant I'll tell her," Kieran says. "I'll tell her and then she has to go. Go for good."

"Tell her . . . ?" Vic thinks straightaway of Jade, what she confided that day outside his flat on Shannon Way, her hair a rippling pink river, her eyes swollen with sorrow. "You mean about Jade?"

Kieran's pale face darkens. "I mean what happened the night of the accident. There's something important you don't know."

"You mean you *remember*?" Ellen's voice shatters over them and, as they turn together, she pulls the gun upwards, pointing somewhere between the two men at about hip height. "Then fucking spit it out, you freak! What is this important thing we don't know?"

And, for the first time since Vic arrived, Kieran acknowledges her directly. He lowers his shoulders, grips his hands together, and looks right at her.

"I wasn't the one driving that night," he says. "Lucas was."

Vic

DECEMBER 19, 2019

WHAT? VIC STARES AT Kieran, stunned, his heart backfiring. *That wasn't what Jade told him.* Aware of Ellen groaning heavily behind him, he turns to check she isn't about to collapse. Even in the dimness, she is hard to look at, emotions crossing her face like creatures in flight: bewilderment, indignation, blackest rage.

"Liar!" Her voice comes at them in a violent shriek, and it seems to Vic she has forgotten what she has in her hand and wants to run at Kieran and attack him with her own body. But she is visibly battling her fear of the edge.

"Stay there," he tells her as calmly as he can, and then, to Kieran, "Don't talk rubbish. Lucas couldn't drive. He'd only had a couple of lessons, he was nowhere near taking his test."

"That didn't bother him," Kieran says. "He knew enough. He drove my car loads of times."

"You don't know what you're talking about," Ellen cries and both men recoil as she gestures again with the gun.

Vic moves smoothly towards her. "Let me handle this. Put that in your bag while we talk, yeah?" He reaches for her arm, steers it back towards the gaping bag at her side. He doesn't dare attempt to wrest it from her, he can't risk her discharging it in panic or incompetence. Meanwhile, he tries to digest this claim of Kieran's, to think it through for Ellen as well as for himself.

"He couldn't have been driving," he says flatly. "He was in the passenger seat when he was found, not the driver's seat."

Kieran nods. "He was in the passenger seat, yeah, that's right, because *I* pulled him into it. The car was blocked on the driver's side and the only way out was through my window, on the passenger side."

Nausea rises in Vic's gullet as Ellen reacts with furious disbelief. "Interesting how you only remember you weren't the one driving *now*, right when it's time to plead for your life."

"She's right, it makes no sense," Vic tells Kieran. "Why would you say it was you if it wasn't? No one in their right mind would want to be put away for a crime they hadn't committed."

"Because I *couldn't* remember. Not then, not for ages. I couldn't remember anything from the time we left the flat." Kieran is becoming distressed. A vein pulses by his left eye, a living thing under the skin, and he paws at his hair. "When I was told he was in the passenger seat and I was driving, I thought it must be right. It was my car."

"But you remembered differently—when?" Vic prompts.

"I learned about all these different therapies at Danstone, stuff that can retrieve memories, so when I was out and had some money, I had hypnotherapy. I remembered that Lucas was the one driving."

"Total crap," Ellen says. "The police checked CCTV footage, I remember it clearly. You were seen driving down Portland Road. *You* at the wheel. Don't listen to this bullshit, Vic."

"I *was* driving when we left, that's true," Kieran says. "We switched when we got out of town. He was begging me to let him take over. Like I say, he'd done it before. No cameras, no other traffic, at least not much. It was just supposed to be a laugh."

"Then what happened?" Vic demands. "He was driving and then what?"

"We started arguing. I told him something I shouldn't have, not then, not when he was driving. He took it badly."

"You told him what?" But this is the one question Vic can answer himself. "That you and Jade were together, right? That's why she finished with Lucas, wasn't it? You'd gone up to Durham to see her and you decided you wanted to be together."

"I don't believe that for a second," Ellen says.

"It's true, Ellen. Jade told me that much herself." She'd wept when she told Vic, the secret she'd been keeping for years.

"There's no way Jade would choose *him* over Lucas," Ellen snaps. She returns her glare to Kieran. "I suppose you've poisoned Freya with these lies as well, have you?"

Kieran's manner grows more combative. "If anyone's lying here it's you. You don't even know it. You only want the memory that suits you. You don't want to know your precious boy was off his head the whole time. You don't want to know Jade couldn't cope with him and wanted to be with me. That time you came screaming at me in that car park, I was there because he was meeting some dealer to get ket! He asked me to pick him up so he wouldn't have to get public transport with the stuff on him."

"Lucas wasn't even there, you—"

"He was fucking five minutes away! But you don't want to hear it, do you? You don't want to hear he was a nutcase who drove a car off the road and killed himself. Almost killed *me* while he was at it! He rang her, you know." Kieran says this with a bitter triumph. "He rang her from the car. He didn't believe me when I told him.

That's why he drove off the road, he was on the phone to her, to *my* girlfriend."

There is an appalled silence. Vic is speechless: Jade had told him there'd been a phone call during which the boys had been arguing, but not that it was actually in progress when the car went off the road. Perhaps she hadn't understood what was happening. She'd imagined a drama, not a tragedy. Not, as Kieran called it, a *laugh*.

"If all of this is true, then it makes what you did even worse," he tells Kieran. "You took your friend's girlfriend and chose the worst possible time to tell him—after he'd taken drugs and was driving a car he wasn't qualified to operate. He must have been completely out of control and yet you watched him make a phone call, you argued while he was speaking, you allowed it to happen."

For the first time, Ellen takes a step onto the terrace. "I want to know what happened underwater, Kieran. You just said you pulled Lucas into the passenger side. How was there room for you both, I don't understand. Tell me. I need to know."

Kieran's fingers are in his hair again, a ceaseless simian fiddling. He speaks in a gush, as if channeling the memory for the first time: "The only window that was open was mine, because I'd been smoking while he was on the phone, and I knew that was the only way we could get out. I undid his seat belt and tried to pull him with me, but there was hardly any space and I worked out I had to squeeze out first and then reach back in. I got him over the gear stick and into the passenger side, but he was unconscious and he couldn't do anything to help. The water was pouring in and I couldn't keep going, it was so cold and my clothes were weighing me down. My shoulder wasn't moving properly. I had to get to the surface, I didn't know how deep we were, how far I'd have to swim."

Though Vic can hardly bear to hear it, Ellen remains rapt. "The police said Lucas survived for almost thirty minutes, he could still have been pulled out of there if you'd got help."

"I did help!" Kieran protests. "I just said, I—"

She cuts him off. "Not in the car, that was instinct, you've just explained. I mean when you were out. Why you didn't you call for help? Did *that* come back to you in your hypnotherapy?"

Kieran flinches. "I didn't have my phone. It came out of my pocket when I was swimming, probably. It wasn't ever found."

It seems to Vic that there is an unnatural dip to these last words, a false note. "The police dragged that whole section of the water," he says. "They'd have found it if it'd just got pulled out of your pocket. Lucas's was in the car. Where was yours, Kieran?"

How can you describe the flicker of recognition when a truth is exposed, that split second before its owner smothers it? Vic can't, but he knows he is seeing it now in Kieran's face. "Oh, God, that phone call between Lucas and Jade. Whatever they were saying, you didn't like it, did you? I bet he was asking her to change her mind, go back to *him*. It didn't sound like good news for you, did it? *That's* why you didn't help. You started to think it through; you were thinking, as long as he was still around, there was a chance you'd lose Jade. And all the time, he was down there, alive, completely at your mercy."

Vic falters then, his brain snagging on something he's missed. Something crucial, not to do with phones or calls for help, but the seat belt. Both seat belts had been disengaged, this has been undisputed information all along. But before this new account of Kieran's, the theory has always been that Lucas, restrained in the passenger seat, had regained consciousness and unbuckled his own seat belt. It has been the sole reason to believe he *did* regain consciousness. Does Kieran's revelation mean Lucas was unconscious the whole time?

That the terror Vic and Ellen imagined him experiencing in his final minutes, that primitive horror of being aware of your own death . . . it didn't ever happen?

He hears himself cry out, feels his blood speeding faster through his veins. "You still had your phone, didn't you, when you got out? They still work, if they've been in the water a few minutes. What did you do with it? Tell me right now or I swear I'll take that gun from her and shoot you myself."

Something dissolves in Kieran's eyes then; something fractures in his mind and releases a final spurt of defiance. "You really want to know? All of that, yeah. Everything you just said. I had my phone and I could see it was still working. I knew I was too injured to go back down and I had to phone for help instead. And I thought, no, fuck him. He's bad news. Jade and me, we don't need him. So I threw it as far as I could, out into the middle of the water. *That's* why they didn't find it."

As Ellen lets out a roar—a truly awful sound of agony, goading, exhortation—Vic feels the energy of it power his body. He puts his face right up to Kieran's and snarls like an animal. "You useless cunt. You evil bastard."

Kieran starts to sob, pleading through the tears and phlegm. "I was wrong, I shouldn't have done it. I'm sorry, I'm really sorry."

"No, you're not. But you will be." And Vic drags him back to the balustrade, takes his writhing body with its kicking legs and punching fists, and heaves him over the top.

For one sublime moment, it feels illusory, the act of a magician: one second there is a groaning, resisting human being in his grip, the next there is absence, silence. Until, one long beat later, there comes the sound of something very heavy hitting the walkway.

Not so much a smack as a clang. A hammer hitting a bell.

Vic

"Vɪᴄ!" Eʟʟᴇɴ's ᴄʀʏ ʀᴇᴀᴄʜᴇs him at a delay, as if she is on the other end of a long-distance call, thousands of miles away. Then, as her voice fades, something new advances: a change of energy in the building, a collective horror. All those people crammed by the open window five floors below, *someone* must have seen the falling man. Some will have heard the sound of his impact on the walkway, felt its vibrations. They'll be crowding to the window to peer down, *right now* they'll be doing this, as he and Ellen stand on the roof, magnetized by each other's shock.

What has he done?

"Vic, come back in." She's retreated back inside the doorway and gestures frantically for him to join her.

"Go," he hisses at her. "And for fuck's sake, get rid of that gun. Chuck it in the river or something. Make sure no one sees you."

"No, you go, Vic."

"What? Don't be crazy. This is on me. You saw what I did. Go, Ellen. You weren't ever here!"

"No, I said *you*." She is behind him now and there is something small and very painful boring into his back, pushing him across the mezzanine towards the spiral. "Take the stairs, then go out through the fire door to the street. Everyone will be on the other side, by the water."

"Don't be crazy—"

"I'm serious, Vic. You've got the baby coming. Get India to say you've been at home all night. Will she do that? Or get Danny to. He'll cover for you."

"I can't let you," he protests, but they're at the top of the spiral now and she's forcing him down. The thing in his back is the gun.

"You *can* let me," she says. "I'll be treated differently. I'm the one with the doctors' notes, the medical history. I'm the one who wanted this, not you."

"But what about Freya . . . ?"

"She has Justin. Go, Vic, you have about ten seconds before it's too late."

He's at the foot of the spiral now. He turns and takes a last look at her face, the face that in the nineteen years of Lucas's life never once resembled his and yet somehow, just this one time, in this crucial moment, does.

And then he puts one foot in front of the other and he runs.

ACKNOWLEDGMENTS

THE HEIGHTS WAS WRITTEN in a year of lockdowns owing to the Covid-19 pandemic, and, reading it again, I detect a particular kind of determination in Ellen's attempt to control her narrative, a control that none of us has had during this period. Publishing it has involved a superlative WFH effort from the teams at S&S. In the UK, I'd like to say a huge, heartfelt thank you to Ian, Sara-Jade, Jess, Alice, Hayley, Gill, Maddie, Dom, Rich, Joe, and Rachel, with special thanks to my brilliant, creative, and always so kind editor, Suzanne Baboneau—our lunch in September 2020 was a true lockdown highlight!

Thank you to Pip Watkins for another beautiful cover and to Susan Opie and Madeleine Hamey-Thomas for a brilliant copyedit and proofread respectively.

At S&S US, I am excited to now be working with Loan Le, Libby McGuire, Megan Rudloff, Maudee Genao, Paige Lytle—thank you to you and all the team. My thanks also to Nita Pronovost, Adria Iwasutiak, Jessica Scott, and your colleagues at S&S Canada; and in Australia, to Rachael Versace and the wider team.

Sheila Crowley and team Curtis Brown have been incredible in

WFH mode—"beyond the call of duty'" doesn't do it justice. Thank you so much, Sheila, Sabhbh, Emily, Luke, Anna, Katie, Callum, and all the gang.

Thank you also to all the booksellers, librarians, bloggers, and reviewers who have somehow triumphed in adversity. Not to mention readers—the point of it all.

Thank you to Andrew at Into the Breach for invaluable research.

The character of Prisca was named following an auction by the 2020 Good Books campaign at CLIC Sargent (her surname, Evans, is fictitious). The real Prisca bears no physical resemblance to her namesake (so I hope she doesn't think I think she looks like a grandma in knockoff UGGs!) but I wanted to give her a substantial character in the story—not to mention the accolade of being one of my rare unambiguous good guys.

A note about inspiration for this book. As usual, I began with the themes I wanted to explore—revenge; the (un)reliability of crime memoir; the condition high place phenomenon; and the particular horror of a Chappaquiddick form of accidental death. As I plotted, I also found myself thinking about the 2001 movie *In the Bedroom*. Directed by Todd Field and starring Sissy Spacek and Tom Wilkinson as grieving parents, it's a wonderful film, both understated and devastating, and must have stayed with me across the years. If you know it, you might hear its echoes in *The Heights*. If you haven't ever seen it, I recommend it.

ABOUT THE AUTHOR

LOUISE CANDLISH is the *Sunday Times* bestselling author of fourteen novels, including *Our House*, which won the Fiction Crime & Thriller Book of the Year at the 2019 *British Book Awards* and was shortlisted for several other awards. It is soon to be a major ITV drama made by *Death in Paradise* producers Red Planet Pictures. Louise lives in London with her husband and teenage daughter.